AVENGING ANGEL

Amanda changed back into her human form and confronted the circle of demons. Her hair flew wildly about her face; only her flashing eyes showing the fury she was fighting to control. She'd fought demons before, but never this many at once. Never so many, so evil. She remembered some of the visions she'd had of their earlier brutal kills and her body shook violently as if she were in the grip of a seizure.

"Let the child go now," Amanda said from between gritted teeth, raising her hand to point at the demon. "Or I'll destroy you. All of you."

"Not likely. You are only one witch, after all, and we are many." The high priest smirked at her, his forked tongue flicking nervously across his lips. He nodded his head at the others. They began to close in.

Amanda forgot all the rules, forgot everything she'd ever learned or believed in a split second of white-hot rage.

She pointed her hand at the leader and a jagged line of crackling fire exploded from her fingertips like a lightning bolt and hit him in the chest. A surprised, then shocked, look rippled across his face right before he burst into flames, screeching like a banshee.

The rest of the coven turned and attacked her.

BOOK YOUR PLACE ON OUR WEBSITE AND MAKE THE READING CONNECTION!

We've created a customized website just for our very special readers, where you can get the inside scoop on everything that's going on with Zebra, Pinnacle and Kensington books.

When you come online, you'll have the exciting opportunity to:

- View covers of upcoming books
- Read sample chapters
- Learn about our future publishing schedule (listed by publication month *and author*)
- Find out when your favorite authors will be visiting a city near you
- Search for and order backlist books from our online catalog
- Check out author bios and background information
- Send e-mail to your favorite authors
- Meet the Kensington staff online
- Join us in weekly chats with authors, readers and other guests
- Get writing guidelines
- AND MUCH MORE!

**Visit our website at
http://www.pinnaclebooks.com**

WITCHES

KATHRYN MEYER GRIFFITH

PINNACLE BOOKS
Kensington Publishing Corp.
http://www.pinnaclebooks.com

PINNACLE BOOKS are published by

Kensington Publishing Corp.
850 Third Avenue
New York, NY 10022

Pinnacle and the P logo Reg. U.S. Pat. & TM Off.
First Printing: January, 1993
First Pinnacle Printing: September, 2000

10 9 8 7 6 5 4 3 2

Printed in the United States of America

For my cherished sisters, Carolyn, Mary, and Dorothy who are in no way witches of any kind . . . good or bad.

Prologue

Near Canaan, Connecticut
August 1694

The witch ran through the sweltering woods, her heavy skirts tangling and catching at the thornbushes and bracken, the tree limbs cutting and bloodying her skin. The woods eerily silent except for the noise she and her pursuers were making.

With a stifled cry of rage, she stumbled to her knees over a low branch. Her blue eyes held more anger than terror as she glanced behind her, as she listened for the sounds of pursuit.

They were close now. Any second they would find her, and they couldn't, not yet . . . not until she'd hidden that damn book. Her diary, the one with all the spells and incantations scrawled through its pages. Black magic. Witchcraft. If they caught her with it, it would be the worse for her. A short trip at the end of a rope.

She pulled herself up from her knees, gathering her drab black skirts in her trembling hands. She was exhausted, could barely stand, much less keep evading them. Her long black hair had come undone and it hung in long sweat-drenched strands about her face.

Her lungs were screaming and her feet were bleeding in her tightly laced boots.

But she kept going. The mob of townsmen and magistrates were right behind her. Six men with hats pulled low over austere faces. She could smell them. Smell the bloodlust that surrounded them like a vile cloud. They were a lynching mob, she had no doubt of that.

And she with no powers to fight them.

Her Master was punishing her . . . punishing her for defying him at the last sabbath when she—heady with her growing powers—had refused to yield to his wishes and kill her married lover, Darcy. She hadn't wanted to. Not yet. Darcy had proved to be a goodly lover and she'd become besotted with him, hadn't wanted to give him up. She'd thought she was being so clever, pretending she would kill him anon, but always putting it off.

Well, now Darcy was dead anyway, the Master had viciously seen to that—and she was soon to follow him, if the rabble led by that witch-hunter, Sebastien, had any say in it. He'd been hunting her relentlessly these last few days and wasn't about to give up now when he knew his quarry was so close, even if the day was waning.

They believed *she* had murdered Darcy. Cut him into tiny bloody pieces and strewn him about his home. His widow had shrieked for vengeance. And everyone in town had known whose bed Darcy had been sleeping in, besides his wife's.

Gasping for air, dizzy, she rested for a moment, leaning against a tree. She could only allow herself a few seconds, she had no more than that to spare. Sweat trickled down her face. It was hot, and she was thirsty. She wasn't accustomed to want. It was hell without her powers. Even her goat-familiar, her beloved Beelzebub, had abandoned her. But then he'd only been on loan to her; he was under the Master's command.

Horses' hooves thundered somewhere behind her through the darkening forest, the beasts snorting and neighing. Coming closer.

If she could hold out until dark, the night would hide her. The night would scare her pursuers away because godly men such as they were afraid of the dark.

In the morning, she could make her way into Massachusetts—if the Indians, bears, or the Master didn't get her first. Massachusetts where there were no sanctimonious Calvinists. She'd had a bellyful of them, witch-hunters, and Canaan.

Shouts rang through the air around her. They'd picked up her fresh trail.

No time left.

She broke through the hedges and came upon a twilight-misted pond sentried by a young willow tree. She knew this place. Black Pond. Her witches' coven had held sabbaths here.

Falling to her knees on the ground under the tree, she clawed at the dirt until a small hole appeared, then tossed the tiny leather-bound book into it, and quickly covered it up again with leaves and grass.

It was done. The book was hidden.

The witch-hunter and his men were nearly upon her. She shoved herself up and away from the pond, sprinting with everything she had left, her breath coming in ragged sobs as she scurried through the trees.

She'd grown soft, depended far too much on her magic. She couldn't escape. They were too close.

Her legs collapsed under her, pitching her to the burnt grass in a weary heap. She could have scraped together a pile of leaves and twigs, tried to burrow under them into the forest floor like a mole. She could have crawled behind a tree. But no, her pride wouldn't let her do that, and she wouldn't give them the satisfaction of seeing her grovel like a beaten cur. She rose to her knees and then to her feet, her chin held up in defiance, to face them, her mind racing.

They wouldn't dare try to touch her. They knew what she was. But they didn't know she'd lost her powers. Perhaps she could bluff them.

Bloodthirsty howls of anticipation echoed and ricocheted through the forest when they discovered her.

Her cold eyes watched as the men on horseback circled her like a pack of ravenous wolves, their hatred—their fear—wavering in their eyes. Death in their grim smiles. They held back.

They were scared of her. Some had seen firsthand what she could do to them. They weren't fools.

"I will give thee one last chance," she snarled, flipping her sweaty hair back from her flushed face. "Leave now and I'll send no harm to thee, thy families, livestock, or crops."

Sebastien rode up, reining in his tired horse within inches of her. "We are not afraid of thee, witch, or thy evil spells," he spat at her. "God's power is greater than Satan's and I am under his protection."

He turned in the saddle to address the men behind him. Blurry shadows in the twilight. "And no harm will come to thee as long as ye are with me."

His fanatical eyes returned to the woman. "Stop thy running. It will do no good. Accept thy punishment, witch. Confess to thy crimes and God will surely forgive thee."

She tried her magic one last time. Still nothing.

Her teeth bit deeply into her lips, drawing blood. She would never renounce her Master, no matter what He had done to her. She knew His power too well. She'd rather die than face Satan's wrath. This tiny meaning-

ess sliver of reality in exchange for eternity. Not a bad
rade.

"Nay, I will never confess," she hissed up into his
ace.

And in that moment, staring into Sebastien's glitter-
ng cruel eyes, she knew that this *was* to be her pun-
shment.

He was a poor excuse for a man, she thought, rake
hin with long greasy black hair, beady eyes placed in
a pockmarked, arrogant face. No wonder he detested
vomen so—none would have him.

They said he'd accused, tortured, tried, and hung
nearly three thousand people for witchcraft since God
had called him to the task.

"Deny Satan, and be cleansed," Sebastien growled
again, bending low in the saddle to peer into her face.

"Never! I warn thee. Leave me be," she whispered,
narrowing her eyes menacingly at one horseman after
nother. "Anyone who lays a hand on me will live to
ue the day he did." Still bluffing, for all the good it
lid.

The horsemen were hedging her in.

Bringing his hand down in a decisive gesture to his
ollowers, Sebastien ordered coldly, "Take her."

When they hesitated, he chided them harshly, "She
annot harm us."

No one moved.

Shadows hid the woman's true expression, but she
vas smiling.

With an impatient sigh, as if the witch-hunter had
een in the same position before, he lifted a coil of
ope from his saddle horn and tossed the looped end
ver the witch's head. She barely had a chance to slip
er fingers between it and her throat before Sebastien
et booted heels to his horse's flanks and took off into

the woods they'd just come out of, dragging the woman behind him.

"There be a pond a ways back. We'll take her there," he yelled over his shoulder as the others trotted their horses to catch up with him.

"She has children, Sebastien, what of them?" one of the men had ridden up beside him to demand, his eyes never leaving the witch's terrified face as she ran behind them.

"Witches' spawn." Sebastien's voice was heartless. "When we are through with her, we will seek them out and destroy them, as well. I will leave no little vipers alive in the nest, Richard."

The woman struggled against the ropes, but couldn't get free.

"I have had no trial," she cried out, stumbling behind the horse through the darkening woods, trying to stay on her feet so she wouldn't be dragged.

"By thine own words thou hast condemned thyself, witch," he sent back at her. "Evil deserves no trial." He beat his horse into a gallop, refusing to listen to anything else she had to say.

She fell to her knees, but the horses didn't stop.

Night beat them to the silent water.

Rough hands yanked her to her feet because she could no longer stand on her own, pulled the rope from her neck, bound her bloodied hands behind her back, and swiftly tied her feet together. By then all the fight was gone from her, her body broken and bruised.

They lifted her from the ground, and carried her to the water's edge in the darkness. Some had lit torches to light the way.

"I will have revenge on thee. All of thee!" she shuddered through gritted, swollen lips right before they flung her body high into the air, far above Black Pond.

"I curse thee!" Her last scream echoed on the air, until

she hit the water with a loud splash and then it was abruptly cut off.

The cold, dark water closed over her head, cutting off the air to her lungs, and her body sank to the bottom.

When the witch could no longer breathe, as water filled her lungs, a great wrath—an eternal fury—lodged deep in her heart and soul like a knife.

And as her life drained away, in those last few agonizing moments when the pain became too great for her to bear, she repeated her curse, her mouth moving silently in the water.

I will have my revenge on all of thee and thy town forever! I swear . . . someday I will have revenge.

The water's surface rippled into a calm, hiding the body and the crime.

Then the night creatures cried. An owl screeched, a wolf howled mournfully at the rising moon, a dirge for her death. Her body would never be searched for nor found.

Some of them stared at the pond, guiltily, the blood fever already dying, as if they expected her to suddenly reappear. In the gloom beyond the flickering torches, the shifting shadows suddenly seemed threatening. Unearthly sounding creatures hooted and whispered, skittering through the underbrush. Vermilion eyes glared at them from the gloom. Watching. Waiting.

And then they remembered whom they had killed. If the rumors be true . . . she had been a powerful witch. *She'd cursed them. Cursed all of them.*

An unnatural chill settled on the air around them, burrowing under their clothes and skin, deep into the marrow of their bones.

One by one, torches held high to keep the blackness at bay, they climbed into their saddles, and slunk home to their families.

All except Sebastien, who taking a few of the men back to a poorly made thatched cottage on the edge of the forest, tracked down the witch's children, and put them both to the knife.

Then, after a good night's rest, he fearlessly rode on to the next town to find, and execute, the next witch, and the next. Never looking back, never feeling the least bit of guilt for what he had done. He never did.

Yet the townspeople, as time went by, grew ashamed, not so much for what they had done—they had all believed she had been guilty—but for the brutal way they had done it.

And for as long as any of them lived, nothing was ever again spoken about the night they murdered the witch Rachel. It remained their shameful secret until the day they died.

But none of them ever forgot.

Chapter 1

The present
A small cabin outside
of Canaan

Amanda knelt on the floor before the hearth, shivering, weak from lack of sleep and food. Her cold hands shook as she laid the wood.

Stacking the kindling carefully, she witched a bright flame from her hand to the wood, fanning the first fragile flames with her warm breath until it caught. Then she added the bigger logs, and the fire roared. She searched its blue heart, trying not to dwell on what she was actually doing.

Outside, the storm grew in fury, thundering at the doors and windows as if it knew what she was going to do.

Sacrilege . . . sacrilege . . . it moaned.

Something thumped persistently against the door. She'd locked Amadeus, her familiar, out. He didn't like it. He knew she was up to no good.

In silence she prepared for the rest of the ritual. With chalk she drew the five-pointed star with alternate points connected by a continuous line—the pentagram. She painstakingly finished the preparations for the ancient incantation she'd begun earlier in the day. A spell that a white witch should never invoke.

Don't do this.

But the flames whispered, *Jake . . . Jake.*

And her tortured, lonely heart ignored the inner voice. The truth.

She sighed, pushing her long wavy hair back from her face. It was tangled and greasy. When was the last time she had washed it? Or taken a bath, for that matter? Weeks? What a sight she must be now, she thought. She must truly look like the witches of the old myths. Smiling wistfully, she tugged the frayed sweater tighter around her.

Since Jake, her husband of ten years, had died she'd had no time except for anger, morbid self-pity, and tears.

Her conscience kept warning her not to go on, but she refused to listen.

You can't call Jake back from the dead. It breaks all the laws of white witchcraft . . . and you are not a black witch.

You will never be able to pay the price.

There was a price to pay for every spell a witch wove, every small favor she asked from life. The bigger the favor, the higher the price.

For every granted wish, there was a price to pay. One way or another. The more precious, or forbidden the request, the higher the final payment. For every push, there was a pull.

Amanda, if you do this . . . you'll damn your soul to hell. Don't go to the dark side. . . .

Not to mention the danger.

But another night without Jake? Another night alone? To have Jake back, wouldn't that be worth it?

The inner voice was mute.

Even witches got lonely. She frowned bitterly in the crowding shadows as she crouched before the fire, her haunted green eyes obsessed. Even witches fell in love. Even she, whom had once believed she would never fall in love. Ever.

But she had . . . with Jake.

She remembered the first time she had met him ten years ago, the way he had looked, what he had said.

He had been so beautiful . . . tall, dark-haired with sensitive, yet piercing blue eyes full of humor and wisdom. He'd had a beard then, in the beginning, and had reminded her for some reason of a medieval tinker. All he'd needed was a leather bag slung across his broad shoulders.

He'd come across her out in the woods one spring day as she gathered mushrooms. The first time she'd looked at him, she knew he would be the one she would love. Something in the soft breeze that cavorted around her told her so.

He'd grinned at her as she'd stared boldly back at him; his eyes had twinkled appreciatively.

"You are . . . lovely. Are you real?"

She'd laughed. "Yes."

He'd reached out his hand, and she'd taken it without hesitation. Love at first sight . . . it had never happened to her before. Before, she'd thought all such talk of love and passion a fable. Worse, she'd always scoffed at it.

She'd had a lot to learn. And Jake had been eager to teach her.

They'd been lovers from the very beginning. No coyness or modesty on her part. Why? They'd been fated to meet, fated to love; it'd been right from the first touch, the first kiss.

They'd made love out in the woods. A warm night. He'd been amused at her that first night, after their

gentle lovemaking, when she'd told him that she'd
loved him before—in another life—and the ones before
that.

"We've both lived before, many times. And were lovers in each one."

"How can you be so sure of that?" he'd asked softly,
not disbelieving, but skeptical.

"I just am. I know many things. Did you think that
I bedded every man I met while walking in the woods?"
she'd teased him gently.

"Well, I'd wondered about that . . ."

For an answer, she'd brought his lips down to hers
and kissed him sweetly.

"What are you, then, to know such things?" he'd
coaxed, holding her close to him in the dark, still teasing. "A witch?"

"Yes, I don't advertise it, but . . ." she'd replied in
a hushed tone, serious. She never told people what she
was. "I am. And witches believe in reincarnation. Spirit-
traveling. What a soul doesn't learn in one life, it must
come back again to learn.

"I've met you before in my travels, my love. And I
have found you again in this life." There'd been happiness and wonder in her voice. She'd known it was
true, amazing as it was. Jake was the one she'd been
waiting so long for and had never thought she'd find.

He'd studied her in the dark, not answering for a
long time. She was afraid he didn't believe her, afraid
he thought her to be just eccentric, or worse yet, crazy.
Then, with the bouquet of honeysuckle wafting around
them in the night, he'd spoken softly to her.

"I don't care what you are, woman. All I know is
that I found you, and I know here"—he'd patted his
chest above his heart—"somehow already, without a
doubt, I love you. Don't ask me how I know it so soon,

just do. You're mine and I'll never let you go. Crazy woman, old maid, witch, or whatever."

"Don't worry, Jake," she'd whispered later. "I'm a white witch. A good witch." And she'd smiled in the gloom. He could just make out the upturning of her lips.

He'd waited for her to go on, but she'd only said, "I've given you enough to think on for a while." And he'd sighed into his strong shoulder, both of them wrapped in her cloak, sleepy, leaning up against a large tree.

"Someday, I will tell you everything, my love. Someday." Touching his heavy eyes, she'd bade him sleep. Cradling his head in her arms, she'd thought about what a difference loving him would make in her life.

Yes, she was a witch. Born a witch like her grandmother before her, and her grandmother before her. The gifts and skills passed down from one generation to another. The power to heal. Foresee the future—sometimes. Shape-change. Control the weather. Each witch had specialties. Her ancestors had all been witches, or warlocks. That simple. White witches, sworn to help humanity. Witches who often believed in a merciful God, and never worshipped Satan.

As the night birds disappeared, and the day creatures began to rise with the dawn, she'd led her love to her bed. From that day on, for ten beautiful years, nothing had ever separated them.

Weeks later, as they had cuddled before a fire in her shack on the edge of the woods, when he had known her better and seen her powers firsthand, she'd told him everything about witchery.

"I'm of the Old Religion, before it split itself into Dualism."

"Dualism?"

"A creed that holds there are two sides to God. The

Diabolic or black witchcraft believes that the evil side, Satan, is stronger. White witches, the pure Old Religion, believe that the good side, God, is stronger, that we receive our powers from Him. It is a very, very ancient, very misunderstood religion. We're not allowed to interfere with the world."

"Ah, like the Prime Directive in 'Star Trek'?"

" 'Star Trek'?" she'd inquired, puzzled.

"That's right, you don't watch much television, do you?" He recalled she had little use for it. "It's an old sixties television science fiction show about these people, Captain Kirk and his crew, who travel through space from one world to another. But they're not—usually—allowed to tamper with the civilizations they encounter, only observe. It would upset the worlds' delicate balances, you see."

"That's it exactly. We witches are supposed to keep a low profile, help from behind the wings, observe. Not call attention to ourselves, never hurt anything or anyone. If we do use our powers to hurt, we pay dearly for it."

"Ah, so the cults, the animal and human sacrificing, Satanic masses, and all that sadistic mumbo-jumbo we read about all the time is the *bad* side of witchcraft." He had caught on quickly.

"The dark side." She supplied the word for him *"Black* magic. Evil people who bastardize the Old Religion's beliefs. Worship Satan and his legions. Sick people who want attention. It's given witchcraft a bad name True witches are healers, not killers. We abhor people like that and fight their evilness whenever we can."

She'd shrugged. "But most people don't know that. Or they don't believe witches exist at all. People are so superstitious, Jake, even in these times, so afraid of what they don't understand." She had sighed unhappily, knowing this well from her own experiences. "I learned early to keep my religion, my powers hidden. It scares people. They think all witches idolize the Devil, drink baby's blood, or cackle over a steaming black kettle full of foul-smelling animal parts. Just like in the dark ages. Warts on your nose and hair like a greasy mop." And with this, she had finally laughed.

But in time Jake accepted what she was, and had loved her more for it. They'd even been married in the old way, just the two of them exchanging their vows under the sacred oak trees. She would have done anything for him.

But fate had something else in store for Jake. One thing a witch must accept was that one cannot defy fate. It was too strong.

What would be would be.

A rainy night, slick roads, and a smashed up car—and Jake was gone.

Now, with her heart breaking, her eyes shut, her hands waving languidly over the fire, she chanted the nefarious words that would bring her husband back from the dead.

"Mandy . . . no, Mandy . . ."

Something crashed against the door, as if someone were throwing themselves against it. Wood splintered, but the door held. Amadeus, who had powers of his own, was fighting mad now. It was his responsibility to protect her, protect her from herself, if need be. She heard him growling at her through the door. *Open up, Mandy. OPEN THE DAMN DOOR!*

"No. I told you, Amadeus, either help me or go away."

The cat mumbled beyond the door, hissed and spat as loud as any big cat, and the battering resumed.

Amanda's eyes flew open, widened as the apparition began to take form inside the pentagram . . . the outline of a man, tall, his arms thrown over his face as if in defense.

"Jake?" she moaned, staring at the thing.

It lowered its hands and a ghoulish, misty face peered out at her . . . a face so full of torment and fear, Amanda fell back in shock.

"Don't do this, Mandy, I beg you! Remember me as I was. I don't belong there anymore," a plaintive whisper, an echo on the still air. Its hands reached out to her. *"Let me go. You don't know what you're doing!"*

But she couldn't stop. The enchantment wasn't complete. It would be better when it was. He was between two worlds now and he would be frightened. Half-formed. *Between two worlds.*

And if she wasn't careful, those unearthly denizens—shade demons, she called them—that haunted that dead world could escape into hers. Dangerous. *So* dangerous. What the hell was she doing . . . opening the forbidden portals like this?

What happened if she was a moment off, a word wrong . . . and the demons came through? If she unleashed them? A disaster.

Amanda steeled herself, wiped the fresh tears from her face with the back of her cold hand. "Damn it, I want you back, Jake. I'll have you back," she swore.

She took up where she had left off, knowing that if she stopped at this point of the spell, it could ruin everything. Everything.

The door groaned behind her under its assault (damn but that cat was strong), the wind screamed outside the windows. The candles placed around the pentagram fluttered in a strange breeze in the shadowy room.

Amanda's heart froze. She stopped in the middle of the spell, her eyes going wide with fear, her hands half-raised before her, and her head thrown back as the flames from the fire glowed more brightly across her tense face.

What was that *word*? *Suureerustus*? Or *Summertus*? Or . . .

She stared at the blurry figure trying to form in the circle. It was yelling at her now . . . something . . . something . . . she couldn't make out the words.

But it was no longer alone.

Things writhed around its melting feet, flew about its head. *Terrible things*. Things from the dead world. *Unholy things*. Gaping mouths with sharp bloodied teeth, glittering fiendish eyes in deformed hideous bodies. Some almost human, some insectlike. Others indescribable. Some growing before her eyes to be taller than she was.

Monsters. Coming through the barrier, crossing the lines of the pentagram, into her world.

She grabbed the nearest thing with which to fight them off, a broom, and started swinging at them.

Amanda was so busy hitting and spewing out new spells to keep the shade demons from coming through that she never heard the door burst open; never felt the cool storm wind enter the cabin until something determined and furry flew by her face toward the pentagram, hissing all the way.

Then Amadeus was helping her herd the malignant spirits back from where they'd come. All claws, teeth, and unearthly glowing eyes. He snarled the word *Sutterus* at her in passing and Amanda quickly supplied it in the spell where it belonged.

The ugly demons began to slowly dissolve in shrieks of rage. *Don't send us away! Don't send us back there! Let us out. OUT!*

Jake's figure returned. A shadow with hanging head.

Just one or two sentences and the incantation would be complete. Jake would be there, solid, before her.

Amanda hesitated. The thing in the circle looked so pitiful. So unnatural.

Then before she could finish, soft, but strong paws clamped tightly around her neck and wouldn't let go. Something howled like a banshee in her ear, as sharp teeth angrily nipped it. She couldn't breathe.

"Amadeus! Get off!" she screamed, tumbling to the floor with the huge cat on top of her, still holding on like a leech, its yowling and screeching enough to wake the dead—instead, it woke her.

By the time she had yanked the cat off, throwing him roughly against the opposite wall so that he yelped in pain, and she had crawled back to the pentagram, Jake was gone. The enchantment broken.

Amanda gazed at the empty pentagram for a long time, suddenly horrified, disgusted at what she had almost done.

She'd almost crossed the line. Almost. Thank God for Amadeus.

She curled up on the floor next to the fire and sobbed. The last of her anguish finally releasing itself. The cat limped over to her and licked the tears from her woebegone face. He didn't seem to be angry with her any longer. Just worried.

"I'm so sorry I hurt you, Amadeus, so sorry . . ." She pulled him into her arms, and hugged him like a baby until he began to purr. "Forgive me?"

Of course.

"Thank you for that, Amadeus. You saved me from making the biggest mistake of my life."

He was smart enough not to answer that one.

She snuggled him, rocking on the floor.

"I had no right," she moaned into his matted fur finally.

"What was I thinking of? I have no right to bring

back the dead. No matter how much I loved him. He's gone now. I must accept it. Go on."

In reply the huge cat purred louder. *About time you wised up*, he huffed in cat language. *About time. I was getting tired of baby-sitting . . . I've got more important things to do.* He reached up with his paws and captured her wet, tear-streaked face between them, his eyes huge, golden, so human and understanding.

It will get better, Mandy. It will. I promise.

Amanda looked at him, his fur still fluffed up from his fight, his ears twitching, as he tried to grin at her. Cats couldn't grin. Made him look funny. Like the Cheshire Cat.

"Amadeus . . . I miss him *so.*"

I know. It'll pass. Give it time. I'll help.

She knew he was right. He was wise. Nodding silently, she stared at the remnants of the pentagram, the broken lines, and the dying flames of the gutted candles. But her tears continued to fall as she held Amadeus.

The cat bequeathed her a cognizant look, his feline eyes shining. He was a huge, battle-scarred Blue Maltese. He was also a very ancient and very powerful familiar. Given to her by her grandmother on the day of her birth, thirty-four years ago. She had no idea how old he was. Only that since she could remember, he'd always been there to guard over her and guide her. He'd pulled her out of many a tight place. She trusted him.

His duty accomplished, he'd had enough of her coddling, and jumping from her arms, stalked away to his favorite spot on the padded rocking chair before the fire. His expression and the stiffness of his tail letting her know he was still a little miffed at her for trying it in the first place.

"You're right to be mad at me, Amadeus," Amanda said contritely.

Outside, the storm had peaked, and she could hear the soft patter of rain hitting the cabin's roof. The snug little cabin that Jake had built her their first year together. Though he'd been a master potter who taught his craft for a living, he'd been a heck of a carpenter, as well. Amanda had always told him that *his* magic was in his hands, and she'd been right. The cabin was the prettiest home she'd ever had.

She touched the wall next to her, memories of the two of them working on it together making her cry more. She could drive a nail and frame out a room with the best of them now. Just another thing Jake had taught her.

On her hands and knees, she scooted back to the pentagram, and with the edge of her skirt, rubbed at the chalk furiously until the star was transformed into a mess of smeared lines. A great shudder rippled through her body when it was accomplished. Now nothing could cross over.

Amanda got up from the floor and, like a sleepwalker, made her way to the door. Stepping outside, she ran to the huge oak tree at the back of the house, and let the October rain soak her to the skin. She felt so worn out and useless. So dirty.

Maybe, it would help wash her clean.

Even in the dark, she could see the silver-outlined clouds stampeding angrily above like crazed animals before a raging fire. The world went on. Life went on. Jake or no Jake.

Standing silently, musing up through the branches at the night sky, she let the rain mingle with her warm tears, her back braced stiffly against the tree's solid trunk.

She did her penance, praying for forgiveness, relieved that Amadeus had stopped her in time. Before she had brought Jake totally back.

Witches usually didn't fool with the dead, the calling up of the dead, or ghosts. You could never tell what you'd get in the end. And some spirits were mischief oriented, some cunningly wicked or just plain evil. It made sense. The people who'd been good in life had gone on to the next life, or to heaven. It was only the troubled spirits that returned.

Jake wouldn't stay in between for very long. His was a good soul.

The night was turning colder, the wind picking up again, the storm finding new energy somewhere, and the rain felt like tiny slivers of ice on her skin, making her shiver.

The house behind her, forlorn as it had become the last few months, beckoned. Safety. Warmth.

She made a dash for the door, slipping back into the house. The door slammed behind her, and she leaned weakly against it in the dark; listened to the storm beat wildly at the outside, wanting so badly to get in.

Though she loved storms, it was good to have shelter. She heard limbs being torn from the trees, crashing into the roof. She heard the trees' agony. All witches could. Trees hurt just like people. It was true.

Only a witch would think like that, she thought, because they, too, were as much a part of the earth as the trees, the wind, the earth. She covered her ears until it stopped, refused to feel their pain. She had enough of her own.

Amanda peered out the window into the rain, caressing the cool windowpane with quivering fingers as the water dripped from her clothes all over the floor.

Jake had loved a good storm.

Touching her way across the tiny kitchen, she opened a cabinet door. She kept extra candles just for such nights. She could have turned on the lights, but she preferred candlelight.

As with other modern conveniences—electricity, tele-phone, and television—she could have just as easily lived without them. Like her ancient ancestors. In the old ways. She chopped her own wood, sometimes cooked her food outside over an open wood fire like Jake had shown her—when the weather permitted.

In the last ten years Amanda had learned to live off the small game and fish that she caught, what grew in her garden, and what she gleaned from the forest, like her great-grandmother, Jessie, had. Ways that she had forgotten years ago during her city life and cringed now to admit that she had forsaken. For a woman who could snap her fingers and have almost anything in the world, it felt good to know she could do it the hard way, too.

She was a modern witch who had come back to the old ways in the last twelve years and was now glad of it, stronger for it. She could make it, she knew she could. Even without Jake.

She lit the candle with a touch of her bare fingers, another witch's trick.

The gentle light fluttered, throwing elusive shadows behind her on the wall, driving the ghosts away.

Drying off, she put on different clothes. She dressed as if she lived a hundred years ago, favoring long dark-colored dresses with full skirts, and shawls. It's what she felt most comfortable in. Out in the woods of Connecti-cut it could get really cold in the winters. But she wore the archaic clothes well, as Jake had always said.

Then she prepared her supper. A large chunk of sourdough bread she'd baked the day before, chilled butter, and cheese. Witched up a bottle of sweet red wine. Then another.

She called softly for Amadeus; searched the unlit cor-ners, his usual hiding places. Contrary thing. He was suddenly nowhere to be found, probably still peeved at her. Just when she needed a friend.

"All right, you little devil, go hungry, then," she murmured dejectedly, and ate alone as the candle's velvet light flickered across her closed face. It was a pretty face, usually, when she smiled. She possessed large eyes the color of new grass, strong cheekbones, pouting lips, and fair skin framed by long curling brown hair, with just a tint of red, that fell to her waist. Not beautiful, but appealing.

Amanda finished her supper, her appetite better than it had been in months. Everything tasted delicious. She drank a little too much wine, and soon she was smiling tipsily at some old poignant memories of herself and Jake. He would always be a part of her heart, her memories. She would always love him.

Someday she would see him again. In another life.

She glanced down and there was Amadeus purring, circling her long skirts just like his old self.

"So you've come out finally, have you? Not angry with me anymore, my friend?" She scooped him up into her arms to hug him. He allowed her to do it, actually continued to purr. She laughed, glad to have things back the way they used to be between them. It was as if a great burden had been lifted from her shoulders. Amadeus knew it, too. He meowed and licked her fingers. No back talk. Acted like a real cat. Which meant he was very pleased.

She took Amadeus and went to sit in the living room in the rocker before the dying fire, Amadeus content in her lap as she petted him and rocked back and forth soothingly. The wine had made her light-headed, carefree.

The storm's winding down outside. Tomorrow morning there'll be a mess outside for me to clear away.

When she went to bed, it was to sleep soundly. There were no horrible dreams any longer, no dreams at all. When she woke up in the morning there was a sleepy-eyed, yawning Amadeus curled in the space between her arms, and a bright autumn sun greeting her cheerfully through her bedroom window.

There was that vibrant mustardy tang to the air that she loved so much in the fall. It filled her with energy. It made her want to get up, and do something—anything—just to prove that she was alive.

For the first time, she thought of her dead husband and was amazed to find that the memories warmed her heart, made her smile. She would always have him. A memory away.

She was finally healing.

Humming, she got out of bed, belted a fleecy blue robe around her thin waist, and with a pesty Amadeus treading on her heels, fixed them a large breakfast of bacon, eggs, and blueberry muffins. Amadeus ate food just like a person, and she'd need all her strength to clean up the storm's debris.

Some of the muffins she saved for her friend, Mabel, an eighty-three-year-old widow who lived past Black Pond on the edge of town, in a tiny trailer. Mabel's arthritis had become so bad, she wasn't able to bake the way she used to and Amanda often took her home-baked gifts. She'd been Jake's friend first, her friend now. Amanda didn't have many friends, so she felt especially guilty for having neglected Mabel as much as she had the last few months. There was really no excuse for it.

Today she needed to see her.

She even set aside a muffin or two for Ernie Hawkins, the mailman, for when he came by later on his rounds. Another friend of Jake's.

Jake had always invited Ernie in for a cup of coffee, something to eat, and the latest gossip. Ernie liked to talk almost as much as Jake had. She'd awake many a morning to hear Jake and Ernie chattering in the kitchen about politics or the state of the economy. They'd always had a running chess game going on. She could still see them hunched over the board, dropping muffin crumbs and slurping down coffee. Another memory that made her smile now.

She watched Ernie trudge past her mailbox almost every day. A short man of around forty or so, with a friendly face, intelligent dark eyes, and long hair streaked with gray. A country storyteller. He knew something about almost everything and everyone. He'd smile and wave at her. But Ernie hadn't stopped in for coffee in a long time.

Maybe, he didn't know what to say to her now. Maybe, he missed Jake, too.

Like Mabel, she'd neglected him.

A plaintive meow at her feet seemed to second the thought.

She cleaned up the breakfast dishes, then went to put some clothes on.

She looked out her bedroom window, shaking her head at all the damage. "Come on, Amadeus, let's go outside and see how bad it really is. See what kind of spell we'll need to clean it all up. What do you say?" She slipped a shawl on and with Amadeus trailing, tail straight up like a flagpole, she went outside.

Outside, she pulled the shawl closer around her shoulders. The morning had a real bite to it. Amadeus trundled across the leaf-strewn ground, hugging the earth and playing with the crinkly leaves. Watching him made her chuckle.

In the sunlight, she could see that the rain from the night before had formed a thin layer of frost, sparkling on the blades of grass and the trees' limbs like winking diamonds. One of the larger trees on the side of the house had been shattered in the storm. Huge limbs had splintered away from the main trunk and crashed onto a section of the roof. But it hadn't seemed to have damaged the roof very much. Jake had made the little house strong.

Strolling slowly around the house, she took stock of the storm's toll. One of the back windows had been broken. Limbs everywhere. Trash from half the country. All in her yard.

Closing her eyes tightly, she began to concentrate on the words of a spell and soon experienced that curious vertigo she always did when witching.

The wind began to pick up, the leaves rustling, cascading about and maddeningly chasing themselves when she raised her hands. There were a series of jarring crashes, loud whooshes.

When she opened her eyes the split tree was whole again. There were no limbs perched precariously upon the roof, no branches or trash anywhere. The broken window was an unmarred pane of shining glass.

All was as it had been before the storm.

Rebecca, her older sister, would have been pleased, she thought.

Triumphant, but weary, she walked back to the house and into the kitchen, plopped down on a chair at the table. As soon as she was able to get up again, she fixed herself a cup of steaming hot tea to regain her strength.

For everything done with magic, there was a price to pay. Magic only took moments, but a witch paid the same price physically as if she'd actually done the real labor.

She laid her head down on the table for what seemed like an instant, but when she raised it again time had flown by like sparrows. Three hours had passed. That's what not eating and mourning all these weeks had brought. Made her weak. It'd taken more out of her than she'd realized.

Ernie would have passed by a long time ago. She'd missed him. Stretching and yawning, she went out to check the mailbox.

It was warmer, and the frost was gone.

The mailbox on the crooked post waited for her. "Amanda Givens" the only name left on its round dented side. She'd removed Jake's name after he'd died.

There were two letters. The distinctive handwriting on both telling her right away who they were from. Her sisters, Jessica and Rebecca.

She opened Jessie's first.

Her husband had been promoted again . . . her two little girls both had the flu, but were getting better . . . she was taking more craft classes up at the community college . . . wasn't the news awful lately, so much killing . . . how could Amanda stand living there all alone in the middle of nowhere, especially with all that terrible cult activity going on—as if Amanda couldn't take care of herself—when was she coming for a visit, or better yet, had she considered the possibility of moving back to Boston?

Aha.

Amanda grinned into the sunlight. Every one of Jessie's long letters ended up the same. Come home. She never gave up.

She tucked the letter back into its envelope. She had two sisters. Jessie was her younger sister, and the only nonwitch of the three. But she didn't miss it, she was really into the wife/mother thing. Jessie had a normal family, a husband named John who was a computer programmer at a local college, and two daughters, Debbie, eight, and Abigail, eleven.

Amanda's father had died when they were babies, and their mother had died when Amanda was twenty-three . . . right before she'd moved here and met Jake.

Her face grew melancholy at the thought of her mother, her heart heavy. Ghastly images of that fatal car crash eleven years ago still came unbidden to torture her. To remind her that the someone who'd been responsible had never been caught. And someone had been responsible. Their mother had been a powerful white witch and she'd had many enemies. One of them had murdered her. The authorities had labeled it an accident, but Amanda had known better. The stench of black magic had been all over her mother's corpse. Whoever had done it had been strong. Strong enough to hide their crime from Amanda, though she had been young at the time and still hadn't come into her own. *It would be different now.*

Afterward, Amanda hadn't been able to stay in Boston. She'd escaped to the woods of Connecticut.

She pushed the sorrow, the guilt away and turned her thoughts back to her sister, Jessie.

Though Jessie had no talent whatsoever as a witch— she couldn't make a pin disappear—Amanda had always been closer to her than Rebecca. They were a lot alike. Jessie really cared about her. Since Jake had died, Jessie had been the one in closest touch with her, the most understanding.

But Jessie didn't understand about this place. It had seemed to call her long before she'd ever found it. As if it had chosen her.

Amanda's haunted eyes drifted around her at the tiny house butted up against the deep woods.

She couldn't leave this place. This was her home. This was where she'd found and loved Jake. She'd never leave.

But Jessie meant well.

Suddenly in her mind's eye, Amanda saw Jessie, with

her wild reddish hair and gleaming green eyes so like Amanda's . . . smiling, as she was probably doing at that exact moment. Sometimes, Amanda could zero in on her sister that easily. There was a strange bond between them, always had been. Even without witchcraft.

Perhaps, she would go and see them all soon. She did miss them. And she wanted to see how little Abigail was doing.

Abigail, a true witch, if Amanda had ever seen one. Did Jessie know that yet? she wondered.

Jake and Amanda had wanted children of their own so much. Jake would have been such a good father. But, for some reason, it had just never happened. It had been the only sadness between them.

Frowning, Amanda took the other letter and opened it. Rebecca's letter was short, plain, and to the point, like Rebecca herself.

Rebecca was divorced again—was that her fourth or fifth? Amanda had lost count. Why did she keep marrying her lovers when she swore she hated men so? Her marriages never lasted. You'd think that at forty, she'd be smarter than to keep making the same mistake over and over. She crashed recklessly through life like each day was her last. How could she ever love another when she didn't love herself?

Rebecca's letter also said that she'd be doing a witch's convention in the area in the next few weeks during her latest book tour and would drop by for a visit.

Well, what a surprise.

Amanda finished the letter and folded it up as she walked back toward the cabin.

Rebecca.

She had the makings of a *great* witch, Amanda brooded, but she played it like some cheap parlor game, milking it for every penny she could. She wrote lurid, sensational books on witchcraft and satanic cults, did seances, sold her spells like a damn Gypsy, and did the whole talkshow circuit like some traveling dog and pony show. It had always been a huge bone of contention between them.

Amanda never made her money by trading on what she was. It was her religion.

They'd never been close. That damned old sibling rivalry—made worse because they were both witches, and Amanda had always been by far the most gifted—had lurked between them, poisoning their relationship and killing any real sisterhood there might have been.

What did Rebecca want from her? To be friends now, because they were both husbandless? Amanda rubbed her eyes, sighing.

At least Rebecca dealt only in white magic. She should be thankful for that. So many ambitious witches went to the dark side.

Amanda dropped the letters into one of her ceramic pots in the middle of the kitchen table. She'd answer them later.

Right now she had a basket of food to prepare for Mabel, and it was getting late.

Thinking of Rebecca and how she made her money reminded Amanda that she was broke herself.

She didn't need much money to live here, but she needed some.

She grew her own food in the summer and canned or froze it for the cold months. There were the fruit trees that Jake had planted years ago. She got by. Being a witch, she knew the ways of fertility, the secrets of the earth. Yet money was nice. She couldn't grow or witch everything she wanted. If she did, she'd be a physical wreck.

In a small wicker basket, she neatly placed a jar of her special peach preserves, the muffins, some tangy cheese and crackers, a roll of Mabel's favorite sausage, and the special herb tea that helped Mabel's arthritis. Tea laced with magic, so the old woman's pain would go away for awhile. With the cooler weather Mabel would need it.

When she was ready to go, she stood in the middle of her front room and murmured a simple spell to protect her house from intruders. Hardly took any energy at all.

Outside, she strolled across the yard to where her workshop sat waiting patiently for her to return. In the beginning, just a large wooden shed that Jake had built to store his potter's wheel, supplies, and pots after he had completed their house.

It'd been Jake who'd suggested, since she was so good with her hands, that she try throwing pots. She'd be a natural. As always, he'd been right. And something unexpected had happened . . . Amanda proved not only to be very good at it, she quickly learned everything he had to teach her and then over the next few years surpassed even him. She grew to love it, learning all about every facet of pottery, its history, and the different styles and techniques. Soon, she not only created the pots, but designed her own intricately patterned pots decorated with ingenious slip designs and glazed in bright colors.

And Jake thought they were so beautiful, so unique, that one day he took some into town and had them placed in a local store, Jane's Gift Shop. They sold like hotcakes . . . and an artist was born. Amanda had been selling them there ever since, and getting a good price for them, too, along with her homemade fudge and candies from her grandmother's old recipe, another idea of Jake's. Now she was known all over the area not only for her pottery, but for her delicious fudge and candies, too.

Since Jake had taught advanced pottery classes in town full-time, he rarely had the time to create new pots as he would have liked, so soon the workshop became her place.

The door stuck like it always did and she yanked at it, going inside. It was musty. The spiders had been busy, she could tell by all the gossamer-thin webs floating everywhere, but their inhabitants were nowhere to be seen. It was getting far too cold, almost November. In one corner, the old potbellied wood stove hunkered, wood still piled up high next to it.

Jake had believed in preparing early. He had cut and stacked the wood months ago in the heat of summer. She could still see him sweating over the large ax as it rose and fell, see the shine on his bare shoulders, the determination on his handsome face.

In the back, hiding in the shadows, there was a place where she kept her witch's pharmacopoeia—dried herbs and plants—in labeled pastel tupperware all lined up on a wall of shelves. She used to spend hours in here while Jake was away teaching his pottery students. Happy hours.

She stared at the place, clutching the covered basket under her arm. Everything was dusty now.

A half-finished pot sat forlornly on the dirty potter's wheel, as if rebuking her for her negligence. She hadn't been in here since Jake had died. She ran her fingers across the caked, dried clay. If she could only go back to the day, the hour, the very minute she'd first started that pot . . . Jake would still be alive. She shook her head.

Suddenly the old familiar urge to feel something taking shape under her fingers stole over her, and a faint smile slipped out.

It's still there. It hadn't left as she had feared it had; soon, she knew, she would go back to work. The shop that carried her creations was out of them. Jane wanted to know when she'd bring in some new things. And Amanda could use the money waiting for her.

She couldn't put it off forever. Going into town. Getting on with her life.

Closing and locking the heavy wooden door behind her, she started the long walk through the woods to Mabel's trailer. She'd never owned a car and didn't care to, though she could drive one and always kept her license up to date. She had a small motor scooter Jake had gotten her last year for her birthday, but she preferred to walk.

She could magic herself there . . . but today she just wanted to feel the earth under her feet, sun on her face. It helped her think. She loved crunching through the burnt scarlet and dun-yellow leaves. Loved the woods.

For a while, coming out of nowhere, Amadeus trailed her, hid playfully behind skinny trees, and jumped out every once in a while—trying to scare her.

"You want to play games, hey?" she teased him, whispering a harmless spell, dissolving into invisibility. There'd be no side effects, unless she stayed away too long. She held her giggles in at Amadeus's antics when he realized she was gone. He meowed pitifully and ran in crazy circles. Searching.

But the witch's cat was smart. She'd played this trick on him before. At first he froze, his whiskers moving, his ears perked, sniffing the air. Then he lunged, rubbing up against her, purring triumphantly. His claws kneaded her sharply in the legs through her skirts, pricking her just enough to make her break her silence.

"You mean puss . . . that hurt." She snatched him up. But not really, and he knew it, purring smugly in her arms.

Visible again, she twirled around slowly with him and

the basket, raining kisses on his head until he protested loudly. Laughing, she put him down.

At a safe distance, he stood indignant, tail straight up like a pipecleaner, and glared at her with yellow eyes, meowing, telling her off. Still laughing, she watched him prance back into the forest.

A snap of her fingers and he would be back in her arms. That really made him angry. But she wouldn't tease him so today. She had other things to do.

She moved through the bushes and the trees, listening to the wind rustling the leaves together. She had on a long dark brown woolen dress belted at the waist, heavy leggings on underneath, a white, warm shawl she had crocheted with her own hands, and a soft hat low over her eyes. Her hair loosely braided down her back.

A little breathless by the time she came to Black Pond, she decided to rest awhile under the weeping willow nearby. It was the largest one she'd ever seen. The pond was so peaceful, so lovely.

Leaning up against the willow's rough trunk, she sat in the grass and daydreamed, skimming fingers lightly over the ground as the gentle wind played about her. She could understand why they called it Black Pond. The water was calm and so dark blue it seemed black.

Tall water reeds and brown furry cattails waved in the breeze as hordes of tiny animals scurried about the water's perimeter and in the pond itself. Waterfowl skimmed its surface and called out plaintively. Insects droned along with the wind. A bluish mist floated oppressively above the pond even now in the brightest part of the day, and made her fancy that to walk into it would be to disappear into another time, another century. It was an eerie, breathtaking place.

A *strange* place. She shivered, and wished that she had worn a heavier shawl. She'd been by the pond many times on the way to Mabel's, but had never stopped. Now, gazing out at the rippling water and a distant line of birds racing high above, she wondered . . . wondered *why* she'd stopped today.

An old place, she mulled over the revelation. But not a happy one, she could sense it. The faintest traces of magic lingered on the breeze.

Was this one of the meeting places of the sadistic satanic cult that she'd begun sensing weeks ago, the cult that everyone was gossiping about? The one she couldn't seem to *see?*

No.

Muted images crowded into her mind of women and men dancing beside the pond in the dark around a bonfire, chanting obscenities and shedding innocent blood, and her face fell into a frown. Yes, long ago a witches' coven had met here. But centuries ago. Yet her skin still crawled. Black magic. Satan worshippers. Then the uneasy feelings were gone.

It had been a long time ago.

The leaves over her laced the blue sky and whispered things she couldn't understand.

Amanda could have sworn she heard someone sigh her name. She listened for a few more minutes, but there was nothing, just the wind soughing through the trees.

Loneliness did strange things to a person. And she'd been achingly lonely these last months, cutting herself off from the world, like a wounded animal licking its wounds. It definitely was time to rejoin humanity. The thought of a hot cup of tea with a friend, just to hear another person's voice again, was suddenly very appealing.

She got up, and as she was brushing off her skirts, she glanced up and saw the shimmering apparition.

It hovered about midway across the pond, above the

water, its face a misty white oval as its arms opened and beckoned toward Amanda.

The specter was so faint, Amanda could barely tell it was a woman. But it was.

Amanda sensed such an overpowering melancholy in the spirit—an aching hunger—that it made her wince, cringe back from it.

The ghost tried to speak, but the words were indistinguishable. As Amanda stared, startled but not really frightened, it dissolved back into the mist, as if it had never been. All that was left of it was a haunting echo on the chilly wind . . .

Amanda . . . Amanda.

It knows my name.

For a time, Amanda stood there on the bank, speculating on the whole mystery. She'd never known a ghost to come *uncalled;* she hadn't summoned it. And it knew her name.

An ominous shiver swept through her body as she recalled what she had almost done the night before.

Had she called something up, anyway? A random haunt that had been sucked into her world?

No, this ghost was *different.* She just couldn't put her finger on why—yet.

A twig snapped loudly somewhere behind her.

If I did accidently bring something out, I'll have to do another spell to reverse the damage, she thought, as she turned from the pond and continued on her way.

Soon Mabel's trailer was looming in front of her.

Mabel was rail-thin, and tiny, not more than five feet tall, with pale blue eyes and wispy hair the color of clean snow that she always wore tucked up with black bobby pins. Her small face was etched with lines. Her eyes seemed to see right through a person. She looked frail but had an indomitable spirit. Thought every day was a gift from God.

When Gus, Mabel's husband, had been alive, they'd had a lovely three-story Victorian farmhouse that had been in her family for over a century, and thirty prime farming acres on this side of Canaan. But she'd lost all of it during Gus's battle with cancer. After his death, she'd had to sell it all to satisfy the creditors, and to pay the hospital and the doctors.

With that familiar look of loss on her thin face, she'd confided to Amanda many times that she missed her old home. The home where a shy girl of fifteen had been courted, and won, by a German immigrant named Gus Sanderson. They'd fallen in love, married, and farmed the place for over fifty years together. They'd hoped to pass it down to their children, a boy named Jon and a girl named Emma.

But as these things sometimes turned out, neither child had wanted the farm when they grew up. Jon had traipsed off to war, never to come back, and Emma had slunk away with a sweet-talking salesman to raise a family of her own far away. She'd always hated the farm, anyway.

"Imagine . . . I've outlived them all, even my children. Never even see my grandchildren," Mabel had said one day when Amanda had been visiting. "Too far away. Since their mother, my daughter, Emma, died all those years ago of pneumonia at thirty-three, I've never heard much from them." Though Mabel believed what she'd really died from had been poverty—too much work, grief, and children too quickly.

"I still write to them sometimes. The letters always come back." She'd shrugged her stooped old shoulders, her watery blue eyes haunted.

"I wonder sometimes what Emma's kids are like. Daydream about them coming and taking me away from here. Back to their home where they'll love me and take care of me. Need me." Her thin body had seemed to sag a little more.

Mabel was all alone, even more than Amanda. Amanda still had family.

Mabel lived on a meager social security check, clipped coupons, and only had her thirteen-inch black-and-white TV for company. For years, first Jake and then Amanda had been trying to get her to move her trailer to one of those trailer parks in town so she could be closer to other people. She never would, because she wanted to stay close to the land and farm she'd lost. Spunky old lady.

And oh, the stories she could tell. She'd spent her childhood in a different world than today's. Her old life on their farm had been idyllic and nostalgically peaceful. Sometimes, listening raptly to the old woman's reminiscings about the hard work, the gatherings with neighbors, their friends, Amanda yearned to be able to walk back into time and somehow become part of it. To have known Mabel when she'd been young and happy.

She'd grown fond of Mabel over the last few years.

Knocking on the trailer's door, she heard shuffling feet, and mumbling behind it. A curtain was shoved over, and Amanda glimpsed a frightened old face, then a recognizing, welcoming smile.

Amanda smiled back at her, waved. The door opened. "Amanda, well, aren't you a sight for sore eyes, child," Mabel greeted her, ushering her into the tiny trailer. As small as it was, it was always as neat as a pin.

"Been a long time since you've visited me, Amanda. I was beginning to think you didn't want to be bothered any longer with an old woman like me. Too much trouble." She clicked her tongue.

She looked very old today, very tired.

Amanda hugged her warmly. The woman was so glad to see her it made her feel even more guilty.

She set the basket down by the door, removed her hat.

"You're no trouble at all, Mabel." A pause. "I've missed you. I'm sorry I haven't been over more lately but I just wanted some time alone. To get my head together. But I'm doing better now. From now on, I won't stay away so long at a time. Promise."

Mabel grinned, showing her empty gums. Amanda'd caught her unaware and she hadn't had time to put her teeth in. They hurt, anyway, she always complained.

"You're smiling," Mabel's voice an ancient rustling. "It's about time. You can only grieve so long, child. Take it from me, I know. No matter how much you loved someone." There was a caring in her that always melted Amanda.

"Being happy now doesn't mean you didn't love him. It's not a betrayal."

"I finally know that, Mabel," she whispered back, as she took her shawl off and laid it on the threadbare sofa. All she had to do was turn around and she bumped into the kitchen table, the rooms were so cramped. She sat down, observing Mabel as she bustled around the stove making tea.

It felt good to be there again.

"Cold out there today, Amanda?" Mabel inquired as she set the steaming cups on the table along with her antique crystal containers of sugar and cream.

"Chilly, but not bad. That storm was a killer last night." Amanda stirred her tea.

"Wasn't it?" Mabel agreed.

"You don't seem to have any damage here, though." Amanda glanced out the window in front of her. "You're lucky. You should have seen the mess at my place."

"Got it taken care of?"

"I think so," Amanda said evasively. "Winter's coming, it won't be long now. The wind's nippy. But the leaves are breathtaking reds and oranges. Beautiful."

"Always is this time of year around here, child," Mabel remarked, good-naturedly. "You walked, then?"

"Yes. I needed the exercise after being cooped up so long in the house . . ." Amanda trailed off, recalling the last weeks and months, the misery and the sadness . . . the loneliness.

She met Mabel's eyes and saw the same feelings reflected back at her. She felt the full impact of her neglect. She'd been without Jake for only a few months, while Mabel had been alone for years.

"I'm so sorry," she divulged, knowing Mabel would understand. "I've neglected you."

"You don't need to apologize to me. I'm just glad you're all right. I was getting mighty worried about you. If my old bones would have carried me, I would have limped over and checked on you myself." Mabel had no car and no telephone; both were luxuries she couldn't afford.

"It's hard, I know, child, being all alone. You must miss your Jake something awful. But the pain will lessen and it'll get easier as time goes by. Just be glad you had someone who loved you as long as you did. Some people never have that. Cherish his memories."

Mabel had thought the world of Jake, too. That was how Amanda had met her, through Jake.

One of his pottery students had belonged to a church in town that took meals and old clothes out to the elderly of the area who could no longer get around. One day Jake had helped the church deliver food to Mabel.

It'd been a vicious winter with lots of snow. Mabel's

furnace had gone out the week before. But she'd had too much pride to ask for help.

Jake had found her huddled in the tiny kitchen, warming her body over the open oven door, trying to stay warm, a blanket wrapped around her and mittens on her frozen hands. He'd felt so sorry for her he'd stayed and worked on the furnace. He'd even gone back to town to buy the necessary parts, out of his own pocket, and wouldn't leave until he'd fixed it. He'd been appalled at the way the woman had been living. Forgotten and destitute.

From that day onward, Jake had cared for her like a son. Maybe because he had never had a mother of his own—his mother had divorced his father when he was just a baby. Then she'd left Jake to be raised by his father and his father's mother, Grandma Cloie. His father had passed away when Jake was fifteen and his grandmother when he was twenty.

Mabel had loved to bake German strudels and yeast breads for him before her arthritis crippled her so.

Mabel had loved Jake, too.

"Being alone's not so bad," Mabel declared, wincing from her arthritis, as she lowered herself into the chair next to Amanda.

She gazed at the cooling cups of tea and the empty table. "I wish I could offer you something to eat, but my social security check is so small it barely gets me through the month."

The basket, Amanda thought.

"I remembered that, so I came prepared. I brought us something to eat. It's in the basket by the door." Amanda got up and retrieved the bundle.

She emptied the basket on the table. "Peach preserves, sausage, crackers, cheese, fresh-baked muffins . . . and that tea you like so much."

Mabel's eyes widened with gratefulness. "You're too

good to me. You're such a kind person, Amanda." She got out plates and napkins and placed them on the table.

The way she devoured the food shocked Amanda. How hungry she must be, and her next check wouldn't come for another week. But Amanda knew enough not to say anything, it would just hurt Mabel's pride.

She'd make sure, though, that she didn't eat much and that she'd leave whatever they didn't eat. That she'd bring more later, too.

When Mabel had devoured enough to satisfy her, she located and put her dentures in and they chatted about trivial things. Amanda poured her more tea. Soon it would make her sleepy, but that was just the magic working. Her pain would be gone.

Amanda suspected that Mabel knew there was something different about the tea, but the old woman never asked questions, never mentioned it, like she never mentioned the rumors spread in town that Amanda was a witch. Mabel believed in such things, Amanda knew that, but she also loved Amanda enough to respect her privacy. They just never talked about it.

"Amanda, I do believe this is the best batch of peach preserves you've ever put up," Mabel judged, yawning, as Amanda fetched her a third cup of tea.

"Reminds me of the preserves I used to can on the farm when I was a girl. We had, oh, about ten acres of fruit trees—apples mostly—and every year my daddy would hire these migrant workers from down south to harvest the fruit when it was ready. Boy, some of them were characters . . . some just strange." She moved her head, rubbing her wrinkled hands down the length of her legs through her faded housedress, as crumbs clung to her chin and a few tumbled into her lap.

"I remember this one old Mexican named Carlos something-or-other when I was about twelve or so. His whole family camped on our property one summer so they could work. There was a mess of them. Lived in a ratty old covered wagon and tents. They had a daughter about my age—can't recall her name at all—so that's why I started visiting them." She squinted her eyes as if she were looking back over the years. "But I remember her grandpa, Carlos, well enough. I can still see him sitting cross-legged, bundled in blankets, before their campfire at night as he spun his stories. He was blind. Eyes were all white. And he wore these bizarre clothes, like a gypsy. Wore all these things around his neck. Magic charms he called them. To ward off evil. He wouldn't talk above a whisper and was always peering around as if he could see. Petrified of some *thing*—a demon he called it—that he wouldn't talk about and that he believed was still tracking him. He was into voodoo, or something like it."

Amanda's hand stopped tapping against her saucer.

"Said he and a friend meddled in affairs he should've left alone and a witch hexed him. He'd never tell me exactly what he'd done to the witch, refused to talk anymore about it, but he did tell me that his punishment wasn't near as bad as his poor friend's . . . his friend was blinded *and* his tongue was torn out in pieces by the demon the witch had sent after them. Then the demon took him away. Grandpa Carlos never saw him again."

"Did you believe what he told you?" Amanda couldn't help but ask. She'd heard of black witches and their demons. They'd call them up from hell, from the world in between, or even from another dimension. All were possible. And the demons were vicious. Unstoppable.

"Not back then." Mabel gestured dismissively with her hand. "I was a child. Innocent of the world."

"Now?"

Mabel stared off somewhere past Amanda. "Well,

now, I'd believe almost anything. I've lived a long time. I've seen ghosts." She brought haunted eyes back to Amanda's interested face. "Saw Gus out in his garden not more than two days after we buried him. He stood up and waved at me. I ran outside, but by the time I got to the garden, he wasn't there any longer."

Amanda thought of Jake and what she'd tried the night before. She shook away the horrible vision of Jake half-formed in the circle.

"Must have been quite a shock for you." Amanda smiled understandingly. She wasn't a hypocrite. She might not scream that she was a witch from the rooftops, but she also never denied what she was, if faced with it; never made fun of other people's beliefs.

"No, not really," Mabel sighed. "It was so good to see him. And it was somehow comforting to know that there was an afterlife of some kind. Not just death." She laid a wrinkled hand on her chest above her heart. "Even though I'm a religious person, it still felt good to know that.

"And I've been looking for him ever since." Her face sadder. "But he's never come back."

"Maybe he will, someday." Amanda patted the old woman's shoulder.

"Maybe." Then she sighed again, drank more of her tea, her eyes getting heavier. She was fighting to stay awake.

"I've been reading the newspapers lately, Amanda," she suddenly said. "This satanic cult stuff is scaring me. They found a family murdered yesterday out by Harbor Light. Four of them. Awful. They were tortured to death. . . ." Her voice fell to a frightened whisper. "Eyes gouged out, tongues torn out. Burned . . . awful, awful." Mabel's sleepy eyes still reflected horror.

Amanda's stern expression covered a growing rage. "I hope they catch them soon." Mentally she made a note to take the time to cast out a spell net for them. She should have long ago, but this was the first time she'd been aware that they were actually hurting or killing people. It would take some work. They had a strong magic shield up against her kind. She'd have to break it down. Could take days.

"Me, too. Amanda, you shouldn't be living out in that cabin all alone."

Amanda almost smiled. "Oh, I can take care of myself, all right. It's you I'm worried about."

"They won't bother an old woman like me. Besides"— Mabel shuffled up from the chair and disappeared into the other room for a few seconds and came back carrying a huge shotgun—"If anybody I don't know comes around, or tries to break in . . . I'll fill all their butts with what's in here." She grinned slyly. "And I'm still a damn good shot. Gus taught me years ago. Haven't forgot. So I can take care of myself, too." She laid the gun against the wall.

"I bet you can." Amanda chuckled and started clearing the dishes off the table, rinsing them in the tiny sink, her back to Mabel. With the talk of witches and cults, something nagging at her subconscious finally surfaced.

"Mabel, do you know anything about a place called Black Pond? About a mile from here?"

"Black Pond?" Mabel responded hesitantly.

Amanda looked over her shoulder at the old woman hovering over the table, and when her eyes met Amanda's, there was an unusual evasiveness in them.

"Why do you ask, Amanda?"

"Well, because today, on the way here, I decided to stop a moment to rest there—by the willow tree—and I thought I saw *something* above the water. Floating . . ."

Then Amanda recognized the uneasiness on Mabel's wrinkled face—fear—and quickly added, "Ah, never

mind. It was probably just my morbid state of mind."
Her thoughts brushed again across the ill-fated ritual
of the night before. "An illusion in the mist. . . ."
Amanda shrugged.

Mabel stared at her. "You saw something?"

"In the mist, I saw a woman," Amanda replied. "She
was calling to me. She knew my name. It was the strangest thing. I just wondered what history was attached to
that place."

Mabel got up to fuss with something at the end of
the kitchen counter. "Place is haunted," she said simply. "You know, it's known by another name. Some of
the older ones still call it Witch's Pond."

"Witch's Pond?"

"Yes. And it has to do with its history. You probably
saw *her.*" Mabel chortled softly.

"Her?"

A thin bony hand settled on Amanda's shoulder after
she'd sat back down. Amanda glanced up at her.

"Her. The witch of Witch's Pond. You've never heard
the stories, then, have you?"

"No. Tell me." Amanda's interest was passionately
captured.

Mabel settled back tiredly into her chair. "When I was
a child my mother warned me about that place. Told me
never to go near it. People *disappeared* there. The children
in town used to dare each other to go there at night
and . . . wait . . . for her. Not me, though, I wasn't brave
enough. There were horrible rumors about that place;
about what had happened there."

"What happened there?"

Mabel inclined her head, her face full of compassion.
"They were supposed to have killed a suspected witch
there. The woman's name was Rachel Coxe, if I recall
rightly. She was accused of being a witch at the height
of the witch scare sometime in the seventeenth century.

You know, though it never got as bad here as Salem or Boston, the witch mania infected the townspeople, right enough. They believed Rachel was a witch, along with a few others, and they hounded her. I don't think there was ever a trial . . . she tried to escape them.

"They say they tracked her, and drowned her in the pond. Her wronged spirit is supposed to be waiting there . . . waiting to take revenge on those who killed her, or win vindication, so they say."

Rachel, Amanda's mind whispered. Knowing a spirit's name was having power over them, like knowing the name of a demon. You could control them.

"Not long after Rachel disappeared, a trapper found body parts strewn all along a section of bank at Black Pond. That was just the beginning. Hideous things have occurred there ever since. Some campers were supposed to have disappeared late in the eighteenth century near the place. Three children drowned there when I was just a girl. Lots of people through the years have seen things there, like you.

"Did she say anything to you?"

"No, just called my name, then evaporated," Amanda intoned, thoughtfully. She'd strolled over to the door, was looking out.

"I can't believe you saw the ghost . . . and nothing happened."

I'm a witch, that's why, Amanda thought. "Lucky, I guess. You really believe that it's dangerous?"

"Things *have* happened there."

Outside Mabel's kitchen the sun was sliding down into the treetops. Everything had that tint of winter pink, like one of those paint-by-number sets she'd had as a child. Night came swiftly in late October.

"Why did they murder her?" Amanda asked, curious. She hadn't felt any danger emanating from the ghost earlier, but then some ghosts could hide their true intentions.

"According to the old stories, she caused the town's livestock to get sick, did wicked things and cast evil spells, was promiscuous—which wasn't all that unusual for the times, no matter what you've read in your stuffy old history books. She was said to be able to see the future. She was a renegade. Very beautiful. The women of the town despised her because all the men wanted her.

"But then they claimed she killed her married ex-lover. And the chase was on."

"So they *murdered* her for it?" Amanda said drily, unable to stop the hair rising on the back of her neck. She'd been treated cruelly for what people had believed she'd done over the years, too, so she could empathize. Boston still haunted her.

"Well, no one knows if they really killed her. The legend went that Rachel was a witch. That she'd killed not only her ex-lover in cold blood . . . but her own children as well."

"She killed her own children?" Amanda echoed.

"They found their bodies, hideously butchered, and some thought she had used them in a sacrifice. I don't recall how many children she was reported to have had, or if they were boys or girls. It's an old tale. She just disappeared one day, some say never to be seen again, while another version went that the vengeful townspeople did catch up with her—and killed her at Black Pond.

"And when the apparition of a woman first appeared at the pond, and evil things began to happen there, people put two and two together and believed the ghost was Rachel. No one knows the real story, except Rachel . . . and those who killed her, maybe. If they did."

Amanda glanced over her shoulder, pretending that the story hadn't affected her in the least. Which it had.

Through the ages, witches had been unjustly tormented, and prosecuted for crimes they'd never committed.

So much evil done in the world through the centuries; the infamous Inquisitions, the heinous torturings, and the mass burnings, had all been performed for, and by, fanatics or men greedy for power, not God, Satan, or the supernatural.

God was a gentle, loving being. It was man who could be the heartless bloodthirsty beast. It was just easier for man to mask his bestiality under the convenient guise of doing what he thought God would want him to do. The atrocities perpetrated on those poor helpless wretches all in the name of religion or fear always made Amanda sad and angry when she heard of them.

After all, she was a witch, too.

It made Amanda sick to dwell on it.

"Do you believe Rachel haunts Black Pond?" Amanda abruptly asked Mabel with candor.

"Black Pond's a place of darkness. I don't know about the rest." Mabel studied her closely. "I'd stay away from there if I was you. You seem especially susceptible to such things."

"Perhaps I am," Amanda said softly.

Amanda's sixth sense was squirming. An uneasiness had started nibbling at her. There was more to this . . .

"Mabel, that's an intriguing story, but I'd better be getting home now. It's getting dark outside. And I wanted to start sketching some designs tonight for some new pots I'm making tomorrow."

"Well, it's about time you get back to work." Mabel gave her a perceptive glance, glad to have dropped the subject of the witch, Rachel, with night coming on.

Fetching Amanda's empty basket, her hat, and her shawl, she didn't utter another thing about Rachel as she said her good-byes.

"Thanks for the company and the delicious food, Amanda. Come by again real soon."

Amanda gave the old woman a strong hug, gazing down at her. She'd left the remnants of their feast for Mabel.

She's so frail and tiny, can't weigh more than a sack of potatoes, all pale skin and brittle bones. She's so old . . . what will I do when she goes, too? Amanda brooded. *I would truly be alone out here, then. Just Amadeus and me . . . and my memories.*

When she walked her to the door, Amanda noticed that Mabel was no longer wincing in pain, or limping. Just very tired. Good.

Amanda left, stepping out into the lengthening shadows of an autumn twilight. The air heavy with the promise of coming frost. Jake and she used to bundle up warmly and take long walks on just such evenings.

For a moment she stood at the edge of the forest and looked back at the trailer. She took the time to weave a protection spell over it and the old woman. If there were any devil disciples around, Amanda wanted to be sure Mabel would be all right.

On her way home, she strode briskly through the woods, snuggled deep in her shawl, her eyes on the ground as the light turned an iridescent mauve and then to dark amethyst shadows. It was very cold and still.

For some unnameable reason, she went a different way home than she had come. Nowhere near the infamous pond.

Or so she thought. She halted for a few moments on a large slab of rock halfway home to take some pebbles out of her shoe.

After she'd tossed the rocks into the tall grass, she was just rising to leave when she blinked . . . and then quickly found herself standing beneath a huge willow tree on the edge of a dark body of water.

The pond. The same exact place she had been earlier when she'd seen the ghost.

In shock, she gazed around. The sun was just a dim crescent on the horizon, the night ready to take over, and the wind was suddenly icy.

"How did I get here?" she demanded aloud to no one, startled, backing away from the willow tree.

There was the presence of danger all around her. The atmosphere glacial. Leaves crackled under her unsteady feet.

The cries for help originated far away in the distance, deep in the darkening woods. A woman's beseeching, blood-chilling screams of fear, pleading for mercy, that grew steadily louder and more horrifying as Amanda listened, holding her breath. There were the echoes of galloping horses, their thundering hooves pounding, bloodthirsty shouts and jeers, like the hunt . . . coming nearer . . . nearer, toward the pond, until Amanda had to clasp her hands over her ears to shut out the worst of the noise.

Then the rabble was surrounding her. The noises so ear-splitting, and the woman's terror so palpable, she could almost reach out and touch it.

The bushes, the leaves were violently disturbed, the dirt splattering up from the ground, stinging and pelting her. So real, she felt a horse's warm, heaving flank slide past her, and she jumped. The scent of the horses, the leather of their saddles, even the sweat of the men was cloying—was *real*. All around her.

But there was *nothing* there.

Phantoms. All.

An eerie trance descended over Amanda as the invisible shades pranced around her. In macabre fascination, she listened as a woman groaned and cried on the ground behind her. Amanda's heart pounded along with the woman's agony. She spun about, sweeping the ground with her eyes and then her hands, but there was nothing she could do to aid the poor woman for there was *nothing* there.

This had all happened in the past.

One last wail crescendoed into the vibrating dusk and then something heavy was flung—she felt the air ripple as it went past her—into the pond's black waters and a woman's final dying scream echoed suddenly into a dead stillness.

But Amanda's ears were still quivering with the unearthly sounds; she couldn't escape them. Finally, shutting her eyes, she shouted out an ancient spell. One that she hadn't had to use in ages. The past released her.

The woods were silent once again.

Amanda opened her eyes cautiously.

Directly in front of her was a dark-robed woman, ephemeral as fog, hovering above the pond's seething waters, beckoning to her. Trying to tell her, or warn her, of something.

"*Rachel?*"

"*Yes.*" The eyes were pools of gloomy emptiness.

"What do you want of me?" Amanda demanded of the apparition. "Why did you bring me here without my consent?" she reprimanded angrily, her firmness concealing a growing apprehensiveness concerning the specter.

The ghost didn't answer her, only moaned. It was drawing closer, as the water began to purl, surging before it in waves.

For a terrifying moment, Amanda couldn't move. She felt the frigid water lapping hungrily at her feet, trying to suck her in. A force so strong, her body could barely resist it.

The wraith was mouthing words, her arms outstretched . . . now almost touching her.

"*Amanda . . . help . . . me . . . find . . . peace,*" the

spirit begged raspingly over the wind that was whipping wildly about them.

"I don't know what you want and I can't help you, anyway. I'm sorry. I *command* you to return to your grave and be at peace!" she yelled back at the spirit.

Amanda invoked another stronger spell that would send the ghost back from where it had come.

It did.

She fell backward, tumbling onto the ground, as if the hold on her had snapped like an overextended rubberband.

The apparition screamed in rage, as Amanda cringed back in startled surprise. Then it slowly faded back into the wet mist until it was gone. But the water continued to churn tumultuously, and the willow tree's branches lashed out at her as if it were alive and trying to beat her.

That wasn't the way a spirit usually responded to a powerful witch.

Amanda turned on her heels and moved purposely away through the darkness. Her steps dragging now from the two spells that had sapped her energy. She had to get home and sleep. She was so weary.

Rachel might have been a white witch, too, her guilty conscience pricked her. Like her. Perhaps she should have helped her.

No, it wasn't allowed. What was in the past, was in the past. It would do no good to resurrect it now.

Later, recovered from the earlier magic, and safe in her warm home before a blazing fire, with Amadeus at her feet, Amanda drew up another enchantment to cancel out any lingering traces of the disastrous one of the night before.

She was sure that would rid her of Rachel for good. But through it all, Amanda couldn't help but feel some pity for Rachel.

Rachel, who couldn't rest. *What torment her poor soul must have endured for its hate to still have so much power after all this time.*

Too much power for a dead woman . . . or a dead witch, if that was what she had truly been.

Rachel. What did you really want?

But Amanda didn't really want the answer . . . because knowing might only cause her more guilt. Interfering with the dead was no business for a live witch.

Amanda's green eyes gazed pensively into the flames.

There *was* something she could do for Rachel's spirit, though.

She softly spoke the words of one last spell, one that would surely give Rachel's soul peace. Forever.

That was the least, and the only thing, she could do for a long-dead sister witch. Even that drained her so much that she fell asleep in the rocking chair, fire still blazing, Amadeus cuddled in her lap; forgetting completely of her vow to search and find the satanic cult that was causing havoc in the area.

Too much magic in one day.

Chapter 2

The next morning Amanda rose from her bed early, disturbing a comfortable Amadeus, and struggled into her heavy robe with cold fingers. Scuffing and shivering into the kitchen in slippered feet, she snapped her fingers at the small wood stove in the corner of the kitchen and crackling flames leapt up inside.

She warmed herself over the stove and gazed out the ice-patterned window. Outside, an overnight translucent blanket of milky ice had attached itself to the ground, and the frozen tree limbs clacked together in the breeze like loose skeletons under a forbidding steel-gray sky.

She tried not to dwell on Rachel or Witch's Pond. It was over. The whole thing was an enigma she would never solve now.

It was Saturday. Seven days from All Hallow's Eve. The night when her Celtic ancestors had celebrated Samhain, the beginning of winter, and thanked the earth for all its bounty of the previous summer. Through the ages the night they'd dance in wild abandon before blazing bonfires in scary costumes, trying to divine the future, and driving all the God-fearing folks crazy. A night when the barriers between human and supernatural forces were broken. A night for witches.

Even the British church setting November 1 as All Saints' Day and a holy day couldn't stop the pagan rites.

But if it stays this cold, Rebecca, she thought of her older sister, smiling, *you'll not be doing any nude cavorting in the woods* this *year.*

As if witches followed those silly rituals any longer . . . well, perhaps, if it would make good fodder for her books, Rebecca probably still did it.

By the time she had finished frying and eating breakfast, the kitchen was warm and cozy. She had a book opened before her and Amadeus was begging for scraps in her lap when the knock came at the door.

"Ernie," Amanda exclaimed, as she tugged the door open. "Long time no see." She grinned at him, feeling a little self-conscious in her robe, though he had seen her in it a hundred times when he'd come over to visit Jake. She pulled at her belt, tightening it.

He stood there sheepishly in his mailman's uniform, clutching a package in his arms. "Hello, Amanda. Got some things here for you. Your Book-of-the-Month club selections." He handed her a brown package. Amanda loved books and read all the time, especially history books, science fiction, and horror. After she'd taken the books and set them down on the table, he lifted a large package up from behind him for her to see, groaning at the sheer weight of it. "And this enormous thing. Whatever it is."

"Heavy, huh?"

"Very."

"Come on in with it," she told him. "It's freezing out there."

"I know," he agreed, chattering his teeth to make her smile again.

Amadeus had scuttled under the table. He curled up in a ball and glared out at Ernie as if he'd never seen him in his life.

"Amadeus, behave," she chided the cat. "Don't know

what's gotten into him. He's never acted that way with you before."

Ernie stepped inside, bringing the cold with him. "Must be the beard. He doesn't recognize me."

Amanda noticed the new growth on his face, streaked with gray. It did make him look different. "I like it. Makes you look distinguished."

"Thanks."

"Why the hand delivery? That's unusual, isn't it?"

"I didn't want to just leave it outside by the mailbox. It's so big, someone might have run off with it. Didn't want it sitting out in the weather if it was important. So I thought I'd hand deliver it, and see how you were getting along at the same time."

"That was nice of you."

"I meant to stop in sooner, but I didn't want to intrude."

"You're not. In fact, I visited Mabel yesterday. It felt good to get out," Amanda said, closing the door. She watched him take the package over to the corner and carefully set it down with a grunt.

He straightened up.

"What's in it?"

"By the size of it and the address it came from—Trenton, New Jersey—I'd guess it was that cake of clay I ordered a while back, before . . ." The words *before Jake died* hung in the air between them, inescapable, dissipating only when Amanda's lips turned up at the corners and she shook her head.

The returning look he bestowed on her was poignant.

"But it couldn't have come at a better time, Ernie," she assured him. "This morning I'd planned to start working again. The clay supply out in the workshop's probably a hunk of stone by now."

"Ah, I was just going to ask how the pot business was doing."

"Growing, and I haven't been supplying the demand enough lately," she couldn't help but banter back.

He chuckled, getting it. "Well, now you'll have no excuse not to. Work, that is. And put me at the top of your list. I'd like another one of those green pots. Bigger than the last one. My rubber tree has outgrown it. But I've received so many compliments on it I want another one just like it. I'll find something else to put in the old pot."

"All right. One large sea-green crackled pot with a Celadon glaze. It'll be the first one I do, I promise."

"Great." Ernie pulled off his dark blue sock cap and stuffed it into his coat pocket, his hair windblown and mussed.

Amanda had never noticed until then how good-looking Ernie was, in a rugged, older sort of way. Ernie was close to forty, she'd guess, though in all the years Jake and she had known him, Amanda had never thought to ask him his age. His once-thick black hair was now peppered with gray, and his humorous eyes were a deep brown, in a sharp-chiseled face. He was much shorter than Jake had been, barely taller than she was herself. He was hometown, born and raised. But he'd always treated her with respect.

He was divorced. His ex-wife and teenage son lived in California, and Ernie rarely saw them. A man with a lot of love to give, he missed his son terribly and missed being a father to him.

"I've got some hot coffee and leftover bacon. Eggs wouldn't take but a few minutes to fry up . . . if you have time?"

A shadow of uncertainty crossed his face; then he glanced back at his mail truck. They'd been friends for so long, it seemed funny that they would be so unsure with each other now.

Ernie's face relaxed and he smiled. "I could use a cup of that hot coffee to defrost me. Today's a short day, anyway. Most of my mail is already delivered. But I don't want to put you to any trouble . . ."

His eyes slid toward the stove and the coffeepot.

"Ernie, it's no trouble, believe me. I could use the company," she confessed.

"Good. I take my eggs sunny-side up. Three will do it. A couple pieces of bacon."

"Black coffee. And my homemade sourdough bread to soak up the egg yolk. I remember. Give me your coat, and sit down," Amanda told him.

He struggled out of his damp coat, handed it to her, and she hung it on the nail behind the door as he settled down on a chair.

"I'll get the coffee," she said.

After she turned on the gas under the skillet, she poured him a cup, and set it down in front of him. He raised it to his lips with a sigh.

"Amanda, I meant to come over sooner." His eyes met hers over the rim of his cup through the steam. "But I wasn't sure if you wanted company yet."

Right after Jake had died, Ernie had been the first one there to console her. And when she'd wanted to be left alone, he'd respected her wishes and had stayed away.

"It's all right, Ernie," Amanda reassured him. "My self-imposed seclusion is over. I'm better. Not so self-destructive anymore. But it's been hard . . ." She turned away for a moment, then walked back to the stove and started breaking eggs over the heated skillet she'd used for her own breakfast, determined not to let the tears win out. They didn't.

Amadeus was scrutinizing her from a dark corner, an encouraging cat smile on his furry face. So he wasn't really mad.

"You do look better than the last time I saw you, Amanda," Ernie remarked from across the room. "But you're a strong woman. I always told Jake he was a lucky man."

"Not as lucky as I was to have him," she replied softly. "He was a once in a lifetime."

Ernie inclined his head. "He loved you more than I've ever seen a man love a woman . . . you remember that, never forget it. That kind of love never dies," he said with kindness.

She regarded Ernie over her shoulder as the eggs crackled in the pan, surprised that he would say such a thing; too touched to respond.

Fresh tears welled up in her eyes. "I'm sorry," she muttered, wiping them away.

"No need to apologize, I understand," his voice sincere.

"There'll never be another Jake for me. Ever."

"No, there won't. But love comes in all shapes and sizes, Amanda, so don't fool yourself into thinking that you'll never *love* again. You might."

"Ernie"—she shook her head—"do you know you're a romantic through and through?"

"Ha, so you finally noticed that, did you?" He looked over at her with teasing eyes.

"Yeah, I noticed it a long time ago."

"How about another cup of that great coffee?" He held his cup out in front of him with a pathetic begging expression on his face that reminded her of the old Ernie.

After he had gotten his coffee, he casually commented, "Isolated like you've been, I imagine you haven't heard about all the Satanic cult activity around here lately?"

Amanda tensed. "Yes, I have. Mabel told me about it yesterday. She's scared." She'd finished the eggs, loaded his plate, and had set it down in front of him. He dug into it as she sat down across from him.

"She has a right to be. They've killed six people now.

They discovered messages smeared in the victims' blood near the bodies, promising more sacrifices. Warnings. I overheard Chief Garren at the donut shop this morning saying that one of the messages mentions that they're followers of a powerful witch. Witchcraft. It's gruesome. How can people do that to other people?" He shook his head, his fork poised halfway back to his plate. "How can they live with themselves?" he growled under his breath.

"There are evil people in the world, Ernie. More evil than you can imagine," was all she said.

Amadeus was hissing under the table, putting his two cents in.

"Well, it's got the townspeople pretty spooked," he continued. "There's going to be a town meeting about it Tuesday night. See if there's any way we can help the authorities find this human filth. And protect ourselves."

"A cult like this won't be easy to find." Amanda's eyes were disquieted, distant. "They know how to hide their tracks." She was uneasy. She'd always had a reputation in town for being a strange recluse. A few people had seen her do things that they shouldn't have seen. She wasn't always careful. She'd even been called a witch before by some of the local children. When Jake was alive, he'd always been her bridge, but Jake was gone now. She was alone. This situation wasn't going to help her bizarre reputation one bit.

"I just hope we can catch them," Ernie swore fervently.

"I hope so, too. Monsters like that give witchcraft a bad name."

Ernie gave her a strange look.

"What is it, Ernie?"

He shrugged, noncommittally. "Nothing much. Just something odd I recall Jake telling me once."

She raised her eyebrows. Her long hair hung loose

and soft about her white face and made her look especially vulnerable. "Yes?"

"Ah, it's nothing." But he still had that puzzled look on his face.

"You better tell me, or I won't give you any more coffee."

Ernie hesitated and then sighed. "He said *you* were a witch. I thought he was pulling my leg. But he was serious. Said he wasn't ashamed of it, and that you were a . . . white witch. Ridiculous, huh?" His nervous smirk faded as she stared at him and didn't try to deny it.

Thanks a lot, Jake.

"There is more than one kind of witch, Ernie, just like, as you said before, there is more than one kind of love. There's such a thing as white witchcraft and *good* witches."

His mouth dropped open. He was one of those people who wouldn't understand, she could tell that. One of those down-to-earth types who wouldn't believe in anything truly supernatural, unless he saw it with his own eyes. And even then he'd still doubt. Doubt his sanity before he'd accept it. Unlike Jake.

She was scaring him, she could tell.

She let him off the hook, trying to act amused. "It was a joke between Jake and me . . . me being a witch. Because he loved me so much, he always said I must be a witch, you know? That I'd put a spell on him? I was joshing you."

He gave a tiny sigh of relief. "You had me going there for a second, Amanda." He laughed, and then glanced at his wristwatch.

"I didn't realize it was so late. I'd better get the rest of my route done or I'm out of a job. Thanks for the breakfast and the coffee, it was delicious—and for the company." He stood up. "Good luck on those new pots. And, Amanda?"

"Yes?"

"I'm glad to see you're feeling more yourself. Making jokes and all."

"Yeah," she responded whimsically. What else could she say?

Amanda retrieved his coat, then followed him to the door.

"Ernie, could you do me a favor?"

"Sure, anything." He'd slipped into his coat, had his sock cap back on, and his hand on the doorknob.

"You know I don't have a phone, and I'm out of stamps . . . so would you take a note to Jane Weatherby for me?"

"Sure. I've got mail to deliver to her today, anyway."

"It'll just take me a second to write it out." Amanda searched for a pen and a scrap of paper and hurriedly scribbled a short note to her friend Jane.

"I want to reserve some kiln time next Saturday morning for my pots and I need to let her know at least a week ahead of time." She hadn't seen Jane in over a month, although, of all the townspeople, Jane, a widow who lived behind her gift shop with her three kids, was the closest thing she had to a real friend.

"I'll be sure to give it to her," he promised as he took the folded note. "I'd better . . . if I want my new pot."

"Yeah, if you want more than a hunk of unfinished clay, I do have to fire it."

She saw him out the door and he was almost to his mail truck when he swung around. The wind tugged at the ends of his hair that poked out from under the sock cap, and he had shoved his hands into his coat pockets. He reminded her of a little boy who didn't want to go to school.

"Amanda, would you consider . . . maybe . . ." he started to ask, faltering, and then rushed on. "Seeing a movie with me one night? Or going out to supper? Just as friends, I mean. You need to get out more."

She gave him a full smile.

"I'll think about it, Ernie. Thanks for the offer." He nodded, content with that, and walked to his mail truck to drive off, waving.

Amanda closed the door, still smiling. Watched the mail truck disappear over the nearest hill.

Then she cleaned up the mess in the kitchen and went to put on some of Jake's old blue jeans and one of his bulky sweaters.

If she was going to be cleaning, she'd want comfortable, warm clothes on.

The morning was the best she'd had in months. She cleaned and swept out the workshop, rearranged things, and took stock of her supplies. She dragged in the new cake of clay.

Then when everything was in place, she built a fire in the potbellied stove and got to work on Ernie's pot, humming contentedly as the sun's strong light slashed through the room.

As she spun the wheel and threw the pot, hands lovingly shaping the clay with her fingers or a wet sponge, her mind didn't wander far from her task, just happy to be working again.

She made it a point not to think about Rachel. But she found her thoughts dwelling on the dilemma of the witchcraft cult and what spells she'd have to perform to flush them out. How hard it would be and how long it might take. She already knew it could be a very perilous undertaking for her, if true black magic was involved. It could destroy her if she went up against them and wasn't stronger than they were.

And she had no way of knowing that until she caught them.

She dribbled more water onto the spinning pot, not taking her eyes from it. The excess clay glopped up on the edges of the wheel and fell to the floor with dull thuds. She wiped straggling hair back from her face, leaving smears of clay on her cheekbones.

Finishing Ernie's pot, she set it aside to dry. It was perfect, even if she was a little rusty. She began another smaller one.

The morning flew by.

Later, when her back began to ache and she realized how hungry she was, she quit, proud of the three pots she'd thrown in her first day. Stretching as she put things away, she scrubbed up the wheel and her tools.

Amadeus materialized and sat observing her with huge yellow eyes from a murky corner under the shelves. He kept growling softly, slinking restlessly around her feet until she noticed him.

"Amadeus, what is it?" she grilled him as she finished the cleanup.

Amadeus was snarling low in his throat.

Something's wrong. I can feel it.

She finally glanced down at the cat. He was crouching there in the gloom, hissing . . . his head tilted up toward the window.

"What?" She grabbed a towel from the table next to her, wiping her hands clean, and cautiously walked over to him. He never acted like this unless he was really disturbed.

Stooping down, she reached out to the cat. Instead of jumping into her arms like he usually did, he met her eyes for a brief second.

Something bad is out there! his cat thoughts insisted. *Something evil.*

Then he suddenly took off, running out the door as if he were in pursuit of something.

"Amadeus . . . Amadeus! Come back!" She walked to the door and shouted after him, "Don't try to do anything without me if it's that bad." She thought of the cult. Her eyes searched for the cat at the edge of the woods where he'd disappeared. No Amadeus.

A shadow wafted across the sun. A bad omen. But no matter how hard she stared, she couldn't see anything out there among the trees that could've upset Amadeus so. She couldn't sense anything, either.

What had spooked him so? Why had he just run off like that, disobeying her? That wasn't like him at all. Must have been really upset.

She called for him, even went outside in the bright afternoon light and looked for him. She cast a spell out for him. It was blocked.

She mulled over Amadeus's strange behavior. He could take care of himself, she wasn't worried. He had powers of his own. And yet it bothered her that her magic wasn't working. It sent ripples of disquiet through her.

Amanda stood listening for him by the window for a long time, but there was only silence. She assumed he was all right. At least, she didn't feel anything was wrong. And she'd always trusted her instincts before, so she had no cause to start doubting them now.

Outside, half the day was over.

Back in the house, she tried to go on as if nothing were wrong.

Maybe, she was thinking, she'd take that meatloaf from last week out of the freezer and make sandwiches out of it, take it over to Mabel's . . . and look for Amadeus along the way.

Soon she'd packed their supper and was headed for Mabel's. She avoided Witch's Pond.

And, though she looked for Amadeus, she didn't find him.

She just hoped he'd be back at the cabin when she returned.

Chapter 3

Amadeus was gone until midnight, which wasn't unusual, although Amanda had looked for him before and after she'd seen Mabel, and had begun to be concerned. She'd been relieved when she'd opened the door before going to bed and he was sitting there.

"Am I glad to see you. I was just about to unleash a minor demon to track you down."

The cat threw her an ugly look.

"I'm kidding. Can't you take a joke?" She tossed up her hands and let him in.

"Well?" she asked him in the dark kitchen as the wind chased itself through the trees and around the house. She was standing there in her robe, her arms crossed, her foot tapping.

Something bad out there . . . something bad coming . . . couldn't catch it. It was fast.

"Was it the cult?"

Could be.

Tried.

Sorry.

Amanda sighed and held out her arms and her familiar jumped into them. He was shivering. "Thanks for trying, Amadeus," she whispered into his ear. "But don't go running off like that on me anymore. You scared the heck out of me.

"Let me handle the cult," her voice hostile. "And I have some homework to do before I can attempt it."

Be careful. He remembered the last renegade cult.

"I will." She laid out some leftover meatloaf and mashed potatoes for the cat and went off to bed.

Sleep was elusive, though. She had to find that cult and stop them. Usually a cult was just a group of people who thought they had powers, but didn't. Then there were always those rare exceptions: the cults that really possessed true witches or warlocks and could hurt her or any other white witch.

That time in Boston had almost done her in. She'd been careless, underprotected, and the Satanic cult had called forth a midlevel demon from hell. . . . She'd won, but had had to spend three weeks in bed healing. She still had scars to show for that time.

Closing her eyes, she could still see that abomination hunkering before her. As tall as two bears, with a head and jaws like a spider and spikes all over its slimy blood-red body. Eight armlike appendages with razor-sharp claws at the ends. It threw acidy venom and breathed fire. The stench of the monster had been enough to make any witch faint away.

Amanda shuddered as she snuggled down into her covers that night, remembering. A close call. The only thing that had saved her was her quick thinking and pure luck. She ran faster than the thing could move and it had bought her the precious time she'd needed to conjure up a shield for herself until she had woven a stronger spell with which to destroy the fiend.

She wouldn't make that same mistake twice.

The spells she'd need to arm herself would take days and drain her of every ounce of strength. But she'd be prepared then for whatever she came up against.

Amadeus believed it was bad, and Amadeus was always right.

In the next few days she prepared her spells and tried to find out more about her adversary. She could not discover anything. No matter how hard she tried, she couldn't locate the cult. There was an invisible brick wall up, protecting them. Hiding them.

But there were no more incidents and as the days went by Amanda began to hope that they'd left the area, or better yet, that they had never existed in the first place. After all, there was no proof that the killings had been done by a cult.

Still, what Amadeus had told her nagged at her.

She wrote back to her sisters, the usual trivial chit-chat, and she wondered when Rebecca would show up. She kept busy.

Her newest batch of pots were coming along beautifully and she found that the work made all the difference in her. She looked forward to getting up every morning and she found herself smiling at things again.

Ernie started stopping by some mornings for coffee, to talk, and to see how her work was progressing. Amanda began to look forward to his visits.

Saturday morning, the morning of All Hallow's Eve, Amanda went into town.

Canaan wasn't big as towns went, with its gently sloping land dotted with old-fashioned houses, and tree-lined streets. It was as picturesque as a quaint postcard. A peaceful anachronism.

But the people were clannish and stayed to themselves. Amanda had never fit in. Never tried to.

She'd lived in the cabin on the edge of town a long time but was still an outsider to them. They didn't treat outsiders kindly.

They had rarely smiled at her as she passed them on the narrow streets, even in the beginning, and especially since that unfortunate incident two years ago. She had virtually become a pariah.

But I couldn't have just stood by and let that man beat that young woman any longer . . . no one else was doing a damn thing . . . I had to help. I just wish I wouldn't have used my magic in front of so many people. Foolish. Broke the rules.

The talk, the gossip, had originated then. It made no difference that she'd helped someone . . . only that she had done something no one who saw it could explain. Magic. They were a very superstitious lot, the towers. Always had been.

Eventually Jake had to be the one to go into town for supplies. The minute Amanda showed her face, some of the townspeople would stare, cross to the other side of any street she walked down, or whisper behind her back. Some even made the sign of the cross silently over their chests. It hurt.

But now Jake was gone and the town had things she needed. Things she couldn't grow or make herself. The shop that sold her pots and candy was in Canaan. Jane was in Canaan.

She'd better learn to fend for herself. It was just a shame that all that trouble with the cult had come about now.

First thing in the morning, Amanda collected the four glazed earthenware pots and packed them carefully in a straw-filled box for the trip. There were two very large ones, including Ernie's, with slip designs, and two smaller ones. She'd decided to preglaze them all and the two bigger ones she'd bring back home to reglaze for another firing later. The smaller ones would be ready to sell after the first firing and she'd leave them with Jane.

Jake had fashioned a simple wooden wagon for her to attach behind the little motor scooter so she could take her wares to town or pick up groceries when he wasn't around. He'd never given up hope that she'd start going into town by herself. She'd never had to use it when he was alive.

Maybe he'd had a premonition even back then that he wouldn't always be around.

Starting the scooter, a blue Honda Passport, she checked her pots one last time and headed off down the road at fifteen miles an hour. In Canaan, it'd draw less attention if she blended in with the rest of them, so she wore blue jeans and a heavy sweater under a blue-jeans jacket that had once been Jake's. She'd woven her waist-long hair into a thick braid that trailed down her back, out of her way.

The morning was cool, the sun dappling brightly on the road before her as a fresh breeze caressed her face. She drove slowly, watching for cars coming up behind, or unexpected bumps; inhaling deeply the heady forest scents and enjoying the morning. She tried not to be nervous.

It'd been months since she'd been in town. And she dreaded facing the townspeople. The town. Without Jake.

But it'd be good to see Jane, she mused.

As she parked before Jane's Gift Shop, Jane waved frantically at her through the large glass window, and ran out to greet her with a hug. Jane's pretty heart-shaped face with the soothing brown eyes framed by curly red hair was a sight for sore eyes.

"I don't believe it. Amanda, you really came. I'd just about thought you'd fallen off the face of the earth, the way you've been hibernating," Jane declared, pushing Amanda away to get a better look at her friend.

"Why, Jane. It's good to see you, too," Amanda bantered back, sliding off the scooter. She started to unpack the pots.

Jane's hands reached out to help her, cradling the received pots in her arms tenderly. Jane wouldn't chastise her for staying away so long; theirs wasn't that kind of friendship. Jane never badgered.

Jane knew what being a widow was like. She understood. Eddie, Jane's late husband, had been dead for
over four years and she still missed him. Still grieved.
But she'd been dating another artist steadily for the last
year and seemed happy enough with him, her three
rowdy kids, and a gift shop to take care of. She had
no plans to remarry, though, she'd adored Eddie. She
was the kind of person you loved to be around. So
alive. So giving.

Jane examined the pots in her arms and remarked,
"Good to see you getting off your butt and back to
work. Best thing for you." Jane should know, she was
an artist as well.

She brushed her fingers lightly over the pots. "These
aren't half bad." That was high praise coming from her.

"I've saved you the whole kiln this morning for 'em.
I had a feeling that you'd have a bunch. In fact, in
honor of the occasion, I've closed the shop for the rest
of the day and thought we'd have a nice visit."

"Thanks." Amanda looked sideways at her friend and
caught her smiling. "But you didn't need to do all that
on my account. You'll lose business." Amanda shook
her head in mock disapproval.

"I wanted to. I needed the rest, anyway. Business has
been great. So come on in," Jane shushed her, and
ushered her into the building.

They passed through a shop full of ceramics, crafts,
and exquisite figurines and into a small space at the
rear of the shop where the kiln, unfinished earthenware, and Jane's potter's wheel sat. Jane was basically a
painter, but dabbled in everything. About ten years before, Jane and her husband had bought the store and
Jane had fought every step of the way to make it work,
even after he had gone. The store and her three young
boys were her life.

"We'll put them here for now and place them in the

kiln right after we get a mug of coffee. I've only had three mugs so far this morning.

"Oh, I've got donuts, too," Jane announced, setting down her armful of pots on a cart next to the kiln.

"I told you not to go to any trouble."

"What's a couple of donuts? I get them discount in bulk and freeze them. The kids love 'em in their lunches."

They made their way even farther back and into the rooms where Jane and her children lived. Three rooms. The largest room was a cozy, but small kitchen/living room area with a television on the counter and a brightly colored couch at the other end.

The other two rooms were bedrooms. The smallest one was Jane's, and the largest one belonged to her boys. She'd fixed it all up so cute, every inch of space cleverly utilized. Her original paintings covered the walls and added a distinctive touch of beauty to the rooms. Jane kept saying that if the boys got much bigger, though, she'd have to either build or find a larger place. It was already a tight fit.

Amanda helped herself to a mug of coffee from the always-perking coffee pot and after Jane got herself a mug and grabbed a couple of donuts, trailed her back to the kiln.

"When are you going to bring in some more of that famous fudge of yours?" Jane queried. "My customers have been asking for it."

"Give me a break, Jane. One thing at a time. They've been asking for it?" She couldn't help but feel a little flattered.

"All the time. Your homemade cookies and candies are addictive. I should know." She grinned widely, stuffing a donut into her mouth. Jane had a well-rounded figure, but it looked good on her.

"Well, maybe," Amanda reflected thoughtfully, "I'll whip up a few batches next week and bring them in."

"Good," Jane said with her mouth full.

They munched on powdered sugar donuts and brought each other up to date on things as they loaded Amanda's earthenware into the kiln. Jane had to show her all the new merchandise in her shop. Tell about the boys and what they'd been up to.

It wasn't until much later that Jane brought it up as they were busy firing the pots.

"You know, there's been a brouhaha raging here in town," Jane's voice deceptively calm.

"I know. Ernie told me about it."

"He sure does get around, doesn't he?" Jane quipped.

"Ah, he's just stopped by a couple of times to see how I was doing. He ordered another pot. This big green one." She picked up one of the larger pots.

They stacked the remaining pots methodically in the kiln on the fire clay stilts in levels and set the timer.

"Well, anyway, then you know about the Satanic cult scare around here lately? The murders?"

"Unfortunately."

"God, I hate to even tell you this—" Jane hesitated, distress coming into her voice. "I mean, I don't see how they can—"

Amanda faced her friend over the kiln, leaning her elbow on the top of it and her chin in her hands. Something she wouldn't be able to do later, when the kiln was hot.

The change in Jane's manner had already alarmed her. "Jane, spit it out, what is it?"

"Yesterday they found another body—up around Black Pond—and along with the body and the usual Satanic symbols this time they found your name . . . in blood."

"My name?" Pain clouded her eyes.

Was it going to happen again?

Was she the target this time and not her mother?

Her mother's agonized, shredded face, as Amanda had vainly tried to save her at the scene of the accident, gazed hauntingly back up at her again through the years. The sounds, the smells of that horrendous night as real as the guilt she still felt. Even though there had been nothing she could have done, more than she had, to prevent it. She'd known her mother was being tracked by a cult, but her mother had said she could handle it. She'd been wrong.

Her mother's death had been no accident.

And for the first time, doubts began to stalk her concerning Jake's crash.

Had that really been an accident?

Jane sighed heavily. "Someone's malicious idea of a joke, I imagine. But the townspeople are spooked and on the warpath. A lot of them believe that because your name is there, you might be part of the coven."

She watched the incredulity dawn on Amanda's features.

"I'm sorry, Amanda. I just wanted to tell you about it before someone else did, or before something happened. There's been some nasty talk about you. It makes me sick," Jane said heatedly. "That they believe you could actually be involved. You. You've lived here for over ten years. That they actually think you're a *witch.*"

"Ridiculous," Amanda agreed, her hands trembling as she lifted her chin from them, and stood up straight.

"I know you had nothing to do with it," Jane defended her fiercely. "I can't believe that anyone could think you did."

"But they do," Amanda said so softly Jane probably hadn't heard her.

"Do you know why your name might have been used?"

"No. No idea at all," Amanda mumbled, her thoughts far away. She looked up at Jane, but the light had left her face.

Amanda didn't know what else to say.

"It'll be a few hours until the pots are done," Jane predicted briskly, changing the subject. "They'll be beautiful. You should be proud."

"I am." Amanda smiled faintly. Suddenly the joy she'd felt in her work just an hour ago vanished, replaced with a foreboding that something terrible was about to happen.

Back in the kitchen, Amanda asked, "By the way, where are the kids? I haven't seen one of them since I got here."

"They're out playing somewhere. Anxious for Halloween and trick-or-treating tonight. But a lot of us parents aren't sure, with these murders and all, if we're going to allow them to trick-or-treat. There's a town party being held and I've already decided the boys are going, like it or not. I just haven't told them yet. You want to come?"

"I don't think so," Amanda answered. She could just about imagine how the townspeople would greet her. "But thanks for the offer."

Jane didn't try to change her mind, but instead rambled on about the children's costumes. Amanda couldn't help but think of Rachel, even though she tried not to. The dead witch. Had people spurned her, too? Misunderstood, feared, and hated her?

Like me.

And had they murdered her for it?

After a while Amanda excused herself. "I have a few other errands to do in town, Jane, some necessities to gather. But I'll be back later for the pots."

"Be careful out there, will ya?" Jane warned her before she left, an uncomfortable reminder of their earlier conversation.

"I will. But I'm sure you're overreacting. This is the twentieth century. People don't *really* believe in bad witches anymore, now do they?" Amanda's tone sarcastic. It was a stupid thing to say and she knew it as soon as it left her mouth.

"You wouldn't suppose they would, but these murders have turned everyone nuts," Jane said in a low voice, her eyes troubled. "I know I'm frightened. I'm locking my doors for the first time in my life. Thinking of getting a gun."

As if a gun could fight black magic.

"Good idea."

Jane and Amanda said their good-byes and then Jane saw her out and watched her walk down the street away from the safety of the shop. Amanda felt her eyes on her back for a long time.

The sun was still shining and the day was still beautiful so Amanda tried to shake off her growing uneasiness. Besides some shopping she had to do, she wanted to eat lunch out somewhere. Treat herself. Walk through the shops.

Jane had paid her for the pots she'd sold the last few months and Amanda felt rich. She also wanted to buy herself some new clothes, but after awhile changed her mind about both.

The first sign of trouble was when the people she passed on the streets refused to meet her eyes. She thought she heard a couple behind her muttering. Then there were those who openly pointed and stared malevolently at her—from a safe distance, of course.

What the hell did they think she was, anyway? A mass murderer?

She strode by the quaint shops and busy stores, her feet moving faster and faster, her head bowed. Still people glared at her. Moved away from her as she walked, as if she had the plague. She caught some of them snarling things under their breath, things that were meant to hurt.

"Hey, witch," someone taunted sullenly from somewhere behind her. "You and your coven celebrating Halloween tonight by cutting up a few cats . . . or will it be children tonight?" Cruel laughter.

Amanda stopped dead in the middle of the sidewalk, spun around. There was no one there.

She studied the stores around her, the dark corners. Whoever had accused her was hiding.

"Go away . . . we don't want you here—"

"Witch," a different voice to her left.

"Witch!" to her right.

She didn't look this time, just turned and continued to walk toward the restaurant she'd been heading for.

Out of nowhere a barrage of rocks pelted her. One stone hit her in the face, just under her left eye. Amanda brought her fingers up to touch her swelling cheek, and felt blood. Another inch higher and it would have hit her in the eye.

She wasn't going to stay where she wasn't wanted. She didn't need anything that badly. She wasn't that hungry.

Amanda turned and headed back to Jane's, her hand still cradling her wounded, throbbing face. The tears trapped behind her eyes. She'd been treated worse. Much worse.

But this had been her and Jake's home for over ten years. She'd been happy here for so long. She'd almost forgotten Boston. The hatred. The loneliness.

Amanda heard the screams and curses behind her, the sound of running shoes, and there was Amadeus at her feet, grinning up at her.

Took care of them, I did.

"What did you do?" Amanda exclaimed, not sure if

she should be angry or not. Wails could be heard going into the distance.

Made many Amadeuses . . . bit bad people. Bit hard.

In spite of herself Amanda laughed, and picked the cat up into her arms. "That wasn't nice." She tried to be stern.

Wasn't nice what done to you. Taught lesson.

"I'm sure that helped my situation a lot."

The cat licked at her injured cheek and suddenly not only was the pain gone, but the cut when she touched it was nearly healed. She kissed the cat on his head and dropped him back to the sidewalk.

"Go home, Amadeus," she told him, not unkindly. "I'll see you there later after I get my pots and the scooter."

Her familiar meowed and then disappeared in a puff of smoke.

Thank goodness there was no one around. The streets had suddenly become empty.

She'd simply collect her ceramics, and get out of town.

She didn't need them. She didn't need anyone. Her home and Amadeus was all she needed. And suddenly that's all she wanted.

God, she missed Jake. He would have taken care of all this mess. Would have chased the culprits down, punched them out. Later would have gathered her into his loving arms to soothe away the hurt.

But Jake was gone.

And moving through the desolate streets of Canaan back to the sanctuary of her friend's shop, she'd never felt it so acutely.

Is this how Rachel had felt?

Perhaps she was stepping on the very same ground Rachel had three hundred years ago, staring up at the very same sky, and weeping inside like she had wept. She couldn't help but feel a sisterhood with the long-dead woman.

"You're back so soon, you just left—" Jane paused, seeing the look in her eyes and her still-puffy face for the first time after she'd let her back in. "What happened?" Jane demanded, her expression concerned.

Amanda looked at her challengingly. "Would you believe I tripped on the way into a store and fell against the edge of the open door? I never even got the things I needed." The ice in Amanda's glance kept Jane from asking any further questions.

"If you say so." Jane shook her head disbelievingly. "But you'd better let me put ice on it. It'll help the swelling."

"I can do it myself."

But Amanda didn't protest as Jane led her into her bathroom and helped her.

Her pots still had another hour to go in the kiln, so eventually Jane pried the whole story out of her. She always did.

"I wish I knew what to tell you, Amanda," Jane murmured. "I warned you to be careful now, didn't I? The whole town's gone bonkers."

"I wasn't doing anything, Jane. Just walking down the sidewalk, for heaven's sake. They taunted me. Threw rocks at me. For no reason. I didn't even see who it was."

"I'm sorry, Amanda. I mean it. I speak up for you every chance I get. I can't believe . . ." Her voice dwindled away, as she met her friend's gaze.

"They talk about me that much, huh?"

"Just lately," Jane said lamely.

They both knew why it had happened and denouncing it wouldn't change anything.

Amanda looked away.

When the pots were done, Jane asked, "How about

supper? We're having fried chicken and there's plenty. You look like you need some meat on your bones."

"Oh, you want to keep me here until dark, huh, so I can slink away unseen—like a criminal?"

"Listen, Amanda, I just want you to get home safe, that's all. I'm your friend, remember? It wasn't so bad until yesterday when the latest body was discovered. It was the worst yet. Then finding your name there didn't help."

"You really think they'll ambush me or something, huh?"

"In the mood the town's in, I'm not so sure they won't. A lot of people are partying tonight, getting into mischief, getting drunk."

"All right, I'll stay. I wanted to see the boys in their costumes, anyway."

Jane's boys burst into the kitchen not long after that, excited over the coming evening. Soon Amanda was busy joking and laughing with them and helping them with last-minute touches on their costumes. On her face now was just a faint bruise.

They made her feel welcome, even if the town didn't.

Ned, the youngest, was going to hide under an old bedsheet and be a tiny ghost. He was four years old.

William, the middle boy, was short, with long red curly hair like his mother's, and the same eyes. He was always smiling mysteriously, like he had a secret no one else knew. He was going to dress up as a tramp and he'd slipped into his room, returning in dark brown trousers with holes in them, a dirty shirt, and one of his father's old worn fedoras on his head. Amanda helped him smear charcoal all over his impish face.

Then she cut the eyeholes in the sheet for Ned.

Jane's oldest, Jonny, a somber dark-haired boy with thoughtful eyes, was going as a ghoul. He'd whipped up some sort of makeup that cracked on his face and after he'd added the finishing touches—red slashes of paint—the overall effect was frighteningly realistic.

At ten, Jonny was tall and lean for his age, but incredibly smart. He read everything he could get his hands on, and was usually nursing in his room some wounded animal he'd found out in the woods. But Jonny was like that, a soft heart for everything and everyone. Jane was sure that he was going to be the first doctor in the family. Or at least a vet. Amanda believed he'd become a writer, the way he loved books. Jonny was just the sort of child, Amanda always thought, she and Jake might have had.

Both Amanda and Jane had noticed that whenever Amanda came over, he'd hang on every word she uttered, asking a hundred questions, and attend to her like a devoted puppy dog.

"Miss Givens," he pressed shyly. "Maybe I could come out to your place sometime and clean up the yard for you? Do chores? For free?" He'd liked Jake and he was trying, in his own way, to ease her sorrow.

"Maybe, sometime. Soon," Amanda answered, hugging him, moved by his caring. "I'll talk to your mom about it. OK?" That seemed to satisfy him.

Amanda guessed she was his first infatuation.

They were great kids. All of them. Jane was so lucky to have them.

Amanda would have done anything to have had Jake's child by her side now. A little boy with Jake's face and Amanda's powers. For years after she and Jake had married she'd fantasized about what their child would be like. But it had just never happened and the fantasies had faded with the years. Now they were dead, like Jake.

By the time the sun had started to go down, they'd eaten supper, broken the news about the town party, and Jane was going to drop the kids off at the village hall for the night. She'd pick them up at eleven.

Amanda was no longer upset. The meal, the laughter

she'd shared with Jane and her boys had scattered it all away. Ned had hugged her, and Jonny had even given her a shy kiss on the cheek before they'd left for the party.

Amanda was feeling pretty good as her eyes followed the children skipping off into the shifting twilight with their mother. There were other shadowy forms to greet them. Giggles haunted the crisp night air. The sharp tang mingling on the cool breezes brought back memories of when she'd been a child. The golden times before she'd realized how the world hated witches. How cruel people could be. How many enemies a white witch could have.

Halloween had always been very special to her and her family. They'd spend the early part of the night giving out candy to trick-or-treaters or going to parties and the later part would be for all of the witches in the family to gather and talk over what they'd done in the last year, to thank God for their gifts and blessings. This night was when Amanda missed her sisters, her dead mother the most. She'd thought of witching herself to where her sisters were, but she didn't know where Rebecca was, somewhere on a book tour, she thought, and Jessie would be wrapped up in her own family. It'd been years since they'd all been together on Samhain.

No, she'd better get used to spending it alone. Or else give up and move back to Boston to be near Jessie, which didn't sound like such a bad idea at the moment. Maybe it was time for a visit.

"You want to leave these two other pots here, Amanda, and I'll glaze them and fire them again for you?" Jane offered later when she'd returned and Amanda was slipping into her jacket. They'd had one last cup of coffee together in the quiet house and had snacked on freshly made caramel apples. Amanda was pleasantly tired and it would feel good to go home, build a fire, and cuddle up before it with the good book she was reading, a science fiction tale called *The Fall of Hyperion,* by Dan Simmons.

"No, I'll take them home and glaze them myself. It's a unique glaze I've perfected that I'm using," she explained. "If it's all right, I'll try to get back in next week to fire them. I promised Ernie his would be done soon."

"I'll let you know when the kiln's available."

Amanda collected her two pots, shifting them in her arms a little.

She strode out into the dark to her scooter and loaded the pots back into the cart. She threw her leg over the seat and settled down on it.

"Amanda, I'm glad you came. Glad we had a chance to visit. I've missed you," Jane confessed as Amanda revved up the engine. "I'm just sorry about what happened."

"Wasn't your fault," Amanda responded, tilting her face up to the night sky. The cool air nipped at her warm cheeks. The wound was almost gone. Jane swore it had been the ice.

"See you next week." And with a wave, Amanda drove off.

She stopped a ways out of town and buttoned up her jacket. Yanking a heavy sock cap from one of her saddlebags, she shoved it down snugly over her head. Glad as she rode down the darkening, winding country road that she had heavy clothes on. It was getting colder by the second, especially in the valleys, as the shadows of night crept down around her. She shivered and sped up, anxious to get home. The little wagon bouncing along behind her. She hoped her pots were all right.

Amadeus must be wondering where she was.

The woods towering around her were ominously hushed. There were no small animal or bug sounds. None at all.

She switched on the scooter's headlight. An owl began to screech somewhere, and the hair stood up on the back of her neck.

Something wasn't . . . right.

She decided to magic herself and the scooter home and a moment later she was parking the scooter with its wagon behind her work shed.

Eerie white lights moved through the gloom of the forest, elusive, but if she turned her head quickly enough, she could just catch them at the corners of her eyes. Wafting about like lost ghosts.

Strange moans and twitterings deep in the woods.

All Hallow's Eve. The spirit world . . . magic . . . the supernatural was at its strongest on this night. Things walked this night that were never allowed to walk any other night. Legend also said that on this night a witch could cross over to the fairy world, join in the festivities of the Fairy Queen's ribald court. Throughout history, witches and fairies were rumored to be close. But fairies were mischievous, troublemakers that would often slip through the barriers this night and bring woe to humans and witches alike.

That was another thing. Lately she'd seen an abundance of fairy rings . . . mushrooms growing in perfect circles. Fanciful people believed it was a place where fairies could cross over into their world, but Amanda knew there was a scientific explanation. Something about two fungi deep in the soil reacting to each other during a bout of unseasonably warm weather. The mushrooms were larger this year than she'd ever seen them. Giants.

She went in and changed back into her usual clothes, made herself something to eat. All the while a premonition battering at her that danger was close.

She paused at the door to gaze at the huge harvest moon rising into the night sky. Strange blood-red clouds scudded across its huge face, yet the winds were still. Bad signs. Amanda frowned at her muted reflection in the glass and inhaled deeply. Outside, the black world was tinged with the blood from the moon.

She sent out a silent call for her familiar. If something was about to happen, if something was out there, she wanted him home. He didn't come.

She built a roaring fire in the front room and tried to shake off the gloominess from her mind.

She stared out the window, uneasy.

Then she heard it. Far away, but coming steadily closer. A cat crying, as if it were fighting for its very life . . . hissing and screeching as if it were in pain.

Amadeus!

She was sure it was him.

She grabbed Jake's jacket which was still hanging on the back of a kitchen chair, dashed outside and into the woods in a frantic search for the cat: One last high-piercing wail. She muttered an invocation, and there he was . . . at her feet, twirling madly in a frenzied circle, his back up and his fangs and claws showing, glaring back at the edge of the woods. Enraged.

"Amadeus!" she ordered, and he was in her arms, shivering and mewling like a lost kitten. Something sticky and cold came away on her hands, and she discovered he was covered in blood.

"How?"

Witch coming . . .

Black witch.

With a moan of despair, Amanda felt the shape of him gently with her fingers. There were deep slashes all over him. One of his ears was missing.

She felt sick and then she felt the anger rise up from deep inside her like bile.

As she held him cradled in her arms, the wind began to moan around her, the trees to sway. A pale luminescence was moving through the night woods toward them. Frost rippled along the trees and ground before it.

Amanda wove a strong spell of protection and let it cloak her and Amadeus like an invisible bubble.

A tall, floating woman in dark clothes surrounded by a misty white light was standing before her, barring her way back to the house. Its arms outstretched toward her.

Rachel.

Amanda was bombarded by pulsations of wrongness from the spectre. This time the evil was so tangible it was an entity in itself.

All that Mabel had said about Rachel flooded back to her. She was believed to have had great powers, suspected of being her lover's and her childrens' murderess . . . a witch.

And after what Amadeus had said, and what the apparition had done to him, it could all have been true. Only a black witch would harm others.

The figure wavered in and out of reality.

"Get out of my way, Rachel. Begone! You have no right to bother the living," Amanda commanded, facing the ghost down with fiery eyes. Her breath freezing on the air before her.

It didn't leave. It was grinning vindictively at her. A ghostly hand sweeping back translucent flowing hair. Bottomless black holes glittering at her.

Help me, Amanda, to stay. I need your powers . . .

The wraith solidified for just one second and the face turned human in the moonlight . . . the countenance beautiful, the eyes haunted. She had long flowing dark hair to her waist, and was dressed in seventeenth-century clothes, a drab, dark high-collared long gown, a lot like the one Amanda had on.

Amanda felt Amadeus grow still in her arms. He needed her attention immediately. Familiars could die. They weren't invincible, just immortal. She tried to walk around the ghost but it kept pace easily with her.

"I can't help you, Rachel, it's not allowed," Amanda

said between clenched teeth. "I wouldn't even if I could, after what you've done to Amadeus. Besides, you're evil."

The spirit laughed wickedly. Its glowing shoulders moving up in a lazy shrug. It was changing in its ire even as Amanda watched. Beauty melting to unearthly hideousness.

Only a familiar . . . a weak one at that. I could conjure you up one that would astound you.

Rachel's ravaged face gazed back at her in the pulsating light, wispy and inhuman. Blackened tree shadows danced behind her, framing her half-formed image.

"A demon?" Amanda hissed. "Something from hell. No thank you."

I can give you anything you want . . .

Amanda was tired of games. Amadeus needed her attention. Now.

"Then go away. Leave us alone!"

Look.

The ghost pointed, and Amanda turned and looked behind her.

Jake was standing there. Her Jake. Alive and solid, tall and handsome. Smiling that smile at her. So real. In the same clothes he'd had on that last day. Jeans and a black sweater.

Amanda's heart nearly stopped. She almost ran into his opening arms before she realized that it wasn't him. It was an incubus. A demon that took human form to entice humans to its bed. Amanda's magic could see through the beautiful exterior and into the nefarious corruption of the creature. An abomination.

It wasn't her Jake.

Amanda's face went hard in the dark, her eyes furious.

"That isn't Jake."

One arm still holding her unconscious familiar, she

raised her hand at the thing and whispered the words of the spell that would rid the earth of the unnatural incubus.

"Go back to hell where you belong!" she ordered it.

The incubus screamed, covering its face with clawlike hands as its form began to shift and dissipate until only an outline remained, and then even that scattered into the night like loosened marbles.

Amanda turned to Rachel's ghost. "Now *you*. Back to hell where you belong. I command it!"

Stupid woman . . . My power is growing more each day . . . I can force you to obey me. I can hurt those you care about . . . hurt you . . . kill you. Take your magic . . .

Amanda closed her eyes, her fury so hot now she could feel it burning like boiling oil under her skin, and started to say the words of one of the most potent spells she knew, one that if used for the wrong purpose or by the wrong person could backfire and the user would find herself tumbling into hell.

At first it seemed it wasn't going to work. Amanda felt her strength draining as she came to the end of the incantation, but Rachel was still standing there. Smirking at her.

The apparition was fighting her.

Startled, Amanda held her breath and began again, her knees buckling beneath her and her head spinning.

Rachel's ghost screeched and her image began to waver.

The face was melting like butter in the sun, the eyes becoming empty holes again, the figure, white bones. For a second a skeleton stood before her and then crumpled into dust.

The noises of the night returned. But the cold didn't leave.

Amanda collapsed to the earth and dried leaves under a crimson moon, Amadeus still clutched in her arms like a lifeless stuffed animal. Rachel's resistance had almost been too much for her.

After a while, she roused herself, as exhausted as she was. She had to get up. Had to move. Had to get inside and take care of her friend, Amadeus, before it was too late. Get free from whatever lethargy Rachel had left her with.

She fought her way to her feet.

The last remnant of Rachel's power slammed her to the ground, with Amadeus awakening and meowing pitifully as her weight fell on him.

When she had caught her breath, Amanda struggled to her knees, then, with the aid of a nearby tree, back to a standing position; she dragged herself through the dark wooded spaces until she spied her open door, threw herself through it, falling into a heap just inside.

Shaking with exhaustion, Amanda reached out and shoved the door shut with her foot, recited another spell to keep Rachel out.

Her witching had totally drained her, she could hardly move.

She hadn't even enough energy left to scream when all the windows imploded, the flying glass slashing through her clothes and tearing her skin and lodging in her eyes. Blood and glass slivers all over her. A thousand tiny cuts along her arms and probably all over her face.

Then again . . . silence. Rachel was finally gone.

Amanda gazed blurry-eyed at the shattered glass and wood all over the floor and shook her head tiredly. A shambles. She'd clean everything tomorrow. She'd used herself up for this night, and she still needed to take care of Amadeus.

Trembling and dazed, she stumbled over to the table and lit the candles to have a good look at him.

"You're a bloody mess, worse than me," she told him, as he opened his eyes and meowed pathetically up at her, laying one bloody paw trustingly on her hand. He was so hurt he couldn't even think human.

Wiping tears from her face, and staring at his beaten furry body, she doctored him the best she could, as well as the worst of her cuts, with a salve she prepared herself with magic.

The ear was gone, and might not grow back. Since black magic had taken it, there might be no magic that could bring it back. Time would tell.

She gently bandaged his other wounds, though, then wearily said some words over him so he would sleep, and start healing. She'd done the best she could. No vet could have done more.

She laid him in her bed. With her last bit of strength, she wove a final enchantment and mended all the broken windows to keep the cold air out. Now, she had to rest.

Climbing into bed, she tucked the cat gently into the crook of her arm, burrowed into the covers, and fell immediately into a deep sleep.

She dreamt of Jake.

"Mandy," he warned her in a loving voice that made her weep in her dreams. "Be careful, my love. There is danger here for you now. Much danger. You don't know. . . ."

"What must I do, Jake?" she asked him, reaching out for him. "What danger? Rachel?"

"Yes. You must find the strength to resist her. Seek help. Damn your pride," Jake told her. "Prepare yourself."

"What does she want with me?" Amanda pleaded of him. "Why is she here?"

"For the coven. For your power . . . so she won't die. Beware."

"Of what?" But he was already fading away.

"Help me," she begged the emptiness he had left

behind. She cried out for him and tried to follow, but she couldn't—he was gone. She was alone again. The ache so overpowering at his going, that she felt her heart would burst.

She woke up. It was barely dawn. Too early to get up, but Amadeus's body cuddled next to her and her pain, vividly brought back the events of the night before.

Rachel. Her threats.

The strange dream she'd had last night with Jake in it. Something about Rachel and the coven. Had Jake meant the cult that was torturing and butchering people in the area?

Was there a connection between the two?

Amadeus was a warm bundle of fur that slept peacefully in her arms, but looked like a war veteran. At least, she consoled herself, he's alive. He'll make it.

She got up, witched a blazing fire in both the kitchen and the living room, and cleaned up the broken glass all over the floor; Amadeus continued to sleep as she did. Poor creature.

She glanced in the mirror at herself. The salve had helped most of her cuts, but she was still a sight. She put on more.

She had just finished when it happened. One moment she was fine and then the next . . . her world was plunged into blackness. She couldn't see.

She groped her way to the rocker and sat down, her heart climbing up her chest. Intoning in a trembling whisper every spell to heal it that she could recall until she was weary all over again.

It still took her three agonizing hours to regain her sight.

It took her much longer to regain her composure.

So . . . she had an enemy she mustn't underestimate again.

So . . . this was war.

She had gone back to bed, snuggled back up against the cat, and was already half asleep when the urgent knocking came at the rear door.

"Damn," she mumbled, dragging herself from under the covers, trying not to disturb Amadeus. Throwing on a robe, she went to answer it.

It was Ernie, of all people. He wasn't in uniform.

There was such a look of distress in his eyes, she gestured him to come in. "Ernie, it's awfully early for a social call, isn't it? And on a Sunday morning. There's no mail today." She sighed, rubbing the sleep from her swollen eyes. Pain reminded her that her face was probably still a mass of cuts; she instinctively lowered her face so her long hair covered most of it.

"I know. And I'm sorry, Amanda, for disturbing you at such an ungodly hour but . . . my news can't wait."

"Want coffee?"

"That sounds good. Please."

"What's wrong? And what news?" she asked. She could tell by the way he was acting that something had really rattled him.

Her back toward him, she hurriedly fixed a pot of coffee, muttering, "It looks like we both need it."

Something in Ernie's silence made her stop before she was done. She peeked over her shoulder at his face.

"Ernie? What *is* it?"

"Amanda, last night something happened in town. Something . . . monstrous. The trees lining Main Street were pulled out by the roots and set back upside down, and all the houses along those streets were shattered and destroyed as if a cyclone had ripped through them."

"There wasn't any storm last night," Amanda exclaimed. "How could such a thing—" But then her voice fell off abruptly and her eyes widened. *Rachel?* The damage done to her own house was still vivid in her mind. She remembered Amadeus.

"I know that. The town knows that," Ernie groaned and wiped his face with his fingers as if he was very weary. Sweat shone on his face and the morning was freezing.

"One of the houses was Jane's. But it wasn't damaged too badly."

"Oh, no," Amanda moaned. "Is she all right? Are the kids all right?" Amanda had walked over to the table where Ernie had slumped into a chair. He looked as if someone had beaten him up. His face gray around the beard, his tired eyes brooding.

"No, she and her kids are fine. They weren't hurt."

"But others were?"

"Yes. They found more dead bodies in some of the houses, Amanda," he murmured, tensely. "But they hadn't died by walls collapsing on them or anything. They were brutally murdered. Butchered like the other bodies that have been found over the last couple of weeks. The Fergusons . . . the whole family. And they had a couple of small kids, too. The Sladers . . . all seven of them. Three adults, two teenagers, and two children under five years old. All dead."

Amanda stared at him, her face icy now. "Oh, no—"

"More cult killings. I can't even tell you what was done to them, it's so . . . horrid. Inhuman." Ernie looked like he could have thrown up. He rubbed unsteady hands over his face.

"The townspeople are scared as hell." Hesitating as if he didn't want to say what he had to say, he looked dejectedly down at his hands folded on the table.

"And as if that's not bad enough . . . there were messages left beside the bodies, in blood . . . to you. In both houses. It's the only lead the police have so far, except"—

he swallowed here as if he didn't even believe what he was saying—"for these strange animal-like prints in the blood that was spilled all over the floor. Kinda like hoof marks, I overheard Deputy Henson say. No other evidence. No fingerprints or shoe prints. As if human hands had never committed the crimes at all."

Fear settled in her mouth, dry and bitter like dirt. *Hoof marks . . . like demons left.*

"And the messages?"

"According to Henson, they all said about the same things in slightly different variations: '*Amanda, come to us,*' or something similar to that. And you're the only Amanda around here."

What did the demons or the cult who'd called up those demons want with her? To join them? Or was it a challenge? The message could be taken either way.

And did Rachel have anything to do with any of it? Amanda wondered.

"I'm pretty sure you're gonna be their scapegoat."

"You're kidding . . . they can't really believe that I had anything to do with any of the killings, can they?" Her earlier conversation with Jane floated back to haunt her.

"I stayed around just long enough to gather that they do think you had something to do with it. They just don't know what."

He nodded his head sorrowfully. "The townspeople are having a meeting right now about it and they're riled up. Got the makings of an angry mob. They're scared and they don't know what to do. It's only human nature to want to strike out at someone. Somebody's going to pay . . ."

Yes, Amanda thought, *and I'm the most likely candidate. What's new?*

She turned and walked back to the perking coffeepot. "Coffee's done," she said in a flat voice. Picking the pot up, and grabbing a couple of mugs on the way from the counter, she moved back to the table.

"Maybe, there's some place you could go for a while until all this blows over?" Ernie suggested carefully.

Amanda laughed, a gallow's laugh as she set the mugs down and poured the steaming coffee in them. "You want me to run away as if I were guilty of something?"

"I know none of it's your doing, Amanda, but just to be safe . . . for now."

Run away again. Just like Boston when it got too hot for her.

She sat down and put sugar and cream in her coffee and then handed the spoon to Ernie so he could do the same, tilting her face up. He just contemplated her with sad eyes, unable to reassure her.

"Amanda?" he suddenly blurted out, seeing her face clearly for the first time. "What happened to you? You're all cut up. Your face?"

She self-consciously put her hands up to cover the cuts. "Oh, it's nothing . . . I had an accident on the scooter yesterday coming home from Jane's," she lied. She hated lying, but there was no way she could tell him the truth.

"An accident?" he repeated stupidly.

She waved her hand at nothing. "It was dark. A car came by going a little too fast for that last curve on Quarry's Hill—you know the place—shoved me too far over and I hit some loose rocks on the side of the road. The scooter went down. I just landed in some thorn bushes, that's all. It wasn't bad. The scooter's OK," she added.

"Must have been some big thorns," he commented suspiciously, studying her damaged face. "Ought to have a doctor look at those."

"Naw," she said lightly. "I've taken care of them already. Put medicine on them. They'll heal. I'll be fine."

Amanda's tone left no doubt in his mind that she wanted the subject dropped. She swung her head and stared at the fire crackling in the kitchen stove. Her heart heavy from what Ernie had told her.

"You really think it would help if I ran away?"

"It couldn't hurt."

"Oh, Ernie," she replied hopelessly. "And do they—do you?—really believe witches are evil and should still be burned at the stake in 1992?" The damning words had just snuck out, she hadn't been able to stop them.

He recoiled visibly at that, a glimmer of hurt in his eyes. "Amanda, it isn't me you have to worry about. I know you wouldn't ever hurt anyone. I know there are no such things as witches. But if there were . . . Jake always said—"

Amanda's eyebrows raised over seething eyes.

And he immediately shut up, probably recalling their last exchange on the issue.

Jake and his big mouth again. So Ernie had believed it, or some of it, no matter what he had said before. "Jake said *what?*"

She had to wait a minute or two before he sheepishly responded, "When he talked about you being a witch, he always said modern-day witchcraft wasn't like what people usually thought. It was your religion. A way of thinking, believing, and living. And most witches were into white magic, not black. He swore there was a big difference." Ernie's brow furrowed as if he'd given all this a lot of thought.

"I'm sorry, Amanda, for bringing it up again," he apologized. "I always thought he was just pulling my leg, but now with all this weird stuff going on . . . I'm not so sure. The way those people were murdered, the destruction done in town last night. None of it's natural."

Amanda smiled bitterly and looked away. So now the

townsfolk—and Ernie—were believers? That was all she needed, as if she didn't have enough trouble already.

Nothing to do but to face it, she thought.

She stared the mailman straight in the eyes and said, just a little angrily, "No matter what you or anyone thinks, if I am a witch or not, it makes no difference, because I had nothing to do with any of what's happened in town, Ernie. Or the murders." *That I know of or could explain.* "It's crazy of anyone to even think so."

"Well, I know *that,* Amanda. I'm just saying that the townspeople don't know that for sure, and I wouldn't put *anything* past them right now."

Then his face grew somber as he confessed softly, "Jake was my best friend. You're my friend. I just don't want anything to happen to you."

"What can happen to me?"

Ernie didn't answer her, but grumbled to himself, rocking his head, as if she were acting like an ignorant child.

"Just think about leaving for awhile, please? Go visit that sister in Boston you're always talking about. Until things cool down."

Amanda sighed aloud. "I'll think about it, Ernie. I will. Thanks for coming to tell me what happened. If you see Jane, tell her I'm sorry about her house. That I'm glad she and the kids are OK I'll come to see her as soon as I can." No need to tell Jane she had nothing to do with it. Jane would already know that.

"And tell the townspeople for me, if you get a chance, that I had nothing to do with what's happening The murders or the damage. That I don't know why my name is cropping up in blood all over the place. *I don't know.* Tell them that," her voice emotionless.

She'd been in this position before, she knew there was little hope, no matter what she did or said. People panicked when confronted with things they couldn't begin to understand. Acted like mindless animals. Snarling and tearing at whatever came in their path.

"Amanda—" Ernie started to say something else, his face troubled, but she stopped him by putting her hand up.

She stood up slowly. "Good-bye, Ernie. Thank you for coming out to warn me. I know you mean well. But I'd like to be left alone now." She firmly ushered him to the door, not wanting to hear another word.

"Good-bye, Amanda." His confused face framed in the doorway was the last thing she saw before she closed the door.

And locked it.

Through the glass she watched him trudge his way out to his old red Chevy, and roar away.

She stood there, back braced against the door like a cornered animal, her mind going in circles.

She didn't want to leave her home. But what choice did she have? Ernie wouldn't have scared her like he had unless there was a good chance she could be in real danger.

They could hurt her . . . just like in Boston all those years ago. Amanda saw herself again at twenty-two, Rebecca and Jessie married already and out of the house, hiding that night behind the door of her home as the crowd of people out front ranted at her. The cult that had arranged for her mother to be killed had aroused her neighbors against her. They'd been afraid of her growing powers and had been determined to get rid of her one way or another. But she'd surprised the cult; she'd been just a little too clever, a little too strong to be gotten rid of as easily as they'd thought they could. So they'd invented bogus evidence and had spread lies. Hurt people with their black magic and had laid it all neatly at her feet for everyone to see.

The mob outside her house had grown ugly, throwing

things, screaming for her blood . . . They'd been good people, just misled, and she couldn't take her frustrated anger out on them. Instead, she'd had to use her magic and sneak out of the house, the home she'd always known, and escape away into the freezing night. Never to go back openly. She'd had to run away like a criminal in the middle of her grief over her mother's murder, though she had done nothing. Hide from her neighbors. Hide from the cult.

That night was etched indelibly in her mind. The horror and loneliness of it. Amanda couldn't block it out. The first time she'd been actually ashamed of being a witch. The first time she'd realized that she wasn't always the strongest in the arena of witchcraft. There were always stronger and meaner opponents. Ones that didn't play by the rules she had to play by.

Only when she heard Amadeus meowing weakly in the other room, calling her, did she move.

Amanda gathered Amadeus into her arms and took him into the front room. His ear was still missing. But the rest of him was healing nicely. Plopping down in her rocking chair, she rocked back and forth, cuddling him, her mind dark as she tried to find a way out of her dilemma. Too disturbed to even witch up a fire.

Ernie right, Amadeus thought at her, licking her hand feebly as she petted him. *Bad evil coming. Very bad. Must leave.*

"Amadeus, do you know who's responsible for the murders?" she asked in a whisper.

Demons. Don't know who sent, though. Cult probably.

"What does the cult want?"

You, Amanda. Your powers. Your soul. He closed his eyes and he seemed to slip away, his furry paw resting on her arm. He was still very weak.

Amanda kept rocking, her thoughts busy. She would make that visit to Jessie now. It'd been a long time since she'd seen her sister and family. She could disappear for awhile until things cooled down, as Ernie had so quaintly put it, or until she could gain some insight on how to find and fight the cult that was most likely doing all this. Until she could stop them.

And until she could decide where Rachel figured in all this—if she figured in it at all. Jessie was always good at listening. Good at seeing things she couldn't see in a situation.

It would also give her some time to think. Sort things out.

Maybe find out why, with all her magic and powers, she still couldn't solve the mysteries or help. Still couldn't see what was going on.

Why she was so . . . helpless. Amanda wasn't used to being helpless, and she didn't like it one bit. Not one bit.

Chapter 4

She didn't give herself much time to rest after Ernie left. She suspected that she might not have much time . . . if someone or something was looking for her. And that did seem possible. Whether it was human or inhuman. She needed to get away for awhile.

But first she had to check on Mabel and make sure the old woman would be all right while she was gone. Make sure she had enough food and enough special tea. Amanda wasn't happy when she recognized the folly of using her magic not only to go to Mabel's, but to get to her sister's in Boston as well. If a cult—with as much power as their crimes seemed to indicate—was challenging or looking for her, using her magic to travel anywhere would leave a neon trail and perhaps endanger anyone she was with at the moment they tracked her down. Magic not only left prints that any other witch or warlock or demon could follow, but it left a personalized scent, too.

So, no magic. Unless it was an emergency.

Amanda put on the blue jeans she'd worn yesterday and a heavy dark blue sweater under Jake's jacket, tied her long hair back in a loose braid, and covered it with an old slouch felt hat, then hurriedly bundled together some extra clothes, a basket of food for Mabel and Amadeus, and packed everything all up in the wagon behind her scooter. She set off through the woods, her breath clouding before her. Amadeus was still pretty sick, so she kept a light touch on the pedal and avoided the most rugged places even though she'd placed the cat on a pile of blankets. She left him sleeping there when she went up to knock on the trailer's door.

Mabel was ecstatic to see her; pulled her right in. But Amanda found out quickly that it wasn't just the food and tea she'd brought that made her friend happy to see her, it was the companionship.

"There was a heck of a ruckus out in the woods last night," Mabel divulged, a shadow of disquiet on her face. "Out by Black Pond somewheres by the sound of it." She was already heating water for the tea.

Amanda had taken her hat and jacket off, placed the large covered basket she'd brought for Mabel on the counter, then sat down at the table. "Oh?" Inside she sensed that what Mabel had to tell her would come as no surprise.

As Mabel looked through the basket, she talked. "Yes. Half the night. Chanting and shrieking. Strange noises as if a herd of something or other were crashing through the trees." Mabel's small frame shivered visibly. "Gave me the willies just listening to it. Believe you me, I had my gun out and laying in my lap. If they would have come skulking around my trailer I would have filled all their backsides with lead." The old lady flashed Amanda a brave grin, showing her toothless gums. She had her dentures out again.

"But they left me alone. Probably rowdy teenagers out making mischief at Black Pond because of its reputation. Halloween and all."

That could be possible. But Amanda didn't believe it had been just kids. Too much had happened last night. And if it had been kids, she prayed that they were all safe at home now, instead of corpses strewn around the pond.

So, Amanda thought, her protection spell had held. Or Mabel might have been a statistic along with the other murder victims this morning. The idea didn't sit too well on her conscience, under the circumstances.

"I'm going away for awhile, Mabel," Amanda told her. "So I don't have much time to chitchat. I just came by to bring you that basket of food and let you know I'd be away." She'd almost slipped and told Mabel where she was going. But that wouldn't be wise. It could get Mabel hurt. Or worse.

"Well, dear, that'll be good for you. A trip. Just what you need after all these months holed up in that cabin of yours. Going to visit family?"

"Maybe."

"How long you going to be gone, dear?" Mabel set a tea cup before Amanda.

Amanda mumbled something.

"You going to tell me how you got those cuts on your face?"

Amanda touched her fingers tenderly to her cheek where the worse of the slashes were still healing under an invisible cream that also toned down the redness. She'd almost forgotten them. "An accident on the scooter." She waved her other hand negligently, telling her the same fib she'd told Ernie earlier. "Just wasn't watching where I was going. Don't worry, the cuts aren't as bad as they look."

Mabel tossed her a questioning glance, but was smart enough not to pry any further. "Go ahead, drink your tea, you have time for one cup before you go, don't you?"

Amanda drank her tea. Without sugar, as she usually liked it. Gulped it down as if it were lukewarm instead of boiling.

"Oh," Mabel said as she sipped her tea, watching Amanda get up and put her jacket and hat back on, "I hate to see you go so soon.

"I'm sorry, Mabel." Amanda tried real hard and produced a weak smile. There was no sense in scaring the old woman any more than she already was. "I'm just anxious to get going. I promise that as soon as I get back I'll come over for a long visit. Maybe we'll even go into town together—I'll borrow Jane's car—and we'll go shopping, catch a movie. Would you like that?"

Mabel's expression lit up. "That would be real nice."

Amanda was at the door when she turned around and said, "Mabel, I want you to promise me that you won't leave the trailer at night while I'm gone? It's not safe. At your age, in the dark, I mean."

Mabel wasn't fooled. "And all the murders. I know. I listened to the news this morning. Don't you worry about me, though, I can take care of myself. I haven't lived to this ripe old age by doing dumb things. Nothing will get me out of this trailer at night."

"Good." Amanda breathed a sigh of relief. "I'll see you when I get back."

"Have a nice trip, and thanks for the food, Amanda."

"You're welcome. Bye." Amanda was out the door before Mabel could wave good-bye.

She debated whether to strengthen the protection spell on Mabel and the trailer as she climbed back on the scooter. It would give her whereabouts away if anyone was looking for it. But then, she was leaving, anyway. A calculated gamble, but one worth taking. She doubled the spell and then rode away, fairly certain that Mabel would be safe.

Amadeus was still in a deep sleep. Still healing. Even the bumps didn't wake him. The day was colder than any before and as Amanda maneuvered through the trees and hanging mist, heard the dried leaves crunching under her tires, she knew winter had finally arrived.

It was no day for a scooter ride. The air froze her face, brought tears to her eyes. It was hard not being able to use her magic to keep herself warm or to get quickly to where she wanted to go. *Never know how much you depend on something until you can't use it,* she thought.

Boston was at least eight hours away. And riding the Passport to the bus station in Shelby—about an hour from where she was—was the best way of losing anyone on her tail she could think of. Catching the bus out of town was just being careful.

So Amanda guided the motorbike to the nearest road and bounced along as fast as she could risk without bumping Amadeus to death, though once or twice she heard a muffled squawk out of him when she hit a rut. She took mostly back roads, some highways, not stopping until she'd arrived at the Shelby bus station. She hid her scooter in a patch of woods behind the parking lot, pulled an animal traveling cage out from the back of the wagon, and gently put the sleeping Amadeus in it, wrapped in a blanket, then lugged the cage and her suitcase up to the bus depot. Bought a ticket for Boston, called her sister Jessie to let her know she was coming, and got on the bus. Keeping her hat tilted low over her lacerated face so no one would ask her any questions, though she could feel the ointment rapidly mending the cuts; by tomorrow the worst of them would be gone.

The bus was practically empty. No one she knew. It was Sunday, after all. There were some filthy looking teenagers in black leather jackets huddled in the back, snickering and bickering among themselves. Amanda couldn't tell the girls from the boys. They all had long stringy hair and earrings. There was a young family seated midway on the bus. A tired-looking plump woman with frizzled hair and a rake-thin husband with his nose in a book as his wife tried to control their two small children, who apparently were whining for something to eat. Two old women napped, their purses clutched to their ample coated bosoms and scarfs on their heads.

The napping part looked good to Amanda.

She was glad to find a seat by the window, place Amadeus's covered cage next to her, and yanking the hat farther down over her eyes, wearily closed them and drifted into sleep. She didn't open them until they were entering the outskirts of Boston proper.

It had been years since Amanda had been there. She'd grown up in Boston, but as she watched the streets flash by from the dirty bus window, all she could think about was how alien it all seemed now with its narrow twisting streets and historic buildings. Once it had been home, now it was just another city.

They rolled past the Boston Common and along Beacon Street and then alongside the State House with its golden dome, King's Chapel, and City Hall. They paralleled endless miles of ancient brick sidewalks on cobblestone streets flanked by rows of stately Georgian houses of rose-colored bricks. Houses and streets that hadn't changed in centuries. And slowly the ageless beauty of Colonial Boston overwhelmed her, as it had years ago.

It was a beautiful city. Whether it had wanted her or not all those years ago. It hadn't been the city's fault, but the fault of the people who had lived in it. Bostonians were as superstitious as the people of Canaan.

Jessie lived on Hanover Street in a monstrosity of a framed house. Three floors. She and her husband had bought it when they were first married fourteen years before, and they were still there. Jessie loved her home as much as Amanda loved her cabin in the woods. She'd spent years fixing it up to be just what she wanted.

A plaintive muffled meow reminded her of her companion and lifting the cover off the cage, she smiled reassuringly through the tiny bars at Amadeus. His wounds looked better, too.

"So you're finally awake, huh?" she whispered.

He meowed back in answer. His thoughts coming

through to her like a radio station still out of range, faint and crackling.

And he *was* feeling better.

"We're almost there."

Where? So low she almost didn't catch it.

"Oh, that's right, you don't know. You were out of it," Amanda said softly. By thought she told him about Ernie's visit, the new murders, her name in the blood, and her decision to take a brief vacation until she could get a handle on the whole affair because her magic didn't seem to be working when it came to the cult.

Good idea.

"Sorry I had to lock you up like a criminal. But those are the rules for taking an animal on a bus these days." She scratched him through the bars and took a good look at what was left of his one ear. His other wounds were healing nicely with the help of her magic, but the ear was still gone and it made him look funny. Lopsided. Maybe it would never grow back.

Amadeus didn't answer but closed his eyes and fell back asleep. Amanda let him be.

She stretched, staring out at the passing scenery, and tried not to let the painful memories of her years there depress her any further than she was. Everywhere she looked held memories. Of her childhood. Her family. Her mother. Of what she was and how cruel some people could be. It had been a long time ago. Perhaps, no one remembered her after all this time. She hoped so.

Then the bus lumbered by the place . . . the very spot where her mother's accident had happened, and guilt flooded Amanda.

Her mother had been trapped in the smoldering wreckage, according to the paramedics who had arrived too late. All her mother's magic hadn't been able to save her. And Amanda still didn't know who had killed her or why, though she'd always had a strong hunch.

Amanda hid her face behind her trembling fingers and fought the awful image of her mother burning alive in a twisted hunk of metal. To die . . . was bad enough. It was the way one had to die that could terrify even Amanda. Burning alive or hanging terrified her. Or being trapped in a car underwater.

She opened her eyes again when they were long past the site.

In the aftermath of the tragedy, she had been very . . . unstable. Had done some stupid things. Tried singlehandedly to track down the killer she sensed was responsible for her mother's death. A black magic cult. She'd riled her neighbors. Of course, she'd had help in that.

She'd loved her mother deeply. But a feeling of contentment suddenly washed over her at the thought of seeing Jessie and her family again.

The last time she'd seen Jessie was at Jake's funeral, not very long ago, but it hadn't been a happy time for her and she hadn't been herself. Before that, Jessie, alone or with her family, used to visit her and Jake about once or twice a year. Jake had heartily refused to ever visit anyone by magic. So Amanda would witch herself to her sister's house a few more times a year in between. Just the house. She'd never wanted anything else to do with Boston other than that. They had never really been apart for long. So this was the first time Amanda had ridden the streets or seen the city in eleven years.

She thought about all the times she'd witched herself places. According to legend, in the old days people believed witches could concoct a special magical salve out of dead things (including innocent baby parts) and when they rubbed their naked bodies all over with it, it would enable them to fly. Or they'd rub it all over a broomstick, and it would fly. Amanda smiled slightly.

On the phone at the bus station, Jessie had been thrilled to hear Amanda was coming—no matter what the reason. Which she didn't know about yet, though she had thought it strange that Amanda was coming in by bus. Amanda had gotten off the phone too quickly for her to ask. She said she'd be waiting for Amanda at the bus station with bells on.

In spite of everything, it would be great to see all of them again. It was what she needed.

The bus roared to a stop and people were stumbling all over themselves trying to get off. Gathering their baggage, stretching, yawning, and grumbling. Yelling through the windows at friends or family as they scrambled down the aisle and disembarked.

Amanda waited until most of them were gone before she collected her bag and Amadeus's cage and made her way off the bus, her hat still shading most of her face. Crowds made her nervous. She took a large breath of relief as she stepped off the last step and stood facing her sister who welcomed her immediately with open arms and a big hug.

"Mandy . . . it's so good to see you! I'm so happy you've finally come, no matter what the reason. The girls can't wait until I get you back to the house. They've got so much to tell you. Show you. Especially Abigail."

"Hi yourself, Jessie."

"By the way, how *are* you doing?" The look on her sister's face made it clear that she was referring to Jake's death and her widowhood.

"I'm doing . . . better," Amanda returned softly. Then smiled. "Much better. In that department, anyway."

"Here, let me help." And her sister tugged everything out of her arms as if she were an invalid.

"I can carry some of it, you know," Amanda said, amused. She took back the cage.

Jessie cocked her head at her sister. "Dressed like all the rest of us today, huh?" She meant the blue jeans and jacket. Jessie had always hated the long dresses, told her it made her look like someone going to a costume party.

Amanda tilted up her head, showing her face, and smiled. "I try to conform, you know, when I need to."

"Been in a war, too, I see."

Amanda's smile dissolved. "Still in one, I'm afraid. I guess I don't look so good, huh?"

"Well, besides being as thin as a stick, huge raccoon circles around your eyes, and having a face that resembles a pincushion, you look all right." Being a daughter and a sister to three witches had taught Jessie long ago that sometimes there were physical hazards to the profession, and she took them in stride, as with everything else.

"Thanks."

"You're welcome."

"But you look great, Jessie."

"Thank you . . . I work hard at it, too." She winked.

"You cut your hair," Amanda declared, finally figuring out why Jessie looked so different. It had always been as long as Amanda's and now it was cropped short around her ears, not tied back as she'd thought at first glance.

"You like it?" Jessie preened, turning her head first one way and then another.

"I do. Soon as I get used to it. Why did you cut it?"

"Got to stay with the times, like the girls always say. Besides, I just got tired of taking care of it."

Amanda noticed that her sister had a few gray streaks in her reddish hair, too, as young as she was, and more wrinkles in her pretty face; she'd gained some weight. But tight blue jeans and an emerald-hued sweater under a tailored short coat of the same color flattered her figure and brought out the green in her eyes. It was the joy of life that danced in the depths of those green eyes, and in her sweet face, that made Jessie beautiful.

They drifted away from the empty bus toward the

street, tromping through the piles of wet autumn leaves along the sides of the road.

"The car's over to your right. I was real lucky and got a parking space close by. Amazing at this time of day."

"Even on a Sunday?"

"Especially on a Sunday."

Jessie grinned and headed them toward a beat-up '76 Ford station wagon that Amanda recognized from their last visit. John didn't make a lot on a Senior Computer Programmer's salary, and Jessie didn't work, so the car's engine had been rebuilt, rust spots patched, and tires plugged so many times it wasn't much to look at. But it ran like a top. John was a wizard with cars, just like he was with computers. As hard as it was at times to make ends meet, Jessie preferred to stay home and raise her two children, run her home, bake cakes and bread from scratch, and have a four-course dinner on the table every night for her family. A woman right out of the fifties. Home and hearth the center of her life. That's what made her so unique in these days. How lucky she was that John wanted her home, too.

"*And* you look tired, Amanda. Worried. You came by public transportation Now that's unusual . . . for you." Her sharp eyes scanned nervously around them. "Something I should know? Is something following you?" Jessie shifted her eyes to Amanda's face after they'd finished tossing the baggage into the trunk and climbed into the front seat.

"I hope not. That's why I took the bus. There was trouble . . . but I think I've given it the slip—for awhile."

Jessie bestowed on her an unsettling look. "Oh, great. Just what I wanted: a witch on the run. Does it have something to do with all those cult murders?"

"Yes. How did you know about them?"

"It's been all over the news all day. About the bodies

discovered this morning and the freak storm damage. They said it occurred in Canaan. Couldn't help but notice that's where you live. Anything to do with you? With your trip here?" Jessie knew that black magic was sometimes attracted to white magic like magnets to metal, and she was very aware of Amanda's suspicions concerning their mother's death.

"I'm afraid so." Amanda rubbed her eyes tiredly, and leaned back against the car seat. "I think the cult—if that's what it is—is baiting me. Wants me to come after it for some reason."

"Oh?" Jessie slid her a questioning sidelong glance. "And there's something else, I can tell." Jessie was very perceptive. Another one of her talents. Along with the fact that it would never have crossed her mind to send Amanda away, even if the devil himself was hounding her. When it came to helping other people, Jessie was fearless. And she'd risk her own life to help her sisters.

"And I'm being . . . haunted by a woman who might have been a witch back in the seventeenth century. A black witch, I'm beginning to believe. Rachel. But I haven't figured out yet if there's a connection between her and the cult and the murders." Amanda was quiet for a few moments as Jessie rummaged around in her purse for the car keys.

"Gonna tell me more?"

"That's one of the reasons I'm here. To talk. To get some advice. A safe shelter in the storm."

"Well, that's what I'm best at, Sis. I might not have any powers, but I have other skills." She waited for her sister to continue.

"I keep coming up against a brick wall, Jessie, my magic is being blocked . . . and someone or something is killing people and making sure fingers are pointing at me. Just like eleven years ago," she commented grimly.

"So keep talking." Jessie started the car and squeezed

out into traffic, her eyes on the other cars lined up bumper to bumper, going out to the main road. Everyone trying to get home before the cold night closed in. Tires screeched. Jessie honked her horn a couple of times as some driver in a white Camaro cut them off and almost caused an accident. Then they were on their way.

Amanda recounted everything that had happened in the last week or so as they drove through the city and nightfall descended. When she was done, she sighed, and fell silent, her head propped in her hand as she peered out at the swiftly fading deep reddish glow of the day. It tinted the whole world like a soft red screen. Lovely, she thought.

There was frost forming on the windows and the temperature must have dropped twenty degrees since she'd gotten on the bus. Dark clouds hung low to the earth, making it seem even darker, and there was the taste of snow in the air. Before tonight, Amanda speculated as she studied the eerie light outside the windows, Boston might have its first snow of the year. Boston was always pretty covered in snow.

Amanda had released Amadeus from his cage as soon as she'd gotten in the car, and now she held him in her arms as he slept. He seemed to be doing much better. His thoughts stronger every time he awoke. She had recounted to Jessie how he had gotten his wounds and Jessie was very sympathetic, petting and cooing at him as if he were a sick baby as he perched between the two of them on the car seat, or purred in Amanda's lap. She was fond of Amadeus. She'd grown up with him and he'd protected her and Rebecca all those years, just as he'd guarded his mistress. Rebecca's familiar, a tiny coal black mouse named Tituba, had never been half as friendly or as vigilant with the girls. Of course, being Rebecca's familiar, he'd never been as powerful, either. And Tituba, or Tibby, as everyone called him, had never gotten along very well with Amadeus, either. He had pretty much kept to himself, only caring about Rebecca.

Amanda had been relieved when the cat finally opened his eyes once the car had started moving, and when he'd looked at her, they'd been lucid. He'd told her the pain was gone, though his missing ear still tingled, and he'd felt almost . . . human.

Amanda had laughed to herself.

Then they were pulling up into the narrow twisting driveway with the sprawling blue house at the end of it. Gravel splattered against the car's sides as it bumped wildly through potholes and ruts and then came to an abrupt stop beside a wraparound porch covered in dying vines. Four wicker rocking chairs sat forlornly on the wooden planks. A child's bike and a couple pairs of mud-covered shoes. A bright rag rug in front of the door with the word *welcome* on it.

It was totally dark outside by then. After the car's engine noises died away, the silence was heavenly. In the murkiness of the car, Jessie twisted toward her sister and said, "You know what I think, Mandy?"

"What?"

"We should ask Rebecca to help you. I know she would if you asked her."

"Rebecca?" Amanda laughed cynically, stroking Amadeus's fur. "Sure. She could sweep in on her motorized broomstick, solve the whole problem in a couple of minutes." She snapped her fingers. "And write a new best-seller on it—then on to the talk shows. If we can even find her with all the séances, private readings, and witches' conventions she attends," sarcasm in her tone.

"Mandy. You're terrible." Jessie chuckled.

"She doesn't know what she's even talking about half the time. She's all show and that's all," Amanda remarked. "We both know she's only in it for the money. She'd never stick her neck out for anyone."

"She would for a sister."

"Would she?"

"Ah, come on. She loves both of us. And I've always thought you underestimated her. And she has written a couple of books on witchcraft and Satanic cults—ghosts. She knows something about them. She might be able to really help you. It's time the petty rivalry between you two stopped, anyway—"

"Whoa," Amanda said. "There's no rivalry on my part and never has been."

"Oh?" But Jessie's voice in the shadows was good-natured.

Amanda shook her head in exasperation, though she had to admit that Jessie meant well.

"It'd be too dangerous for her, anyway. Her powers are limited. I would never be able to forgive myself if she got hurt because of me. I just don't think she can help me."

"Then who can?"

"I don't know . . ." Amanda muttered and pushed open the car door to get out, Amadeus clutched in her arms. "I've got to think about it."

She helped Jessie get her luggage from the rear of the car and followed her to the back door. Jessie unlocked it and they stepped into a large entry hall filled with wood, windows, and plants everywhere. High ceilings. Lots of space. A huge stained-glass window that Jessie had created and installed herself fanned over the top of the massive door. And cats. She had pictures and ceramics and stuffed cats everywhere. Jessie loved cats. She had five living, breathing, purring felines herself—Tomas, Kitty, Felix, George, and Rory. Though, Amanda noticed, they always seemed to scatter and hide when Amadeus was in the house.

Amanda trailed along behind her sister into the roomy old-fashioned country kitchen and set her bag on the round oak table, dropping Amadeus to the floor where he sauntered off underneath and curled up by one of the fat table legs. The kitchen smelled like fresh-baked bread. Cat wallpaper above and warm brown paneling below on the walls gave the place a homey look. White ceilings. An antique cabinet housing a tiny television and dishes, and oak cabinets lining two whole walls gleamed warmly. There was a cat-shaped family cookie jar in the corner of the counter. One of the ceramics Jessie was now into and taking classes for. Amanda commented on how pretty the cookie jar and matching mugs were that she'd made. In the middle of the table sat one of Amanda's pots, brimming over with a collection of dried autumn flowers.

Amanda and Jessie slipped out of their coats and Jessie took them into another room to hang them up while Amanda slumped down into a cushioned chair and stretched out her cramped legs.

Jessie returned and started a pot of tea. As she ran the water, she said casually, "You know, Mandy, there *is* another solution to your problem." She looked at her sister over her shoulder and her expression was thoughtful.

"And what is that?" As if she didn't already know.

"You could just stay here with us. Never go back. There's no reason to any longer, is there? Jake's gone. The town has never really accepted you, anyway . . . and now with all these murders, it seems they're never going to. We'd love to have you stay here with us." She smiled hopefully and her gaze roamed around and upward. "We've got plenty of room . . . three stories. You could have the whole third floor. The loft. I've just finished remodeling it."

"Jessie . . ." Amanda raised her hand and started rocking her head back and forth. "I couldn't impose—"

"You wouldn't be. Please, just think about it? Isn't it time Abigail and Debbie got to know their favorite aunt better? And"—she paused a second, an apprehensive look in her eyes—"our mother was killed by a renegade cult. I don't want to lose you to one, as well."

"Oh, Jessie . . . don't do this to me," Amanda chided, but couldn't help but be touched at her sister's generous offer, her love. "You know how I feel about my home in the woods . . . my memories."

"Amanda, that's just it. They're just memories. That's all they are now. And with all the rest of this trouble, wouldn't it just be easier to leave it all behind? Be with your family. Stay here and start a new life. There are lots of men in Boston and maybe you could . . ."

Amanda cut her off as if reading her mind. "No, Jessie. There'll never be another man for me, but Jake. I told you that and I meant it. I'll never love another man as long as I live." There was steel in her voice. "And that house back there in the woods is my home, it always will be. I miss it already."

Jessie refused to give up completely, though. "Well, promise me you'll at least think about it?"

"That I'll do. And that's all I'll do. And while I'm thinking about it . . . I'd prefer it if you didn't mention any of this trouble and why I'm really here to the girls or John. I don't want to scare them. Let's just say I'm here for a long overdue visit. I was lonely for all of you, which is partly the truth. I've missed you all."

Jessie poured them two cups of steaming hot tea into mugs with pictures of cats scampering all over them and brought them to the table along with a plate of chocolate-iced pumpkin cookies and some Polaroid photos of the kids from the night before dressed in their Halloween costumes. She plopped down next to her sister, one leg crossed under her and reached down to gently stroke Amadeus as he brushed past her leg.

"OK. You're right. It would just scare them and there's nothing they could do to help."

Amanda leaned over and grabbed her sister's hands in a quick, strong grip, her caring face breaking into a smile.

Jessie squeezed her back and then met her sister's eyes, her expression lighter, too. "Except sometimes that Abigail . . ."

"Ah, so you know?"

"I was hoping she wouldn't—"

"Have the family curse, huh?" Amanda supplied knowingly and nibbled on one of the cookies. She realized for the first time that she was hungry. A good sign. "Though, it's still too early yet to tell." Which was a barefaced lie, and they both knew it. Rebecca had known she had powers by the time she was six. Amanda even earlier.

Amanda had already begun to wonder about obtaining a familiar for her niece. There was this one raccoon that Rebecca had mentioned in one of her last letters, who was now without a mistress. She'd died—natural causes—a while back and they were looking for a home for it. She ought to speak to Jessie about it soon. If Abigail was a true witch, she'd need training and protection soon from all the evil forces that would be drawn to her. A tinge of guilt rested on Amanda's shoulders briefly. She should be training the girl. Preparing her. After all, she was her aunt.

"Do you really think she is?" Her sister's face was comical, the look of distress so apparent.

Amanda nodded, her eyes mockingly grave.

Then they both laughed.

What would be, would be. There'd been witches in their family for centuries. Someone had to do it. The world needed more white witches, not less, or evil would run rampant.

Amanda looked at the pictures. Abigail dressed as a colorful gypsy, complete with ten pounds of golden jewelry, and Debbie made up to look like a female construction worker with hard hat and tool belt dangling from her small waist. The pictures made Amanda laugh again. "I wish I could have been here and seen them." She handed the pictures back to her sister.

"Me, too. We had a great time last night."

"Is that where the cookies came from?" Amanda teased, trying not to let the memory of her Halloween night ruin her good mood. "Leftover trick-or-treat goodies?"

"Yeah, how'd you guess? Don't you like them? They aren't stale yet, are they?"

"Oh, no. They're delicious—but that's because I'm starving." To prove it, Amanda picked up another and started munching on it. "You make the best cookies."

"As good as yours," Jessie retorted.

"They should be. They're my recipe," Amanda reminded her. "Talking about the kids, where are they? And John?"

"They're at the new science center over on Seventh Street, gawking at the stuffed dinosaurs. It opened a few weeks ago and Abigail had to go visit it for a school project." Jessie was gobbling down her third cookie as she talked. "So I sent them all away for the afternoon so I could have some time alone with you before they all swoop down on us." She grinned sweetly. "Selfish of me, I know. But the minute you called, I knew something was wrong. I thought it would be easier on you if we could talk in private first. Uninterrupted."

"Thanks. You were right."

"Come on." Jessie stood up, grabbing Amanda's right hand in one hand and Amanda's traveling bag in the other. "I want to take you up to your room and settle you in. Show you what I've done to it since the last time you were here. You won't believe it."

"I'll bet," Amanda answered and allowed her sister to tug her up the two flights of narrow steps to the loft at the top of the house, gabbing at her all the way about the home improvements she'd made in the last couple of months. Showing her the crafts she'd made herself, hanging all over the walls and sitting on shelves. Macrame cats. Ceramic cats.

Amadeus, feeling more himself, padded along behind them and played with the shadows. Hissing every time he thought he'd discovered one of the real cats. But they were nowhere to be seen, as usual.

"Jeez, I still can't believe you wallpapered the whole second floor yourself . . . and laid all the carpeting," Amanda said in awe as they got to the top of the stairs. "You've been a working fool, haven't you?"

"Well, John helped," Jessie reminded her.

"I hope so."

Jessie dumped Amanda's bag right in the middle of the quilted bedspread on the four-poster bed. It was a beautiful old-fashioned loft room decorated carefully like the rest of the house. There was muted pink and blue wallpaper with roses on the short walls, and a window seat under the narrow windows that were covered in heavy lace curtains. There were paintings of cats (what else?) on the walls and a massive cherry-wood country chest of drawers and matching bureau with a large round mirror in two of the corners, an overstuffed chair next to the bed and a love chest at the end where Jessie stored extra blankets. On top of the chest was a small television. A plush oval area rug of azure blue lay on the wooden floor and disappeared under the bed. Amanda wanted to take off her shoes and rub her bare feet through it.

"The room is beautiful," Amanda exclaimed, overwhelmed as she sat down on the bed, looking around. "You did a great job with it." She gazed up at her sister's proud, anxious face. "You really want me to stay, don't you?"

"Yes. I'd be a liar if I didn't admit it." She spread her arms. "I did this all so you wouldn't be able to refuse."

Amanda lowered her eyes that were filling with tears, and just shook her head. A simple thank you wouldn't do it. Jessie had put her whole heart into this. Her fingertips brushed over the soft bedspread that had once belonged to their grandmother, Jessie. It was one of her sister's prized possessions.

"When do you expect the horde back home, anyway?" Amanda inquired, sniffing the tears away and looking back up.

Jessie peered at her wristwatch. "Another hour or so. Just enough time to get supper going. Homemade stew and corn bread. You said you were hungry. Want to help make supper?"

"Sure. Just tell me what to do."

"OK. You peel the potatoes, carrots, and onions while I fry the meat. Just like old times."

"Yeah, just like old times." Amanda shook her head again. Then, "Jessie . . . it's sure good to be here."

"Well, it's sure good to have you here, Sis. I've been worried about you. Especially since I heard about those murders."

"I know," Amanda whispered just loud enough for her to hear.

Amadeus was unexpectedly in Amanda's lap.

Bad thing going to happen.

Got to go. See. Be back soon.

Then he dematerialized right before their eyes.

"That cat," Amanda complained, as if she didn't know what to do with him. Though she was glad to see him back to his old self.

"Will he be all right?" Jessie asked, sitting down on the bed next to her sister.

"Sure. He can take care of himself," she said like she always did. But a tiny frown creased her brow. Lately she wasn't really sure he could take care of himself, not since last night. But he was gone, doing whatever he thought he should be doing. And Amanda knew better than to try to call him back. She'd seen the fanatical glint in his feline eyes. To him the game was afoot. She'd just have to wait until he came back and let her in on it. But his warning continued to disturb her. What was coming? And was it coming here? Could it hurt her family? The frown deepened and spread to her eyes and Jessie caught it.

"You know, Sis," Jessie said somberly. "I've been thinking about that cult, too. I had this crazy idea. It just popped into my mind when we were talking earlier."

"What?"

"Has it ever occurred to you that the cult may not be all human acolytes? That that dead witch you've been seeing has gathered together a coven from hell?"

"A coven of demons?" Amanda was astounded that Jessie could stumble onto such a bizarre notion.

"It would explain the butchery of the killings, and the inhuman powers that have been demonstrated, wouldn't it?"

The hair on the back of Amanda's neck was prickling, her face stricken. Yes, it would explain a lot of things.

Oh, my God, she thought, *and am I the one who has helped Rachel call them from hell in the first place with that damned spell I wove last week to bring Jake back from the in-between world? Oh, no . . .* If so, she was to blame for all the hideous deaths so far. The destruction. It was her doing!

"Amanda, are you OK?" Jessie was clutching her sister's arm, a worried look on her face.

"Yes, I'm fine," Amanda lied, putting a fake smile on her stiff lips. If the coven was headed or formed, even partly, by demons . . . even she might not be strong enough to fight their combined power. There'd be more deaths. And worse. Soon. It was a thought that drove shivers of ice through her already guilty heart.

And if it was true, her staying away would only make matters worse.

She had to go back. Stop them. Fight them. Before they began their real killing spree. Demons soaked up strength from torturing and killing. The more they maimed and killed, the stronger their power would become.

They went back downstairs and started supper.

And later that night, surrounded by Jessie's noisy family, eating the delicious stew they had made together, Amanda was unusually quiet. Her mind was full of the horror she might have released, and the horrors to come. Her heart was heavy; her mind indecisive to what she should do now. She wasn't a coward, but she wasn't sure if she was strong enough to fight what was waiting back in Canaan for her. And though she didn't care if she died herself in the trying, she did care if she failed and the hellish cult (if there was one) was left to terrorize her family and all those she cared about, and to ravage the world.

That she couldn't allow to happen.

After the rest of the family had gone to bed and the house was quiet, Amanda stood in the dark by the loft windows in her nightgown and robe and gazed out into the wintry night. She had been right and now the snow, light and wispy, swirled silently outside. It brought back memories of other winter nights in the snug cabin with

Jake. It made her lonely, even with all those people sleeping below her.

She wondered if Mabel was all right. Oh, if only she could use her magic to see.

But she'd watched the late night news with Jessie and John and there hadn't been any more incidents reported back in Canaan. So far.

Again . . . if only she could risk using her sight. But she didn't dare.

Well, Amanda thought, dropping her robe to the floor and slipping into bed, she'd have to go back sooner or later and fight them. She plumped up her pillow, and lay back, watching the window and the drifting snow. The room was full of a pearly light from it, lifting the darkness. And there was a draft in the room, so she snuggled deeper under the covers and tried to stop her shivering. Old houses had drafts; it was part of their charm.

She fretted over Amadeus's absence. Where had he gone and why hadn't he asked her first? Should have asked her, she grumbled to herself. She was the witch, and he was the familiar. He was supposed to be doing what she wanted him to do. Not scouting out on his own. But Amadeus had always been a rebel. Always acting on his own. And, she begrudgingly had to admit, he had saved her butt many times just because he was that way.

Everything she was worried about kept chasing around in her mind like mice in a box. She just couldn't seem to stop them. She couldn't ignore the tiny stirrings of fear. It'd been a long time since she'd been afraid of anything. She didn't like it.

She tried to dwell on the nice evening she'd had with her sister and her family. The kids and John had come home right about the time the stew had finished simmering, and they'd all sat around the big round table and eaten it, along with freshly baked sourdough bread and tall glasses of milk. Chocolate pie with whipped cream on top for dessert.

They'd all mentioned the cuts on her face and she'd trotted out the same lie as before, much as she disliked lying. But by evening the wounds were nearly healed from the special cream she'd been putting on them and it was easy to convince everyone that they weren't that bad.

The two girls had talked about what they'd been doing in school, and John, a short balding man with wire-rimmed glasses and a subtle wit who'd always had a special brotherly fondness for Amanda, had bragged happily about his promotion and what his new duties were. Jessie had woven humorous stories of her craft classes at the college and some of the sights her and the girls had seen while out trick-or-treating the night before.

They'd asked about Amanda's going back to throwing her pots, and about Mabel. The last time they'd been there before Jake's death, Jake had driven over and picked up the old woman so they could all meet her. She never got out much and Jake had wanted to treat her. The two girls had taken to Mabel right off. Now they always inquired about her.

Then all of them had gotten cozy in the living room with a big crackling fire and watched rented science fiction videos until it'd been time for the girls to go to bed. The adults had stayed up longer and talked.

The night had been fun, except for the gloomy thoughts churning around in Amanda's mind And Jessie, sensing this, walked her up to her room at the end of the evening and again suggested trying to see if Rebecca could help.

"We might try calling her agent or her publisher tomorrow morning and have her tracked down," she'd said. Jessie was sure she was on a book tour somewhere in the Midwest. "Someone must know where she is. And if Rebecca can't help, she might know someone who can. Another witch or a warlock. You don't have to be alone in this, Mandy."

Amanda, like earlier, had protested. She was afraid to pull anyone else into the eye of the storm with her. They might not come back out. After all, she was one of the strongest witches she knew of in the United States and if she couldn't handle what was going on, she didn't know of anyone else who could.

Amanda might have slept, or she just might have thought she had when she felt another presence in the room.

"Who's there?" she said, peering into the dim room with sleepy eyes. "Amadeus?" She sat up.

"No, Aunt Amanda . . . it's just Abby," a small voice said next to her. "Did I wake you?"

Abigail. "Not really . . . I think I was only half asleep." Amanda switched on the dim lamp on the stand next to the bed, and yawned. "What's wrong? It's late."

The little girl in the blue flannel nightgown and fuzzy slippers stood at the foot of the bed, clutching one of the stuffed cats, Paws, that her mother had made her. She was eleven, still loved stuffed animals, but in every other way was older than her years. Her innocent face was flushed from sleep, her long hair mussed. A striking child because of her bright red hair, glittering dark green eyes, and perfect heart-shaped face, but there was also something different about her. Amanda had seen it years ago in her strange gaze; the way she listened and seemed to understand things most children never did. As if she weren't a child at all. She probably saw things most children didn't see, either.

That the child was a born witch, Amanda had no doubt. Or something close to it. In their family, through the generations, there'd also been seers, psychics, and healers.

"I had a nightmare. Just now. I'd fallen asleep and . . . and . . . I had to warn you, Aunt Amanda. I just had to!"

In the faint light from the lamp, the girl's face was full of foreboding, her sensitive eyes troubled.

"Do you have these nightmares often?"

"Sometimes."

"How long have you had them?"

"Oh, for years. I've told Mom about them. And usually they're just dreams . . ." her voice hushed. "Aunt Amanda . . . sometimes they come true."

Ah, so she was psychic.

"Come here, Abigail." Amanda patted the spot next to her on the bed. "And tell me all about the nightmare."

The girl slid into bed with her and Amanda gave her a hug. Abigail propped Paws up on the pillow next to them so he could watch.

"Amadeus hasn't come back yet, has he?" the girl asked.

"No, he hasn't."

"I hope he's OK. He was in the nightmare, too. But he was just a regular cat." Abigail stroked her inanimate feline, her child's voice unsteady. Abigail, unlike the younger Debbie, knew that Amanda was a witch. Her mother had explained all of it to her a year or two ago when Abigail had asked point-blank. Abigail had suspected it for a long time. She'd had *dreams* about her aunt.

The child shivered.

"Are you cold, Abigail?" Amanda tucked the extra blanket she'd had on the bed around the girl's thin shoulders.

"No," the child's voice sure. "It was just the dream. It frightened me."

"Tell me about it, then."

The girl swung around and looked at her aunt solemnly. "It was about you, Aunt Amanda . . . I think you're in some kind of trouble, aren't you?"

It wouldn't serve any purpose to lie. Not if the girl was clairvoyant, as Amanda suspected. "Yes, Abigail, I am. But you needn't worry, I'm handling it."

"Ah, I thought so. Then at least that's true. I wasn't just imagining things." It seemed to soothe her. Amanda was reminded of herself long ago as a child and how crazy she'd felt when she'd started to discover her powers and her gifts. Before she knew what she was, before her mother had told her. It was easy to believe one was going insane when things first began to happen.

When you saw things and heard things—could do things—that others couldn't do.

"No, you weren't." Amanda, fully awake now, smiled tenderly at her niece cuddled in her arms. "What was the dream about tonight? Don't be afraid to tell me, I'll understand. We're alike, you and I."

"Are we?"

"Yes, we are. Don't ever be ashamed or afraid of your dreams, Abigail. They're part of what you are. I'll help you. I'm here for you."

The look Abigail sent her then was one of grateful relief. They were kindred spirits and she understood her. Abigail's head averted, her eyes closed. Long dark eyelashes against pale skin.

"In the dream you were out in the woods somewhere. You were begging me for help, but you were dressed . . . funny."

Amanda's eyebrows went up and her eyes danced. "More than usual?"

Abigail frowned. "Yes. It was like"—Amanda could see her mind searching for an explanation—"like you were in another time, Aunt Amanda. Like the pilgrims or something. You know? And people were chasing you . . . trying—I think—to hurt you."

"Are you sure it was me? Not someone who looked like me?"

"Oh, I'm sure. You called out my name and everything. There was this awful man who was beating you . . . he called you a witch and said he was going to punish you." Her small face wrinkled up and she started to cry softly. "Oh, Aunt Amanda, it was horrible. Horrible. He was hurting you so bad . . . and I couldn't help you. I couldn't do a thing. What does it all mean?"

Stunned, Amanda rocked her as she wept, and looked out into the falling snow, uneasy. That was the second warning she'd had. What was going on? Had it been just a dream, or a vision? A warning. It was just too coincidental that Abigail should dream such a situation, considering that Rachel had been accused of being a witch and probably executed in a time that might look like the pilgrim's time to a child.

Was Rachel trying to get to her through her niece? Trying to scare her?

But Abigail had seen her—Amanda—in the dream and not Rachel.

"What does it mean?" she repeated again, timidly.

"I'm not sure yet, sweetheart." Amanda decided to tell her some of it, she owed the girl at least that.

"There's another witch who's trying to hurt me." There was no need to mention the cult murders and the rest of it.

"Another witch? Why would another witch want to hurt you? I thought you were all like sisters?"

"She's a black witch, not white like me."

Abigail nodded her head slowly, comprehension coming. She knew the difference and what it meant.

"She's dead now, but she lived around seventeen hundred."

"Oh, she's haunting you?"

"You might call it that."

"And you think she had something to do with my nightmare?"

Smart child. "It's possible."

"I wish I could help you, Aunt Amanda." Abigail sighed, and tried to stifle a yawn. Then another.

"There's nothing you can do, except," she admonished affectionately, "get yourself back to bed. Now. Off with you."

"OK, Aunt Amanda." Abagail slipped out of the bed and headed for the door under Amanda's vigilance. At the last second she spun around and said, stuffed cat cradled in one arm, her face sorrowful, "Be careful, Aunt Amanda. Something real bad's going to happen. I'm afraid for you. Promise me?"

Amanda nodded gravely in response. "I will. Good night, Abby. I love you."

"I love you, too," the girl added at the last moment and disappeared into the hallway. Her footsteps pattered away to soundlessness.

Amanda switched off the light and lay back down, her mind a jumble of thoughts—her present situation and memories of her childhood that Abigail and Debbie always set off.

She'd been so much like Abigail. Wanting to be accepted. Not wanting to be so different that she didn't fit in with her peers. Afraid of what her differences meant. Scraps of her strange childhood came back to haunt her. She could see herself as a little girl about Abby's age, standing in the schoolyard the first time she'd realized how cruel children could be to those who were not like them. There'd been times, growing up in a family of witches, where she'd forget herself at school. The day got suddenly chilly and she'd forgotten her sweater, she'd simply witch one up. To her it had been so natural. She recalled vividly the girl at the desk next to her, all eyes and disbelief, and then her gaze had reflected fear. A look she'd come to know very well over the years.

And much later, an incident with a scrawny boy named Andy, who'd been a friend of hers for a while, and had a bad home life. He usually wore raggedy clothes and never brought anything to eat for lunch. One day, feeling so sorry for him, she broke the rule about not letting outsiders see what she was, she'd wished him something to eat—an apple and a sandwich—right into her hand. The look in his eyes as he backed away. "Get 'way from me. My mom's tolt me about people like you. Witch . . . you're a witch!" And he'd scampered away like a rabid dog was chasing him.

Amanda had hidden the hurt she'd felt. Like always. She forgot her lunchbox one day and thinking that no one was around her to see, materialized a full lunchbox for herself. But someone had seen. A mean-spirited girl named Sandy. Who'd blabbed to everyone that she was strange, unnatural . . . spooky. *Stay away from her.* And they did. Amanda was ostracized from then on.

Was Abby's life like hers had been? She hoped not. Of course, did things ever change? Not really. She studied the dark room. A loft room so much like the room she'd shared as a girl with Rebecca and Jessie. Memories.

"I'm going downstairs," a pudgy Rebecca out of her past was saying stubbornly. Same dark fuzzy hair. Sly eyes. "I want to show them what I can do . . ."

"Becka, you know Mom said for us to be good and go to sleep. It's late," her small child-self was whining, sitting up in her bed, the moonlight flowing in over her. "It's late. Go to sleep, would ya?" crossly. Downstairs their mother was busy with her guests. All other witches. It was a Sabbath. She could hear the soft chanting rising and falling like waves. It was strangely comforting. She'd heard it so often. Lulled her to sleep.

Jessie was only a curled up knot under the covers of

her bed, only her shiny red curls poking out and her stuffed dog, Spotty. The youngest, she was still a baby. She slept a lot. Rebecca would have little to do with her because she couldn't do the things she and Amanda could. Make things disappear. Appear. Float. "She's not a witch like us," Rebecca would always whisper disdainfully, her nose awfully high.

That night Rebecca did sneak down the steps in the dark, but she was back up in bed in a flash. Magiclike. One second not there and the next there, angry, huffing and puffing because the women downstairs had been too busy to watch her perform all her tricks and her mother had unceremoniously barred her from the gathering.

Amanda had laughed and laughed. Rebecca never listened. To anyone. Never thought of herself as a child. Always needed to be the center of attention.

And she'd never changed.

Amanda sighed in the dark, remembering them all as children. Shy Jessie. Peacemaker Amanda. And pushy, obstinate Rebecca. Wondering why she was remembering. The loft, she reasoned. So like that old bedroom. It seemed so long ago now. So simple in some ways. Ah, to be a child again . . . with only a child's problems.

It took her longer to fall asleep the second time, but it only took her a heart-stopping moment to come to full wakefulness. Sometime right before dawn, when the darkness in the room seemed to be dissipating, she opened her eyes.

There was something in the room with her. On the end of the bed. She could see a darker shadow gleaming there. About the same size as a small cat.

Not Amadeus.

There was a funny scent in the air. Magic. Amanda sat up.

A flame appeared, held in the claw of a tiny black

creature. Its crimson eyes glittering back at her from a furry dark face peered at her almost as if she intrigued it. The face reminded her of a bat, and then she observed that the claw that held the mysterious flame was really one of two folded up wings. It crouched on two bony paws under a shiny fat belly.

As she watched it started growing in size. Until it was as large as a small child. It grinned at her then. A mouth full of razor-sharp teeth. Pointy ears.

"Who are you?" she whispered.

"Gibbiewackett," it croaked like the rustling of dead leaves. The creature tilted its ugly head, and lowered the flame away from its face. It didn't like the bright light.

"What do you want?" Amanda asked, her heart slowing back down to normal. She'd recognized the odor. The thing had offered its name. White magic. Gibbiewackett was someone's familiar.

"To warn you," the squeaky-hoarse voice croaked on. "They know where you are, witchy. If you don't leave soon, people down there"—he gestured downward with a bony appendage—"will die. Many people will die." It had an accent, British, if Amanda wasn't mistaken.

"Who knows where I am?" Amanda was burning with interest now. She rose to her knees on the bed and looked the thing right in the eyes.

It laughed, cryptically.

"Your non-witch sister was right . . . a cult of demons led by someone or something so evil even my own all-powerful master cannot see it. Yet."

"And why should your master want to help me?" she probed sharply. "Who's your master?"

It turned its head. She thought it was laughing again.

"Let's just say a . . . friend. One of the Guardians. That is all I'm allowed to tell you."

The Guardians? Amanda's mouth was open, she knew it, but the knowledge had taken her that much by surprise. Every witch had heard of the legend of the Guardians. An ancient group of the most invincible white witches and warlocks ever born. Said to watch over and protect all witches from the worst of evil. But she, like every other witch she had ever met, had always believed it just a legend. No one had ever really met a Guardian. Ever. No one had needed a Guardian. They were only supposed to surface when the very stability of the world was at stake. Only when evil that sinister was afoot on the planet.

"Yes, the Guardians truly exist. My master is one." The beast nodded its head. Grinned again. "Very, very powerful." Pridefully. It popped the flame into its mouth and the room went dark again, but not as before. Dawn's feeble rays were sneaking into the room from the windows.

"Need to go now. Remember. Leave soon." The familiar had began to shrink. Its beady red eyes blinking at her like a broken stoplight. The size of a dog. Cat again. Tiny kitten. "My master says be careful." A kitten-sized purring voice. "Fight them. Call me if you need me. I might come," a mouse voice.

Then the familiar was the size of a bug and in a sudden glow of light, poofed out completely.

Amanda rocked back onto her bottom and collapsed full-length onto the bed, wondering why she had been warned. Wondering what was going on. *My God, a cult of demons . . .*

If they know I'm here . . .

She bolted upright again and jumped from the bed. The morning light was streaming through the windows now. Bright pink and yellow.

I have to get out. Now. Jessie, John, Abigail, and Debbie are in danger as long as I'm here.

I can use my magic. It felt good to know that, but she

had to conserve as much of her strength as she could for the coming fight.

She started tearing off the robe and nightgown and wiggled into some clothes she pulled out of her traveling bag.

It wasn't until she was all dressed and ready to leave that she remembered Amadeus.

He still wasn't back. She sent out an urgent silent call for him. No answer. She couldn't wait for him. He'd just have to find her. Amanda quickly settled the strongest protection spell she knew over Jessie's house and on the people who lived there. That would help.

She was bouncing down the steps when she heard the phone ringing into the silence of the early morning house. But the noise stopped in mid-ring and as she came into the kitchen she saw her sister, Jessie, standing in a robe, hair mussed, with the phone in her hand, talking. The coffeepot was plugged in and perking away on the kitchen table, and the pungent aroma of fresh coffee was wafting across the kitchen. Newspaper unfolded and open on the counter. Monday morning. Jessie always got up before the rest to prepare breakfast. The kids had school. Her husband had a long commute to the college.

Jessie's eyes widened when she saw Amanda. She handed her the phone. "It's for you. It's Jane," was all she had time to say before Amanda grabbed the phone and put it to her ear.

"Amanda," the frightened weepy voice on the other end said. "Jonny's gone. Gone! Oh, Amanda, help me find him, please?"

How had she known she was here? Ernie maybe.

Amanda didn't hesitate. "I'll be there. Hang on. I'm coming now." She put the phone back in its cradle and looked at her sister.

"The cult knows I'm here, I've been told. No sense in hiding anymore." Her lips curled up in a sneer.

."They're determined to get me back. They've taken one of Jane's children as bait."

"Oh, no." Jessie's hands went to her face, her eyes stricken with sympathy. She could imagine what losing a child could do to a mother. She didn't ask any questions.

"Jessie, you were right. The cult's not all human. And I've got a hell of a fight on my hands." She smiled derisively at her choice of words.

"I have to go. No more time to waste. Or prepare. If I don't find the boy soon, they'll kill him." *Butcher him,* was what she was thinking. *Not Jonny. Sweet, innocent Jonny.*

"If Amadeus returns, tell him where I've gone."

Jessie nodded, and didn't try to stop her. "Be careful, Amanda . . . and God protect you."

But Amanda was already gone. She'd witched herself to Jane's front door.

Chapter 5

When he opened the door and found her standing there, Ernie's eyes went round with incredulity, then bafflement. "Wasn't Jane just talking to you on the phone at your sister's house?"

"Yes," Amanda said. She wasn't surprised to find Ernie there. Ernie and Jane were friends, too. He'd gone to high school with her, and if Amanda recollected right, they had even dated during those years. His usually friendly face was lined with weariness and his eyes were shadowed. His clothes, blue jeans and a gray and blue plaid flannel shirt, were disheveled and coated with cockleburs and dried mud. She'd never seen him looking so unkempt.

"Doesn't your sister live in Boston?" he insisted.

"Last time I looked, she did."

"Then you are a witch, aren't you?" a mere whisper, his expression priceless. Not fear, exactly, but cautious wonder that such a thing could exist in the world.

"Yes." She exhaled it in one breath, stepping through the front door of the quiet, closed ceramic shop. He clicked the door shut silently, as if he was trying not to disturb someone. "With what's ahead of us, Ernie," she continued in a low voice, "it's only fair that I tell you the whole truth. I'm going to need all the help, the backup, I can get. Human and supernatural."

Ernie's face reflected an almost stupid look. "Well"—
he rubbed his beard with a shaky hand—"I'll be da—"
He caught himself before the word had completely escaped, and flashed her an embarrassed grin. "I guess
I'd better believe you, since you're either a liar and you
weren't in Boston at all, but down the street somewhere, or you were in Boston and only magic could
have gotten you here that fast."

Not to mention he'd seen the storm damage when
there'd been no storm, and he'd heard the police of-
ficers talking in hushed tones the last week or so over
their coffee in the local donut shop about the murder
scenes. He'd overheard some mighty strange stories.

His eyes appraised her sternly. "And I don't believe
you're a liar, or Jake was a liar. I know you both too well."

"Before you go thinking anything else, Ernie, I want
to tell you that I'm what you would call a good witch."
Amanda was talking as her eyes roamed the empty shop,
taking in everything. The stench of evil hung heavy over
the whole place. They'd been here, all right. Demons.

"Have you ever seen the Wizard of Oz?"

"Sure, lots of times," Ernie replied as she walked past
him.

"Remember there were three witches in it? The
Wicked Witch of the West, and the Wicked Witch of
the East, I think . . . but there was also a good witch
called Glinda?"

"Yes." He spoke slowly, his eyes looking at her as if
he'd never really seen her before, studying her face
closely in the dim light of the shop.

"I'm like Glinda. That's the easiest way to put it."
She smiled softly. "Though unlike the Land of Oz, we
good witches aren't supposed to interfere with mankind, except under extreme circumstances. We're not
supposed to call attention to ourselves."

"Didn't ever believe in witches before, much less in

two kinds. Good and evil, huh?" His voice, she noticed, quavered.

"You got it. There's good witches—white magic—and then there's the evil—black magic." Her eyes narrowed with fury and met his. "What we're dealing with here with this so-called cult is black magic. The blackest. And even worse than an evil witch . . ."

"I'm listening."

They made their way through the chaos of the partially damaged gift shop, stepping carefully over broken glass and shattered pottery, talking in low tones about what she'd learned. The black magic cult and Rachel. Amanda told him just what she thought he could handle, nothing more. Nothing about the cult consisting of hellish demons. No sense in scaring all the wits out of him. She needed him sane.

The inside of Jane's Gift Shop wasn't as bad it looked; the destruction was mainly on the outside of the renovated house. Someone had already begun to clean up, but it looked as if they'd stopped halfway. Maybe when Jonny had been discovered missing.

Ernie absorbed everything she said with little comment. She could tell he was having a hard time with it. But then, what normal person wouldn't?

They came into the bright kitchen, used coffee cups strewn all over the table and a fresh pot perking on the counter, dirty dishes piled high in the sink as if a large hungry crowd had just left.

The first thing Ernie did was steer her firmly to a chair, pour her a cup of coffee, and then start clearing off the cluttered table.

"There doesn't seem to be any damage in here."

"No, only in the shop and on the outside. She's luckier than the others. Peterson's and the Carden's house were demolished." He'd finished cleaning off the mess and was at the sink now, washing the mound of dishes.

Amanda looked up at the crucifix hanging on the kitchen door that emptied out into the shop.

"And no one here was hurt or murdered, either. Even though they were all sleeping back there." He gestured toward the rooms with a sudsy hand.

Amanda didn't want the coffee, but she drank it anyway. It'd help steady her nerves. "Where's Jane?" she asked between gulps. The coffee tasted really good, she thought.

"She was just given a mild sedative," Ernie explained. "So she's sleeping in the back room. She and everyone else around here were out all last night, hunting for the boy, and Doc Ellis felt she needed some sleep before the next round. She was practically in hysterics by the time he gave her the shot. Her other two boys are at their grandmother, Helen's house for awhile. Get them away from the circus that this is going to become here pretty soon. Couldn't keep it away from the press any longer, I'm afraid. We've already had phone calls from all the television and radio stations. I expect them to come snooping around here any minute. I was almost afraid to answer the door just now." His back moved slightly as his large hands washed the dishes, rinsed them automatically, and laid them in the plastic rack for air drying.

"But Jane has already decided to go on television to plead for the boy's return—as soon as she has a little rest. Channel Four's setting it up now."

Oh, boy, Amanda thought, television crews and rude anchorpeople will be swarming all over in no time No one will have a moment's peace. Not even her . . . once someone opens their mouth about a neighborhood witch. This was the kind of crap the television stations loved. Satanic cults, witchcraft, sacrifices, murder and mayhem.

"Everyone else has gone home, too, for awhile, and

then they'll be back here and at it again. State boys as well as our own police are still out there searching in the woods. They're calling in more reinforcements even now."

"How long has Jonny been missing?"

Ernie had finished the dishes and came and sat down next to her at the table, a cup of coffee held tightly in his hands.

"We're not real sure. Jane didn't start worrying until he never showed up for supper last night. He and a couple of his friends had gone off to play yesterday morning and had been warned not to go too far or to go into the woods—the murders, you know—and his friends had returned long before nightfall, but he hadn't. They said they'd last seen him strolling off for home through the edge of the forest over by Gacy's Funeral Home. He never showed up.

"By full dark last night Jane was frantic. Said Jonny wouldn't scare her like that. Staying away after dark, what with everything that had been going on. She said she *knew* immediately that something had happened to him. Mother's intuition.

"She called the police about seven-thirty last night and the search has been on ever since." His gentle eyes looked at her, as he started rubbing the side of his face again, a nervous gesture.

"Usually the police wouldn't have been as worried as they were, so soon after a youngster's disappearance, but with all these cult murders and stuff, they're being extra cautious."

"They should be."

Amanda laid a comforting hand on his wrist. Closed her burning eyes. She was already exhausted. Worry, fear did that. Ever since Jane's call she'd been petrified of facing her; she didn't know what to say to her. Even her brief respite in facing her friend face-to-face just made her edgier.

What do you say to a mother whose child has been abducted by a sadistic murderous cult? Especially one as unearthly as the one that was plaguing Canaan. She had no idea. Not the total truth, certainly. It would drive her mad. For Amanda had no doubt that Jonny was with the cult. That they'd stolen him. To lure Amanda back. To have something to fight her with. She loved Jonny and the other boys. They were almost like family to her. So Amanda's mind worked feverishly on what she should do next. Should she wait to see Jane, talk to her? Or should she just start looking for the boy on her own?

There wasn't much time. Not much time at all.

"How long have you been here, Ernie?" Amanda inquired, looking up finally.

"Since she first realized he was missing last night." There was a moment of slight embarrassment on Ernie's part, and then, "She called me first thing . . . I should have mentioned it before, but I never had a chance—we've been kind of seeing each other, you might say. It started out just as a friendship, and I've grown very fond of the boys." Ernie loved kids, Amanda knew that just by the way he'd grieved over the loss of his son since he'd moved to California with his mother after the divorce. It made sense that Ernie would turn that love to Jane's children. They were sweet boys.

"You know she's had a steady boyfriend?"

"Yes, I know." Amanda had even met him. A nice guy. He was a painter. Oils. He was tall and skinny. Wore his hair in a ponytail and liked fancy clothes. But he'd never warmed up to the boys the way Jane would have liked. His only drawback. Amanda had thought Jane loved him, but . . .

"Had, I should say. She stopped seeing him about a month ago. We've been dating ever since."

Amanda's eyes glinted back knowingly at him. "You have? Oh, I knew you two were friends, but I thought she was serious about that artist friend of hers. She's been dating him for over a year." She wasn't hurt that neither of them had mentioned it to her, she was just happy for them. Probably not telling her had something to do with Jake's death and not wanting to hurt her. She patted him on the hand. "I'm glad. You two are a lot alike." Steady, giving, and level-headed. Loved children. Jane had never acted like the usual scatterbrained artist. She was too down-to-earth. "Be good for each other."

Ernie smiled faintly, but his eyes were still sad. "Thanks. I've really come to love her and the boys, you know?"

Amanda nodded her head. Yes, she could see that.

"She's the one who suggested I ask you out with us for supper and a movie sometime. Said it would be good for you to get out. She worries about you."

Ah, so Jane was behind that strange invitation she'd gotten from him last week? Amanda should have guessed. Ernie had never shown any romantic designs on her. He was truly just a good friend.

"We were so happy . . . until this. I don't know what to do now. We've called all the right authorities. Searched everywhere for the boy. No traces at all. No ransom note. Nothing. Jane's devastated. So am I. I love the boy. He's a good kid."

Amanda could hear the pain in his voice and she could see his desperation. He was talking on and on to help disguise it.

"It's like he's just disappeared off the face of the damn earth. God, Amanda, I'm worried sick now with all you've told me. I had hoped, like Jane, that Jonny was just lost—anything but to have been taken by the ones that you think have taken him. And Jane, well, she can't take much more of this . . . not knowing. But I can't tell her what you think, either. It'd kill her. All her hope would fly out the window. That's all that's keeping her going now, anyway. Hope that they don't have him." There were traces of tears in the corners of Ernie's eyes. His shoulders had slumped, his face hangdogged. He rubbed his bloodshot wet eyes with trembling fingers.

Amanda sighed heavily, not knowing what else to say, turning away so Ernie could have some privacy in his grief, and drank some more of the coffee.

Ernie went on talking in low painful tones about the search and what they were planning to do next.

"Is he still alive, Amanda? Do you know that?" He was trying so hard to believe she could help.

She concentrated, using her magic.

She could see Jonny's innocent little face in her mind and her sight glimpsed something so awful that she didn't want to face it. In the swirling mist of her magic, she saw a bloody altar and a knife dripping with a child's blood. She heard a child screaming in agony.

Amanda glanced violently away from Ernie's gaze so he couldn't see the terror written all over her white face. Her heart felt like someone was tearing at it.

Had it happened already? Or was it yet to come? Her sight didn't always answer that. Present and future sometimes merged together and she had to decipher the clues. Something prevented her from seeing any more. Damn them! She pounded her clenched fist angrily on the table, causing Ernie to jump. Then like a brief clearing of storm clouds during a deluge, some of the truth slipped through the barriers the cult had erected and came to her.

"Amanda?" He put his hand out to her. "What is it?"

She knew where Jonny was. She knew. They had him. They were going to kill him. Soon. Then the rage rose like bitter bile inside her and she couldn't stop it, didn't want to stop it. Didn't for once even want to control it. A killing rage like she'd never experienced before, even worse than when her mother had died.

And there was no more time to waste, she realized with a sinking feeling in the pit of her stomach. No more time to sit here talking with Ernie. No time to wait for Jane to wake up and comfort her. *No more time.*

"Amanda?" he reiterated, growing fearful at the odd way she was behaving. "What's wrong?"

She stood up. Mustn't let Ernie suspect how close to death the boy was. Must take care of this herself. Now. Her way . . .

"Tell Jane when she wakes that I was here. I'll be back." She shoved her arms robotically into Jake's old jacket. Put on her hat and her gloves. As much as she'd need them. For Ernie, for appearance's sake. Old habits died hard.

Ernie suddenly blurted out, "I'll give you some advice. Don't show your face in town, Amanda." As if he had forgotten momentarily what she was and what she was capable of.

Amanda glared at him, a quick ugly frown skimming her lips. "You mean the town still thinks I might have had a part in murdering all those people?" she asked acidly. "Maybe a part in Jonny's disappearance?"

Ernie evaded her eyes. "Yes, just like I was afraid of before," he said quietly. "They were in a frenzy before Jonny disappeared and now, with no one else to blame and strike out at . . . you've become their prime suspect. Prime target. Especially since they discovered you'd left yesterday. They all have kids, too. I heard them whispering about it when we were out looking in the woods last night. I think they'll come after you as soon as they know where you are. They think you're part of the coven."

And how were they to know that the coven was not even human? And even if the townfolk knew . . . they wouldn't believe, just like Ernie wouldn't believe.

"I'm sorry, Amanda. I'm ashamed of the town I've grown up in." His face was full of disgust. "But if they see you now, they'll come after you. So don't take any chances."

"Looking for someone to lynch, huh?" There was bitterness in her voice, but no real anger. She'd been there before. Anger was a waste of her time and energy.

"Amanda, they're just scared. Everyone is. I am. Jane is. And we're terrified for Jonny."

The ice went out of Amanda's stare. "I know they don't mean it." Ernie was right, they were just frightened. They were like people all over the world at any time in history. Anyone who was different, or acted differently, was a good vent for their hostility and fear.

"Thanks for the warning. But I can take care of myself." No one would see her, anyway. So she had nothing to fear.

She was just about to leave when Jane came stumbling out. Dressed in a loose robe, her hair uncombed, her fingers clutched at her throat, she moved slowly into the light of the kitchen like someone in a trance.

"I heard voices out here . . . Amanda? I thought it was you." Her face was blank, her eyes moved erratically, her mouth drawn into a taut, colorless line. Amanda recognized shock in her actions as she shuffled across the distance between them. She made it to a chair and then stood there swaying like she was drunk. The sedative. Jane didn't even mention, like Ernie, that she had just talked to her from Boston on the phone.

"Sit down, Jane." Amanda took her friend's arm firmly and coaxed her into the chair.

The woman turned dead eyes on her. "Have they found Jonny yet?"

"No, not yet," Amanda said softly, her heart aching for her friend.

"No news?" now a monotone.

"No. I'm sorry, Jane." She couldn't tell the poor woman the truth, it would only make her torment more unbearable.

Amanda didn't sit back down. She had to go. Quickly.

"I knew you'd come and help us look for Jonny. No matter what they said. The townspeople think you took him." Jane shook her head sadly. "They don't know you. They don't know anything." She laid her head on her arms on the table, staring through Ernie. She was out of it.

Amanda threw Ernie a meaningful glance. "You ought to put her back to bed, Ernie. She's in shock. I've got to go," she whispered to him, aware of the precious time slipping through her fingers.

Abruptly, Jane sat straight up. Her eyes widening. "Amanda . . . have they found my boy yet?" she cried again. Her lips were quivering and her face was screwing up like a child about to weep. Then tears slid from her eyes and tracked down her face. "They're going to kill him, I know," she sobbed. "Kill him. Like all those other poor bastards."

Amanda knelt down next to her and grasped her hands, looking gently into her stricken eyes. "I'm going to get your son now, Jane. Don't worry. I won't come back without him," she promised fiercely.

A small spell to help put her friend to sleep wouldn't weaken Amanda that much. She wove it. "Sleep, Jane. You need sleep."

Jane uttered a low moan and slumped against Amanda, her face finally peaceful.

"Tuck her in, Ernie," Amanda said flatly.

Ernie picked her up and turned to Amanda with Jane asleep in his arms. "Are you really going to get him? You know where he is?" His eyes filling with a wild hope.

"Yes, I think so."

"I'll come along. I'll help."

"No, I have to do this myself. It's too dangerous for you."

He looked disappointed. Only because he had no concept of what he would have been facing. If he only knew, thought Amanda.

"Good-bye, Ernie . . . wish me luck, I'll need it." Amanda's chin tilted bravely up and then as Ernie looked on in amazement, she disappeared into thin air right before his eyes.

"Good luck, Amanda . . ." he murmured in her wake.

He carried the sleeping woman back to her bed, still shaking his head in disbelief at what he'd seen. Maybe he was going over the edge, too.

Amanda knew that the coven and the boy were somewhere in the woods, but from the moment she'd left Jane's house the walls had come up again and she could no longer see the boy. But he was somewhere out there, she knew that. She did something she rarely did and changed into a huge black panther with glittering ruby eyes and sped through the forest under an obscured dim sun. It was swifter than her human form. The day was heavily overcast and storm clouds hovered close above her as she raced along the ground, frantically trying to find the boy before they killed him.

She searched for most of the dark day among the leaves and trees, creeks and hillsides. She even tried Black Pond. They were nowhere and her strength began to wane. A hard, steady rain began to pelt her and the woods misted up until she could hardly see three feet ahead of her even with her keener animal vision.

Finally, as true dusk began to settle and the rain fell harder, she slunk back to the cabin, weary and heart-sick, her paws cut and bloody. She'd failed. Not all her magic had enabled her to find him.

But they were out there somewhere. She knew it.

By the time she got to the cabin and had trans-formed back into her own human shape, night had come, bitterly cold, dark, and wet. The rain continued as the wind soughed through the grabbing trees. She wondered if it would snow like it was in Boston.

Inside the cabin, she dragged herself around and lit the fires. Put out candles. She found some dry clothes, another pair of Jake's old blue jeans and a heavy flannel shirt, and put them on woodenly.

Her stomach growled, she was hungry, but she didn't eat. No time. She had to find Jonny.

She sat down cross-legged before the fire in the living room and went into a trance, first to check on Mabel and make sure she was all right because she didn't have time to go over there.

Mabel was eating a supper made from the supplies she'd brought her a couple days ago, watching her tiny television in the dimly lit trailer; humming softly to herself and half-asleep. All was well.

So Amanda returned to desperately searching for Jonny as the minutes drained away like the blood of a dying man. Some urgent sense deep inside her telling her not to give up. Still, she was kept from seeing.

It was the scratching at the door that aroused her.

Amadeus was back. He didn't wait for her to open

the door, though; before she knew it he had it swinging on its hinges and was in her lap. His fur was wet and he was shivering. His missing ear had never returned, but other than that, he seemed to have fully recovered. She hugged him tightly until he squirmed out of her embrace.

"Amadeus, where have you been? I've been worried."

Looking for Jonny. Like you.

Amanda caught her breath and stared into his clever cat eyes.

"What have you found out?"

Found coven. At Witch's Pond. Now.

But I was there, she thought, confused.

They were coming. Just missed them.

"They have the boy." It wasn't a question. Amanda knew. She stood up.

Yes. Going to kill him. Hurry. Amadeus headed for the door, which opened before he even got there and as he scooted through and out into the rainy night, Amanda metamorphosed back into the giant panther and slipped out after him.

She followed him through the blackness and the swirling rain to Witch's Pond. Her great paws skimming the ground, ebony fur flowing over steel muscles, her eyes glowing crimson with rage. If they had hurt Jonny . . . *she'd kill every one of them.*

And there under the old willow tree gathered around the churning waters of the pond stood dark-robed figures chanting and moving slowly in the heavy rain. The fog curling about the dreamlike shapes and settling on the pond was as thick as soup, but the foul stench of evil was so overpowering, Amanda could have found them by that alone. How could she not have located them before? She had no answer. Unless she wasn't meant to until now.

There was an eerie glow about the whole place, a

faint flickering light, but she could see no source. She edged in nearer, her razor-sharp claws sheathing and unsheathing from under the black fur of her paws, as she readied to spring.

Then she saw Jonny. A small bundle in one of the cowled figure's arms. He wasn't moving. The figure had laid the body on a makeshift altar, a flat slab of rock close to the water. As it spun around slowly to speak to the rest of its coven, Amanda caught a glimpse of its shadowed face as the head came up and the cowl slipped back. Only a man, or so it appeared to her at first. A lean, sharp-eyed, brutal face, pockmarked, with a hook of a nose. It smiled cruelly, showing blackened teeth. Long stringy dark hair. The high priest, no doubt, by the imperious way he was acting.

But then a mere second later as it spoke, the chiseled planes of its face began to melt like wax set over a flame . . . until what glared down upon its sycophants was a drooling, fang-toothed, hideous monster with demon-red eyes and a serpent's tongue that flicked out of wet leathery, deformed lips. It laughed, a hellish sound, its shoulders hunching and stretching, and its body shifting under the robe like huge worms moving under a thin blanket. With every movement it grew taller and larger until she could see ghoulish, thickly muscled legs peeking out from under the fluttering robe and cloven hooves at the bottom of them.

At least a mid-level demon. Someone very powerful had called him from his place in hell. And he would be very difficult to fight, even for a witch as strong as she.

Out above the misty waters of the dark pond Amanda spied a small glimmer of light, also growing in size and strength, drawing nearer as the coven's chanting increased. Rachel. Amanda had the feeling that if she didn't act soon, the odds would be even more against her.

She was crouched behind a tangled thicket of vines and brambles. She didn't know where Amadeus had gone to, but she was sure he was somewhere close by, waiting for her signal.

The rain had formed a curtain hiding away the rest of the world, except for the coven and the altar.

The circle of hulking vultures converged around the child on the stone. Grunting and hissing spiced the feverish chanting. Unearthly tongues lolled hungrily from inhuman mouths. A hazy steam rose from some of the robed creatures in the rain and Amanda realized at that moment that some of the followers, but not all, were demons.

Her eyes locked back on the child and to the demon that held the knife. She followed the gleam of metal as it raised the serrated long-bladed dagger, and her muscles bunched for the attack.

If this kill was like their others, it wouldn't be a merciful plunge of the knife, but a slow and heinous butchery. But still, alerted as she'd been, she didn't pounce swiftly enough, and as her panther shape leapt through the heavy air, the child released one long piercing cry.

Amanda exploded into their midst like an avenging angel, slammed down one of the robed demons at the edge of the circle and with a swipe of one of her huge paws, took a clawlike hand off. It shrieked a shrill bellow and as she came in again for another attack, its image wavered a moment and then faded into a column of black smoke, spiraling up, up, and into the black sky until it was gone.

She'd taken care of one, twelve to go. She spun on her paws and growled at the rest of the coven, barring her fangs, her slitted feline eyes on the boy as the high priest glowered over his shoulder at her and raised the knife again. He halted its descent when it kissed the boy's already bloody cheek. Jonny was conscious, shuddering with terror, whimpering, his childish wide eyes fixed on the demon hunkering above him. Scared speechless.

"One more move, witch, and the boy will die," a hoarse guttural order full of arrogance and intense hatred. It wrinkled its snout in disgust. White magic smelled just as bad to it as black did to her.

The rest of the coven hesitated in the mist, repulsive faces expectantly turned toward her, some human, some fiendish. The humans were wild-eyed, their faces distorted with blood lust and evil. Some of the demons had the features of reptiles, others were a grotesque combination of a person's worst nightmares—snakes, rats, or huge snarling bugs with snapping mandibles. Some reminded Amanda of gargoyles. Ugly, ugly monsters.

Somewhere off in the dark beyond the pond, earthly nocturnal creatures mourned as if they sensed the coming battle between good and evil. Frightened, as always, that the evil would win. The willow tree's branches sang a song of loneliness as they brushed against the night winds.

Amanda changed back into her human form and confronted them. Mustn't let them see her fear. That would be her downfall. Her hair flew wildly about her stony face; only her flashing eyes showing the fury she was fighting to control. She'd fought demons before, but never this many at once. Never so many, so evil. She remembered some of the visions she'd had of their earlier brutal kills and her body shook violently as if she were in the grip of a seizure.

"Let him go, now," Amanda said from between gritted teeth, raising her hand to point at the demon. "Or I'll destroy you. All of you." Her gaze traveled coldly around the circle.

"Not likely. You are only one witch, after all, and we are many." The high priest smirked at her, his forked tongue flicking nervously across his lips. He nodded his head at the others. They began to close in on her.

"But I have God on my side," she told them calmly. "And you have only Satan."

The demon with the knife slashed upward on the child's thin arm and the long wicked gash splurted blood all over the monster's face. Jonny screamed and fainted. The demon's long tongue darted out again and lapped up the warm blood greedily, a look of pure pleasure on its beastly face.

Amanda forgot all the rules, forgot everything she'd ever learned or believed in in that split second of white-hot rage. How many other innocent victims had they tortured and murdered? How many children slaughtered? How many more?

No more.

She pointed her hand at the leader and a jagged line of crackling fire exploded from her fingertips like a lightning bolt and hit him in the chest. A surprised, then shocked look rippled across his countenance right before he burst into flames, screeching like a banshee.

The rest of the coven turned and attacked her.

From out of the blue Amadeus was at her side then, all teeth and claws. All over them. He was no match for the demons, but he did a good job keeping the human followers busy while she attended to the others.

The fire bolt struck again and again and the yells of the dying filled the night . . . and the horrible stench of burning human and demon flesh.

She heard Amadeus's bloodcurdling screech as he was smacked against a tree and his body fell into the undergrowth. But she was too busy keeping the demons away from Jonny to go to his aid.

She destroyed all of them. Every last one. Murdered them all.

Until there were none left. Just piles of smoldering burnt flesh that once were human. Those called up by Rachel evaporated into smoke and scuttled back to where they had come from. Hell.

When it was all over, she stumbled over to see if Jonny was still alive. He was. Barely. But blood was flowing everywhere. If she didn't help him soon, he'd surely die.

She checked on Amadeus. He was battered and beaten, but already moving around when she found him in the brambles. She picked him up and took him over to where the boy was. She laid down the cat and gathered Jonny's frail body into her arms.

With grieving eyes she took in the carnage around her, what she had done . . . and was horrified at it. She had broken the greatest rule. She had *killed*. Not the demons, they didn't count. But the human members of the coven. Six had been definitely human. And she had killed them.

The guilt swept over her like a beating. She bent over and threw up in the grass. She'd never felt so sick. Slumping to the wet ground next to the stone altar with Jonny in her arms, she wept. Great racking sobs.

She'd done the worst thing a white witch could do. She'd murdered. And she knew that somehow, someway, she would pay for it.

The rain poured from the skies around her, soaking her, the unconscious child, and a shellshocked Amadeus even as they crouched under the canopy of the willow.

The eerie illumination had died with the coven. It was pitch black.

"You did a fine job helping me, Amadeus. Thank you," she breathed.

A triumphant meow came from her right somewhere

and then a furry head came up under the palm of her hand. She was very cold all of a sudden. And so weary, she could almost lay her head down in the wet weeds and sleep. So dizzy. No. Must stay awake, she told herself.

"Can you make it, Amadeus?" she asked him in a weak voice.

No answer except his wobbly rubbing against her. Then he meowed throatily and she knew he'd make it one way or another.

"Then let's go."

She didn't have time for self-pity. Glaring over her shoulder, she could see the ball of light that was Rachel's ghost still floating over the middle of the lake, coming closer.

If the coven would have completed its sacrifice, what would have happened then? She looked back down at Jonny, not wanting to even dwell on it, ignoring the spectre suspended between worlds. She wasn't sure, but in the newborn silence she could have sworn she heard laughter from somewhere in the mists. Then her preoccupied mind trudged on to other more urgent matters.

She must tend to the child. Get him out of the wet, deadly cold. She had nothing to wrap the boy in, so she lifted his pitiful body gently up from the stone and hugged him close to her shivering frame. He was so small, so weightless. Her hands were filled with a warm sticky substance. Jonny was bleeding heavily.

She laid a hand on him and whispered the right words to heal. Nothing. Again. With a gut-wrenching feeling, she knew that she wouldn't be able to witch him well. Couldn't help him in any way. Now.

Because she had used herself up fighting the coven and the demons, or because she had broken the Great

Law and taken life? She wasn't sure. One would be temporary, the other . . .

No matter, she warned herself angrily. She had to get the child somewhere warm and dry immediately. Safe. Somewhere where they could stop the bleeding, suture the wounds. A hospital.

Shaken, she tried to witch them all to the clinic in Canaan. But again nothing happened. Nothing.

Amadeus, she sent out the thought, *can you hear me?*

No answer. Not even a meow, though she could dimly see his fuzzy form curled at her feet.

Her powers were gone. All of them.

For every asking, there was a payment. For every sin, there was punishment, her mind nudged her vindictively.

She was huddled in the rain in the dark night under the rustling willow tree with the boy in her arms. Rachel's ghost behind her, half-formed and drifting nearer to the shore.

She had to get away now. Had to hurry.

She couldn't wait for her powers to return—if they ever would—so she cautiously, painfully stood up with the boy nestled in her arms and began the walk back to town to get Jonny help. Carrying the child, Amadeus limping behind like a wounded soldier, coupled with her exhaustion and the inclement night, she calculated, the journey could take hours.

Another punishment she deserved, she decided numbly, not the boy.

She prayed that he would live through it, and then started walking, Amadeus trailing drunkenly behind her, his tail dragging.

Chapter 6

After a couple of miles plodding through the soot-dark woods, Amanda's legs began to quiver and her muscles to cramp, but she only pushed herself harder, staggering along with the boy in her arms while the shadowy limbs scratched and tore at her face and clothing. Without her magic she was vulnerable to fatigue, cold, and hunger. None of which she was used to. The rain had plastered her clothes to her body and her teeth chattered. She wore just what she'd had on when she'd bolted out the door after Amadeus: jeans, shirt, and tennis shoes. No coat, gloves, or hat. She wished fervently that she would have grabbed her coat on the way out. But there was no changing it now.

The boy, who had in the beginning been as light as a feather, soon felt like an iron anvil clasped in her arms; her arms became numb, like her mind, yet she ignored all the miseries of her body and her heart and dragged herself on. She couldn't let Jonny die. She just couldn't.

Amadeus fell farther and farther behind. She tried stopping every so often to let him catch up, but he was holding her back and Jonny's heartbeat was dwindling. His warmth seeping away into the frigid night. He'd never come to. So she had to keep going. What she wouldn't have done at that moment to have had a dry, thick blanket to wrap the boy in.

And Amadeus would make it back to the cabin some-how; he hadn't been that badly hurt.

It wasn't long after that when Jonny began to thrash in her embrace, moaning and choking. Taken off balance, she toppled to the wet ground and sat there rocking and soothing the child until he quieted.

Then low in his throat she heard the dreaded death rattle . . .

"No, oh, no, Jonny," she cried aloud, drawing his chilled body tighter to her breast, tears welling up in her eyes. "You can't give up now! You can't die now!"

The ominous gurgling grew louder. Jonny was dying. She tried her magic one last time. Nothing.

"Oh, God, please don't let him die!"

Then Amanda remembered the Guardian's familiar who had appeared to warn her back in Boston, and the last words he'd uttered.

"Gibbiewackett! *Gibbiewackett!*" she shouted into the rainy night, her voice almost lost in the wind. She screamed his name over and over, her face raised to the sky, her whole body straining to send the message as far as she could. "I'm calling you . . . not for me . . . but for *Jonny.* Please, if you hear me and you or your master can help him . . . *help him!* I *beg* of you. Don't let an innocent child die. I'm the one who did wrong, not him!" she wailed despairingly, her voice finally turning into sobs. She bent her cracked lips to the boy's face and cried against his clammy skin.

The rattle stopped. Jonny grew still.

And as Amanda peered frantically into the boy's face in the dark, she thought he opened his eyes and smiled at her.

"What are we doing out in the woods in the rain, Miss Givens?" The timbre weak, but steady. His frail arms rose up and wrapped around her neck trustingly. "I'm cold," he said in a tiny voice. "Hungry." He nuzzled up against her neck and became motionless once again.

But this time she could hear his soft sleepy breathing and his body seemed warmer. At ease. He was not going to die, after all.

Amanda thanked God and Gibbiewackett and his master. She had no doubt that someone had saved Jonny. In fact, she was sure of it. And it hadn't been her.

She continued her trek through the woods, her joy at Jonny's miraculous recovery giving her new spirit, if not the energy she needed. She had to fight to keep awake and moving one foot in front of another. Jonny mentioning he was hungry had reminded her that she hadn't eaten since the night before, either. The hunger pains gnawed at her insides like a little beast.

Once or twice she stopped. Afraid she was lost. It was so dark. Had she come this way yet or not? She wasn't sure. And she hadn't seen Amadeus for a long time. She prayed he was home and not lying in the bushes somewhere, sick and hurting.

Leaning against a tree for a few minutes because she could no longer go on without rest, she first smelled the smoke. The rain and the wind had abated, and the pungent odor of burning wood hung on the night air like a misty curtain.

With Jonny in her arms, she followed the scent of the smoke until she saw the flames licking the sky above the trees ahead. A huge bonfire.

Here? In the dead of a freezing night in the middle of the woods?

People. People to help her and Jonny.

She heard the shouts and howls of an angry mob and her hopes were struck down.

Amanda was drawn to the maelstrom of noise and destruction like a starving woman to a feast. But when she got to what was burning, she was so stunned at what she saw that she fell back against a tree, her mouth gaping open and her eyes glazed. Unaware that she'd been spotted.

The townspeople were burning her cabin! The cabin Jake had built for her so many years ago. Her home.

Ashes to ashes, dust to dust . . . just like the cult.

More punishment. A loss of power, a house, for all those lives. What next? She deserved worse and yet her heart broke as she watched the fire hungrily devouring everything she owned; the last part of Jake that she had. All her furniture, clothes. Her coat. They were even torching her workshed with pottery wheel, pots, and medicinal herbs. Herbs she'd spent years collecting.

"No!" she heard herself shouting at them. "No. No. No," the last falling to a whimper as the men with hateful faces came toward her.

She gently laid the boy's body on the ground, and stood up unsteadily, preparing to explain to them what had happened. Explain that Jonny was all right and that she'd saved him from the cult. That he needed to be taken to a hospital right away. But before she could open her mouth, the crowd of perhaps eleven or twelve men surged toward her with blood in their eyes, and clubs in their fists. Shouting awful things at her. Throwing rocks and sticks.

"There she is!" one of them yelled excitedly. "And look . . . LOOK! She has Jonny! She did take him, I told you so. She's . . . murdered him. . . . GET HER!"

"Wait, wait," she tried to interject, putting her hands up to protect her face from the thrown rocks, but her words were drowned in the cresting wave of screaming vengeance as the mob charged.

Frozen for a split second with the feeling that she was in some awful nightmare and this wasn't happening to her, Amanda stumbled backward, tripped on a branch, and sprawled full-length in the weeds.

For a moment she gazed at Jonny's body lying at her feet.

He'll be all right now, her befuddled mind reassured her. *They'll get him to a doctor. They'll take good care of him. You don't have to worry about him any longer.*

Worry about yourself.

Get up and run!

Gasping, Amanda scrambled to her feet and darted back into the forest on stick legs that didn't seem to want to move; leaving Jonny's battered body in the grass behind her.

Her only thought was survival. As she plunged through the hostile night world, attacked by trees and sharp brambles, slipping in holes and tripping over dead branches, she tried her magic one last time. Still nothing.

She didn't have time for regrets or anger. All she could do was run. Escape. A miracle that she could even make her legs move. Amazing what fear could do.

The mob was breathing down her neck.

Amanda was gulping air, her body crying out against the abuse after everything it had been through already that day. Holding her side in pain, she raced on blindly.

She knew the woods far better than they—but then it was as dark as a grave, and they weren't as exhausted as she was. Her body was used up, spent. All she longed to do was collapse into the leaves and sleep. Sleep. Instead, she crouched down behind a bush, held her breath, as the mob streamed around and past her.

She took off in the other direction, unsure of where she was going or why. Knowing just that she had to get as far away from them as she could.

She'd thought she'd given them the slip when she heard the shouts again behind her and to her left. She couldn't seem to lose them. They were determined to catch her.

She kept running, tears creeping down her face, her

heart pounding wildly in her chest like a runaway
freight train. What would they do to her if they caught
her? Beat her up? Burn her? She stifled a cry of terror.
This was the nineteen nineties, not the sixteen nineties.
Witches weren't hanged and burnt these days. People
didn't do that anymore.

Did they?

Amanda fell again and as she lay in the wet grass for
a second, panting and trying to quell the fire raging in
her lungs, she listened. Above the sounds of human pursuit and the forest noises there arose other sounds. Unnatural sounds. Horses whinnying, hooves stamping . . .
strange voices in another dialect fading in and out.

She'd heard those sounds and voices before . . . and
she recalled where and when. The noises she'd heard
right before she'd first seen Rachel.

Rachel. She'd almost forgotten her.

That's when she began to look around. She was back
at Witch's Pond, she was sure of it. She recognized the
towering willow tree she was poised under, the tree she
was braced up against. Where she'd discovered and destroyed the coven; where she'd last seen Rachel.

The stench of burning flesh and malevolence still
hung over the place like a pall. In the darkness she
could see the ghostly outline of the slab of bloodstained
stone that had been the altar.

She tried to get away, but her legs buckled under
her and her vision blurred. She clung to the tree or
she would have passed out.

"Rest just a moment . . ." she groaned, wheezing
like a sick horse. The whole damn town must be able
to hear her. They were not that far behind. She could
hear them. Then the decision of what to do next was
literally swept from her hands.

The sounds of men on horseback had grown louder.
So near now they sounded as if they were almost on

top of her. Trapped. She didn't know whether she should go to the left or the right. Hide or start running again. So she scrunched down beside the willow's trunk, forcing her breathing to quiet, as she scrutinized the section of blackness from where the din was originating.

God, she missed her powers!

A glowing, pulsating shroud of light was coming toward her. Pale and translucent. Larger and larger until she could see that it contained men on horseback, half there, half not . . . in archaic garments of cloth and buckskin with billowing dark cloaks. High boots and long hair. Wide-brimmed beaver hats cocked low on one side. Flint-lock muskets sheathed alongside their saddles. Torches held aloft. If Amanda recalled her history correctly, their costumes were late seventeenth century. The horses reared as the men whipped them about sharply, bellowing and cursing, working their mounts into a foaming lather . . . stampeding them . . . right at her.

They could see her!

My God, who are they? Amanda thought, backing away past the tree, her eyes full of confusion and then filling with fear as she comprehended their meaning. Phantoms.

They can't hurt me. They're only ghosts of what once was. Then she thought of Rachel and the real physical damage she'd done.

Maybe not. Amanda turned and ran blindly.

Go away! she growled at them under her breath as she fought through the thicket of tangled brush and vines.

But they kept on coming. Closer. Glancing back, she could even make out their faces. Shadowy, grim, and bearded. Righteous, like the townspeoples' faces.

They bore down upon her in a cloud of noise and dust and knocked her to the ground, the thundering hooves narrowly missing her as she rolled and dodged under them, clinging to the earth.

She sprinted to her feet after they had passed, and kept on running.

They doubled back and charged her again.

She lost them and hid behind a low hedge of bushes, panting. What the hell did they want from her? What had she ever done to them that they were pursuing her so avidly? These apparitions from the past.

Here they come again, she thought as they discovered her new hiding place and she scuttled out of their path.

The clicking of bridles and the straining creak of leather told her how close they were. Too close.

Something lashed out at the side of her face, drawing blood, giving pain, and she reached up a shaking hand to touch the warm blood. One of them had caught her with a whip.

This was real, she absorbed the truth with a jolt. Real!

Amanda evaded the next lash, and scurried the other way. But the townspeople were in front of her. Searching the woods. She could hear them.

Where to go!

Then a man broke out of the woods directly in front of her and she almost collided with him. A man she recognized from town.

He had a gun.

"Here she is!" he yelled to those behind him. "I've found her!"

He aimed the large shiny pistol at her, it went off, and a sharp burning pain lodged in her right shoulder as the impact rammed her violently against a tree.

She couldn't help herself and cried out with the pain, as she clamped her hand over the wound and blood gushed freely.

She couldn't believe that they'd actually shot her. It was unbelievable. It was . . . impossible. She melted away into some bushes and away from the man. Then ran.

If it hadn't been so excruciatingly painful, at that mo-

ment, she would have burst out laughing. They were
so damn scared of her they'd actually shot her. With
no real proof, no trial. They'd burnt her cabin, tracked
her down like a common criminal, and were shooting
at her. The implications make her head reel. Or maybe
it was the loss of blood, she wasn't sure.

And with a panicked gasp, she realized where she
was. Witch's Pond. Again. The willow loomed like an
unholy sentinel high above her as she knelt in the watery mud along the bank, feeling her strength ebb
swiftly away.

Hurt, bleeding, getting weaker . . . and they were all
closing in. The past and the present.

Now she knew what the damn fox must feel like.

A horse whinnied. Tree limbs cracked. More shouting
and gunshots.

She tried to witch herself out of harm's way one last
time, but it didn't work.

Something warm and furry brushed against her leg,
but she was already losing consciousness, even as her
tingling fingers reached out for it. She fell to the
ground, clutching her shoulder, pain ripping through
her body. She couldn't move another step, her vision
was revolving, the world was spinning. "I need a place
to hide," Amanda whispered, her cheek kissing the
mud. "A place to hide. To rest for just a little while."

The last thing she saw or heard was the nebulous
figure that had come up behind her. A woman in a
somber long dress with huge empty eyes. Hovering at
the edge of the pond.

"Amanda."

Amanda could only stare up at the ghost. She
couldn't move. Or talk. Couldn't escape.

The spectre smiled a mocking smile, soft as a raven's
wing. It put a white hand out to Amanda. "Sister . . .
thou art in great danger.

"They are almost here, Amanda . . . they would kill thee." A grimace of hatred masked the ghost's features.

Amanda shook her head, trying not to look at Rachel. *She's putting a spell on me,* Amanda thought dreamily. *A spell. There's not a thing I can do about it. My powers are gone.*

And for the first time she wondered: Rachel's doing?

"Come." The spirit reached out and captured Amanda's hand and yanked her to her feet. Like touching ice.

Amanda couldn't resist, though she tried. Could only follow mindlessly as the ghost led her toward the water. "I know a place thou can hide where they cannot hurt thee. Will never find thee." Laughter that could have been a sigh of the wind.

The rest of the world disintegrated as Amanda was drawn into the blue mist of the pond. The cold water lapped around her feet, her legs, and then up around her shoulders . . . dragging her down into its murky depths . . . and then . . .

Echoing wet darkness . . . so cold . . . so endless . . . Then nothing.

Amanda came to gradually, layer by layer until things were revealed in startling clarity. Trees, sky, grass. Her clothes were soaked and muddy, her hair loose, tangled, half-dry—and she lay at the edge of the pond like a beached whale. The sun high in the sky. A sparrow was warbling happily on a limb above her.

She must have passed out last night from her experiences and the gunshot wound, and somehow been overlooked by the mob that had been stalking her. All of them. Lucky. So damn lucky. A miracle.

So someone *was* watching over her, huh? She strug-

gled to sit up. Too weak at first to even accomplish
that small feat.

Her head pounded as if she had a tremendous hang-
over.

And then all the rest of it rushed back at her. The
cult and what she'd done to them. Jonny. Her cabin
burning. The phantoms.

The angry townspeople; her crazy run through the
woods. She'd been shot. Amanda touched her chest
where the bullet had entered. There was nothing there
now. No wound. No blood. No pain.

Had she dreamed it?

Rachel. Now that hadn't been a dream, had it?

She'd tried to bewitch her. Amanda was sure of that.
Had dragged her into the pond . . .

She lurched up and, eyes glittering madly with confusion, she studied everything around her. Listened intently.

No. She was alone. Totally. No frothing at the mouth
townspeople. No charging manifestations. No Rachel.

All gone with the night?

She remembered her last minutes of awareness and
a small warm animal body rubbing up against her.

"Amadeus?" she called hoarsely. Her throat full of
cotton. "Are you here, Amadeus? Don't play games with
me right now, puss," her voice broke. "I'm in no mood
for it." She kept looking at her surroundings uneasily
as she talked.

He was nowhere to be seen. In her whole life she
could never recall being separated from him longer
than a few hours. He'd always been there for her.
Maybe he'd gone back home, though that even seemed
out of character for her familiar. Unless he'd been hurt
worse than she'd suspected, he would have come back
looking for her. She knew it. Thinking of home had
brought instant sadness. Her home was gone. Gone.

Or had that been a dream, too?

She crawled to the nearest tree, circled her arms around it, and hauled herself to her feet. As far as she could see, she wasn't hurt in any way. Other than feeling so tired she could hardly keep her eyes open.

She'd go to Mabel's. Find out what really happened last night. Find out if Jonny was all right. She'd take her in, if no one else would.

The tree on the edge of the pond's bank she had her arms around was a willow tree. A *small* willow tree. Amanda gawked at it, amazed, lost her grip, and slid back to the ground. She lay there for a long time, unable to make sense of what she was seeing. No. It wasn't possible. It just wasn't. The willow at Witch's Pond was much, much older. Much, much larger.

But the willow she was looking at was a young one. Barely a sapling with a circumference of maybe eight inches.

Her eyes examined the length of the pond tediously, noting every detail. It looked the same, yet, it didn't. It had rained heavily last night. Why wasn't anything wet?

But it was Witch's Pond, she was sure of it.

And why was it so warm? It was November, but it felt like July.

Amanda forced herself to get to her feet, to get moving. She had to get to Mabel's. She was either dreaming, mistaken, or insane. Then the thought crossed her bewildered mind that maybe none of last night had occurred at all. Wouldn't that be a relief.

But her powers were still gone. She tried an insignificant spell. Nothing happened. So that hadn't changed.

They could be gone forever, after what she'd done.

There was nothing left for her to do but to make it to Mabel's somehow. She started wobbling among the trees, even though she was as weak as a baby. She'd gotten to know the woods well over the last ten years, yet as she moved through the forest, she didn't want to admit that it looked different to her somehow today. Alien. The landmarks she was familiar with were no longer there.

She continued to call Amadeus as she went, but he never answered.

A creeping suspicion had begun to haunt her, but she kept shoving it away. Insane notion. Insane.

She didn't get too far before the heat and her poor physical condition caught up with her. She dropped to the sunburnt grass under a tall oak tree and, exhausted, ravenous, and weak, she curled up at the base. Laying her head on a pile of soft leaves, she fell asleep.

She was awakened sometime later by a sandpaper tongue on the side of her face and a bundle of warm purring fur snuggling up against her.

"Amadeus," she cried out gratefully, gathering him into her arms and smothering him with kisses and hugs. "Thank God you're OK. I thought I'd lost you."

Left you behind, was more like it.

Amadeus blinked at her. But said nothing. Just like a regular cat.

No. It was her. She couldn't understand him anymore.

She knew what that meant. Without her powers she was no longer a witch, but Amadeus was still a witch's familiar. He was talking, probably a mile a minute right now, but she just couldn't *hear* him.

She held him in her arms, happy to have him with her, anyway, and got back on her feet. She winced at the unusual stiffness throughout her body. It was as if it wasn't her body at all, she felt so . . . disoriented and odd. But the rest had helped her. She did feel a little better.

She took a deep breath, made a promise to herself not to become hysterical until she knew more, and started walking again. Amadeus was content just to be carried along in her arms.

First toward what was left of her home, just to prove something to herself. And then to Mabel's.

Amanda knew the woods like her own backyard.

But she never found her cabin, or even what was left of it.

There was nothing but woods.

That was her first big shock.

The second revelation was that—though she was positive she was in the right place—Mabel's trailer was no longer where it used to be, either. Just deep, thick woods.

Amanda paused in the exact spot where Mabel's kitchen used to be and mumbled to herself.

Wherever she was, she wasn't home.

"This isn't Kansas, Toto . . ." she said sarcastically to no one in particular, then chuckled at the old cliche, as Amadeus stretched in her arms.

"Well, I guess we should see if Canaan's still there. Don't you agree, Amadeus?" Her voice held no emotion and a little fear. The cat didn't answer her, just gave her a knowing look. Amanda suspected that Amadeus already knew what she'd find, had all along. For once she missed his constant jabbering.

"But first," she went on, speaking half to Amadeus and half to herself, "we need to find something to eat. I'm starving." Amadeus seconded that motion with a strong meow. She let him down and he scooted off into the dense foliage to catch something small and furry. He seemed to have recuperated well enough from his battle with the coven, but then he had stayed away from the demons and he was a hardy little creature.

She found blackberries everywhere and gathered them in the front of her shirt, gobbling them as she searched for more. The food gave her strength and kept her from dwelling on her predicament. The thought crossed her mind, too, that if it was November how come there were ripe blackberries everywhere? It wasn't long before Amadeus came traipsing back, a large fish in his jaws and a proud swagger in his walk.

"Yes, you're the great hunter," she complimented him, taking the fish from his mouth. "Now all we need to do is find some way to cook it."

Amadeus used his paws to scrape together a few twigs and dry leaves and then touched them with his paw. A tiny flicker of flame leapt up and Amanda quickly added more twigs and small sticks of wood of her own until the fire was going strong.

"So you still have some powers left, huh?" she asked her familiar, plunking down cross-legged before the fire.

He looked back at her innocently. Lifted his paw up from the ground ever so slightly. Amanda got the message.

"A little power, right?"

He bobbed his head *yes* like a person would have.

"How about cleaning the fish? You got a knife of some kind up your sleeve, too?" she inquired.

He shook his head *no*.

"Too bad," she said, and looked at the scaly fish distastefully. Her mouth was already watering. Hot food in her stomach was all she could think about at the moment.

Over the fire she built a homemade stove of piled rocks and laid the uncleaned fish in the middle. It baked slowly, but it baked, and soon she and Amadeus were feasting, washing it down with water from the stream where Amadeus had caught the fish.

It was the best meal Amanda had ever had.

After they were done eating, Amanda rinsed her hands in the stream, stood up, and said, "Well now, my friend, it's time to go into town and see if it's still there."

The six miles into town stretched ahead of her like a thousand. Amanda took it at a leisurely pace and

Amadeus dogged her trail, checking things out and sniffing at everything.

There'd been a different face reflected in the water when she'd been washing her hands. Not a bad-looking face. Pretty, really, and a lot like hers in many ways. But not hers. And now that her clothes and hair had completely dried, she'd also noticed that her jeans and shirt were a lot roomier, that her hair's texture and color were . . . different. The ends of the hair she held in her hand and stared down at were black. Thick, straight black hair. Not wavy brown. For some reason, she hadn't been too surprised by her appearance. Amanda had gulped, breathed in deeply, and turned away.

"Amadeus," she queried later as they were heading toward town under the broiling sun, "I don't look like myself anymore, do I?"

The cat stopped at her feet and glanced up at her with a look she could easily read. He swayed his head negatively.

"I look like Rachel," she murmured. And she didn't need her familiar to tell her she was right. Though she'd only seen Rachel's ghost, she knew approximately what the woman had looked like. Just like the woman she'd just seen in the water. The implications of her new appearance, along with everything else, didn't make her happy.

"Thank God I've got you, Amadeus." *And I'm not alone.*

They were hiking through thick underbrush, lush trees interlaced above their heads, sometime later when Amadeus grabbed at her pant's leg with his claws and tugged her to a standstill. His eyes fixed on something hidden in the next thicket.

Amanda slid back behind a tree, and waited.

She didn't have long to wait. Indians. A whole mess of them were moving gracefully and silently through the bush. Lean as whips, bronze as dark copper, with braided hair adorned with feathers. Faces sharp-angled and predatory like hawks. Bows slung across naked shoulders, arrows clicking in leather quiver pouches, they marched within twenty yards of her and never blinked an eye.

Amanda held her breath until they were long gone, and then released it in a relieved, but muffled sigh. She looked at Amadeus, her eyebrows raised high on her forehead, a hand massaging the area above her right eye as if she had a nagging headache.

"Oh, boy," she whispered. "Somebody else's forest, somebody else's body . . . and wild Indians, too. Just what I needed. What else, Amadeus?" she asked, tiredly.

The cat had no answer.

"Let's get out of here before they smell us on the air and come after us." Amanda swung around—and froze.

Not more than eight feet away from her, standing perfectly motionless in the shadows of the tree was an Indian brave. Not much taller than her with a long, morose face that could have been of dark stone, and black shining eyes that seemed to delve into her soul. He was garbed in a buckskin breechcloth and unadorned moccasins, necklaces of shells and animal teeth hung around his neck, and there were a few feathers stuck in his loosened long black hair. It was difficult to tell his age. Not old. Not truly young. Maybe thirty. She had no idea what tribe he was of.

Amanda had seen hundreds of Indians. All in books. But no picture had ever prepared her for the real thing. He was so . . . fierce-looking. Savage, yet beautiful. The Indian studied her for an eternity, not moving. Amanda didn't know what to do. Should she run, or stand still? She remembered reading somewhere that Indians respected bravery. So she lifted her chin and tried not to look too scared. He wasn't actually threatening her in any way. Just staring at her. Must be her clothes.

Amadeus was at her feet, snarling at the brave, back arched and eyes flashing. The Indian's gaze shifted from her to the cat and then back again. He didn't seem afraid, which was more than she could say for herself.

Amanda bent down and scooped the cat up into her arms, shushing him. She didn't want the rest of the tribe back here. One Indian was enough.

"What do you want?" she asked the Indian.

He just looked at her.

"I mean you no harm. Just go about your business and leave me to mine." She made sure her tone was friendly, but firm. Even if he didn't understand her, it was all she could think of to do.

The Indian's lips curled slightly at the corners in a flat smile which might have been either cruel or merely playful, and he said something in a guttural language, gesticulating with his expressive hands.

"I don't understand you," she said sadly, shaking her head.

The brave moved swifter than she could react, taking one of his necklaces from about his neck and slipping it around hers.

Then he was gone. Vanished back into the woods as if he'd never been there at all.

Astonished at the whole experience, she gazed down at the necklace. Panther teeth. She smiled.

What had that been all about?

Amanda didn't really care. The Indian was gone and she was unharmed. She hurried through the forest, Amadeus trundling along behind her, and as far away from the Indians as she could get. Toward town.

She hadn't gone too far when she spotted the turkeys. A large flock of them scattered as she approached, gobbling in alarm, and waddled away into the next clearing.

Wild turkeys? She'd never seen so many wild turkeys

together at one time. Hunters had depleted them long ago in this area.

Again her inner voice pinched her—wild Indians and turkeys? Her worst fear was seeming more and more possible. She was no longer in her body, no longer in her time.

Amanda kept walking. Her clothes were too warm for a sultry afternoon, and were soaked with sweat. Her hair was all tangled and loose, damp underneath. Pausing for a short rest under a spreading maple tree, she rummaged in her jeans' pockets until her fingers discovered one of a few rubberbands that she always carried. By touch alone, she quickly wove her long unruly hair into a tight braid, rolled up the sleeves of her flannel shirt, and then continued her expedition. There, that was better.

As the sun glared down at her from a lower position in the clear blue sky, she finally arrived at the outskirts of Canaan proper.

And stared at it, her mouth agape.

"This doesn't look like my Canaan, either . . ." she breathed, putting her hand up to her throat, her eyes growing hard as flint as the final piece of the puzzle dropped into place like a tomb being sealed.

She *was* in another time. At least a couple of centuries past. She recalled what Mabel had said about Rachel and when she was supposed to have lived. Around seventeen hundred. The town, or village she was inspecting before her could easily be from that time period.

It had one main dirt street, cabins of rustic wood or small houses of clapboard squatted close to each other along it on long narrow plots of fenced-in land. The fences she recognized from history books as being split-rail zigzags . . . or what the pioneers of the time referred to as snake or worm fences that kept the cattle each family owned from straying at night and out of the gardens. During the day the livestock were taken to graze in a common village green which, if she guessed correctly, would be somewhere ahead of her at the end of the main road.

There were gardens before almost every house. Small orchards behind. The gardens were full to bursting. Harvest time must be near. Amanda spotted apple and persimmon trees.

Her eyes traveled farther. She counted at least three inns or taverns or did they call them grogshops? She did remember from her history books that drinking and drunkenness had been very common in these times. Too common. Drinking and public punishments had been the main social events.

She scrutinized the sleepy village before her thoughtfully.

The end of the seventeenth century. They actively persecuted witches, she frowned, so she should feel right at home. And that realization made her even more uneasy. She couldn't recall whether Calvinists or Puritans had settled early Canaan. No matter, one was as bad as the other.

She wondered what kind of money they used, English? Shillings and stuff like that. Gold? She didn't know. But she did suspect that barter was a more widespread way of buying things in this time. Real money would be hard to come by.

What did the people of these times eat? No supermarkets here. They'd have their own livestock. Pigs. Cattle. Crops? Corn, she remembered, was real big. Beans. Most households would have their own gardens.

And the Indians would still be savage and untamed . . . she'd read of terrible massacres as late as eighteen hundred in this part of the country. A chill stirred up her spine at the memory of the Indian with the brooding eyes who'd given her the necklace back in the woods. Why hadn't he killed her? What had it meant?

Just another mystery. She sighed softly.

Unless he and some of his friends were trailing her right now.

The notion unsettled her and made her walk faster.

What's the matter with you? Then she reminded herself, *I'm in town. Safe.*

And if he'd wanted to hurt you, Amanda, he would have back there. He'd had weapons on him. Calm down.

Yep, she murmured to herself, as she watched a couple of women in long homemade gowns and bonnets leave one wooden building, heads bent together, chatting, baskets hanging from their arms, and briskly stroll on down the street, leaving little puffs of dust in their wake, *this is definitely not modern times.*

No electric lights at the corners to illuminate the highways—no highways. No cars. No telephone lines strung up everywhere, because there were no telephones. No televisions, no microwaves, no VCR's, no vacuum cleaners, or computers . . . it was mind-boggling.

A fever or an infection could kill you. Women died every day in childbirth. There would still be epidemics of influenza, smallpox, and typhoid. Thank goodness she'd had all her shots. She didn't even laugh at that thought.

A town truly out of the distant past . . . might as well be Mars, she mused glumly, as strange as it all seemed to her.

Her eyes stared down at her clothes. Of all times to not have one of her long dresses on . . . she'd stick out in these clothes like a raving heretic in a church congregation.

Which meant she couldn't chance being seen until she'd done something about her clothes. But what? How? She didn't have any way to buy different clothes, and even if she'd had money right for the times, she couldn't just waltz into a general store and purchase something. Too risky. A stranger. Looking the way she looked. Talking the way she talked. They'd think *she* was from another planet.

She'd tarried too long in the middle of the street apparently, daydreaming, and the wagon was almost upon her before she realized it. Amadeus, smaller and quicker, made it into the bushes alongside the road, but Amanda was left to face the suspicious-eyed people crowded in the wagon as it slowed down to roll past her.

A family, it looked like. Mother in demure homespun gray dress and snow-white cloth bonnet. Father, reins in work-chapped hands, in a loose-fitting shirt, dark trousers, and floppy hat. Three children of different ages, two boys and one girl. The boys dressed exactly like their father. The girl, like her mother, even down to the bonnet. Poor people. You could tell at a glance by their worn and simple clothes. But well-fed and clean. A cow was tethered behind the wagon, following along docilely.

Whispers. "That Coxe woman . . . says she be a witch . . ."

"What is she doing out here . . ."

The wagon drew closer and the voices, Amanda had no doubt, were meant to be overheard by her.

"Why I never . . . look at the way she be dressed, Matthew. Shameful. Trousers on a woman." More whispers. "Not fit to associate with good people . . . madwoman . . . witch, that is what she is. The vicar is right. We should turn her in to the local magistrate . . .

"She has gone too far this time."

Their stern faces peering down at her mirrored their disapproval. And their fear. Some things never changed.

The wagon jostled past her and left her in a cloud of dust. But the insinuations floated back to taunt her.

That Coxe woman.

They thought she was Rachel because she *looked* like
Rachel. And the last piece of the mystery was accounted
for. It was true and her worst fears were now a reality.
Somehow she'd been transported back to seventeen
hundred and had taken Rachel Coxe's place. Rachel
Coxe, the local and much maligned witch.

Taken her place for what? To die the way she had
died? *No.* Amanda felt the sobs rising up in her throat
and couldn't stop them from escaping.

The pounding of hooves, a horse snorting, yanked
her back to reality and she ran back into the shadows
under the trees.

Here she was, running away and hiding like a thief.
She was a stranger in a strange, hostile land with no
home, family, friends, or powers. Lost in time. And
worst of all, no one had the slightest idea where she
was. So rescue, outside of a miracle, was not an option.

She was trapped here. And unless she regained her
powers, maybe forever.

Sliding down against the side of a tree, her eyes
blurred with her crying, a lump in her throat, the tears
came, even though she fought them.

But when a horse whickered, very near, she opened
her red-rimmed eyes.

"Mistress, be there something wrong? Can I be of
help?" a man's deep voice inquired.

Startled, and painfully aware of how odd she must
look in her modern-day clothes, her face grimy, and
her hair a mess, Amanda lifted her teary eyes to the
man's face.

"I was behind that wagon and couldn't help but over-
hear how they mistreated thee . . ." He was sitting
astride an enormous ebony-colored horse, but dismounted immediately and strode toward her.

His horse followed and Amanda, ill at ease at being
caught at such a vulnerable time, downcast her eyes

and reached out to touch the lovely animal. She'd never had much dealings with horses but, like all animals, she loved them and they loved her. The horse nudged her and whinnied, wanting more attention, as she petted him.

"He likes thee," the man declared, astounded. "Gabriel rarely lets anyone near him but me."

Amanda took her hand away from the horse's warm muzzle. She stole a quick glance at the man.

He was tall, as large as a bear, with long wavy chestnut-brown hair to his shoulders. Dressed in some kind of leather vest and white gathered shirt; leather pants, high boots, and a three-cornered hat with some sort of plume cocked rakishly to one side. A thick mustache hung low over a sensuous smile—and he was smiling at her as she caressed the horse's arched neck, a smile full of intelligence and amusement, and something else. Unease and bewilderment? Why?

In one hand he toted a musket and he moved like a big cat, easy and sure-footed, exuding an immediate and impressive sense of grace and power. A military man, perhaps.

"Mistress . . . did they hurt thee?" His fingers were gentle as he wiped the tears from her face and tilted her chin upward so their gaze met. His eyes, a shining deep brown, bore down into hers and touched off a tiny spark of unexplainable recognition. Unexpected pleasure. Uncanny how much he reminded her of someone she knew. But she couldn't put a finger on who.

"No."

"I would not have bothered thee, but I heard thee crying . . ." He seemed embarrassed, at a loss of what else to say, as if a woman crying was such a rare sight. Or as if her crying had been a rare sight. She studied his face from behind lowered lashes, knowing she should be cautious. She didn't know him from Adam.

But something about the way he was looking at her evaporated all her fears. There was gentleness in his brown eyes, even if his jaw was pulled taut.

She imagined this was a man whose ways were usually sterner, a man of strength and few weaknesses. A man of the times. She could tell sympathy was new to him. He seemed to be struggling with the feelings she was creating that were obviously making him uncomfortable.

So his kindness, at this time of all times, after all she had been through the last few days, was too much for her to handle. The straw that broke the camel's back. The tears fell harder even as she swiped angrily at them and ordered herself to stop acting like a stupid helpless woman and pull herself together. She couldn't. Finally she gave up, hid her head in her hands, and let the tears seep from the corners of her eyes.

"I'm all right," her voice muffled by her hands. She was about to say something else, but realized who she was talking to. "Just . . . weary." There was no way she could tell him why she was really crying. That she was from another time that hadn't wanted her, either, and that she was hungry, exhausted, and frightened. Alone. Didn't know where she'd find shelter, or what she would do next.

When the silence went on too long, she peeked through her fingers. He was staring at her clothes.

"Mistress Coxe, dost thou know thee are dressed most peculiarly?" he asked softly, his face a study in control.

"You *know* me?" she blurted out before she could stop herself.

"Aye," he replied, his expression becoming puzzled. "Thou art Rachel Coxe."

So she truly had taken Rachel's place. She wondered where Rachel was. In her time, taking her place? And was she without her powers, as well? If she wasn't . . . it was a horrendous thought. Amanda felt sick.

"The whole town knows thee." His voice had turned cynical. "Thou hast been the topic of gossip for years."

Amanda's brow furrowed. So he didn't actually know her, just by sight and word of mouth. *The evil witch that lived among them.*

"So why did you stop?" she asked, unrolling her right sleeve and wiping her wet face on the back of it.

"I thought thee needed aid . . ." lamely. Clearly he didn't know why he had stopped. Probably regretting it now.

She sighed, and biting her lip, she turned her head away.

"I can take thee home," the stranger offered kindly. "It is on my way."

Rachel had a home. Of course she would have. And if Rachel was not here then Amanda could use it. A sanctuary where she could stay until she figured this whole mess out and found a way back to her own time. It would be better than sleeping out in the woods, wouldn't it? As much as she disliked the thought of living where Rachel had lived, sleeping in her bed, Rachel's house was better than no house. But she didn't know where Rachel lived. How could she? But the townspeople would, and her helpful stranger seemed to.

"That would be kind of you."

He remounted his horse and came up beside her. From one of his saddlebags he brought a bundle of material and handed it down to her. "To cover thyself," he said with a twinkle in his eyes. " 'Twill halt the further wagging of tongues." Now he was dead serious.

For a moment Amanda was almost tempted to laugh. She must look very strange to these people. And sound strange, also. It suddenly occurred to her that her speech was very different from theirs. Not just her accent, which was far more Americanized, but her choice of words, as well. The man must think she was touched in the mind, as they would have said back then. Back . . . now.

Amanda slipped the black cloak around her shoulders and fastened it. She smiled for the first time at him then, and he smiled softly back.

"I go by Joshua Graham," he told her as his strong hand clasped hers and pulled her into the saddle before him. His arms encircled her as they tugged at the reins and his boots lightly tapped the horse's flanks, and got them moving. Sitting so close to him, feeling the warmth from his muscular body, sent shivers down her spine. It'd been a long time since she'd had a man's arms about her. It felt good. Too good.

"I will get thee home soon. Surely, thy children must be missing thee."

Children? That's right. Rachel did have children. Girls, wasn't it Mabel had said?

Who were supposedly murdered by her. Sometime in the future.

She couldn't believe what was happening. It seemed impossible that she was in another time. In another's place. In the shoes of a possible murderess, so to speak. It was a nightmare.

Then she remembered Amadeus.

"My cat," she said aloud. "I can't leave my cat."

"Cat?"

"Yes, he ran off into the woods when the wagon drove by.

"Amadeus," she called out. "Amadeus, where are you?"

And the cat was in her arms, purring. She hugged him close to her, glad to see him, but more than a little perturbed that he had arrived the way he had.

The man's shocked eyes found hers for an uncomfortable moment, but he didn't say anything, just looked at Amadeus, who was staring back at him from

behind the edge of the cloak. He was snuggling
mistress's lap, his one ear perked straight up.

Amanda clenched her teeth, remained silent, and
squeezed Amadeus a little too hard. He reciprocated by
nipping her.

The man guided his horse between two trees, shaking
his head. Then he laughed low in his chest and again
Amanda was hit with a big dose of *déjà vu*. Where had
she heard that laugh before? She had this unnerving
sense of having known him before. The knowledge
washed over her like a gently building wave and lulled
her. Insane.

They made their way silently through the woods for
a while in the dappled sunlight until Amanda's curiosity
got the better of her.

"Are the Indians around here dangerous?" Careful to
speak as little as possible. The less she talked the better.

Joshua seemed taken aback at her question. " 'Tis rumored the Pequot have a camp somewhere deep in
these woods. The townspeople leave them alone. They
are not friendly." He was looking down at her as he
talked. And she was very aware of him behind her.
Strong and solid. Familiar somehow. Unbelievable as it
sounded, she knew she was safe with him.

Amanda reached up with the hand that wasn't holding Amadeus and touched the panther teeth hanging
around her neck.

She had the feeling that Joshua had noticed the
necklace, but again he asked nothing.

Amanda could feel his intense eyes on her. Feel the
stiffness take over his body. And she asked no more
questions. Something had upset him and she wasn't
sure what it had been. Maybe it was her clothes, her
speech, the way she was acting. Maybe she'd been odd
enough to arouse his suspicions.

They eventually came to a crudely built clapboard

cottage on the outskirts of the town. Amanda spied a small anxious face peeking from a window at them. One of Rachel's little ones.

"Thou art home, Mistress." Joshua wrapped his arm tighter around her waist, lifted her from the saddle, and lowered her to the ground right at the tiny cottage's doorstep. The horse moved back as if the man was anxious to be on his way.

"Thank you, sir," Amanda murmured, evading his sharp eyes. She was so tired she was weaving. Aftereffects of her journey through time, or just emotional, she wasn't sure. She hoped it wasn't some extra spell Rachel had put on her. Like drugging someone who's going to the guillotine. She had to brace herself against the side of the house or she would have fallen asleep right there.

The man was studying her closely, as if he was deciding something about her.

He leaned over the saddle and whispered into her ear, "I am a planter, a small landowner of some means, who lives up at Settler's Pass. If thou ever hast need of me, just send a message. Joshua Graham. I will come."

Then he galloped away without a look back, merging into the forest, leaving her standing there at a stranger's door.

She let Amadeus down and he started exploring the outside of the cottage.

It was then she thought of the cloak; she'd forgotten to give it back and he'd forgotten to ask for it. She unfastened the clasp, slid it off her shoulders, and draped it across the inner crook of her arm.

The door opened.

A girl about ten or eleven years old appeared in the doorway, squinting at the harsh sunlight, shading her eyes with her hand. Amanda's first impression was one of an emaciated scarecrow standing there in rags. Her small face pitifully white and in strange contrast with

her large dark eyes and coal-black hair that hu..
stringy clumps nearly to her waist. She had on a shape
less dress belted with a coarse piece of rope. She reminded Amanda of a homeless, starving waif. The kind
you'd see in those Save-the-Children ads where the foreign children were all hungry eyes and bones sticking
through their skin. She was barefoot.

"Ma, where hast thou been so long? Lizzy and I were
worried," a cowed voice whined in an oddly restrained
manner. Too polite. And the girl hadn't exactly rushed
out to greet or hug her. Was this the way a child acted
toward her mother? So distant.

Amanda met the girl's eyes only briefly. Afraid she'd
see right away that she was an impostor. "In the woods.
I had an . . . accident, I think." Remembering not to
talk too much.

"Ah," the girl said. As if she were used to such vague
explanations.

"The gentleman is not staying, then?" The girl's eyes
cut sharply to where the dust kicked up by the man's
horse was just settling. Then she looked back at Amanda.
Her eyes perplexed.

"No," Amanda answered, not understanding what the
girl was getting at.

The girl seemed at a loss. But she didn't question
further.

She was gawking at Amanda's clothes.

"Ma, why are thee wearing such strange clothes?"

"They are?"

The girl's face had a grimace on it. "They are. Men's
clothes."

Now it was Amanda's turn to be at a loss. She was never
good at lying, especially on the spur of the moment. She
decided that pretending she didn't know might be the
best course of action. Convenient amnesia. "I'm not
sure . . ." She raised her hand to the side of her face

and tried to look confused. Which wasn't all that difficult in the mood she was in. "I was so hot . . . I think I fainted out in the woods. When I came to"—she waved her hands lazily in the warm air—"I was dressed like this."

Then she made a great show of staring down at her clothes in surprise. "I don't know where these clothes came from." The corners of her mouth twitched up slightly at the corners. "Then that nice man came along and brought me home."

She could tell that the girl didn't believe any of it, but she merely inclined her head as if she did.

"Well, come inside, Ma. The sun is hot." There was no real empathy, though, in her sad eyes at the words or in her voice, as if she either didn't care or as if she was used to her mother coming home in such a questionable state.

"I have saved supper for thee."

"Thank you." She didn't even know the girl's name. She was supposed to be Rachel and this was supposed to be her child. How, she fretted, was she going to fool her?

Alert to the strained emotions drifting around them, Amanda asked, "Is everything all right here, then?"

"Aye." The girl gave her a sly sideward glance. There was something she was deliberately leaving out, but Amanda knew when she was getting the brush-off and let it drop.

Amadeus sauntered past them and into the cabin.

"Ma, thee brought home a cat? Where is Beelzebub?"

"Beelzebub?"

The girl's voice drifted to a whisper and her eyes darted around to be sure no one was around to hear. "The goat. Thy familiar?"

"Oh." So Rachel's daughter knew all about her being a witch. Which wasn't so unusual. Living in such close quarters she would have had to know what her mother was. Or had been.

Amanda hesitated, searching for some plausibl̲e̲
Because, of course, she had no idea where Rachel's fa̲
miliar had gotten to. He was most likely with Rachel.
Wherever she was.

"I don't know really. He left."

The girl just gawked at her, then shrugged as if she
didn't care either way. "I did not like him, anyway. He
had a nasty temper. Is the cat your new familiar, then?"
The child had turned and was heading into the darkness of the cottage. Amanda followed her in, stooping
because the door was so short and narrow.

"Ah . . . yes," she answered. Well, that would make
it easy.

They were inside. That it was hot as blazes was the
first thing Amanda noticed. Hot and stuffy. There were
only two miserly windows covered with what looked to
Amanda like some sort of waxed cloth, instead of glass,
and they let in only a little light. Heavy shutters surrounded both windows ready to be bolted shut—protection against Indian attacks. One large room with a
simple fireplace made of logs plastered together with
clay in one corner and shelves around it filled with
cooking kettles and dishes. A wobbly looking table, and
three chunks of shapeless wood served as simple chairs.
For beds there were mattresses stuffed with something,
probably rags or corn husks, in two corners. She
counted two smaller ones and a much larger one.

Either Rachel liked room when she slept . . . or (and
Amanda finally recognized the girl's earlier confusion
over Joshua leaving so soon) Rachel had shared her
bed at times. The floors were packed dirt. A tattered
rag rug lay in front of the fireplace.

The walls were raw wooden timber, the cracks filled
with some sort of mud or something. The house itself
had a thatched roof. Very primitive. A chamber pot was
snuggled next to the beds. No indoor plumbing here.

But when Amanda's eyes had become accustomed to the dimness she also saw that the cabin was filthy. Uncared for in many ways.

If Rachel had been such a powerful witch why had she had to live like this? So poorly? Another mystery.

Amanda couldn't help the compassion from welling up inside of her and spilling out toward the children. If she'd had children, she would never have treated them like this. Never.

Amanda nonchalantly wandered around the cabin as the girl picked Amadeus up, and cuddling him, took him to a corner of the room where she sat down next to one of the stuffed pallets. He let her, and soon Amanda could hear him purring from across the room. Heard the girl talking to someone in soft tones.

There was something delicious cooking over the fire in a hanging kettle and Amanda walked over to the hearth and stoked the dying fire back up into a strong flame. It brightened the dark interior of the cottage and that was when she saw the other child. She was holding Amadeus and cooing over him happily as she sat talking to the other girl in the corner.

Amanda walked over. A very young child with an angelic face and empty bright blue eyes stared up at her. Not much more than a baby, really. Three or so, and as blond as the other child was dark, with a perfect heart-shaped face and curly golden ringlets. Lizzy, the dark one had called her before. Short for Elizabeth, perhaps?

Rachel's other child.

The smaller one was hugging the cat and laughing and Amadeus was licking her face contentedly, when he wasn't wanting the other girl to scratch him under his chin. He seemed to have adopted the two already. And they him. The younger one was squealing with delight, and even the older one was smiling. Amanda in a flash of insight knew that for these two children life had been hard. Loveless. It was written all over their faces.

Looking down at them, Amanda felt a surge o~~f~~
These were the two children whose destiny—was to b~~e~~
butchered. Oh, no . . . not these children. Not these two
innocents. Not if she could help it. She'd watch over them.
She couldn't deny that she felt, almost against her will, a
bond with these two. A bond for another witch's children
whose fate, she prayed, wasn't already written in stone.

"I see you've made friends?" Amanda smiled down at
the girls.

The older one glanced up. "Aye, he is a bonny cat." Her
eyes glittered in the murkiness. A piercing sharpness to
them. A knowing. The girl was smart. Very intuitive.

The littlest one continued to stare emptily up at
Amanda, no acknowledgement whatsoever. No expression,
nothing. A chubby fist came up and rubbed her eyes. She
yawned, showing perfect little teeth. A soft wistful smile
came and then faded.

Amanda passed her hand in front of the child's face. No
reaction.

With dawning sadness, Amanda realized that the child
was blind. She couldn't see her. She couldn't see anything.

"Lizzy." Amanda sighed. The name sounded sweet on
her lips. Amanda knelt down, and unexplainedly drawn to
the child, she took her into her arms and cuddled her.
Rocked her gently as if her caring could change the fact
that she was blind. At first the girl seemed to resist her but
as Amanda continued to hold her, the feeble struggles
ceased and the child responded cautiously by hugging her
back.

The older girl was watching intently, her dark eyes narrowed, as if she was trying to pierce Amanda's disguise.

"Mama?" The small voice, astonished, was full of desperate want and . . . fear? It struck Amanda as unbelievable. But the child was actually afraid of her.

Her own mother. Hadn't Rachel loved her children,
then? Hadn't she shown them any affection at all? Amanda
had no way of knowing.

She hadn't known Rachel.

"Yes. It's me."

The child held on to her tighter and planted a soft, sloppy kiss on her cheek. Hot as fire, like her whole body. Fever. The child was sick. Amanda thought, *I'll have to gather some special herbs from the woods and make her some medicine.*

As she drew away, an urgent longing—a painful tug— lodged in her heart and began to take root. She wanted to protect and love this child in her arms. Forever. The child shone like a diamond, her soul as bright as the sun.

A special child, this one, Amanda thought to herself. *Good. Not a child who should belong to a black witch.*

"Are thee truly well, Ma?" the older girl pressed. Doubt and suspicion again evident. Distrust.

"Thy speech . . . be strange." In her eyes, Amanda could read much more that was unusual to the girl than just that. But the mistrust was stronger. "Thy actions, too," a meek observation.

Amanda knew exactly what the girl was alluding to. Yet she had to pretend she didn't.

"Yes, I'm well," Amanda replied, laying the child in her arms back down on the pallet; even then, the tiny fingers sought and found hers, refusing to relinquish her totally.

"I am just weary." She wished she knew the older girl's name. She must find some way to trick it out of one of them eventually.

The girl continued to stare at her with uncertain eyes, but backed off. Again a decision seemed to have been made and the girl, sitting there still stroking the dozing cat, mused aloud, "What shall we call him? Hath he a name? Look, he hath but one ear . . . it makes him look so funny." Amadeus covered his mutilated ear with one of his paws. "We are going to keep him, are we not?"

Amanda was relieved for the change of subject. She was too spent and still in shock over the day's discoveries to have put up any more of a fight. She was tempted to just tell them both the truth and get it over with. Throw herself on their mercy.

But they might think she was insane and shun her completely. Or turn her over to the authorities. She wasn't sure of the older one yet.

Maybe, she brooded, she was Rachel after all and her mind had just snapped? The thought frightened her. She—Rachel—was insane. This was how being insane felt.

No. Impossible. Her other life wasn't some sick dream.

Not Jake, her home, family and friends. Canaan. The past she remembered so vividly. They *weren't* all just figments of her imagination. They all existed somewhere ahead in time. And so did Amanda Givens . . . and somehow she would find a way back. She frowned and then recalling where she was, she reached out to pet Amadeus, turning a cheerier face to the watching girl.

"Yes, Amadeus is staying."

The girl threw her a quizzical look. "Ama—?"

"Amadeus," Amanda repeated slowly for her benefit.

"A most uncommon name for a cat, Ma."

Amanda looked at the cat. "He loves classical music. And Amadeus is the middle name of a very famous composer. Wolfgang Amadeus Mozart." Then she paused.

The dark-eyed girl stared at her as if she had gone mad and again Amanda was struck with the shakiness of her position. The girl probably didn't even know what classical music was. Rachel, either.

And had Mozart even been born yet in seventeen hundred? Amanda didn't believe he had. But the girl wouldn't know that and Amanda was suddenly too tired to play any more games and tiptoe about. So let the girl think she was mad. Did it really matter?

"Amadeus," the girl echoed haltingly, "it shall be, Ma. Though, I think One-Ear would be better." A tiny smile.

Amanda returned the smile. "His name is Amadeus."

"As you say, Ma." Accepted with a curt nod of her head, the smile gone, as she went on petting the purring cat.

"There be stew in the kettle," the girl offered. "And freshly baked bread. Would thou want me to serve it to thee now?"

Amanda couldn't help herself again and smiled warmly at the eager-to-please face. "Yes, that sounds delicious. But I can serve myself. Have you and Lizzy eaten yet?"

Again the girl flashed her a questionable glance. Taken aback.

Now what have I done wrong? Amanda thought perturbed.

"Nay. Thou knows we always wait for thee to eat before Lizzy and I. Remember?" As if she were talking to someone with a simple mind. "But I did give Lizzy a wee bit of it earlier because of the fever. I am sorry." Nervous. Her eyes downcast. As if the child's condition were a crime. The girl had stood up and was wringing her hands, guiltily. As if feeding a sick child was a crime, too.

"Then she must have more right away. And afterward, I'll go out into the woods and locate the right medicinal herbs to brew her some special tea to bring down that fever."

Amanda turned away too soon to see the look that crossed the girl's face at that remark.

And sooner or later, she thought, she'd search for Rachel's stash. If Rachel had been half the witch she was reported to have been, then there was bound to be a stockpile of healing herbs somewhere close and Amanda would find it.

Lizzy piped up, "Maggie, can I eat now? I am so

hungry." Lizzy's voice was racked with fever. She started to cough miserably and the older girl bent down to comfort and hush her.

Maggie. The older girl's name was Maggie.

"Aye, Lizzy, we shall eat now. I will bring thee some right away. Hold the cat so he will not be lonely and I will fetch supper." Real love and devotion softened Maggie's voice.

"Tea, too, Maggie?" Lizzy begged. Still hacking and sniffling.

"Aye, maybe tea, too." Maggie hesitated, sliding another wary look toward Amanda, who nodded.

"Plenty of it," Amanda agreed.

Lizzy giggled happily between coughs and snuggled the sleeping cat so tightly that Amanda was sure he would wake up and tug himself free. But he didn't, he kept sleeping in the girl's tiny arms like a baby.

He reminded her how tired she was herself.

Amanda barely made it through supper. She trudged over to Rachel's stuffed mattress, settled down on it, and leaned back with a sigh. She'd rest just a moment, she told herself. Just a moment.

Maggie was scrutinizing her, but Amanda didn't care anymore. She felt curiously at home here with them. Safe. It was the nightmare outside the door that scared the hell out of her.

"Shall I help you dish it out, Maggie?" Amanda asked sleepily.

Maggie was already at the fireplace, hovering over the kettle, dishing out stew onto what looked like handmade wooden trenchers. Her back instantly went stiff, but she continued her task. "Nay, Ma. Thou need not help me."

Though half asleep, Amanda still heard the girl's angry grumbling under her breath. "And why is tonight any different than any other night?"

Maggie brought Amanda a steaming plate of stew with a huge hunk of crusty bread and a mug of hot tea.

"Thank you."

The girl nodded and then went to feed her younger sister. Both ate from the same plate.

She had placed a small plate of the stew on the floor for Amadeus, and he was awake and happily slurping it up, purring loudly.

Amanda gobbled down the food in a few moments. Not realizing how hungry she had still been.

"The stew was delicious. What was in it?" Amanda asked the girl, her eyes heavy as she set the empty plate on the floor next to her. So tired she could hardly think straight any longer. The world was turning all fuzzy.

"Vegetables from our garden. Rabbit. One I caught this morning out in the woods, Ma. I watched the traps carefully just as thee bade me to."

"Any more?"

"None, Ma. I am sorry." There was that damn fear in her voice again. She held out their unfinished plate. "Here, have the rest of ours. We are not that hungry."

Lizzy whimpered, but didn't say a word.

Amanda met the girl's eyes and it all fell into place. The girls *were* terrified of their mother. Rachel. Terrified.

And Amanda wondered again what had been done to them to make them so.

"No. I've made a mistake . . . I'm not that hungry, after all. That stew really filled me up. Go ahead and eat yours." There was a firmness in her tone that wouldn't let them contradict her.

Maggie's face was indecipherable, but Lizzy clutched at the plate as if she were starving, as her older sister hurriedly spooned the rest of the stew into her mouth.

Amanda had stretched out on the bed and couldn't stop yawning. The food and tea were warm in her stomach and consciousness was slipping away. Amanda's eyes drifted shut for the last time.

She slept.

When she awoke again, she sat up slowly, her thoughts muddled and her heart racing as her eyes roamed about her. A crude cottage, a low flickering candle, and two small human lumps sleeping on the mattresses across the room from her.

Damn, it hadn't all been a dream.

Another woman's bed; another woman's children.

Another woman's life.

For a brief moment she let the horror of her situation and all that it meant overwhelm her. Then, with a strangled sigh, she lay back down and stared into the darkness at nothing. Her battered body aching. Thinking furiously. Trying to figure out what she should do.

Maybe, if she really was irrevocably trapped here in this dangerous time, she should run as far from here as she could. Escape. This was where Rachel's murderers lived.

Or she could find a way to change history, and escape Rachel's grisly death . . . if Rachel's fate was really to be murdered at all. She couldn't even be sure of that, really. Which one was it to be? Her eyes rested on the sleeping children's forms.

If she ran away, she'd have to abandon them.

Through the cloth-covered windows she watched a large shadowy moon ride the velvet skies and she mulled over her dilemma.

She missed Jane and Ernie. Missed Jessie and her family, and yes, even Rebecca. Had Jonny made it? Was he still alive? And she worried about how Mabel would get along without her. Two hundred and ninety-six years from now.

Amanda rose from her bed and stepped outside into the moonlight. She traveled a little ways into the woods and relieved herself. Then she recalled the herbs she was going to look for to help bring down Lizzy's fever. And even in the dark, they weren't that hard to find. She had excellent night vision and knew the herbs well. She stuffed them gratefully into her pockets. She'd brew the tea first thing in the morning. It was more important if the child were allowed to sleep the night through. Tomorrow or the next day she'd find that cache of medicinal herbs she knew Rachel must have hidden somewhere. Maybe Maggie might know where.

She came across a small pond glimmering in the moonlight not far from the house and with a groan of pleasure, stripped her clothes off and waded in to rinse the filth from her body. The bath and the cool water did wonders, she almost felt human again.

Then she went back to sit in front of the cottage in the dark and let her hair dry out in the cool breezes. Amadeus popped up at her side, but she'd suspected he'd been following her since she'd first left the cottage. She'd heard him cavorting in the weeds as she'd been bathing.

"Still watching over me, huh?" She chuckled. "Can't break the old habit. Even if my powers are gone and technically I'm no longer a witch."

The cat meowed and rubbed against her. Amanda did miss talking to him.

"What am I going to do now, old buddy?" she asked him softly. "In this terrible time?"

He meowed again and jumped into her lap.

For some reason, she couldn't get that man off her mind, either. Joshua, he'd said his name was. Joshua Graham. He'd been so familiar somehow. She was surprised to realize that she hoped she'd see him again. Soon. She'd really liked him.

She studied the bright moon and listened to the familiar noises of the woods around her, trying to collect the rest of her scattered thoughts. Where was Rachel?

In *her* time causing trouble? Or was she in one of the other in-between worlds, waiting until Amanda was dead and she could take her place without challenge? Amanda had no way of knowing. Like she had no way of knowing what tomorrow would bring.

But the day's vicious heat was gone and it was cool and tranquil and Amanda was enjoying it. The solitude. The woods felt like the woods she knew back home. That hadn't changed. Nature rarely did. The leaves of the night woods rustled and whispered secrets she still couldn't understand.

Being a witch, she imagined she was probably accepting this whole thing a hell of a lot better than a normal person would. But she'd seen some bizarre things in her life, that was for sure. This was a shock, but then she'd had other shocks almost as bad—and she *had* broken the Law.

Her powers were still gone. She pined for them, felt positively lost and vulnerable without them.

The bottom line truth was that without them, she had no protection in this threatening world. She was at its mercy.

After a while, she went back into bed and slept fitfully, her sleep full of her old lost life and her crimes . . . and the nightmare that she had stepped into unwillingly.

And, in her dreams, too, the mysterious Rachel. Laughing at her. Maliciously telling her how her powers were greater than Amanda's and how she had won.

That she was living in Amanda's body in the present, weaving black magic with which to torment her friends and family. Living Amanda's life as she left Amanda to perish in her old one. That Amanda would die soon.

The next morning Amanda woke and prayed that it had just been a dream.

Chapter 7

The next time Amanda opened her eyes, it was day; though in the cavern-like twilight of the cottage it was hard to tell.

And she was still in the seventeenth century.

Real soon, she made a mental note, *I'm going to redo those windows so they can be opened in good weather. Let the sun in.*

She got up from the lumpy mattress, stretching, rested for the first time in days and tiptoed over to look down on the two girls. Both were sleeping peacefully and curled up in each other's arms like kittens. It touched something tender deep inside her, made her feel like she'd never felt. If she was here to stay, these would be her children. For the rest of her life. It was a sobering thought. There was a lot of damage she had to undo, a lot of damage done by Rachel.

Amadeus was already out romping in the woods, scoping out the new terrain, or chasing down rabbits.

As she stood poised in the doorway, pulling her fingers through her tangled hair, she looked for him, but didn't see him. *Wish I had a comb or a brush. A toothbrush and some toothpaste.* She walked out the door into an overcast day and worked her way down to the edge of the pond. Using twigs, she brushed her teeth as well as she could with the cold water, and then washed her

hands and face. She wanted to wash her clothes, but
she had nothing else to wear. So she had to leave them
on, dirty as they were. Rachel must have clothes somewhere in the cottage. She'd have to find them, too.

Above her clouds were gathering—burnt marshmal-
lows—and the temperature was dropping. She could
feel it on her skin and shivered. A storm coming.
Maybe it would break this suffocating heat, she contemplated, lifting her hair off her neck to catch the breeze
and tugging her fingers through it again. Hopeless.

She clumped back up to the cabin and caught Maggie lurking before the door, waiting for her. She had a
hand-carved wooden comb in her right hand and held
it out to Amanda.

Amanda had decided last night before she'd fallen
back to sleep that when she had to converse she would
try to talk more like the people of the time. Using thou
and thee whenever she could remember. No contrac-
tions. Her survival depended on making people believe
she was Rachel, but a changing Rachel. Slowly and cautiously she had to whiten Rachel's tarnished reputation.

"I thank thee. I need it, do I not?" Amanda agreed,
as she took the comb and started yanking it through
the rats and knots.

Maggie disappeared back into the cabin and came
back with a piece of thin rope which she offered her.
"Here, thee can tie thy hair back with this."

"Thank thee," Amanda muttered, again. She had the
rubberband she'd taken out of her hair the night before and more in her pockets, but it seemed easier to
use the rope than have to explain where she'd gotten
the rubberbands. After weaving her hair into one thick
braid, she tied it and flipped it over her shoulder and
down her back. On one hand, she would have liked to
have had a mirror, but on the other, not. It wouldn't

be her face looking back at her. She was still acutely uncomfortable about that.

Then Maggie handed Amanda a bundle of cloth. "And one of your dresses. 'Tis time thou put on a proper dress."

"I thank thee again." Amanda unrolled the cloth. It was a lovely blood-red dress with a thin waist and a full skirt. Beautiful. Amanda's eyes widened as they stared at the dress and then back at the thing Maggie wore. She had to bite her tongue, remember who she was supposed to be, or she would have given herself away. The dress explained partly the poverty in the house. If Rachel had always dressed this well, no wonder her children had to wear rags. Live in a dump. There were soft slippers tucked inside the dress and a fancy petticoat.

"I took it from thy chest there in the corner. It be one of thy favorites." There was just a pinch of anger in the girl's voice, a hint of red in her cheeks that matched the defiant gleam in her then-quickly lowered eyes. But Amanda caught it, anyway.

This will have to change, Amanda thought to herself. *As soon as possible.*

"I will go gather the eggs from the chickens as thou dresses and then we will eat breakfast," Maggie announced.

Amanda's face went blank.

"The chickens, Ma. Those we have in the back pen next to our garden . . . remember?" There was amusement in the girl's tone that again made Amanda feel like the child. How could the girl be so young and think so old? She must have had plenty of practice.

"Oh, those chickens." Amanda rubbed the side of her face absent-mindedly. "That knock yesterday on the back of my head must have addled me some, Maggie."

"Aye," Maggie threw over her shoulder as she

traipsed past her and out of sight around the side of the cottage, a basket in her arms for the eggs.

Amanda followed her silently and saw where she was heading before she turned back toward the cottage to slip on the dress, and check on Lizzy.

A small chicken coop was crouched behind the house, along with a large, well-tended garden. So she knew where some of the food was coming from now. Fresh eggs sounded delicious. It was strange how the idea of a simple hot meal could bring up a person's spirit.

Of course, the dress and slippers fit perfectly. Rachel had been a smaller woman than Amanda, but the dress had been made for her. After Amanda had put the clothes on, she found the chest Maggie had spoken of and went through the clothes and things in it. Her irritation grew as she took out one beautiful dress after another. At the very bottom of the large chest she discovered a box of jewelry, fine handkerchiefs, bonnets, and accessories. Clothes and jewels fine enough for a princess.

She made a decision then and there that she'd take most of the dresses and cut them down for the girls to wear. Sell or barter away the rest of the stuff in the local marketplace—if there was one—for other necessities. It was silly to have such things when the children needed so much. She'd always been good with a needle and thread and she was sure she could do it. The children deserved better than what they had and she was going to see that they got it. She didn't need all these fine clothes and jewels, but they needed better clothes. She kept out two of the prettiest dresses of thinner material and laid them on the table. She'd start cutting them down and sewing new ones right away.

She laid the comb on the shelf by the fireplace and quickly built up the fire for cooking. She'd noticed that

Maggie never let the fire go out, even in this hot weather. There were always tiny burning coals or a small flame.

Lizzy was sleeping, Amadeus curled in her arms. He must have snuck in when Amanda wasn't looking.

The girl's eyes opened.

"Good morning, Lizzy," Amanda said, stooping down to lift the child into her arms. She was as light as a bundle of clean clothes. "Are thee hungry, too?"

The little girl hid her head against Amanda's shoulder and mumbled that she was. Her arms stole around Amanda's neck and tightened. The child seemed to trust her completely already.

If I had my powers, Amanda brooded, *I could help this child* . . . if the damage to her eyes weren't too bad. But her powers were gone, so she couldn't do anything. Again the loss of her powers caused her regret and pain.

Though she'd have to hide her healing gifts here in the past, anyway, she reflected, just like in the future. Here, because any sort of unexplained healing was often attributed to Satan much quicker than to God, and in the future because contrary to what most people would have assumed, the medical community and the medical authorities would discredit or simply destroy any person who had such a healing power, if for no other reason than it would jeopardize their immense profits. Sickness in the twentieth century was big business.

So long ago witches learned not to advertise their healing abilities just like their other gifts. It was far safer that way.

Amanda had never approved of the greed she'd found in most so-called health-care professionals or the life-prolonging procedures that some doctors and hospitals resorted to, or when a brain or body died but machines kept the shell alive long after hope was gone. A sin to do that. Yet the medical community and the courts allowed it because of the vast sums of money concerned. The longer a hospital could keep a dying person alive, the higher the final bill would be. Sometimes advanced technology wasn't always good.

Amanda was sitting at the table, giving the child sips of the special tea she'd brewed from the medicinal herbs, relieved to hear the cough and the congestion breaking up. She was marveling at the child's brightness for her age when she heard the sound of a horse's hooves, and a shadow from the doorway fell across her. A big shadow.

She moved her gaze up and was startled to see Joshua Graham standing there, and then was even more surprised by the joy that burst upon her just at the sight of the man again. She looked up at him, a grin spreading across her face; her eyes shining, her heart skipping beats. He was so handsome. Dressed in a white shirt and leather jerkin, tight-fitting leather breeches and the high boots again. That long hair glinting with streaks of brilliant brownish-gold swept back from a strong face. He'd trimmed his mustache. He carried the old flintlock musket in his left hand and a sack in his right.

Everything else faded into oblivion. Except for his piercing brown eyes and his somehow hauntingly familiar smile.

Amanda's smile faltered, she trembled.

It had come to her finally. His smile, his mannerisms, his eyes . . . were *Jake's. How could you not have seen that yesterday?* Maybe, an inner voice told her, because you were so upset? It was such a shock she just sat there gawking up at him like an awestruck child who'd bumped into Santa Claus in person on Christmas morning. In physical appearance, except for his height, he was little like Jake had been. Such sharp features. He seemed much more guarded than Jake. Yet, it was Jake.

We've both lived before, many times. And were lovers in each one, she'd told Jake once long ago. And now she had found him again in the far past. It was incredible. Imagine the odds. Or, another thought hit her, was it fate? Was he here for another reason? For her. To help her.

Again she had the strange premonition that someone was watching over her. Even here, so far from her home and own time.

"Mistress Rachel? I am sorry to intrude like this . . . but I—"

"Came for your cloak," Amanda finished for him, taming her grin, and ordering her heart to stop hammering wildly in her chest. This wasn't her time, he wasn't her Jake. Just because Jake's soul resided in this body before her, didn't give her any rights to him. They didn't know each other. She'd be wise to remember that.

He paused. Amanda had the feeling that the cloak wasn't all he had come back for, as his eyes self-consciously met hers, then traveled to the dress she was wearing and clearly registered approval.

"Aye, for the cloak, to be sure, but also to see if thee were feeling better today."

"I am," Amanda responded.

His chiseled jaw clenched and his voice fell. "And to apologize for my rude behavior, as well. It was unforgivable."

Amanda shook her head slightly. "You helped me, what is there to forgive? I should thank thee."

He seemed to accept that.

Outside, it began to rain softly. A soothing sound.

Amanda got up from the chair with Lizzy clinging to her hip like a monkey and went to fetch the cloak.

When she handed it to Joshua, she said, "You may come in, sir, out of the rain. It is the least I can do after what you did for me yesterday."

He hesitated, thought about it as Jake would have done, and finally stepped into the cabin and sat down on one of the two other chunks of wood that passed for chairs. The cloak he laid across his lap, the sack he lowered to the floor, and the musket he propped on the floor against his thigh. She noticed his work-roughened hand never left it.

His eyes scanned the place and Amanda felt shame at the poor condition of the cottage. What he must think of her.

"It does not always look like this." She felt the need to apologize for something that wasn't even her fault. She promised herself the next time he stopped by the cottage would be spotless.

If he came by again.

He shrugged, and said nothing.

She gathered the dresses from the table and folded them neatly to one side. "I was about to cut them down for the girls," she found herself making another excuse.

"Thou were?"

"Yes."

He placed a burlap sack on the table before her and explained nonchalantly, "We butchered some of our pigs this morning and I thought with the children"—he nodded toward Lizzy as she hid her face against Amanda's chest from the stranger who seemed to frighten her—"thou might have use of a slab of fresh pork." Amanda couldn't help but catch the fleeting glimmer of kindness that the man then tried to conceal with a stern face.

So like Jake and yet not.

Amanda smiled at him. A feeling of happiness she couldn't contain lightening her mood. "I thank thee.

The meat will be put to good use. But, thou must stay and have some of it along with fresh eggs for breakfast." The invitation snuck out before she could stop it. She hoped she was putting her thees and thous in the correct places.

"I could not—"

"I insist.

"My daughter, Maggie, is out even now stealing the eggs from the chickens." She chuckled softly.

"Then"—he spread his arms in a capitulating gesture—"I would be honored."

Lizzy was begging for more of the tea and Amanda put the cup's rim back to her lips, gently helping her to drink. The girl hadn't coughed since Joshua had first arrived and the hotness of her skin had cooled. She was getting sleepy. Good.

Amanda glanced up in time to see Joshua regarding her and Lizzy with compassion, and admiration mixed with a touch of confusion. Anyone who studied the child for a while could tell she was blind.

"And this is my daughter, Lizzy," she introduced the two.

"Nice to meet thee, Lizzy." He spoke softly to the child and made no comment on her condition, just smiled understandingly over her head at Amanda. "Thou art a lovely child."

Lizzy burrowed against Amanda's breast again. Amanda could hear her tiny heart thumping against hers. But she was no longer afraid of Joshua, she could tell that. Just tired and shy.

Joshua met Amanda's eyes directly for the first time and held them. "Thou dost look better this morning. In fact, quite fetching."

Under his intense observation Amanda could feel herself blush. Glad that she'd had the time to pretty

herself up before he'd appeared and then amused at
herself for caring so.

His tall muscular frame remained rigid, as if he was
uncomfortable sitting across from her. He was a fighter,
she could tell. Like a hawk, his sharp eyes didn't miss
a thing. His movements lethal as a panther.

So like Jake, and yet so unlike him.

Lizzy had fallen asleep in her arms. She took her
back to her bed and settled her down on it. Sleep now
was the best thing for her. So the medicine could work.

She laid a kiss on the child's brow before she stood
up.

When she returned to the table, she remembered her
manners. "Tea?" she offered the man.

"Aye, and the stronger the better," he answered. His
eyes, enigmatic and sardonic, gleamed at her from under dark brows.

She fetched the boiling tea kettle and another cup
for her guest and then poured both of them some regular black tea. She missed the sugar she usually put in,
but there was no sugar or honey or whatever they used
back in these times, so she supposed she should get
used to it. Joshua drank the tea without asking for
sugar.

And he was staring at her again.

"Why dost thee look at me that way?" she asked,
unable to restrain herself any longer.

His voice was filled with gentle amusement. "Surely,
thou jests with me? Surely thou knows the answer?"

And Amanda understood. Rachel's evil reputation, of
course.

"Because they say I am a witch, true?" her voice quivering. "And thou hast never seen a witch close up?"

Joshua's face showed no emotion, but his eyes
watched her closely.

"Thou cannot believe that I truly love my children,

that I don't eat baby parts for breakfast or drink human blood in my teacup—that I am not a devil." Anger had crept into her voice and she couldn't help that, either.

He leaned forward then and suddenly there was a mischievous glint in his eyes. "Mistress Rachel, thou must be aware of the rumors spread about town concerning thee . . . that thou practices black witchcraft. Lays spells on helpless chickens, sheep, and cattle so that they waste away to skin and bones if thou hast been given offense by their owners. That thou sells, for coin or souls, love charms, potions, and incantations. Poisons. For evil purposes. That thou hath powers over the elements and can bring hail and terrible thunderstorms to wreak destruction on thine enemies. That thou can heal any sickness of mind or body—or cause it." He paused, dramatically. "And that thou sacrifices human babies in the name of Satan to gain these accursed powers . . . a strumpet who bewitches and then steals other women's husbands . . ."

Amanda, now livid, came slowly to her feet, her eyes flashing. She had to keep reminding herself that he wasn't Jake. He wasn't anything to her. And it was hard. She wanted to strike out at him. But it was not just at him, she realized sadly, that she wanted to lash out. It was her predicament. It was Rachel.

Then Joshua started to laugh. He raised his hands up in front of himself as if to ward away her ire. "But I never believe what others say. Only what I see with my own eyes. Find out myself. Thou art no black-hearted sorceress."

And Amanda's fury scurried away like rats hit by a spotlight; catching the joke, she plunked back onto her seat of wood and began to laugh, too.

He had been baiting her, teasing her. He was trying to tell her that he now believed not a word of any of it.

His face became serious, his eyes soft as his hand reached out to touch her hand. "And thou art no evil siren, no bride of Satan, I would warrant. All falsehoods, as well. Aye?" Oh, he wanted so to believe that, she could tell.

"Aye," she repeated his word, and sighed. "I am not evil." And from her lips—Amanda's—it was no lie. "I try not to hurt anyone intentionally." The image of the rogue coven she'd destroyed in the twentieth century pricked her conscience like a monstrous thorn in her side, and she still felt gut-wrenching guilt over the human members she'd had to dispose of. But they had been evil. Corrupt. She was sorry for it. But it could never be undone.

Joshua smiled, then nodded. He seemed to be satisfied with what he had heard. Her sincerity. "I believe thee."

They were touching. Their faces so near each other's. Again Amanda experienced the electric shock of recognition as their eyes met. By the bewildered look in his gaze, the way he jerked backward abruptly away from her, and dropped her hand, she wondered if he'd felt it, too.

Amanda felt reckless, and asked, "What else do they say of me?" She'd need to know if she was to right things.

His eyes shifted toward Lizzy asleep in the corner and then to Amanda's face.

"Since I have been back from King William's service and his bloody war in France this last year I have been hearing the rumors—but they have increased tenfold of late since Master Darcy's wife has discovered her husband's infatuation with thee."

Amanda almost protested, *Not with me.* Caught herself just in time. Instead, she remained silent and listened.

"I can see why he might be," a hoarse whisper, his

eyes gleaming with open appreciation. "I can see why the women of Canaan be jealous of thee. I believe, though, after having met thee and seen thee like this, that it be only spiteful jealousy that spurs these women's hatred."

"Then thou would be right," she confessed bluntly.

"But, do not fool thyself, Mistress Rachel," he said ominously. "Whether the gossip concerning thee be true or not. There be many hereabouts who hate thee vehemently and swear that thee be a witch, and would have thee punished for it. I know. So I would warn thee . . ." He again extended his fingers and slid them in a soft caress down the side of her face, then pulled away just as quickly. Confusion warred in his eyes. "They have sent for the infamous witch-hunter, Sebastien Goodman. He will arrive before another fortnight passes."

Amanda's face drained and her breath rattled through clenched teeth. She crossed her arms and her fingers dug into flesh. So here it was. The dreaded, hated words: *witch-hunter.*

This was why Rachel had brought her here.

"Who is this Sebastien Goodman?" Amanda's voice was as cold as ice. Her fingers were plucking nervously against the arm seams of her dress.

"A swaggering nobody who swears God hast called him to the task of rooting out the evil of witchcraft and all those who follow Satan. What blasphemous drivel," Joshua spat out in disgust. "He hast left broken bodies and corpses throughout Connecticut and Massachusetts—all in the name of God. But God would not condone the cruelty he uses to extract his confessions."

There was a darkness in Joshua's face now as he talked, and he was no longer looking at her, but at something invisible beyond her. She noted how his fists kept clenching and unclenching as they lay on the table. There was someone he wished he could break in two.

"Thou hate him. Why?" Amanda tilted her face and waited for him to explain. She didn't have to wait long.

"My brother, Jacob, was in Cambridge last fall to find buyers for our tobacco crop and saw firsthand the malicious mischief Sebastien conjured up. He himself was waylaid, arrested, and falsely accused of witchcraft. Probably for the gold coins he carried," Joshua snarled, his lips curling away from his teeth. "But by God's grace he escaped and made it home again, yet hast not been the same since. Stays alone in his room and will speak to no one but me and our mother." He would tell her later that his mother, a widow, had been an Irish bonded servant who'd stolen his father's heart thirty years before and married him. Joshua's voice was always full of love as he spoke of the feisty woman who also cherished the land as much as he.

"My brother be so tormented now. He saw such horrors in the dungeon he was captive in that his mind cannot bear to think upon them, or what was done to him before he broke free. He swears that the witch-hunter be a devil himself. My brother says Sebastien loves too much the stench of branded flesh and the sight of fresh blood."

Joshua shook his head and returned haunted eyes to Amanda.

"Now the beast will be here in Canaan soon. Protect thyself, Mistress Rachel, if thou can. He hast powerful friends. To be truthful, thy children and thyself might be wise to leave this place for a while. Visit relatives. It will not be safe here for thee."

Amanda shuddered as if someone had trodden on her grave. She'd heard almost the same words out of Ernie's mouth just days ago. Centuries from now. Her new life was uncannily paralleling her old one. She was about to answer him when a noise made her look toward the doorway.

Maggie was standing there, a little damp; in her arms a basket of fresh eggs. She was glaring hatefully at Joshua.

She turned to Amanda and insinuated, "I suppose thee wants me to take Lizzy now and go out to wait in the woods while thee entertains the gentleman here?"

"In the rain?—Of course not." Amanda declared, and smiled innocently back at her. "All of us"—she looked at Joshua, who was watching Maggie with dry humor—"will be having breakfast. Together."

Maggie, flabbergasted, gaped at Amanda as if she had lost her mind.

"This be Joshua Graham, Maggie. Thou remembers him. The one who helped me home yesterday after my . . . accident. I have invited him to breakfast. Look, he hast brought us fresh pork. We will have it with the eggs."

Talking and being with these three people was becoming easier all the time. If she hadn't been found out this far, she was most likely safe enough. They truly believed she was Rachel.

"Please, Maggie, hand me the eggs and I will start breakfast while thee heat up some more water for tea. Thou must be hungry after wrestling all those eggs away from the chickens."

Amanda took the basket of eggs easily from the girl's hands and transported them and the slab of pork to the hearth, lifted a large black skillet down from one of the shelves, and hung it by the arched metal handle over the fire. She searched for and found a well-used knife lying on the bricks by the fire, wiped it off on the edge of her skirt, and as the skillet began to heat, she deftly sliced portions of the pork into strips and tossed them in.

"The tea?" Amanda mouthed over her shoulder to Maggie as the delicious aroma of sizzling bacon filled the small cottage.

"Aye, Ma." And the girl did what she had been told.

They all sat down to a large breakfast, Maggie silently regarding Amanda the whole time as Amanda held Lizzy in her lap and fed her, fussed over her.

Joshua, after he was pressed for the third time by Maggie, finally recounted some of the stories of his service to King William of Orange. Amanda had been right. He had been a soldier, though he avowed he was a farmer by birth. She could see just by the way he talked that he loved his land and the growing of things far greater than worthless bloodshed and vain glory in far-off lands. He'd had no choice but to go to war, or go to prison. Amanda remembered that about these times, as well.

He'd been in France, fighting England's war to gain control of lands in India and North America, and had loathed every moment of it. He'd been many places, including the court of fiery Queen Mary. But had grown disillusioned and weary of the fighting and the rapacious royal court and when his time had been put in, had come home.

He'd been away from Canaan long enough that he was considered an outsider. A stranger with strange ways. Amanda felt an immediate affinity with him.

The morning and the breakfast went by swiftly and before Amanda knew it, Joshua was standing up to take his leave.

"I have crops and field hands to attend to. And my mother will be worried." His father had died when he'd been off at war and now, with his only brother hiding in his room, his mother needed him to run the farm. To care for and oversee their corn and tobacco crops.

He said nothing about coming back, but as Amanda

watched him from the open doorway get back on his horse and ride off into the forest in the steady rain, he pivoted around in his saddle and waved good-bye, smiled, and Amanda had the strong premonition he would return. She caught herself smiling radiantly back at him, an almost forgotten sense of well-being and joy making her feel so wonderful she could have danced around like a crazy person. She hadn't felt that way since before Jake—she stopped herself.

No, don't get too attached to him, her heart counseled her. *As soon as you get your powers back, you'll be gone. Back to the time you belong in.* She looked around her at the cottage, at the girls. *Don't get too attached to anything. Anyone. You don't belong here.*

The words Joshua had spoken about her leaving for awhile crossed her mind again. But what happened if someone in her time was looking for her? Wouldn't she be wiser to be close by, to be where Rachel was supposed to be—if they came looking for her?

If *who* came looking for her? No one knew what had happened to her. No one knew where she was. She was being foolish. Worse, stupid. *No one was coming.*

And what of the children? She couldn't just leave them. They would be in danger, too, when the witch-hunter arrived. They needed her. Even if she took them with her . . . to where? Where could she go with two small children? One blind. How would she feed and shelter them?

She lowered her head and rubbed her eyes. What a mess she was in.

After Joshua had gone and Amanda had seen Lizzy settled down on the rug with a crude homemade cloth doll that Amanda had thrown together to play with, she turned around to find a suspicious-eyed Maggie confronting her.

"Who *art* thee?" the girl demanded to know, her face earnest and troubled.

Amanda was about to answer with the lie, *I'm your mother, of course.* But before she could utter a syllable the girl narrowed her eyes and said in a measured, steady tone, "Do not lie to me. Thou art *not* my mother. I am sure of that now. Thou look like her, aye. Thy voice be the same. Thee might fool anyone, *but* me and Lizzy, you be so like her. But thou art not her. I have suspected so from the first when thee showed up yesterday in those queer clothes, speaking strangely. Acting strangely.

"And now I see that thou art nothing like her. Thou art too kind and gentle-hearted. She never cared for Lizzy or me, much less our comfort and welfare. She was a whore, slovenly and hateful. Vengeful. She slept with every man who rode up to the door and had gifts of money to pay her. And she *hated* me." The look on the girl's face was unreadable, stone, but Amanda guessed it covered a lifetime of pain and hurt. She'd had a lot of practice covering her true feelings.

Amanda, stunned by the girl's keen insight, what she had pronounced concerning Rachel, and seeing that she was not to be fooled, sighed softly and sank back down onto the chair she had just vacated. The game was up. Time to face the music.

"No, I'm not your mother," she replied simply, firmly locking eyes with the child. It was almost a relief to admit it. A relief to say it aloud. To stop pretending. To stop using those damnable "thees" and "thous."

"I also didn't ask to be brought here, to be in her image—and I haven't done anything to hurt her, I swear."

The girl's demeanor was alive with apprehension as she moved away from Amanda a little. "Art thou a demon sent from hell to torment us?" she croaked.

"No, I'm human, just like you." Amanda smiled gently at the girl and it seemed to pacify her.

"I thought not," Maggie whispered, almost to herself, visibly relaxing again.

"Maggie, you know what your mother was?" Amanda had decided to trust the girl and tell her everything.

"Aye." Revulsion lay heavy and flat in the girl's dark eyes. "She be a witch. What others say of her be true, well enough," Maggie hissed. "She be evil, and hast done many of the crimes accused of."

"I, too, am a witch. My name is Amanda Givens."

"Thou art a witch like my mother, then?" Expression hardening. Her eyes growing wide and wary.

"No, not like your mother. I'm a white witch. I don't worship Satan; my powers come from God."

"A *good* witch?" Maggie exclaimed, with a quick intake of breath. "I never knew there be such things."

"There are. Good witches, I mean. I'm one of them."

Maggie searched Amanda's open face with some confusion. Trying to accept what she was saying, but having a difficult time of it.

"Maggie," Amanda said, "I'm telling you the truth. I'm no threat to you or your sister. I would never do anything to hurt either one of you. In my time I lived a solitary life, tried to help people if I could without drawing attention to myself."

"In your time?" Maggie's voice rose a pitch higher. Might as well tell her *everything*.

"I'm from another time, child. The future. Nineteen hundred and ninety-two. Your mother somehow kidnapped me from my time, my home, and my friends to take her place when I was vulnerable—to take her place for some reason I can only guess at."

"Oh, dear God in heaven," Maggie's childish voice squeaked as she jumped to her feet, trembling. She crossed herself and backed away, nearer to Lizzy, as if she felt there might be a need to protect her. "Thou art not lying to me, are thee? Not having fun of me?" she asked angrily. "How can this be true?"

"No," Amanda answered wearily. "I wish it weren't true. This whole thing is a nightmare for me.

"Except for you and Lizzy," Amanda amended her last statement. *And Joshua.* "Because not only am I in someone else's body in another time, but I'm in a time that is extremely dangerous for witches. Good or bad. I don't know what is going to happen, Maggie. I'm without my powers and helpless. I want to go home . . . but don't know how." Amanda stopped, afraid that it was all too much for a girl as young as Maggie to comprehend.

But she would understand this. "And I'm frightened," she murmured weakly.

The empathy on Maggie's young face told Amanda that she had finally touched the girl with that confession, for her expression softened. She didn't seem afraid anymore, either.

Amanda asked, "What year is this, Maggie?"

"Why 'tis the year sixteen hundred and ninety-four of our Lord." She scooted over and sat back down.

The Salem witch trails had been staged in sixteen hundred and ninety-two, Amanda recalled. The witchcraft hysteria would be in full swing. She couldn't have come at a worse time.

Maggie leaned her head into her hands. "Do thee know where my mother is?"

"No." Amanda hesitated, unsure how much to actually divulge to the girl. She wouldn't tell her about Rachel's legend in her time. The legend of Black or Witch's Pond: that Rachel was probably murdered for being a witch. Too cruel. And Amanda herself wasn't even sure what had really happened. No one knew, except Rachel.

"She's either in my time, in my body, or she's in between . . . waiting."

"What is she waiting for?"

"I don't know." *Waiting for me to die.* But Amanda couldn't say that to Maggie, either.

"In between?"

How to explain other dimensions or the outer fringes of hell to a child? "Like when you're dreaming. That kind of in between."

"She cannot hurt us in our dreams, can she?" Again that fear.

"No. She can't touch you. You're in the real world. There's a wall she can't come through." Which was a lie in a way, too. Because Rachel had broken through somehow into her world, her time, and done this. Yet there was no sense in frightening Maggie any more than she was. Amanda was sure that her crime against the coven had somehow aided Rachel's scheme and created the momentary pathway between the worlds. Rachel had no reason to come back here. Not until what she had set out to achieve had been accomplished.

"Are you that afraid of your own mother?" Amanda questioned. Lizzy was humming some tune to herself and playing with Amadeus, who was affectionately bumping against the child and actually purring.

"Aye," the timbre of her voice uneasy. "She hurts people. Puts curses and hexes on them. She loves to see others suffer. She lays terrible spells upon people who cross her or make her mad. I have seen her do it. She has great power, my mother, and has made many enemies. The whole town despises us. I dare not even show my face these days." The girl was obviously bitter.

"I care not if she *ever* comes back," Maggie spoke harshly, her eyes hard chips of flint as she glared at Amanda. "And I am not like her. Not anything like her!" She was standing again. Trembling.

The last piece of the mystery fell into place. The girl did fear and hate her mother and what she had been.

"She is a whore," she condemned. "She always makes me and Lizzy leave when the men come. So she can be alone with them. Sometimes we even have to sleep outside. It makes little difference be it hot or freezing or raining or snowing. That is why Lizzy is sick now. *I hate her,*" the girl stated with vicious malice, pounding her hands against her sides.

Amanda walked over and touched the child's arm soothingly. She wanted to take the girl in her arms and hug her, reassure her, but she was afraid the girl wasn't ready for that much caring yet. "I'm sorry she was so mean to you and Lizzy. I'd never do that if I were your mother. You don't deserve to be treated so poorly."

The girl turned her bright eyes away to hide the sudden tears. Amanda was right; she wasn't used to kindness, didn't know how to take it.

The girl sniffled a few seconds later, wiped her hand across her wet face, and asked, "What is your time like?"

"Oh, in some ways very different than yours." Amanda's gaze traveled thoughtfully around the simple room and at Lizzy playing noisily in the corner with her familiar. She remembered with longing the electric lights, the gas stove, the beautiful furnishings. Then her memory recreated the people of Canaan and their cruel treatment of her, her ostracism. Their ugly faces in the light of the blaze that had once been her home and the way they had chased her through the woods that last night. "And in some ways, very much the same.

"I miss my family . . . my friends. My life." Canaan and its people aside. Amanda shook her head and stared moodily into the shadows of the cottage. Outside, the rain continued, the inside of the cottage growing murkier.

Lizzy whimpered because Amadeus had run off somewhere, and Amanda collected her, cradling the child in
her lap.

"Thee do speak strangely," the girl blurted out
abruptly. And Amanda laughed. The dark-headed girl
joined in, her laughter sounding rusty from little use,
and finally came to sit next to her again at the rickety
table.

"What should I call thee?" Maggie inquired shyly
then.

"Amanda, if you want."

Maggie seemed to think about it seriously for a moment and the corners of her lips slid up slightly in
what could almost be called a smile. "Perhaps it would
be best if I continued to call thee Ma, as before. In
case someone should ever be around and I would slip
and call you . . . the other name. It could raise questions."

Amanda looked at the child. If she wanted to pretend
she was her mother, then so be it. It couldn't harm
anyone. Amanda might be here for awhile. A long
while. She thought again how clever Maggie was for as
young as she was. An old woman in a child's body.

"Tell me about your time," the girl requested again.
Amanda had the feeling that Maggie still didn't believe
she was from the future but was humoring her.

And Amanda did. About who Amadeus was. About
her time and her life, her family, and everything that
had occurred to her right before she was swept into
the past. What it was to be a white witch in the twentieth century. Just leaving out the things that might
scare the girl too much or things Amanda believed she
didn't need to know, or wouldn't understand. After all,
she was only a child.

Outside, the rain had turned into a mild storm, sift-
ing through the trees and drumming harder against the

house. The temperature had fallen even farther. Amanda and Maggie built up the fire together and Maggie kept asking questions about the twentieth century.

As the time went by, Maggie became spellbound with the stories Amanda was telling and ceased the questions, content just to listen as Amanda sat at the table, working on their new dresses, and talking.

Later over supper of homemade succotash and more strips of the bacon Joshua had brought them that morning, Amanda asked about Rachel's store of medicinal herbs.

"Tomorrow, if it stops raining, I will show thee the root cellar," Maggie said. "It is where my mother keeps all her witchery things. Herbs and medicines. These *things* in bottles." She shuddered. "And her book of spells."

"Her book of spells?"

"Aye, a small book covered in black leather where I think she kept record of all her black magic, though she never let me near it." Maggie's voice was uneasy. "As well a record as she could keep, she could write very little. 'Twould be our death warrant if it were ever to be found here. So she kept it hidden well. Perhaps it might help thee?"

"I don't see how it could. Rachel's magic and mine are very different." As different as black and white. Then Amanda thought about it some more. Maybe it could help her. Give her more insight into the woman who had turned her life upside down. "But it wouldn't hurt to have a look at it."

They finished supper, discussing the Canaan of sixteen ninety-four, and then Amanda's plans for the next few days: about cutting down most of Rachel's dresses for the girls, cleaning and fixing up the cottage, and bartering away Rachel's jewelry and some of her fancier clothes for food and things they'd need.

Maggie at first seemed astounded that she would do all that for them, but Amanda finally convinced her it would be done.

"There be so much Lizzy needs. More blankets. Warmer clothes. Though her fever and cough seem much better today," Maggie said.

"Both of you need things."

"All of us need things." Maggie grinned at her then like the child she was.

"Maybe even a few real toys for Lizzy." Amanda was looking at the raggedy cloth doll with button eyes. "And something special for you, Maggie. What would you like?"

"Nothing," the girl answered flatly, as if she'd never given any thought to it. But her mind was already busy on their other problem. "We could trade for what we need in the marketplace on Saturday. Once a week merchants and the local farmers come into town to sell their livestock, vegetables, and wares. If they do not stone us the moment we set foot in town." The girl's grin had vanished, a frown taking its place on her plain face.

"Well, we'll have to see, won't we?" Amanda finished hopefully.

The girl merely shrugged her shoulders.

The next morning when the sun glowered bright overhead, she followed Maggie around behind the cottage, about sixty yards into the forest, and down some dirt steps into a dark, cool root cellar full of canned fruits and vegetables. She had the egg basket hanging on one arm.

"I canned all the fruit and vegetables myself," Maggie said proudly. Amanda had already guessed that.

And far in the back behind a false wall, Maggie

showed her where there were shelves full of dried herbs
in messy piles strewn everywhere and stuff in small
wooden bowls or bottles, all unlabeled.

Rachel had not been organized at all.

Amanda shoved the basket back on her arm and lit
a candle, swiping at spiderwebs. She studied what she
found as Maggie lingered on the other side of the false
door, refusing adamantly to come in any farther.

"I will not set foot in that wicked place. The *things*
in those jars. Sometimes I think they be staring at me."
Maggie crossed herself, her face white as a ghost; her
eyes peering cautiously into the inky corners of the cluttered cellar.

Amanda had never seen such a collection. She ran
her fingers lightly over the dusty bottles. Some of the
contents she thought she recognized.

Foxglove roots. One-fifth of a grain was so lethal it
could slow and then stop a heart's beating. She reached
out and poked a clump of hedgerow or nightshade as
it was sometimes called. Fourteen of its berries could
easily kill, and less would induce delirium. There was
curare and the dried fruit of hemlock, both of which,
in varying doses, could inflict gradual or complete pa-
ralysis.

Amanda studied a strange-looking dried plant. If she
was right, it was tansy . . . a magical plant that was
believed to be able to prolong life, though it was very
rare and she had never seen any except in pictures in
old dusty books. She laid a hand reverently on it and
wondered where it had come from. Where everything
had come from.

There were rows of what appeared to be exotic potions, poisons, and ghastly looking monstrosities (parts
of slain animals?) in some bottles. Blood-colored liquid
in others. Some of them made Amanda queasy. They
were so grotesque.

She never used such things in her magic.

But there were also the more common medicinal plants and herbs that Amanda was more familiar with that were used for healing fevers, chills, and other ailments . . . and on and on.

A well-stocked witch's pharmacopoeia. Heavy on the black magic ingredients, though. Real heavy.

Amanda could only imagine what the townspeople would do if they found this forbidden cache. What they would believe. Just the thought of it made her nervous.

Her skirts disturbed the dust around her and she began hacking. Put a hand over her mouth. The dirt stung her eyes.

"Where's the diary?" She coughed.

"She has it hid. There." Maggie reluctantly moved up behind her and pointed with a shaky finger to a flat rock right under Amanda's feet. "Under that rock, buried a little under the dirt."

Maggie handed her a stick, sharpened on one end, that had been lying on one of the shelves; then she edged back closer to the entrance.

Amanda crouched down and lifted the heavy rock, set it aside, and started digging.

"Are you sure it's here?"

"It is. Dig deeper," she encouraged Amanda.

Amanda raised her eyebrows and then started to dig harder in the moist, loose soil. Finally she hit something and she tossed the stick aside.

Her fingers brushed something smooth and hard, covered in a scrap of coarse cloth. She tugged it from the ground and unwrapped a delicate leather-bound and clasped book. "Got it."

She got off her knees and hid the diary in her basket under the herbs she'd already collected to help Lizzy shake the last remnants of her fever. She'd study it later when she was alone. She could tell that Maggie was very uncomfortable in the cellar and wanted to get out of it as soon as she could. She knew how she felt.

"All right. We can go now," she told the girl, and shooed Maggie out into the sunlight and back toward the house.

Maggie didn't utter a word once they'd left the cellar. And Amanda was too preoccupied with her own thoughts to notice how quiet the girl was.

She couldn't wait to examine Rachel's book of spells. Maybe then, she'd know more about her nemesis. Know how to defeat her.

If she could. Perhaps, Amanda had the sudden hope, there was even a spell in the book that might let her go back home. Break the enchantment Rachel had put on her.

But for now, she tucked the little book away in a safe place that Maggie showed her under a loose brick of the hearth and spent the rest of the day cleaning the cottage from top to bottom. Tomorrow she'd try to fix the windows. If the right tools were available.

That night in the soft glow of candlelight Amanda and Maggie worked on the children's new dresses and became friends. Amanda had begun to realize how lonely the girl had been.

She never mentioned her mother. Not once the whole night. But Amanda thought of her quite a lot. Where was she? In her time, or in between? Or still haunting Black Pond? She asked Maggie about Black Pond and Maggie gave her general directions to it. It was about six miles away toward the west.

That night, as the two girls slept on their pallets, Amanda retrieved and opened Rachel's book of spells by candlelight. Amadeus was perched in her lap, for some reason very unhappy at what she was doing. If she could have understood him she probably would have had an earful. He clearly didn't want her to have

anything to do with the book. Twice he actually tried
to snatch it away from her, and once, when she'd taken
it away from him for the second time, he actually
nipped at her.

She couldn't understand, though, what he was fussing
about. As she turned page after page, her bewilderment
grew. If the book was full of spells it wouldn't have
mattered. Wouldn't have helped her one bit. She
couldn't read a damn word of it. It was in some sort
of code or arcane language, indecipherable to her.
Whatever secrets it held would not be for her to learn.
A chill tingled along her spine. As only another witch
would sense, she sensed that the book in her hands
was evilness itself. In the end, she hated to even touch
it and hid it away again under the brick.

When she and the children were long asleep and the
fire in the hearth was burning low, Amadeus stealthily
dug it out. He silently made the door open with his
fading magic, and holding the book carefully between
his teeth, he scampered out into the rainy night.

When he returned a while later he spent a lot of
time meticulously cleaning away the dirt clumped between his claws and around his sore paws until there
wasn't a trace of where he'd been or what he'd been
doing. Then, with a huge smug grin plastered across
his furry face, he laid his weary head on his paws and
fell instantly to sleep.

Chapter 8

"Rebecca! Great, I've finally gotten ahold of you. . . . You are a difficult woman to track down, Sis." Jessica's usually placid voice sounded breathless on the other end of the receiver.

"Yeah, when I'm on a book tour like this, I am. Two one-horse towns a day, three hick radio station programs with ungracious and unprepared, arrogant hosts, inadequate lodgings, and discounted Greyhound bus tickets keep me hopping, all right. My messages, urgent or not, don't always catch up to me. Sometimes never. You're damn lucky . . . yours just caught me by a hare's whisker." A self-amused chuckle crackled across the line, but Jessie caught the tiredness behind the voice, too.

"And I had this sudden whim to call my answering service this morning." Rebecca didn't tell her sister that it had been more than a whim, but almost a driven compulsion. Even her mouse familiar, Tibby, had urged her to call her younger sister. Pronto. So she had shuffled down to the phone booth on the lower level of the hotel complex in her robe, curlers, and fuzzy kitty slippers, and had sleepily dialed the number. When she wasn't even awake yet, and Tibby chattering on like a magpie in her housecoat's roomy pocket. She didn't know what had gotten into the critter lately. He had

woken her at dawn with a lot of nonsense about someone close to her being in real danger. *Call your sister.*

And since the only sister she knew of who had a
phone was Jessie, she'd called Jessie. As silly as Tibby
could be sometimes, he had his connections. There was
a whole network—worldwide—of witches' familiars and
they jabbered and gossiped over the miles with their
magic like servants once gossiped in the downstairs
kitchens. Maybe he knew something she didn't.

"What can I do for you, Jessie?" her voice purred.
She was tucking her short dark hair back up into the
large curlers as it escaped. Her face round and her eyes
a startling blue as they scanned the surrounding doors,
all with numbers on them. Most of the guests were still
sleeping, but some were already packing up their suitcases in their cars and going off to breakfast at one of
the local restaurants. Breakfast made her mouth water,
she was starved. There were only two places to eat, as
far as she could tell, a Denny's and some sort of truck
stop, in this godforsaken tiny town. Somewhere in Ten-
nessee, but she wasn't sure exactly where. It was like
that sometimes on these whirlwind book promotion
tours. Two towns a day and she never could remember
where she was half the time.

"It must be an emergency, Jessie, if you've gone to
all this trouble. Your messages—all ten of them—
sounded desperate." Rebecca shivered a little. She'd left
her sweater in the hotel room. It was cool outside for
November, but not yet cold.

"Yes, I think it's an emergency." A gulp of air and
only a split second pause before Jessie launched into
everything like a freight train on a fast track.

"Amanda's in a whole hell of a lot of trouble, if you
ask me, and I'm afraid—*really* afraid—for her . . . and
that was before . . . before the Satanic cult stole Jane's
little boy and Amanda went to get him back . . . before

the townspeople found the boy, mutilated and half-dead, at Amanda's feet last night, burned her cabin to the ground, and chased her through the woods . . . Now, according to Ernie, Jane's boyfriend, she's disappeared on top of it all . . ." A sharp intake of air and she plunged on again before Rebecca could stop her. "I told her she'd gotten involved in this thing way over her head with this long-dead witch, Rachel . . . and, Rebecca, I tried to warn her . . . tried to get her to wait until we could locate you to see if you could help her or try to get *some* kind of help . . . but you know Amanda . . . headstrong and always thinking she can handle every damn thing alone . . . But she couldn't wait because she knew the cult was going to kill Jonny and the townspeople thought she was one of them—"

"WHOA! W . . . h . . . o . . . a!" Rebecca interrupted forcefully, her head spinning from information overload. "Slow the bejesus down, Jessie! I don't know what the hell you're talking about . . . remember me? The left-out sister who might as well have been on another planet for the last couple of months and doesn't know what's been going on? The black sheep sister of the family? Amanda may have let you in on all the scuttlebutt, but not me." Underneath all the bravado in the lilting voice there was a thin veneer over the hurt of being left out.

Jessica, even upset, but ever-observant, caught it. Like she usually did.

"I'm sorry, Rebecca." She sighed wearily. Rebecca could almost see her rubbing the side of her forehead, as she always did when she was losing it. "I guess I just got carried away. Just worried, that's all. Time is essential. I might not be a real witch like you two are, but my woman's intuition is pretty good. I know Amanda's in real trouble. I *feel* it in my bones. I need your help. I can't do a thing by myself. Please?"

"All right," the voice on the other end of the phone grumbled. "You can count on me. What are sisters for, anyway? But we have to talk face to face. As soon as possible. Phones won't cut it. Too many ears listening."

There was an unusual caution in Rebecca's manner that puzzled Jessica. It wasn't like her sister to be afraid of anything or anyone, even though with her limited powers, at times, her sister thought she should be.

"I'll come as fast as a plane can fly me," Rebecca said.

Rebecca, unlike Amanda, had never perfected her appearing and disappearing act. She could use magic to get places, but only at her own risk. Short distances usually were safest. She didn't always get where she was aiming. The last time she'd tried, she'd ended up on the icy wing of an airplane—in flight—and after that had given up traveling that way. She took public transportation now. It was safer.

"You can cancel the book tour?" There was relief in Jessie's voice.

"Sure. Who's the best-selling author, anyway? I'll tell my agent screw the damn book tour 'cause my sister comes first. The book seems to be doing bloody well without me hawking it all over the airways, anyway." Rebecca was a born Anglophile and spiced her conversation with British dictum whenever she could. She had friends and colleagues in England and flew over all the time. At times, she even affected a slight British accent that drove Jessie nuts.

Then Rebecca commented sarcastically, "Satanic cults and dead witches, huh? What has little Amanda gotten herself into," she trailed off, thoughtfully. But underneath her sarcasm there was concern. She didn't possess the powers her sister Amanda possessed, but she had the knowledge. She'd written two books on Satanic cults and their followers and she'd learned long ago that they were nothing to fool with.

From her pocket, Tibby was chattering hysterically again. Something about him being afraid. Not wanting to go. *They should just as well drench themselves in gasoline and light a match. Be done with it.* His little hairy black face was peeking out at her from the darkness of her pocket, his whiskers jumping like tiny antennae and his beady black eyes bulging. He was always scared. What a wuss. Rebecca shushed him. She could only listen to one conversation at a time. "I'll talk to you in a minute, my pet," she whispered down at him.

A man in a tacky plaid sportsuit passed by and gawked at her. She stuck her tongue out at him.

Her attention came back with a start to what her sister was blabbering on about at the other end of the phone.

"I can't wait until you get here."

Rebecca could almost hear the fear in Jessie's plea; it fell heavy on her senses like a descending blanket.

"Put on the coffeepot and something to eat . . . and I'll see you real soon, Sis."

"OK . . . good-bye."

"Good-bye."

Then right before the click came she added softly, "Don't worry about Amanda, Jessie. I'll find her and bring her back . . . even if I have to go to hell itself. I promise. No matter what it takes. We'll find her."

Then she cut the connection.

Even if I have to go to hell itself.

As Rebecca replaced the receiver on its hook, she frowned. The words hung before her like ghosts on the air. A sudden chilling breeze had caressed her face and as sure as she was standing there in her tacky robe and curlers, an ominous forewarning settled on her shoulders like a shadowy cloud.

And Rebecca knew. *Amanda's crossed someone or something that has a hell of a lot of power. Malevolent as all get out. I can feel it, as weak as my magic is. And it ain't just a cult or a witch, neither. It's more. Much more.*

It's BIG.

But that was as far as she got with the premonition. Any further probing after that was like hitting a blank wall.

Something doesn't want me to know.

My, my, Amanda. You are in deep shit, aren't you? You've crossed somebody very, very powerful and heaven knows what the price is gonna be to get you out.

Rebecca just hoped that it wasn't already too late. She sure had a bad feeling about all this.

What the hell had happened back there in Canaan, anyway, and where the hell was her sister? She couldn't stop the horrible thought from seeping through: was she even still alive?

Tituba had crawled out of her pocket and was perched on her shoulder as she trudged back to her hotel room. He was babbling a mile a minute about how if she tried to save Amanda *she'd* be in way over her head.

And Rebecca listened because Tibby was usually right, even if he was a little coward at times, but he knew what he had to say wouldn't stop her. And she proved him right.

"I'm going, no matter what you say. No matter how dangerous it is. She's my sister, damn it." Her jaw set, her eyes blazing.

Tibby gave up.

Rebecca dressed in her black stretch pants and long black blouse, and hurriedly packed the rest of her clothes. Her pentagram necklace glittering around her neck. She always wore black. Part of her witch show.

She's still alive, Tituba told her with his thoughts. He

was sitting on the edge of the hotel bed. A small ebony dot on the huge white chenille bedspread. *But hurry, mistress . . . you haven't a hell of a lot of time to save her. If you can.*

And that worried Rebecca more than anything Jessie had had to say.

She called her agent and canceled the rest of the tour. Her agent didn't like it, but then Rebecca didn't give her much time to complain before she'd hung up on her. She made plane reservations and called a taxi after she'd finished with the agent, and then headed out the door after slipping on her black sweater, munching on one of the candy bars she had stashed away for emergencies as she went. No time for breakfast now. She had fifteen minutes to drop off her room key, settle her bill, and get to the hick airport and catch her plane. Maybe she could get some food on the flight. She hoped so. It was hard to stay plump when you ran as much as she'd been doing lately.

Five minutes later, she was running toward the yellow taxi pulled up in front of the manager's office.

She just made her plane. Barely.

Chapter 9

As the days drifted by, Amanda became sure of three things: She had to hide or get rid of the cache of potions and black magic paraphernalia that Rachel had left behind, destroy the book of spells, and learn to fit into the society she had found herself thrust into. There was no telling how long she would be there, and without Rachel's or her own powers with which to protect herself, the cellar was too dangerous to leave as it was.

Yet when she pulled the brick away over the hearth, the book was gone. She had no doubt that Amadeus had taken it and gotten rid of it, remembering how he had reacted the night she'd been examining it. But if he had taken it, he wasn't about to cough it up.

She cleaned out the cellar the first week with Maggie's help, only rescuing the herbs she might need for medicinal use and some of the rarer plants. She carted away and tossed most of the repugnant evidence into the pond close by or buried it out deep in the woods. Soon the cellar only contained canned vegetables and fruit. The secret room held only the basic herbs most midwives or healers might possess. At least she'd never be accused of practicing *black* magic.

Lizzy had gotten better every day until her cough and fever were gone and her cheeks were a healthy pink. She'd loved Amanda almost unconditionally from the very beginning, which amazed Amanda. It took Maggie a little longer, she'd had to learn to trust her, but soon she was a different child, as well. They both were. In the lovely but simple dresses that Amanda made for them and the moccasins she fashioned from the soft leather that Joshua brought, Amanda realized that even Maggie could be a stunner.

Amanda became attached to both children, more so every day, no matter how she tried to rationalize the reasons not to. She did. They needed her and she needed them. They gave her life a purpose she'd been lacking for a long time.

And Joshua. He visited them in late afternoons when his chores were done, arriving with either food or other small gifts. Leather for moccasins. Bonnets for the children. A shawl for Maggie. Meat for the table. A helping hand. Sometimes he would stay for supper. He was kind and gentle to the girls and Maggie developed a crush on him.

Amanda couldn't help but love him, drawn to him not only because he was her Jake, but because the attraction between them was too strong for either of them to resist for long.

As insane as it was, they were soon lovers. Discreet, because of the children, but lovers all the same. When the girls were asleep, they'd take a blanket and go out into the woods and make love under the warm night skies. And then they'd talk about the things all lovers talked about. Except about Amanda being a witch or her previous life. As much as she hated lying to him, inventing a personality and past that really wasn't hers, she had to—to Joshua she was Rachel.

He asked her to marry him one night as they lay in each other's arms and gazed up at the stars. He wanted her and the girls to live with him on his farm. More than anything in the world Amanda wanted to say yes, but she couldn't. What happened if she did marry him and then suddenly found herself whisked back to her own time? Or if she regained her powers and was able to go back, but had to leave him behind? He had a destiny to complete here and Amanda could destroy the fabric of time by yanking him away. He no more belonged in her time than she did in his.

And most importantly, he didn't know what she really was. A witch. The very thought of confessing that made her heart constrict. She already knew him well enough to know that he would never accept what she was. He was, after all, a man of his times and lived in a small world bound by his strict upbringing and religious beliefs. Jake had been an atheist. Joshua was a full-fledged Christian who went to church every Sunday with his mother and brother. He believed she wasn't a witch, wasn't what the townspeople accused her of being. She left it at that.

She was content and accepted every day as a gift from a somehow sardonically humorous God who let her be sent back into harm's way, just to present her with the long-lost love of her life. A bittersweet happiness.

Her old life in the twentieth century was becoming more the dream with each day. By the second week she could go a whole day and not even think of it. Though she missed her sisters and friends, her pottery, she often found herself smiling blissfully and was always caught off guard by it. There were times when Amanda would look around her, rub her eyes, and shake her head, unable to believe that any of it was real. That she was still there, playing house, playing mother to another woman's children, and falling in love all over again with Jake. It was a miracle. It was hell. And she believed deep down in her soul that there was some *reason* she was there, besides to take Rachel's punishment. That belief kept her sane.

With Maggie's help, Amanda also fixed the windows so they could be opened and shut. She redecorated the cottage as well as she could—with Joshua's help. He was a generous man. In a week it didn't even look like the same dwelling.

She visited Black Pond once out of curiosity, not that she expected to find Rachel there—she didn't. There was nothing there except the supple young willow tree. The serene water and the pond animals. No Rachel, no ghost, just as she had suspected. The place, in all its brooding oppressive silence, was empty, though the mist, as Maggie had warned her, was black and heavy as pea soup. A cursed place even then, Amanda could feel it all around her like a dark cloak. She didn't stay long. If there were any answers to her problem, they weren't there for her to find. Not yet.

Maggie informed her that it was July, though the girl couldn't read and she wasn't sure which day exactly. Amanda made another mental note to teach Maggie how to read, if she was there long enough. The days were scorchers, bright and vividly blue, but the nights were cool under the forest's trees. After she'd been with the children for two weeks, Amanda decided that the next Saturday was the day she'd finally venture into the town marketplace and try to barter away Rachel's jewelry for the other things they needed. She was dying for real sugar to put in her tea. Coffee, if it was available. Flour so she could bake more than cornbread. More plates. Featherbeds for the girls. Amanda was sick of seeing them sleeping on bags of cornhusks. Maggie tried to dissuade her from going into town under the present conditions, but Amanda was determined to begin on Rachel's new reputation as soon as possible. The townspeople must not be allowed to keep believing that she was evil. She had to start somewhere and sometime. Maggie was overruled.

And it was in the second week that the Indians came.

One morning when she opened the door, a wooden bucket in her hands to go for water at the creek, they were standing there before the cottage, staring at her. No telling how long they'd been there waiting. Two braves and a squat, stony-faced woman in white buckskin with pitch-black eyes and hair laced with gray.

One of the braves was the Indian who'd given her the panther-tooth necklace.

"Ma?" Maggie's voice behind her was frightened. "What do they want?" She was cringing behind Amanda in the doorway. She lowered her voice almost to a hoarse whisper and muttered, "They are Pequot. Last spring it was Pequot who massacred the settlers down at Mustang Creek. Every last one. Even the children."

"It's all right, Maggie," Amanda answered, never taking her eyes off the Indians. "They don't mean us any harm." She was sure somehow of that just by the calmness of their movements, the desperation in their faces. They needed something. Help.

The brave she'd met in the woods walked up to her and gestured with his hands toward the woods. His hands air-molded what she believed were teepees or dwellings. Then he pointed at her, himself, and the other two Indians and toward the woods again. His dark velvet eyes were worried. She noticed that he was older than she had thought. There was gray in his hair, too.

"You want me to come with you to your village?" Amanda speculated aloud. He didn't understand. She duplicated his earlier gestures but pointed at herself first.

He nodded solemnly. His expressive hands described a person lying down. He made little circling motions on his skin. A rash? Touched his forehead and acted as if it were very hot. Fever. Someone sick. By the fear in his expression, someone very dear to him.

"Someone is ill back at his village," Amanda explained to Maggie, who was distrustfully peeking out at the Indians, Amadeus in her arms. He jumped down.

"They want me to come."

"Ma, thou art going with them? Savages? What will we do if thee art not allowed to return?" Maggie hissed, grabbing at Amanda's arm as she moved through the doorway toward the Indians.

"Don't worry, Maggie, they won't hurt me. I know they won't." She turned to look down at her charge. "Can you manage here by yourself for a while?"

"Aye. I always have before," the girl retorted, straightening herself up to her full height.

The brave urgently motioned for her to follow as if he was trying to hurry her. The other two Indians were already tromping back into the woods.

"I'll try to be back as soon as I can," Amanda promised, hugging Maggie quickly.

The brave touched his necklaces of feathers and teeth and looked at her bare throat.

The necklace, she thought, *he wants me to put on the necklace.*

"It's in the house," she said, pointing behind her.

He crossed his arms, and waited, his dark eyes impatient.

Putting the bucket down by the door, she reentered the cottage, retrieved the necklace from where she had stashed it away that first night, and slipped it around her neck. She'd need medicines, so she grabbed the egg basket and walked past the Indian toward the cellar with Amadeus underfoot, staying close.

The Indian understood that there was something she needed to collect before they could go. He waited for her as she entered the cellar and searched through the hidden back room with a lit candle until she found what she thought she might need. She had no idea what awaited her at the Indian village, so she took the basic medicines for whatever she might find, hoping that her limited knowledge of the healing arts would suffice. Healing had never been her strong point.

When she came back through the door, the brave tossed one glance back at her and then set out through the trees at a killing pace. She had to run to keep up with him.

Amadeus galloped along behind them to protect her.

It seemed as if she followed the Indians for hours along the sweltering paths and down the dusty trails before they came to their village. It was a small village. Not more than ten or twelve round bark-covered wigwams huddled in a clearing. The thick trees spread a lush canopy of foliage overhead, covering them in shadows, hiding them. She strode behind the brave past the bark dwellings. Even though she could see the other inhabitants of the village, standing or squatting before the other wigwams, it was strangely quiet. Their faces were blank, their eyes full of dread.

Somewhere ahead of her someone was coughing violently.

There were no other signs of life, no children playing, no one working. They were all just watching her as she approached, her eyes down, the basket clenched nervously at her side. A huge blue-gray cat with one ear, sidling along behind her skirts.

Amanda, even without her magic, sensed something was direly wrong here.

Her guide halted before one of the wigwams, pushed the piece of hide used as a door covering to one side, and gestured for her to enter. She did.

Inside, once her eyes became accustomed to the dimness, she found a young woman lying under a fur pelt on a raised wooden structure, moaning. She would have been lovely, but now she was obviously very sick, her face sprinkled with sweat and angry pus-filled sores. Amanda knelt down next to the woman and felt a great surge of pity, compassion. The woman could have been the brave's wife, or even his daughter, she was so young. Once, she had been pretty.

The brave hovered above them like a bright-feathered bird and observed closely everything she did.

She examined the woman with her gaze. Red oozing pustules scarred her skin and fever had turned it a shiny red and coated it in a fine sheen of sweat. She knew enough not to touch her. Whatever she had could be contagious. Amanda wasn't sure, but she feared it could be smallpox. The great killer of these times. It had wiped countless settlers and whole Indian tribes off the face of the earth. A sickness that caused a slow, repulsive death. The victims would sometime slough off whole layers of skin if you tried to so much as turn them over in the later stages of the disease. A hideous way to die. Amanda fretted over where the woman had contracted the disease. How. She prayed it wasn't rampant in the village.

"I think it's smallpox, Amadeus," she asided to her familiar, a large furry shadow crouched in the corner behind her. "It's bad, too. How many more in the village have it?" she asked him. He meowed and shook his head. *None,* it seemed like he was saying but she couldn't be sure. She could no longer talk to him.

She had to make the Indians understand that they were not to come near this woman. If it was smallpox, a virus, then it was highly infectious. The woman had to be quarantined, and then the village had a chance.

Tediously, she sought to make the brave understand what she wanted with hand signals and mime. Using pushing motions at him, at all beyond the wigwam, and gesturing back at her patient, she thought perhaps she had gotten her meaning across when he nodded and silently slipped out the door.

They expected her to heal the woman. Now she understood why the brave had given her the necklace. In their tribe it was the sign of a healer. The brave who had brought her there was the tribe's medicine man, but he had failed to save the woman and was asking for her help. They thought she was a healer. Which wasn't really true. Without her powers, she could only do so much for the woman. But she would try, like with Lizzy, using only her knowledge of the medicinal herbs and her modern-day common sense.

She spent the whole day and that night, caring for the sick woman. Lancing the infected pox, preparing special salve for them, and a sleeping potion so the woman could get the true rest she needed. A potion to bring down the fever. She had all clean clothes and blankets brought in after she'd washed the woman and had burned the filthy bedclothes. Amanda knew that her skills alone wouldn't save the woman, but if she had been healthy before the illness struck, she might yet live. If Amanda could bring down the fever and get her through the night alive, she might make it.

Amadeus helped all he could. He touched the sick woman on the forehead with one of his paws and instantly she calmed, the heat radiating from her skin considerably lowered. Amadeus had little of his magic left, but Amanda knew he'd given the woman some of what he'd had. Maybe it would be enough.

By morning the fever had broken, the woman had come to briefly and fallen back into a real sleep. She'd gotten past the worst of it, Amanda was sure. She might recover now, depending on how great her will to live was. It was in God's hands. Amanda and Amadeus had done all they could do.

Exhausted, as dawn's golden rays tinted the earth, Amanda left the wigwam. The brave was sleeping outside and she woke him. He offered her fresh water out of a gourd. Amanda gulped it down thirstily.

"I think she's going to make it," she said softly, looking back at the wigwam where the girl was sleeping, smiling at him. The smile is what got through to him. *She's all right.*

He reached out and touched her hand gently. His eyes were shining with gratitude and he said something to her in his own tongue. Amanda couldn't understand a word, but she understood his meaning well enough. He was thanking her for saving the woman's life.

"I had help," she answered, still wearing her tired smile, and looked upward. "Now, take me home, please?" she asked, swaying. She was so weary she could have lain down right there and slept for a week. But she had to get back to the children. They must be worried sick over her.

He led her back to the cottage, Amadeus sleeping in her arms, tired, too, and left her.

Maggie was ecstatic to see her back alive and in one piece. Lizzy cried with happiness. Amanda, after she had assured them both she was fine and cleaned herself up with soap and as hot water as she could bear, fell onto her pallet and slept the rest of the day. It was good she did.

That evening as she opened the front door at Joshua's knock, she looked down. Outside, the Indians had left her gifts. Freshly killed rabbits and fur pelts. Payment for her services.

When she met Joshua's eyes, she knew something was wrong.

"What is it?"

"Please, can thee come?" his voice a wretched plea. He reached out a hand toward her. "There be a terrible sickness at the farm. These last two days many of the laborers have come down with it and the physician is busy fighting it in town and will not come."

Smallpox, Amanda thought with a heavy ache in her chest.

"Now my mother has it." He stopped. His huge black horse restless behind him. Animals could sense when their masters were disturbed. Sense when death was nearby.

"They say thee can cure anything. That thee have the power . . ." A strange light gleamed in his troubled brown eyes.

A witch's power, Amanda mused sadly. So Joshua did still believe, in part, that she was what they said she was. What they said *Rachel* was. He was desperate, though. He couldn't help but grasp at any straw he could. Inwardly, Amanda cringed, but kept her face impassive.

"I will come," was all she said. She went to tell the girls she was leaving again, and to gather what she would need for her journey and the task at hand.

Then Joshua, already remounted, pulled her and Amadeus (who insisted on coming along) up into the saddle and they galloped away in the creeping twilight from the small cottage.

Maggie watched them ride away, a grim set to her thin mouth. *Something terrible will come of all this yet*, she thought. *Something terrible*. She had these *feelings* at times. Almost visions. Most of them came true. Though she'd never told a soul about them, especially her absent mother, who would be jealous of her for them. Amanda . . . she hadn't decided yet if or when she would tell her about them. Or the other powers she had begun to acquire these last few years. Until now, she'd always been ashamed of them. Hated them for what she thought they made her. Wicked, like her real mother Until Amanda had come. Now she wondered if possessing powers was as evil a thing as she had believed.

Standing there in the evening's growing shadows, Maggie whispered a prayer that Amanda would return safely. Maggie had grown to love the woman from another time. She recognized a good heart and pure soul when she saw one. Unlike her true mother who could never see anything but blackness and spite. Never be anything but bad. Amanda was different. Amanda was *good*.

Too good to die a senseless death.

Chapter 10

They'd been talking since Rebecca's arrival and they were both fatigued, and disturbed over their absent sister's fate. Outside, the snow was now a full-fledged blizzard descending upon a sleeping Boston, and the large house creaked and moaned as the winds tore at its outer shell. But the kitchen, where Rebecca and Jessica, with bloodshot eyes, conferred over hot coffee at the kitchen table, was warm and cozy.

Rebecca had arrived about eight-thirty that evening on the last plane to slip through before the bad weather. Everything, the man at the departure desk had told her as she'd waited for Jessica to pick her up, was grounded. No more planes would fly in or out again until the weather conditions let up some. Too dangerous. Ice formed on the wings and down they'd go.

John and the girls had gone upstairs fairly soon after Rebecca had gotten to the house. The two sisters wanted to be alone so they could talk freely, and John, knowing what was going on, had taken the girls to watch a late movie on the television up in the den. John couldn't help them with their problem; he knew nothing about witchcraft, though he'd been a believer since the day he'd met Amanda and she'd done her disappearing act right in front of him. He prayed, like

them, that Amanda could be found. John had always
liked Amanda.

By now, as silent as the upstairs was, they were probably all long asleep.

Rebecca had sat stiffly in the chair, her head in her
hands, shaking it back and forth as Jessica recounted
all she knew.

Tituba, Rebecca's familiar, had paced around the table, pulling out his whiskers and acting nuts like he
always did when he thought they were heading for danger of any kind.

Mistress, he had warned her, *sister or no, it's too dangerous for us to be involved with. Something bigger is behind
all this. Not just a renegade witch-wraith. My contacts feel so,
too. REAL evil is behind Amanda's predicament. Big.*

What exactly are you implying? Rebecca had demanded
to know with a tinge of sarcasm as she rolled her eyes.
*Next thing you'll be whining about will be that it's a first-level
demon or even Beelzebub himself, I suppose?*

And, though she hid it, it had unnerved her when
her familiar just glared up at her from the tabletop
with his coal beady eyes and had refused to answer,
swishing his mouse tail back and forth like an angry
whip. Instead, he'd gone back to pacing the rim of the
table, his tiny furry body quivering and bristling with
anxiety.

Rebecca had waited until he got close to the edge
and then with a well-placed flick of her chubby finger,
shoved him neatly off the table. An indignant squeak
and then a burst of angry chattering had dwindled off
into the next room.

"Now you've made him mad," Jessica had said, covering her mouth so as not to laugh. But she hadn't
asked what the two had disagreed about. If Rebecca felt
she should know, she'd tell her.

"He'll get over it," Rebecca had sighed. "He's been

real uptight over this whole thing." Then she had let it drop.

Jessica swiveled her head and was looking out the window at the snow, her face lit strangely by the eerie whiteness.

"You actually think that Amanda's lost somewhere in the seventeenth century?" Rebecca's voice was skeptical when she got back to what they had been talking about before. "Why do you think so?"

"Abigail dreamed it. She's always had this special *connection* with Amanda."

Rebecca's heavy dark brows arched up. She'd known about the bond between Abigail and Amanda and she'd also suspected for quite a while that Abigail was probably psychic, so the news didn't surprise her much. She rubbed her cheek and then pushed her dark hair back from her face. She always took the time to curl her hair, but rarely afterward did she fuss with it, or even comb it. So usually it was a tangled mane going every which way, giving her a wild, crazed appearance.

"I know I don't have powers like you and Amanda, but Abby, I believe, is psychic. Early stages yet, but it's growing. She dreamed of Amanda two nights ago and last night, she told me, and both times Amanda was dressed in long dresses—which isn't really unusual for her—but she was surrounded by people dressed the same way. In a quaint village that was definitely not in our time, Abby said. There were horses, carriages, no cars. Men in tricorne hats with feathers on them. Abby and I went to the library and looked up the costumes for seventeenth century New England and Abby says the clothes were quite similar."

"Well, if Amanda's really gone back in time—which I have never heard of, though that doesn't mean it's not possible—how do you suppose she got there? And what is she doing there?"

"Abigail doesn't know. But I think it has something to do with the black witch, Rachel. The one I've told you all about. Amanda said she'd lived in the seventeenth century and probably had died a violent death. Unjustly executed for being a witch. The legend concerning Rachel and Black Pond, which is sometimes called Witch's Pond, has been around a long time. It might have something to do with that. It's just awful strange that Amanda's haunted and harassed by a long-dead witch named Rachel from the seventeenth century who wants her for something—no one knows what—and suddenly Amanda is tangled up with this sadistic cult, and then she's . . . gone."

"You don't accept that she could just simply be dead?" Rebecca asked.

Jessica winced. "No. For some reason I feel she's still alive. Somewhere. In trouble. Powerless. I think she's calling for help. Our help. Abigail feels the same way."

Rebecca smiled faintly. "I think so, too. I've had glimpses . . ." Her voice faded away, her face closing. She fingered the pentagram at her neck absentmindedly. "Now some of them almost make sense."

Rebecca was silent for awhile as she ate the rest of the roast beef sandwich Jessica had fixed her an hour ago, and watched her sister drink another cup of coffee before she went on.

"And you also believe Amanda annihilated the members of that Satanic cult that took Jonny?"

"Abigail suspects so. And Jane called again to tell me that after Jonny was rushed to the hospital and came to, he talked about it. Said Amanda *saved* him from the cult. Sent fire bolts and incinerated every one of the cowled fiends. Then Ernie, she said, went out to the site and found the charred remains of six bodies, the bloody stone altar, and the knife.

"I myself have no doubt that she did it."

"Amanda has the power, all right, to do such a thing. Never thought she had it in her, though." Rebecca snorted, amazement then concern changing her features. "But I can hardly believe it of her. Amanda knows the Laws better than anyone. She wouldn't do anything wrong, much less take another life. Six lives. Even though they deserved it, after what they did to that boy, and all the others. Still . . ." She shook her head again, a pained look in her eyes.

Even Jessica understood the ramifications of what Amanda had done and her face was unhappy. "There wasn't a sign anywhere of Amanda. But some of the townspeople swear they saw her walk into Black Pond that last night and just *disappear.* They've dragged the pond—no body. No sign of her anywhere."

"Humph." Rebecca seemed lost in thought for a moment or two, and then said, "Amanda's the strongest witch I've ever known . . . but if she had no magic left of her own it could explain how another witch could overpower her."

Outside, the storm whispered, the wind moaned like someone was dying. Upstairs, footsteps echoed as if one of the occupants was up and padding around for some reason. Behind them, the coffeepot grunted and hissed as it perked away.

Rebecca sighed and her hand reached out to touch Jessica's cold hand lying on the table between them. "I've listened closely to everything you've said . . . and, I've got to be honest with you, Sis, it doesn't look good. Not good at all. This is way out of my league. I'm going to have to have some help. Right now, I just don't know where to go to get it. I have to think on it."

It shocked Jessica to see there were tears glistening in her sister's eyes. She had never seen Rebecca cry. Ever. Not over any of her bad marriages or her divorces. Not even when their mother had died.

"I imagine that Rachel somehow got to Amanda when she was vulnerable, perhaps . . . after she, er, had taken care of those Satanists. And cast a spell on her. I've just got to discover which one, and how to break it." She nodded her head, got up to fetch another piece of apple pie, and refilled her coffee cup. She sat back down with a heavy plop. Dressed all in black like she was, she looked like a huge crow.

"I've studied and come across a lot of ghosts and queer beings in my research . . . but none so powerful that they could manipulate a mortal witch from the grave. Especially a witch like Amanda. Now, that takes power. Black witchcraft of the highest level. Never seen anything like it."

In the other room Tituba was still whining and talking frantically to himself. He'd tried to sneak back into the kitchen a couple of times to put his two cents back in, but Rebecca had always lifted her finger and sent him back with a grunt of protest and a whoosh of magic.

"Maybe Tibby knows more than he's telling," Rebecca remarked, her tightened lips and face reflecting her worry.

"What are we going to do, Rebecca?" Jessica exhaled. It'd been a long couple of days since Amanda had first arrived and told her about Rachel; it'd been an even longer day since she'd talked to Rebecca about it all on the phone that morning. She was exhausted and irritable, and upset because she couldn't do anything else to save her sister.

"Well, as soon as this storm lets up, I'm flying out to Canaan and to Black Pond, work some spells, and see what I can find out. The connection with Amanda should be stronger there. The signs of what really happened easier to read. I'm not as good a witch as Amanda was . . . but I'll give it the best I have. I'll

seek help, if I can figure out where to seek it at. There
are some people who can help me, if I have need of
them." *At a price,* she thought somberly. *Always a price,*
especially when dealing with black magic.

"I'll bring her back if I can."

Jessica hadn't forgotten the rivalry between Amanda
and Rebecca. Wounds that had scarred all their child-
hoods. The fights. The cold silences and tension. What
Amanda had said about Rebecca just the last time she
had been there.

Remembering all that, Jessie smiled thoughtfully at
her older sister. "I've always thought Amanda underestimated you, Rebecca. I believe you have power that
you haven't even tapped yet."

Rebecca returned the smile with pleasure, though her
eyes stayed sad. And Jessie thought, as she had many
times before, that she was almost pretty when she
smiled like that. Almost. She just didn't do it often
enough, that's all.

"Sure. You say that because you have a soft spot for
your older sister. Always have. I don't know why. We
both know that Amanda is the gifted one, the beautiful . . . the special one. Always. Mom loved her best.
Everyone loves her best." Rebecca's eyes lowered, but
not before Jessie caught the hurt still festering in them.
After all this time. Not that Amanda had ever treated
her badly. She never had. Even though Rebecca had
played a lot of cruel tricks on her as they were growing
up out of pure spite and jealousy. Amanda had never
repaid in kind. Perhaps Rebecca was remembering that
now, too.

"I feel so bad," Rebecca's voice a whisper as she
looked around them. "So helpless." She pounded her
curled-up fist on the table, making the coffee cups rattle.

"You'll find a way, Rebecca. I know you will. I have faith in you. In the meantime, what can *I* do?"

Rebecca eyed Jessie pensively. "Nothing, right now." Then, seeing her sister's face fall, "I'm not going to lie to you. We're dealing with powerful magic here, Jessica. It's extremely perilous. Soul-losing perilous. Especially to you, a non-witch. I can't take a chance of losing you, too, so I'm going to ask you to just stay out of it for now. Let me handle it. I'm going to have to be clever . . . and very careful. If I make a mistake, it could mean my disappearance, as well. Loss of my immortal soul."

Jessica understood. If a larger evil was mixed up in this, the winner would take all. Satan and his legions collected souls as trophies, not just lives. So there was more at stake than just living and dying. "All right. I'll stay here and wait. Maybe Amanda will try to contact us. Maybe," she mused hopefully, "she might get out of this on her own, yet."

Fat chance of that. Rebecca leaned back in her chair. "Maybe. But I wonder . . ." She seemed suddenly far away.

"Wonder what?"

"Wherever Amanda is, as we discussed before, it's possible that she *is* without her powers. Can't get back. Can't *protect* herself. And, if I'm correct, she's right in the heart of witch-hunting country. Smack dab in the witch-burning times."

Both sisters looked at each other, their faces drained.

Rebecca got up first. "But now we had better get some sleep, Sis. I have a lot of traveling and work to do yet tonight. I need some peace and quiet. And rest. Tomorrow I'm going to need all my strength."

Jessica inclined her head and rose, too.

"I'm frightened for her, you know?" A weak plea.

"I know," Rebecca replied, but thinking to herself

that if Jessica knew what *she* knew about black witch-craft—if she had been a true witch like Amanda and herself—she'd be even more afraid.

The two sisters walked through the dark house and upstairs, arm in arm, each with their own tormenting thoughts as the snow whirled around outside on the night air and the ice-coated trees knocked softly against the frozen windowpanes. It wasn't the kind of weather Rebecca cared much for, especially when there was so much to do. The closed airport hung over her plans like an albatross of doom, and she knew deep inside that she didn't have much time. Not much time at all.

Not that that should matter as much as the rest of it: she hadn't the slightest idea how she was going to find Amanda or, even if she did find her, how she was going to get her back. Didn't know who to go to for help. Not a clue. Everything had been all bluff so far—for Jessica's sake.

I'll think about all that later, she mused tiredly. *Later and tomorrow. I'll grab a little shut-eye and then right after midnight, when magic whispers loudest, I'll send out a call for help. Like an SOS beacon into the night.*

Maybe someone might answer.

Chapter 11

Amanda kneaded the bread dough leisurely, thoroughly, and every so often glanced up to make sure Lizzy wasn't straying too far away. Then the child was at her skirts, tugging and laughing up at her like a little imp. Her round chubby face glowing with health and happiness. Her lengthening blond hair wispily plaited down the back in a miniature replica of the braid Amanda sometimes wore.

"Mama . . . Mama." The child giggled and held on tighter as Amanda tried to playfully smear flour on her cheeks.

"I am gonna get you!" Amanda laughed back and pretended to chase the girl around the table with her floury hands. Lizzy ducked and slid under the table, to peer up gleefully at her from her cave as Amanda made a great deal over looking for her.

The child was a different child than the one she had first met. Now there was no more fright in her face when Amanda picked her up. No more distrust or melancholy. Maggie, too, had changed. For the better.

Amanda had begun to take them for long walks in the cooler evenings as the summer died, holding Lizzy's tiny hand and Maggie's and leading them through the woods, talking to them about particular plants that they passed, and their medicinal properties. She presented

Lizzy with flowers and pebbles to touch and hold in her small hands as Amanda explained what they were and their colors. Lizzy loved the walks and so did Maggie, and often during the walks Maggie would still ask for stories about Amanda's time and friends, never tiring of hearing about them.

"Our real mother never took us for walks. Never had time for talking and sharing. She never wanted to bother with Lizzy," Maggie had mumbled one time, and the words *or me,* unspoken, had lingered on the warm air anyway. "The way Lizzy be and all. Her blindness." Then she'd looked ashamed for saying such a thing.

Amanda had begun to question if Lizzy was completely blind. She discovered that she was able to see shapes, at least blurred outlines.

Lizzy wanted to be with Amanda all the time. She'd even started crawling into bed with her at night and Amanda would cuddle her until she fell contentedly asleep.

The child came out from under the table, toddled into Amanda's arms, and hugged her close. "Love Mama," the child cooed, as Amanda rocked her gently in her arms.

Tears rose in Amanda's eyes at the words. The little girl really loved her.

Lizzy released her and crawled off to play with one of the cloth dolls Amanda had sewed for her. Dusting off her hands, Amanda strolled over to the door to gaze out into the woods, her thoughts turning more serious.

She'd been here in the past for over a month now. It seemed like a lifetime ago that she had been Amanda Givens. Alone. Her life had changed so dramatically. She looked back fondly at Lizzy as she rocked her cloth doll with the yellow yarn hair and blue button eyes. Until Amanda had come, she'd never even had a doll of any kind or much of anything, as far as Amanda could tell. Rags for clothes and bugs for pets. An absent mother and little caring. Under her tender care and good cooking, both children were blooming like wild roses, Lizzy a fragile yellow rose and Maggie a blood-red rose. They'd filled out, laughed more, and worked hard to please her.

With her hands she smoothed down the new soft gray dress she'd finished for herself just the night before. A white cloth bonnet, similar to some of the caps she'd seen women wearing that first morning in town, covered her head and the prim bun she wore her hair in these days, and tied under her chin. She'd done a fine job with the dress and couldn't wait for Joshua to see her in it.

Joshua. She no longer thought of him as Jake. He was Joshua. A complete and independent person in his own right. A man she loved now with every fiber of her being.

Weeks ago she'd helped nurse his family through the smallpox. His brother, weakened in body and soul by his earlier experiences at the hands of the witch-hunters, hadn't made it, but Joshua's mother and a good deal of his workers had. Joshua, even in his grief, believed that she had been the one to turn the sickness away with her herbs, her caring. Her magic. And wouldn't listen to anything she said to the contrary. He would be forever in her debt, he'd promised her.

And, like a miracle, the smallpox took no more victims. The town itself had been spared. When Amanda was sure it was safe, she'd gone back to Rachel's cottage, to the children and her new life.

Rebecca had been a lot on her mind lately and she wondered why. Maybe, she'd speculated, she was much on Rebecca's mind. For the first time in her life, Amanda wished that she and Rebecca had been closer, like she and Jessie. She found she missed both of them more than she would have thought.

Her new life had made Amanda both happy and sad, but she'd stopped feeling guilty weeks ago. She was still there and nothing had changed. Except that she was happier than she had ever been. How dare she be happy. But she was. Amanda sighed softly and canted her head to watch Lizzy play with her doll.

She had Joshua and she had the children. A roof over their heads and food in their bellies. All was well, except . . .

Their endeavor at bartering off Rachel's jewelry in the marketplace a few Saturdays before had reaped an unexpected and alarming harvest. The day had begun well enough, though the townspeople had hung back, barely acknowledging her and the children. Yet with her appropriate clothes, carefully spoken speeches, and demure smiles, she'd eventually coaxed a couple of the merchants in their stalls to trade the pieces of jewelry for a priceless ten-pound cone of white sugar called a *loaf,* more tea and coffee, and featherbed mattresses for all of them. The sugar, tea, and coffee she'd carried away with her, but the mattresses she left to be picked up later by Joshua in his buckboard, per an earlier arrangement she'd made with him. The merchant knew Joshua well, he'd said. The whole town did. So that venture had gone well.

But it was the chance encounter she'd had with the infamous witch-hunter, Sebastien Goodman, and his friends, late in the afternoon that had ruined and sullied the day and had given Amanda nightmares ever since.

Thank goodness she hadn't taken Amadeus along. That would have been even more suspicious-looking. People had been burned to death just for having an animal that could be considered a witch's familiar. And

Amadeus, with his arrogant behavior, wouldn't have helped matters.

She and the girls had just begun their trip home and were walking alongside the main street, with their packages clutched tightly in their arms, when a gaunt man in a dark cloak rode by on a bony horse with three other men.

When the men slowed down their mounts to come abreast of her and the girls, Amanda had looked up and, with a foreboding shiver, met the man's manic eyes hidden in the darkness of his hood. Saw his face as he glared down at her and the cowl slid back.

That face . . . that face was someone she *knew.* Instant feelings of doom and chilling terror had lodged firmly in her chest, heavy as stone, and no amount of telling herself that she had no reason to be frightened would dislodge it. It had clung like a leech, sucking the strength from her and making her behave like an idiot.

Amanda had quickly lowered her head and pretended to go on her way, dragging Lizzy and Maggie behind her.

Then the man astride the horse had spoken to her and she'd been obliged to stop, raise her head, and answer against the silent warning screaming in her head the whole time.

"A woman alone should not be unescorted out in public. It be unseemly, Madame," he'd drawled, as his horse had come abreast of her, tugging at its bit and snorting as it pawed the ground. "Where be thy husband?"

His three friends, all dressed like him in somber-colored clothes and cloaks, stared down at her coldly, but seemed content to let the other man do all the talking.

"I have no husband, sir," she'd replied carefully. The less she said, the better. She just wanted to get away from them.

"What be thy name?" She'd noticed he had a cruel voice to go with his cruel eyes. A smile full of arrogance and threat, and more of a scowl than a smile, showing a mouthful of bad teeth, a curse of the times.

"Rachel Coxe," Amanda had replied; her heart had been beating so wildly in her chest, it'd made her dizzy. She'd had to support herself against Maggie to keep from swaying like a drunkard.

The man had been leaning over her from his horse's saddle, squinting at her in the falling shadows, taking stock of her as if she were a bug under a microscope— one he wanted to dissect. His companions had ogled her in silence. All four of them put her in mind of drab-feathered vultures. Their noses beakish, their faces humorless, and their stares predatory. There'd been a sly viciousness about all of them that had made Amanda, always attuned to the good or evil in people, cringe immediately. They'd made the hair on the back of her neck rise.

The man had smiled wider at her name, his pretentious gaze had flicked across her and the two children, and then slyly around them at the people who were already gawking. He'd liked the attention.

Amanda had also recognized the fear in those faces before they'd turned swiftly away.

"Mistress Rachel Coxe it be, then?" His face had screwed up as he'd seemed to search his mind for something, and then his eyes glittered wickedly. "Aye, I know of thee. Thy reputation has preceded thee."

She'd sensed something very dangerous about them. Their intense scrutiny of her wasn't normal.

The man continued to study her for a second or two longer in the same strange way as he calmed his nervous horse with a slap of the riding crop he'd held in one hand.

Get away from them. Now, her mind sang.

"Excuse us, sir. We were just leaving," Amanda had said respectfully, her eyes traveling past him to the other dour-faced men with him. "It be late."

He'd ignored that, too. He maneuvered his horse before her so she couldn't leave. His eyes had roved away from her and the girls, toward the setting sun, and then back to her expressionless face.

A hint of importance tinged his gruff voice as he leaned down closer to her and mouthed, "They say there be many witches in Canaan causing decent God-abiding folk to tremble in their beds at night. Laying evil spells and hurting the good people of this town.

"I have come to rid the town of them and bring God's grace back to this accursed place." His sudden declaration had cut her like a knife. Then abruptly, he'd sat up straight in the saddle and had grinned down at her startled face.

"I am known by the name Sebastien Goodman, witch-hunter of some fame . . . do thee know of me?"

Sebastien! The witch-hunter. The beast who had imprisoned and tormented Joshua's poor brother . . . and nameless others.

Amanda had simply shaken her head, so angry and unsettled she hadn't trusted herself to speak. Here was the worst of all her nightmares come true . . . in living, breathing flesh right before her. Like a monster come suddenly to life. It had made her want to run away screaming in panic; it'd taken every ounce of strength she could muster not to.

"I have just come from the coast cities." He'd tossed his head, his straggly, greasy hair fluttering in the slight breeze. "And proud to say that there be no witches left from whence I have come. I have imprisoned or hung them all. God will not abide a witch to live, so they say, and I am God's man." He'd laughed sadistically, then, enjoying her obvious discomfort. The man enjoyed inflicting fear and pain.

Catching her off guard, he'd dismounted from his horse and had faced her, grabbing her hands viselike in his so she couldn't escape. He was a tall, thin man who'd towered over her; up close, his face was ravaged with pockmarks and his breath foul—like his heart.

"Are thee one of *them*, Mistress? A witch?" he'd come right out and asked her boldly. His eyelid drooped lower over his left eye than the other, giving him a deceptively lazy, harmless look.

"Nay, sir," Amanda had whispered back, gritting her teeth, trying to keep her terror from showing. She'd *wanted* to scratch his eyes out. Instead, she'd kept her gaze lowered in a pretension of humility. Any sign of rebellion would only have incited the madness in such a man.

He'd reached out to touch her face, nodding at what she'd said, and then had murmured in a dead voice, "But beware, Mistress, if thou be not what thee say. God despises liars and will punish the guilty." His eyes had had that glow again.

Amanda, realizing he was truly insane, had finally snapped out of her trance, yanking her hand from his grasp, and had moved away from him as if he were a leper.

But she'd been careful to cover her loathing and her dismay under an icy face. To have let him seen her fear would have been like signing her own death warrant. He'd been waiting for that.

"Then I am sure God will protect me, as I am what I say I am," she'd managed right before she'd rushed off down the street and away from him and his friends.

She'd heard laughter as she urged the girls on faster toward home.

"Good day to thee, Madame. We shall meet again,

Mistress Coxe, be sure of it," he'd yelled from behind her. From his lips, it'd sounded like a threat, pure and simple.

It was only then she'd known she should never have given him her true name. God, what had she done?

If only she'd still had her powers! But she didn't, so instead, she'd fled from the marketplace and the silent crowds, shaking so hard, she could hardly keep her teeth from chattering.

At first, she'd been afraid he'd follow her, so with Maggie leading the way, they'd swiftly disappeared into the nearest alleyway and had scurried home as inconspicuously as they could manage.

But he didn't follow. He didn't need to, did he? He knew her name.

A frown settled on Amanda's face at the memory of the witch-hunter and their meeting. Since then, she had placed his evil face.

Impossible as it seemed, he'd looked like the high priest of the cult that had taken Jonny . . . his face the face of the demon she'd destroyed that night almost three hundred years in the future. And the knowledge terrified her. Was Sebastien a man or a demon? She didn't know.

But that incident with the witch-hunter and his magistrates had been weeks ago. She'd told Joshua all about it. Yet nothing had come of it. So perhaps she was safe. Yes, perhaps it was all right. Her growing reputation as a healer and a good woman, and Joshua's patronage, must be protecting her.

Amanda went back to the table and finished the loaves of bread and laid the pans carefully on the grate she had fashioned over their hearth fire. It was as if she had been born to this time. Everything she'd learned so eagerly years ago from Jake and by doing things herself as a way of going back to the land held her in good stead here. She fit in and found she even liked it. She liked the hard work. The sense of accomplishment.

She made her way outside into the stifling heat, after taking Lizzy's hand to draw her along, and went behind the cottage to check on their growing garden. She wondered wistfully what the townspeople did think of her. The tongues surely had been wagging night and day since her visit to town. Had they softened toward her at all since they had seen that she cared so well for the children? Had helped so many people? Maybe. She hoped so.

Amanda shaded her eyes with one hand and smiled as she watched Lizzy playing in the tomatoes—smiled as she thought of Joshua. He would be with her again tonight. Like most nights.

She knelt down to do her daily weeding. The garden was also thriving with her expert, loving care, and she was planning to plant some late summer crops, starting tomorrow.

Who knows, she chuckled to herself as she stared at the brilliant summer blue sky and wiped the sweat from her brow, she might become a full-fledged farmer and plant a field of tobacco or corn or anything. Get some pigs and some cattle. Joshua would help her. She could even add another room on to the cabin so Maggie and Lizzy could have their own bedroom. She was sure she could swing a hammer well enough to do the job.

The Canaan she had known just months ago never seemed so far away. Though she still fretted over poor Mabel and what her family was going through over her disappearance, there was nothing she could do about it. She prayed for all of them, as well as herself.

As she poked and tugged at weeds and threw out rocks, Amanda daydreamed about all the things she still had to do. She might never be able to go home. Maybe she'd have to stay here forever. Except for that meeting

with Sebastien, she didn't miss her powers much anymore. Her old life and her powers in exchange for all
this. Lately it had seemed a fair trade.

She gazed at Lizzy and sang happily to herself a song
that Maggie had taught her. The child had Amadeus
in her lap and was stroking him. Amanda could almost
hear his purring from where she was. It seemed the
longer she was without her magic the less she understood Amadeus. She could tell at times he was angry
with her because he couldn't communicate. At times,
he seemed to be trying to tell her something. But she
could no longer understand.

Sometimes she felt sorry for him.

It was late when the knock came at her door that
night, long after she'd given up hope of him coming.

"Rachel, let me in, it be Joshua."

Glad as always to see him, she fell into his open arms,
but what he had to say made her body go stiff and her
mind reel again with a feeling of *déjà vu*.

"I was in town this night on business and heard the
rumors in the Blue Boar Tavern. 'Tis talked of everywhere about Sebastien Goodman, the many arrests, and
the trials that are to begin soon. The jail be full of
accused witches already and each day more are dragged
before . . . Sebastien's inquisition."

Amanda pulled away as he slumped down onto one
of the new wooden chairs he'd made for them. He was
shaking, and in the light of the hearth fire, his eyes
were full of hate. His handsome face was as threatening
as a storm cloud. He yanked off his three-cornered hat
and laid his musket against the rim of the table. "It
also be rumored that they are torturing the poor creatures to extract their confessions, just as my brother
once told me of," Joshua spat.

"When I first heard the stories of the atrocities in-flicted on the victims . . . I could hardly believe . . . now with what I have been hearing . . ." he muttered, covering his face with his hands. Between his fingers came, "My good brother was right—God rest his sweet soul—that Sebastien be not human."

Amanda felt a tingle of dread run up her spine, re-membering who Sebastien had reminded her of. A de-mon.

She stood rigid above him. "What else, Joshua?" Amanda closed the door quietly so as not to wake the girls. The candle on the table had burned down to nearly nothing.

He met her eyes and she saw him flinch. He hated having to tell her. He reached up with a large, work-worn hand and caressed her face tenderly. His long chestnut-colored hair was drawn back in a ponytail. A queue they called it. He was dressed in his nicest town clothes. A broadcloth long jacket, white linen shirt, and tight fawn-colored breeches tucked into chocolate-hued tall boots. His mustache had recently been trimmed. She knew that when he kissed her next, it would prickle her skin.

"They have posted a list of more suspected witches he wants brought in immediately for . . . questioning. He is giving them the chance to come in on their own and submit themselves to *God's will,* as he puts it," his voice scornful. His hand took hers and squeezed pro-tectively.

"Thy name, Rachel," he said with horror, "be at the top of the list."

Shocked, Amanda could only stare at him empty-faced. Speechless. Then the anger began to seep in. *Next thing he's going to say is that I should leave town. Like Ernie advised months ago. No, centuries from now.*

He misunderstood her muteness and smiled bravely

up at her. "Do not lose sleep over it, Rachel. Do not be afraid. Thee are safe. I plan to petition the chief magistrate to have thy name dropped from the list. I know him well and we are friends, and I am sure he will oblige me. Thee are no evil witch, but a healer. Aye, and I would fight any man who says different." He angrily pounded his fist against his muscled thigh.

Then he gathered her gently into his strong arms, settled her onto his lap, soothed her, whispered lovingly into her hair words meant to reassure her. But Amanda gazed at something only she could see, preoccupied with truths he would never be able to comprehend.

From the murky corner of the cottage where he was curled in the arms of a sleeping child, Amadeus was awake, listening, his cat's eyes glowing like two yellow embers.

So fate would have its way, she thought, follow its preordained path, no matter what she did. The whole thing was almost amusing. Rachel had been thought a witch. She was thought a witch. Rachel had been accused of witchcraft and so she shall be accused. And Rachel had . . . there her mind stopped dead in its tracks, refusing to go any further, like a stubborn old mule.

She could still change history, if she tried, couldn't she?

Could she? And there were really only two alternatives: To run away or to stay and fight for the life she had come to cherish.

Joshua was still talking and she slowly began to come back, closer, to understand the words. "He shall not touch thee, my Rachel, that I promise. I shall stand by thee and make sure no one hurts thee. I have much standing in the community. Surely they must listen to me before a stranger so hated as he be."

So feared as he be, Amanda's mind supplied. If Sebastien really decided she was a witch, could Joshua save her? Could anyone?

Amanda had been lulled these last weeks into believing she was too smart to fall into any trap, that she could change Rachel's gruesome fate. Now she wondered if she could. If she dared to try. She was scared. She'd be a fool not to be. Without her powers she was helpless. Just as Rachel had wanted her to be. And she'd grown too fond of the children to endanger them—or leave them. Too much in love with Joshua. She was caught right in the middle.

She had the needling premonition that if she stayed here she'd have to *prove* her innocence. That would be hard, but it was possible. She'd been so good since she'd arrived. Had taken loving care of Rachel's children. Her reputation had changed in the community. Was changing still. Since she'd nursed the Indian woman and Joshua's people during the smallpox, since she'd stopped creating mischief as the real Rachel had, people spoke of her differently, Joshua had told her. She'd even had hesitant visitors to the cottage (usually at night when they wouldn't be seen) the last week, asking for potions or advice on this malady or that. She'd given out cold remedies and fixed poultices, prescribed what would bring down their children's fevers, end their coughs, and cure their arthritis. The townspeople were surely aware of her new compassion. Her caring. That should count for something, shouldn't it?

But in the wee hours of the night long after Joshua had left her, she lay tossing on her featherbed, trying to capture sleep. Debating with herself whether she should run away or stay and fight. Fear had settled like a heavy yoke on her shoulders but the unreality of the whole situation and her safe twentieth-century thinking kept her from believing that the worst could happen to her.

If she left, where would she go? She had no money.

The jewelry was gone and there was nothing left to barter, except what they grew in the gardens and that only for a few more weeks. Winter was coming around the bend. Hard currency was almost nonexistent to the poor of these times.

And she'd have to take the children with her because her running away would be a sure sign of guilt, and Sebastien might harm the girls if she left them behind. A lot of the witch-hunters of the time were known to destroy not just witches but what they called the witch's spawn. They'd kill the children like unwanted mongrel pups, and with no mercy.

Lizzy and Maggie were just beginning to be healthy. If they ran someone might come after them. How could she subject them to a life on the road, running and hiding like common criminals? And lastly, how could she leave Joshua now that she had found him? She couldn't, she just couldn't. Not unless she was *absolutely* sure she was in real danger.

Sebastien only wanted to question her. Surely she could handle that; could she handle him? She was no longer a witch, she had no powers, so how could he make any of the charges—whatever they might be—stick? She had nothing to hide. She'd done nothing wrong. Then again, perhaps Joshua could sway the chief magistrate to intercede on her behalf. At least there was hope.

She had time yet, she thought.

In this Amanda made her gravest mistake. She didn't realize how short her time would be.

Still agonizing over what she should do, she eventually found sleep, but she imagined she could hear Rachel laughing at her again from somewhere. Wherever she was.

Chapter 12

No one answered Rebecca's SOS that night at Jessie's. Nor the next night, as she was waiting for the snow to stop and the airport to reopen. So, for now, she was on her own. Maybe the clues would come more readily concerning her sister's whereabouts once she was back in Canaan.

Two mornings later, Rebecca checked into one of Canaan's Holiday Inns so she'd have a base of operations, a bed, and a shower when she needed it. She was still tired what with the small amount of sleep she'd allowed herself back in Boston in the last few days and the catnap she'd stolen while in the air on the plane. But there was no time for any more sleep. She had a lot to do if she wanted to discover what had happened to her sister.

The first thing Rebecca had to do was get out to Black Pond and go into trance at the last site where Amanda had been seen; use all of her limited witch's powers to find out what she could. She'd never cursed her lack of skill more than she did now. Oh, she had always been jealous of Amanda's great natural gifts, but she had learned to compensate in her life for not having them. She'd worked hard; studied her craft and its every facet in a scholarly fashion; her knowledge was impressive, but she still couldn't do half the things

Amanda had been able to do. She was a handicapped
witch. She smiled whenever she thought of the term,
but it was appropriate. Though she wasn't envious of
her sister any longer. She'd gotten over that years ago.

So Amanda had been able to project herself anywhere in the world and heal people with the touch of
her hands, and under limited situations, see the future
or the past and weave great spells . . . but Rebecca was
the famous one with all the money in her bank account
and public recognition. That was what she'd wanted all
along. She'd learned over the last few years to be content with that. That was what made her happy.

She enjoyed her life now. Since she'd dumped her
last loser husband, Frank, she'd begun to see herself
differently. And she had begun to discover that just having a man—any man—didn't make you a woman. That
she hadn't known herself at all, and she'd decided from
now on she would remedy that. She wondered if Jessica
and Amanda knew she'd changed. That, at forty years
old and after five husbands and countless lovers, Rebecca was finally satisfied with herself and her life.

Mulling over the last year, as she had flown high over
Connecticut earlier, with Tibby quietly tucked away in
her coat pocket, she knew she would no longer have
traded places with Amanda for anything. Especially now.
Rebecca was a lot smarter than others gave her credit
for. She'd come to see that those who had the greatest
magic were often the malevolent targets of the black
powers and were always in danger of losing it. Amanda's
present predicament was a case in point. Amanda had
something that someone else desired and would kill for
to obtain. And if Amanda was without her magic, as
Rebecca conjectured, how exposed she must feel.

Rebecca had come to understand something else,
too . . . knowing Amanda was in dire trouble had

jolted her into looking at her innermost feelings for her younger sister.

The love bond, though often strained in the past, was stronger than she'd given it credit. Yes, the sibling rivalry was what had initially formed Rebecca, painfully but solidly, into the very person she was today. It had finally dawned on her, that without someone as special as Amanda for a rival, she wouldn't have strived so to get to where she was today. A success.

The truth was, she'd always loved—no—adored Amanda since they'd been scrawny children back in that house of witches. There wasn't anyone else in the world like her younger sister. Amanda was special.

Even as children, looking back, Amanda had never lorded her greater powers over anyone, least of all Rebecca, who had wanted so badly to be as good or better than her. Amanda had always taken her unique gifts for granted. Given them away generously—for nothing—just for the pleasure of making other people happy, and had been nothing but loving and considerate toward Rebecca.

We aren't Gypsies, she'd maintain adamantly, her sea-green eyes flashing. *We are witches, Sister. True witches. Witches don't sell their gifts for mere coins.*

Ah, Amanda! So naive. So well-meaning. So *good.*

Rebecca slowly rose from the motel bed and dressed warmly in heavy jeans and layers of sweaters under her coat. Thick gloves and a pulled-down woolen cap.

Tibby wasn't speaking to her anymore, he was so angry that she was going through with her stupid plan to save Amanda. That was the only bad thing about her familiar, he didn't have much of a heart. But, in the end, with an exasperated groan, he refused to be left behind and scurried into her coat pocket where he continued to berate her intelligence and be a bodiless nag.

There was ice forming on all the trees outside the

hotel and layering the windowpanes. The forecast called for snow here in the next few hours and she had to get out to Black Pond. Wherever in the hell that place was. Out in the damn woods somewhere. Why did Amanda have to live out in the middle of a godforsaken wilderness, anyway? Never could understand that. And with her luck, she'd be out stomping around through the toolies during another blizzard. It had followed her from Boston, no doubt.

She'd have to get Ernie or Jane to show her where Black Pond was. Boy, she couldn't wait.

Then she'd have to try to command up the black witch, Rachel, from her watery grave, confront her, and trick her into divulging where Amanda was. Beat her at her own game. Find Rachel's weakness and break the powerful spell she had cast on her sister—and bring Amanda back.

Rebecca knew as she knocked on Jane's door a little while later that if she didn't succeed it would mean Amanda's death.

"Jane Weatherby?" Rebecca asked the short woman with the leery brown eyes, standing before her in the open door.

"Yes?" Hesitantly. The hand brushed curly red hair back from a pretty face. A tall older-looking man came to pose protectively behind the woman, hand on her shoulder, and examined Rebecca, as well.

He stepped up front and demanded, "What do you want? If you're selling something, we don't want it." His voice was deep, curt, and firm. Unwelcoming eyes.

Rebecca's eyes had turned back to the woman, ignoring the man. "Jane, I'm Rebecca Givens. Amanda's older sister? I'm here to find her. Will you help me?"

"Rebecca?" The two had never actually met. Tears of relief suddenly flooded the other woman's eyes and without further ado, she reached out a hand and yanked Rebecca into the house.

"Oh, thank God Jessie found you . . . and you're here. I'm so frightened for Amanda! She's been missing for five days, and we know"—her eyes glanced up to the man's softening face—"that she's in terrible danger.

"And yes, we'll help," she breathed. "Ernie and I would do anything for her." She leaned back against the man with his hands on her shoulders.

"She saved my Jonny from those awful, wicked cult people, and somehow got rid of them. I owe her more than I can ever repay. The whole town does. If not for Amanda, my son would be dead and probably scores of others." The woman was crying openly now and the man was inspecting Rebecca, searching her face for traces of the Amanda he knew. He eventually smiled at her encouragingly. Amanda was his friend, too.

"Good." Rebecca smiled for the first time. "We have to talk first. There's a hell of a lot I need to ask both of you."

"All right. We'll talk over fresh coffee and something to eat?" Jane offered kindly. "You look hungry and exhausted to me, Rebecca."

Rebecca was thankful. "You're right—on both counts. I haven't had any breakfast yet, either, come to think of it, and I'm starved. So that would be great. I could use a cup of hot coffee. It was freezing hiking over here from the hotel. Don't go to any real trouble, though."

"It's no trouble, believe me," Jane said as she led her through her ceramic shop and back into a small, cozy kitchen and put on the coffeepot.

"How is Jonny doing?" Rebecca questioned first thing.

"He's doing well," Jane replied, her face tender at mention of her son. "The doctors said there'll be some

scars. Physical as well as emotional . . . but that he'll
recover in time. He's still in the hospital, and my other
boys are still with their grandmother." She gave Rebecca a soft smile as she got some things from the re-
frigerator. "Mom thought I needed a few days of rest."

"I'm really glad your son is OK," Rebecca responded.
"I know how dear he was, all the boys are, to my sister."

Rebecca turned to the man and shoved out her hand
for him to shake. "Hi. You're the mailman? Ernie,
right?"

"Right." He nodded in affirmation.

"Amanda wrote me all about you in her letters."
Jake's friend. But she didn't have to say that; he knew
she knew.

Rebecca settled down in one of the chairs with a tired
sigh, Ernie next to her, watching her with an amused
twist to his lips. He'd never met anyone who looked
more like a witch in his life. In the last few days since
Amanda's disappearance and what he'd seen at Black
Pond, he'd been doing a lot of thinking about what
Jake had once said about Amanda's being a real witch;
about what Amanda had revealed, and then Jane and
Mabel. He'd never believed in witches and such before,
but things had sure gotten weird lately. Real weird. And
somebody had cremated those cult members into piles of
ash and gritty rubble.

Then Rebecca's familiar crawled out of the pocket of
her coat, which she'd hung from the back of her chair,
climbed up and sat perched on her shoulder. Ernie's
eyes widened as the tiny ebony mouse glared through
Rebecca's wild hair at him with beady eyes, his whiskers
twitching, and winked at him. Looked at him as if the
creature was fully cognizant of everything that was going on. Like it had intelligence. Ridiculous.

"My familiar, Tituba," Rebecca introduced him to

Ernie and Jane, smiling. Seeing Ernie's open mouth, she added, "He won't bother us. He just wants to listen. So he can help." Which wasn't quite true. Tibby liked to make mischief as much as magic and soon he was aggravating Ernie by appearing and reappearing first in one place and then, a poof later, in another. It seemed to drive Ernie nuts. As if he couldn't believe his eyes, but then couldn't not.

Jane, who seemed to accept Tibby quicker than her boyfriend, made the coffee and threw on some fat slabs of bacon before she started recounting her story. About Jonny's abduction by the cult, the search, and how the town mistakenly chased Amanda to the pond after burning her cabin to the ground. Jane's fears over Amanda's continued absence. Everything.

Rebecca's face was grim as she listened, but it felt good to be sitting with Amanda's friends around her, people who knew who and what she was and what was at stake. Not just some of her witchcraft-crazy fans wanting something from her. These were real people. Friends that she knew well from all of Amanda's chatty letters. The comfortable surroundings, and the smell of bacon frying and coffee brewing, hung sweet on the air, and Rebecca, even though the subject they were discussing was serious, felt like she was in heaven.

She'd been on the road far too long, Rebecca thought cynically, when a home-cooked meal could mean so damn much.

After this was over, observing the homey kitchen and how expertly Jane had broken the eggs into the frying pan and had popped some rolls made from scratch into the oven, maybe she should see about settling down some. A home of her own. Maybe, even buy a house around here somewhere. Darn, if this was where Amanda really wanted to live, if she cared for these people that much, it must have its good points. Sisters should stick together, shouldn't they? Especially when they both lived alone.

A house all her own . . . hum . . . it had never appealed to her before and yet . . . now suddenly it did. She was sick of living out of suitcases. She was sick, to tell the truth, of being a celebrity witch. Sitting backstage at talkshows and being stared at by so-called stars with about as much brains and off-screen personality as cantaloupes. Lounging before radio microphones still half-asleep because it was earlier than a human being should ever have to get up and having every nutcase in the world call and ask the most stupid questions—was that really living?

"Tell me all about . . . Rachel. The legend of Black Pond," Rebecca finally requested as they ate.

Ernie and Jane exchanged looks but it was Ernie who answered.

"I don't know everything about Rachel and the legend, just what I've heard through the years. But after Amanda disappeared I went to see another friend of hers. Mabel."

"The old lady in the trailer?" Rebecca tossed in.

"Yeah," Ernie said. "I was hoping Amanda, scared at what the townspeople had done, was maybe hiding out there. But she wasn't, of course. That's when Mabel told me about Amanda—and Rachel's visitations to her. Told me all about it. It seems impossible. A vindictive ghost and all."

Witches seem impossible to most non-witches, too, Rebecca thought, amused, as she recognized the look in Ernie's steel-gray eyes as he talked to her. The man still didn't completely believe in Amanda or her. Or ghosts. Yet.

At that moment Tibby appeared on Ernie's arm and when Ernie neglected to notice him fully, the mouse nipped him and then scuttled away down his leg, chuckling. Ernie just stared after him like *he'd* seen a ghost.

Then he scratched the side of his head and grinned in embarrassment as if he'd just decided that he liked the little fellow, after all. Then, without skipping a beat, he finished what he had begun to say before Tibby's little stunt.

"But Mabel's a pretty level-headed old gal. Not prone to fancies. So it's hard not to believe her."

Rebecca paid careful attention to everything Jane and Ernie had to say, filing away anything she thought would be of importance later. Sometimes a puzzled glint wavered in her eyes, or dismay, surprise, and sometimes even alarm as they unfolded their tale.

They'd done their homework and had talked to a lot of people in their search for Amanda. They still didn't know what had really happened to their friend. There was no body in Black Pond. The sheriff had conducted a thorough investigation prompted by the townspeople's guilt. No body. Nothing.

When they were finished with their story and the food, Rebecca was studying the ceiling, burdened with knowledge and conclusions that she alone had patched together.

"Where is Amanda?" Jane broke into her reverie. "I know you have your suspicions, don't you?"

Rebecca slid her eyes from the ceiling to Jane's face. "Jane, if I told you, you wouldn't believe it. So let's just say that she isn't where she's supposed to be, and that if I'm right about everything . . . it'll be a hell of a story.

"And, yes, I'll tell you all about it—when it's over." *If I'm still here and alive myself,* Rebecca thought, letting out a great sigh, and then slowly stood up to pull her sweaters, coat, gloves, and cap back on. The talk was over. She'd learned all she was going to learn from Ernie and Jane. Now it was showtime.

"You have a car?" she asked Jane.

"Yes," Jane said, her eyebrows raising in a question. "Can I borrow it and one of you to get out to Black Pond?"

"Of course," she agreed. "But we're going with you, Rebecca. We want to help." Jane's eyes were determined as Ernie took Jane's small hand in his to show his support.

"I only need one of you to drop me off near Black Pond. Direct me toward it. And you don't come with me. You stay in the car and wait. I don't have a car, and I don't know where it is. Just one of you." She looked at Ernie. Ernie, Rebecca had observed, was the strongest of the two. Whether he knew it or not, he had an inner strength that would protect him far better than Jane.

"You, Ernie. I'm afraid it's too dangerous for Jane in her . . . condition."

Ernie didn't notice Jane's shocked expression; he was still looking at Rebecca. So the moment slid by.

"But she saved my son's life," Jane insisted strongly. "And Amanda's my friend, too—"

Rebecca cut her off with a sharp gesture. "Jane, you've helped enough already. I think you've given me what I need . . . to go after Amanda. And I don't want either of you going along for another reason. There are things I need to do and I won't be able to do them if I have to protect you two. You and Ernie have no concept of what we're really up against here—and you have absolutely no defenses against it—but I do. I'm a witch," she said with obvious pride for maybe the first time in her life. "I'm the only one who can fight Rachel on her own terms. I don't want any more people in harm's way than need be," Rebecca finished, turning serious eyes on them both.

But the truth was: *Rachel would kill both of them quicker than a person would step on a fly that was bugging them,*

Rebecca thought glumly to herself. *And she didn't want their deaths on her conscience if she failed.*

They didn't give her any more trouble. Jane took her car keys from her purse and handed them to Ernie.

"I'm ready to go anytime you are, Rebecca." He grinned, shrugging into his coat, and kissing Jane good-bye lightly on her lips. She still looked like she needed another week's rest. "We'd better hurry, too. Worse weather and subzero temperatures are heading this way even as we speak. You wouldn't want to be caught out in the storm that's coming."

Which storm? Rebecca pondered, thinking not only of the weather, but of Rachel.

"Good luck. Be careful, Rebecca. I pray you find out what happened to Amanda. I pray you find her. God protect and speed," Jane admonished at the door after she had kissed Ernie good-bye again.

Lovers were so sweet. It was a shame, though, Rebecca thought, that Ernie was taken. She liked short men with beards, and gray-streaked longish hair.

She and Ernie didn't talk much on the drive out there. Rebecca hadn't let either Ernie or Jane in on the real reason she had to get out to Black Pond because, as she had said, they wouldn't have believed it. It'd been easier to use the excuse that she just wanted to examine the last place where Amanda had been seen. Search for tracks of any kind. Inspect the remnants of the cult; the scene of the crime, so to speak. See if there were any vibrations left. It'd have served no purpose to tell them that she was going to try to call up a dead witch and trick her into confessing what she'd done with her sister. If she could. It would have just scared them more. God knew, it scared the hell out of her. But it had been the only thing she could think of.

She'd placed a few long-distance telephone calls from

Jessie's and had been dismayed and genuinely baffled
to discover that most of the witches and warlocks she
knew and who she'd asked for help had turned her
down cold. Too dangerous, some of them had said in
strained voices, as if they'd known something she didn't.
Too much black magic to go up against, some had said.
Signs are bad. Very bad. The word had spread quickly
and so, it seemed, had the cowardice. None of them
had fooled Rebecca one tiny bit. They were afraid. But
of what? Rachel—or what stood behind her? And what
exactly was that? The cult was gone, so it couldn't be
them. Rebecca didn't like to dwell too long on that
problem.

The woods were brooding, silent, as the '82 black
Chevy station wagon rattled down the narrow road.
They drove by the ruined and blackened shell of
Amanda and Jake's cabin and the pathetic sight caused
Rebecca's eyes to harden. Damn superstitious towns-
people. Small-minded and vindictive. Things never
changed, did they?

Miles farther down the country road, Ernie pulled
over onto the frozen shoulder. "Well," he said, glancing
over at her and pointing over her right shoulder,
"Black Pond is about a mile through those trees there.
Can't get any closer in a car. Up that hill and down
on the other side. Can't miss it. A big pond. There's
a massive willow tree that guards the place. And the
mist. It cloaks the pond like a shroud. As cold and icy
as it is. So watch your step," he cautioned.

"Thanks for the ride, Ernie. And the concern. But I
can take care of myself." She leaned forward toward
him. "This could take awhile."

"I'll wait. You sure I can't be of any help? Can't come
with you? I'm pretty handy in the woods."

"I imagine you are. But no, Ernie, I wasn't fooling

before when I said that this could be dangerous. I have to do it myself."

Ernie's eyes were the color of the flat gray sky outside "You'll holler if you need me, won't you?"

"Sure will." Rebecca opened the car door and slid out. The frigid air took her breath away. She lowered her chin, tugging her coat tighter around her shivering body, and crunched away from the black car and toward where Ernie had said the pond could be found. The sky was filling with thick slate-colored clouds and her breath froze the second it left her mouth. Never got this cold in the city, she grumbled to herself. The trees must suck all the heat off.

Her feet, boots or no, were lumps of ice before she'd scaled the hill. It was getting colder every minute, yet the snow was holding off and she was relieved for that, anyway. She stopped a moment at the top and waved back down at Ernie as he sat smoking a cigarette behind the wheel. He waved back and gave her a thumbs-up for luck.

She could feel Tibby shivering in her coat pocket. So far, he'd had nothing else to say. Figured. He was all griped out.

Rebecca turned and stumbled down the other side of the hill toward the wall of bluish fog shimmering across the field before her. She could see the towering willow tree, and plodded on through the icy-slick weeds.

With her witch's intuition, she knew immediately she'd arrived at Black Pond the moment she broke through the hedges and spied the frozen body of water. Under the thickening smoky-rimmed clouds, she stood surveying the pond critically, her head cocked to one side. Every nerve in her body tingling: *Beware. This place is evil.*

Tibby was strangely quiet.

The smell of smoke permeated the place. The stench

of burning flesh still caught at her nostrils when she moved. She found signs of where the charred bodies had once lain, circles of black under the thin layer of new ice, and she shuddered. The bodies, or what had been left of them, were long gone. Cleared away earlier by the police, according to Ernie. Boy, she'd love to have been able to read *that* police report, she chuckled to herself.

The ambience of the whole place was malignant. Even Rebecca was enough of a witch to sense that. It was an ugly place, too, she mused, as she looked down upon the glittering sheet of dark ice surrounded by grieving, dead gnarled trees. She could tell by looking at it that the pond wasn't solid ice. It was too early in the winter for that. If she stepped out on it, she'd crash through.

She trod to the edge of the water, closed her eyes, and whispered the words of a spell she'd learned for beholding the recent past. It took every bit of power she possessed. She peeled her gloves off her hands and stuck them in her empty pocket. Backing up, and stretching her arms out to touch the stark willow tree with her bare fingers, she made a link with the place and allowed the images to flow into her mind.

She saw the cult as misty phantoms milling around her. Nebulous shadows of what was past and gone. Figures cowled in black robes. Chanting. Torches held high. With strange auras. Bright red and yellow emanations. Rebecca tensed up, the shock of her next discovery nearly knocking her over.

They hadn't all been human . . . the ones Amanda had destroyed . . . some had been *demons*. The High Priest most assuredly.

They'd had a terrified boy with them. The specters scuffled by with the speed of light, their time different than hers because they were traveling now in another dimension. A child's pitiful scream. A knife's flash. They were torturing the child.

Then a monstrous panther with bared fangs and human eyes burst into their midst and attacked the High Priest . . . her sister, breathtaking in her righteous anger and her power as she had pounced down upon them and had extracted her gruesome retribution.

Human-shaped torches. *God.* Cries of agony and rage.

And after all was done, Amanda, now in human form, gathering the boy's small still body into her arms, and staggering away.

And Rebecca understood why Amanda had done what she had done. She *understood.*

In her dream trance the time fled by as Rebecca searched for the rest of the truth. And waited, shivering in the frigid air, her bare hands long since numb. Then it grew darker. The clouds dissipated as she went back in time to a night five days past, and the trees moaned around her like living beings lost and in misery. She waited.

Eventually Amanda's ethereal form returned, running, out of breath in the twilight that represented night, to the edge of the water which was now a liquid pool, no longer ice-coated. All around there rang a clashing and clanging. People shouting in anger and blood lust. Horses neighing. Amanda was being pursued.

She was fleeing from the townspeople . . . and from something else. But Rebecca couldn't see it. The odor of burnt wood clung to the ghost as she scrambled past her. Amanda held her shoulder in pain . . . blood gushing between her fingers . . . someone had shot her.

Rebecca, so close she could see the terror and exhaustion on her sister's grimy face, ached to step out of her vision and run to her sister's aid. Yet she knew she couldn't . . . it was only a dream.

It was true, then . . . Amanda had lost her magic. She hadn't been able to fight back.

Then Rebecca watched in awed silence as a woman with long black hair and beckoning arms arose from the water and after speaking with Amanda beguilingly— Rebecca couldn't understand a word that was said, though—lured her back into the depths with her. Rachel's ghost. *And something else.*

And the water closed over them. The night became an overcast day again. The woods hushed. All the ghosts were gone. Rebecca moaned out loud, her heart lurched in her chest. *My God . . .*

Rebecca had seen as much as she had only because it had happened to Amanda. She usually wasn't this receptive. But love is a strong bond, a strong conductor. Shivering like a frail leaf in a storm, she let her hands fall from the tree, rubbed her eyes, dazed. Drained. Frightened. She tried, really tried, to call the wraith back so she could question her.

Where's Amanda? What have you done with her? But she couldn't make Rachel come back. She didn't have enough power.

Either Rachel was resisting her, or she was no longer there. *I wonder where she is,* Rebecca worried, as she slipped her gloves back onto her stiff hands.

Tibby was tugging frantically at her sleeve from the ledge of the pocket where he'd been clinging. His eyes as wide as saucers. He was chattering in terror. Rachel had scared the bejesus out of him. He wanted to go. Now. He was raving something about the Devil being there. Watching them.

She smiled down at him and was about to lift his furry body into her hands when his little body froze, his eyes turning glassy. A shadow crossed the dim sun, turning his eyes as red as fire. Suddenly her familiar jumped from her grasp and landed on the ground with a soft plop. He ran toward the base of the willow tree and started to dig like a beaver.

"Tibby, what are you doing?" she burst out, crouching down beside him. But it was plain to see that he was trying to dig something up. That he wanted her to dig, too.

Something was there. Something under the ice and dirt. Rebecca picked up a stick, shoved Tibby aside, and furiously began to dig at the base of the willow tree. Puffs of cloudy air escaped from her open mouth. The dirt was frozen solid but that didn't stop her. She got a bigger stick. Used her magic to turn it into a small shovel. Even she could handle that.

She dug and dug, Tibby observing . . . until she held the small leather-wrapped parcel triumphantly in her hands, which were so unfeeling from the cold that she could barely unwrap what she'd found.

A book of some kind.

Whose?

It was old. Very old. No telling how long it'd been there. A marvel that it was still intact. She leafed through the pages. She couldn't read a word of it. It seemed to be in an ancient language.

What did the book have to do with Amanda?

As Rebecca stood up with the book cradled in her hands, the uncalled vision came like a train out of the fog and answered her question.

She saw a dim, filthy cell. A prison. With people wailing out in fear and pain . . . in chains . . . the scent of fresh blood curdled her stomach . . . and somewhere in the shadows Amanda cried. Alone. Forsaken. She'd lost her powers, was helpless. Rebecca was sure it was Amanda. But in the flickering candlelight she didn't look like Amanda . . . she had long black hair and piercing blue eyes. She and the people around her were dressed in peculiar clothes.

Another time . . .

Then as swiftly as it had come, the image dissolved. So Abigail's psychic dream had been accurate. Amanda *was* trapped in the past. In another woman's body. A woman who resembled the ghost that had taken Amanda into the water. Rachel. But why was Amanda in Rachel's body? Startled, Rebecca believed she knew the answer. *To take Rachel's place . . .* and legend said that Rachel was probably killed for being a witch.

So that's why Rachel had wanted her. To trade places with her. To die for her? No wonder Rachel's ghost was no longer haunting Black Pond. It was most likely waiting in the world in between. Waiting for Amanda to die. Then Rachel could possess her twentieth-century body. Wound and all.

Good God. Rebecca whistled out loud. At least Amanda's wound, the one she had when she'd been sucked into the pond, hadn't killed her.

Rebecca collapsed on the ground by the tree's trunk and regarded the book in her hands. It was the key. She knew it. The book had something to do with where Amanda was now, and had something to do with releasing her. If Rebecca could figure it out. Amanda must have touched the book or held it at some time for such images to have come from it. Sometime long ago. And . . . somewhere in the past Amanda was still alive and something very powerful was keeping her there. Not just Rachel.

You're in way over your fucking head, Rebecca, she told herself, mulling over Amanda's predicament.

Who the hell do you think you're fooling, my dear, really? You're no damn Amanda . . . You're just a fortune-telling, book-writing, sniffling nobody of a witch. Telling fortunes and reading tarot cards are more your speed. You're no match for evil such as this. No match at all. How are you going to get Amanda back? You stupid witch.

But the thought of Amanda drove her on relentlessly. Her lips had settled into a thin, grim line of pure defiance. *I'll find a way. I swear it. I'll get you back, Amanda.*

Could be a hell of a book, too, if it was all true. Another best-seller. Rebecca's eyes glittered.

Picking Tibby up from the ground, she pulled herself back to her feet, and set him on her shoulder where he snuggled up against her neck. Amazingly, he seemed to be asleep. As if his experiences had knocked him out. How did he know there had been a book at the base of the willow? Hummm. When he awoke, she'd have to ask him.

As she dragged her feet back through the darkening woods toward the black station wagon, Rebecca thought about the book in her pocket and how she was going to decipher it, and the evil presence which had hunkered behind Rachel's ghost as she had drawn Amanda into the water in her vision. Rebecca, even now, wasn't sure she'd really seen what she thought she'd seen. A huge shadowy beast of some kind behind Amanda's abductor . . . impossible. Right? Even a midlevel demon wouldn't have cast such an forbidding aura . . .

Every nerve in her short, plump body was aquiver as she recalled the fiery-red nebula. *Only Satan would create such a sign.*

Her body stiffly braced against the rising winds, she kept trudging away from the frozen pond and toward the man waiting in the car. By the lowered sun, she guessed she'd been gone at least two hours.

"How'd it go?" was the first thing Ernie asked after she'd gotten back in the front seat. God, it felt good to get out of the cold. Ernie had the heater on and

Rebecca took off her cap and gloves and tried to rub some life back into her hands.

She slid her puffy eyes over to look at the man calculatingly. "Do you really want to know, or are you just making polite conversation?"

There was a hint of anger in his voice when he retorted, "I really want to know."

She was ready now to take any offered help she could get. To hell with her pride. There was too damn much at stake. So she told him. Everything. The look on his face when she expressed her budding suspicion that the formidable force behind Rachel's strength could be Satan himself was worth it. It almost made her laugh, as frightened as she was, and helped take some of the pressure off her.

"That's impossible," Ernie exploded, but his face again betrayed him. He'd listened to everything Rebecca had said and she knew that, though he didn't want to believe there were such things as real witches, ghosts, and the Devil, he could no longer pretend, after what he'd seen and heard, that there weren't. The cult and what they'd done had almost been enough to convince him.

Now Rebecca did laugh out loud. "Well, impossible or not, if I want my sister back . . . I'm going to have to fight the Devil for her. The cult and Rachel, I believe, are Satan's creatures all."

Rebecca pointed her finger at the starter of the car and the car roared into life. She waved another finger and the stick shift moved into drive. Ernie had to grab wildly at the steering wheel as the car lurched forward or they would have ended up against a tree.

A new lit cigarette had mysteriously appeared in his mouth. With two fingers he took it out and gaped at it. Then before Ernie could sputter a word, his mouth still gaping open in surprise at what she'd done, she asked sweetly, "Could I talk you into giving me a ride to my hotel so I can pack, and call the airport for plane reservations? I need to take this book to an ancient-language specialist I know in England. Right away. I think it might help us get Amanda back."

"Sure," Ernie said without hesitation, putting the cigarette back between his lips as if nothing had happened, and concentrating on steering the car.

"I'll do anything to help you get Amanda back safely."

He turned a pair of tenacious eyes on her, his jaw going hard. "Anything. But you have to let me help. In fact, I insist. I'm a God-fearing man and I'm not afraid of dead witches—or Satan. And it sounds to me as if you're going to need help. A lot of help."

Rebecca got the message and just nodded tiredly right before she slumped back against the seat. Tibby was still sleeping on her shoulder, and she took him in her hands and gently tucked him back into her coat pocket. "OK. You can help. I'm too weary to fight you anymore. But don't say I never warned you when the shit hits the fan." She had to get to London and talk to someone. Find out what was in the book. She had to get some sleep sometime, too.

"Good," Ernie grouched, as he turned left down another road and drove them back to the hotel. "About time you listened to somebody. Witch or no witch."

Rebecca smiled, crossed her arms over her plump coated stomach, and fell immediately asleep.

It was nice to have friends.

Chapter 13

Once Ernie dropped her back at her hotel, she called
the airport and booked a flight on the next plane out to
Heathrow in London, which left in four hours. Ernie left,
saying he'd be back to drive her to the airport. Outside,
the daylight was being replaced by twilight. Still no snow.

Then Rebecca took a long hot bath, as Tibby slept
like a dead mouse on her pillow. She curled up on the
bed next to him later and scrutinized what she'd dug
up from under the willow tree. With the faint light
from the bedside lamp pouring over her, she scanned
the yellowed pages. She still couldn't make head nor
tail of it. Could even be in the Old Language itself. It
still gave her strange vibrations when she held it. Just
being in the same room with it gave her the shivers.
Black magic always did that. She was beginning to think
the book was a book of spells. That would explain her
reaction to it. She couldn't wait to have it decoded.
One of the spells might be the one Rachel used on
Amanda to pull her into the past; one of the other
spells might be the one that explained how to get her
back.

She frowned deeply, shook her head, and leaned it
back on the pillow with a weary sigh. She desperately
needed a nap and her body was vocally rebelling from

that lovely trek she'd just taken out in the boonies. Every muscle she had was moaning.

There was only one person she knew who could probably decipher the thing: Winifred Harris, her book researcher. An old, eccentric, but highly skilled professor of ancient English languages at the London University. She'd met Winifred a score of years ago after one of her own books on witchcraft had come out. The woman had bluntly written just to inform her that she had some of her facts wrong.

Amused by the woman's gumption, Rebecca had written her back and soon they'd become transatlantic pen pals. Winifred Harris lived in a London suburb. Eventually they'd met in person. It turned out that the woman was a treasure, one who was familiar with a lot of witchcraft's ancient history and its writings. Her specialty, the Old Language. The language of the witches. Long ago Rebecca had also begun to suspect that Winifred was even more than she let on. That she was connected with a lot of influential, powerful people in the witch world, and that she kept those contacts secret for a reason. Rebecca had come to depend a lot on the professor's approval and advice. She was very wise.

Rebecca sat back up with a groan—time for some sleep after she called Winifred—and pawed through her purse for her address book. She located Winifred's telephone number and dialed the phone.

"Winifred? Hello, this is Rebecca Givens."

"Ah, funny you should call, Rebecca," the woman's husky voice chirped. "Just been thinking about you. Got that copy of your latest book that you sent me. Looks good, even if I say so myself. Many times as I've seen it before publication, that is." She cackled, sounding like a witch herself. Winifred had done most of the research for the book.

"Thanks, Winifred. But I'm calling for a very special

purpose and I don't think I have a lot of time, so I'll get right to the point. My sister, Amanda, a witch, is in deep trouble. You remember I've talked about her before?"

"Yes, dear, I recall. What's the problem?"

"I'll tell you all about it when I see you—"

"Oh, so you're actually coming to see me?" It'd been almost a year since her last visit.

"Yes, I catch a flight leaving here in about four hours. I've stumbled upon a very strange find here in Canaan, where my sister lives. I think it's a book of spells. Black spells. I found it buried by a place called Black Pond, under a huge willow tree." Rebecca held the book in her other hand and studied it thoughtfully.

The voice on the other end of the line was quiet.

"It's in this ancient script . . . perhaps, the Old Language of the witches. I need to get a translation if I can. I'm sure it has some connection with my sister's plight."

"Ah, sounds very intriguing," the voice crackled over the long-distance line. "And getting it translated is so important that you're bringing it in person instead of just sending it first-class insured post as usual, eh?"

"Well," Rebecca agreed, "I can't let it out of my hands. It's too valuable and time is of the utmost importance. I need a translation . . . yesterday." Rebecca could almost visualize Winifred's white eyebrows rising straight up in that way she had, her black eyes blinking. She was a queer old bird, a dowdy heavy-set woman with pure-white hair and one leg shorter than the other, who lived alone in a two-hundred-year-old English thatched cottage, grew twelve varieties of rare English tea roses, drank at least three pots of tea a day, and never seemed to sleep. Oh, and she loved hot scones with orange marmalade. Nonetheless, she was also the undisputed expert in her chosen field. She taught an-

cient languages part time at the university and helped
Rebecca and about five other novelists with their research. She was accurate, dependable, and diligent. The
best researcher Rebecca had ever found.

"So you should be here around high tea time, I cal-
culate," she sent back with good-natured amusement in
her voice. In England high tea was sometime between
supper and bedtime. Except Winifred stayed up half the
night and her idea of high tea could be the middle of
the night.

"About then."

"I'll put on the crumpets and tea. I'll see you soon.
Ta, ta!" And then the old woman hung up. She wasn't
one for telephone chatting.

After Rebecca hung up the telephone, she set her
traveling alarm clock for three hours from then, lay
back, and fell immediately into sleep.

When the alarm's shrill buzzer awoke her, she dressed
in a whirlwind, hurriedly packed, and was ready when
Ernie knocked at the door.

She positioned Tibby gently back into her right coat
pocket because she still couldn't wake him. He must
have had quite a jolt out there at Black Pond for him
to be so out of it for so long. She was beginning to
worry about him, but she decided to just let him sleep
it off on the trip. She'd interrogate him later. Apparently he needed the rest. It never occurred to her that
there might be something else wrong.

In the car as they raced to the airport, Rebecca stared
out into the frosty night as she and Ernie discussed
plans. She was to call him or Jane as soon as she knew
she was coming back and one of them would pick her
up from the airport. Rebecca had no doubt that she'd
be returning to Black Pond to finish what she'd started.
It only made sense that if she discovered from the book
what she had to do, that she'd have to do it there. The

retrieval spell would have to be cast at the last place
Amanda had been before the other spell had been cast.
There was most likely a portal between Rachel's and
Amanda's times somewhere above or in the pond.

"They say that big snowstorms's coming in by tomorrow sometime." Ernie made conversation a while later
as they bumped down the road. "Hope you don't get
caught right in the middle of it."

"Me, too. As long as I can get back here before it
locks us all in again," she replied with a quick smile,
her mind preoccupied with what she was going to do
if the snow did keep her from returning to Canaan.
She could take a chance and try getting back with her
magic. Maybe she'd land in a soft tree somewhere. God,
if only she had the power to safely transpose herself
from one location to another as Amanda had been able
to do and didn't have to take airplanes. If for no other
reason, that was why she hated snow. Always had. Yet
here she was, still living in New England, land of long
white winters. Florida or the Bahamas sounded real
good to her about now.

The car's headlights slashed through the dark gloom
and illuminated a pair of gleaming eyes for a split second. Ernie pointed them out, thought they'd been a
deer's.

Uneasy on the seat next to him, Rebecca didn't contradict. She knew it hadn't been a deer's eyes, but the
eyes of some of hell's denizens tracking her progress.
They knew she had the book.

Ernie got her to the airport with only minutes to
spare and after waving good-bye, she sprinted through
the gate and boarded her plane.

God, she hated flying, too. And this was her third
flight in a week.

She found a seat in the back. Always in the back.
Someone had once told her that the safest place was

in the back, in case the plane broke in half in midair
or some such thing. It was probably nonsense, but she
couldn't take the chance if it wasn't.

She would remember later that it was when she first
sat down in her window seat she felt that someone was
still watching her. Or something. Outside the plane it
was dark. And out of the corner of her eyes, when she
passed them across the window, she thought she saw . . .
something. An elusive glimmer of red, blinking. But
when she looked harder, nothing. *Must be my imagination. After Black Pond and all that mumbo-jumbo. I'm just
really tired.*

A middle-aged man with silver-tipped hair and metal-
framed glasses, wearing a business suit with matching
briefcase, settled down in the vacant seat beside her,
nervous and jumpy. She ignored her disquiet and him,
popped a mild tranquilizer, and tried to sleep like Tibby
was doing. But the man kept praying so damn loud, it
wasn't easy. She hoped he wouldn't clamp onto her like
a leech if the plane jolted on takeoff.

The plane rolled and lifted off into the air. The man
next to her didn't move an inch. Like a stone statue.
Rebecca felt sorry for the guy. She was unhappy in an
airplane, but he was petrified.

After a few minutes of smooth flight, Rebecca drifted
off.

She had no idea how long she'd slept before the
violent turbulence of the airplane brought her to with
a stomach-wrenching start.

"What the hell's going on?" she just had time to cry
out before the rocking ceased. The plane leveled off
and everything returned to normal. Her heart sticking
somewhere up in her throat, her hands claws on the
armrests, she looked at the guy next to her. He'd
fainted.

The rest of the passengers were in various stages of

panic. Some were still shouting, some had fallen from their seats and were crawling around in the aisles, laughing or weeping in relief, some were in shock or had passed out like the man beside her. There was litter everywhere, exploded suitcases, purses, briefcases, and other assorted odds and ends.

Tibby was awake, gibbering like a mad mouse in her lap. She hushed him without taking the time to understand what he was trying to tell her, and asked the nearest person to her, a young teenage girl with short blond hair, "What *happened*?"

The girl, who had obviously been scared out of her wits, answered in a squeaky voice, "Don't know. The plane just began bucking like a wild horse. The captain came on the intercom and explained we were experiencing some . . . difficulties. But before he could say anything else, it got worse."

She let out a long breath, her whole body shuddering. "Jeeze, I thought we were goners for sure.

"Is it going to be OK now?" she begged of Rebecca as if she had the answer.

"I hope so," Rebecca said with a false courage she didn't feel. The back of her neck was tingling. They were under somebody's nefarious surveillance again. Something was still wrong.

"I thought I was gonna die." The girl laid her face into her hands; Rebecca could hear her relieved sobs.

The plane was flying right now, the ride soft as a baby, but Rebecca's inner voice was in high gear. *Danger. Danger.*

She happened to peer out the window on her right and discovered why. There were eyes peering back at her. From *outside* in the night. Red, glowing, bestial eyes. She blinked and they were gone. That quick.

Jesus. Demons. That was why her witch senses were on overload. She was being watched. Or followed Or . . .

Targeted for elimination. Her paranoia about being observed back in the woods and when she first boarded the plane made sense now.

The other people around her whispered and talked, picked up their scattered belongings, and tried to calm themselves down as she contemplated the darkness racing by her window. Endless blackness. But there was . . . *something* . . . out there. The wings of the large airplane, an L10-11 Widebody, were just barely discernable and, as Rebecca squinted her eyes into tight slits and shaded them from the interior lights of the plane with her hands, she wasn't sure she was seeing what she thought she was. Blurry shapes were scuttling along the wings. Outlined shadows against the inky sky.

But she wasn't completely sure.

She closed her eyes and evoked a spell that would allow her to see in the dark. When she reopened her eyes, she had to cover her mouth to keep from gasping out loud in horror.

There *were* creatures sitting, clinging, and running on the wing. Hairy, scaly beasts with fiery eyes and lots of teeth. Lots of arms and legs. Spiderlike. All different sizes. *Demons.* A huge hulking one with glowing eyes as big as dinner plates ambled up to the window and grinned lasciviously in at her so that she jerked back in her seat in surprise. He tapped on the window and snarled at her. Wanting in.

"*Good God,*" she whispered to herself. "What do they want?"

The book, Tibby hissed at her from her lap. No one else could see him, he was hiding in the folds of her coat, which she'd taken off and laid across her lap.

She glanced down at him. His little face was scrunched up in anger.

They want the book? she questioned him in her mind.

*The book we dug up at Black Pond?—By the way, how did
you know that book was there?*

*Yes, they want that book. And no, I don't know how I
found it. A voice in my head told me it was there. Made me
dig it up. So why do they want it?*

*It belongs to their Master, that's why. He wants it back. It
has a lot of magic. Black magic.*

Oh, Rebecca mind-murmured. *There's something in it
He doesn't want me to learn of. Something very important.
So I was right about Satan being behind the cult and Rachel
being behind Amanda's abduction?*

Of course.

Oh, boy. Rebecca stared back out at the things outside
the window.

Are you going to give it back? Tibby demanded peevishly
when she was silent too long.

No. Firm. *I need it to get Amanda back. I have a hunch
that without it I won't have a chance.* She shook her head,
still regarding the threatening shapes. They were fading,
her spell wearing off, leaving her light-headed and even
more tired. The price she had to pay for concocting
enchantments.

With it, Tibby snapped back at her, *we won't have a
chance, either.*

What do you mean?

Tibby sighed an almost inaudible groan. *They*—he
could still see them—and he tossed his head at the
demons crowding now outside the window—*came for the
book. And if they don't get it*—he made a sharp cutting
gesture with one of his tiny paws across his neck—*we'll
get it.*

Rebecca's blood went cold. *Oh, boy. That was what
she'd been afraid of.*

She made herself look away from the window. Made
her heart slow down. Said a prayer. The strongest magic
she had would come from God. And from anyone else

out there who would hear the silent plea she was sending out. Help. *Help me.* She'd need it.

I'm not giving back the book. No way.

Tibby sputtered, *Stupid witch.* Then he fell silent.
Maybe he realized that even if they did give back the
book, they might die, anyway. Demons lied all the time.
Just like their Master.

The plane abruptly began to pitch all over again.
More violently than before. Rebecca grabbed onto the
arms of her seat and held on. The passengers began
to wail and screech. The lights began to flicker and the
captain's terrified voice boomed out over the intercom
for the second time with empty promises for their complete safety. No one believed him as the plane began
to jump around like a giant was shaking it. All the lights
on the plane went out, leaving them in total blackness.

People screamed. Prayed for God to save them. Went
nuts. There were terrible noises coming from the engines.

Outside the window from the darkened interior, Rebecca could see the demons clearly again; they were
bouncing up and down on the wings like they were on
a goddamn trampoline . . . and now there seemed to
be more of them. Lots more. Covering the plane's
wings like a blanket. They were going to wreck them.
Rock them into pieces.

They must have heard what she said about not giving
the book back. *Damn.*

One of the engines exploded. Probably choked on a
demon. The plane plummeted from the sky like a fa-
tally wounded bird.

Do something! Tibby yelped in terror, scurrying up,
grabbing at her hair, and hanging on for dear life as
the descent grew steeper. Rebecca was slammed back
against her seat so she could hardly move. The muscles
in her face grew taut with the pressure and her mind

began to fall apart. She'd never been so scared in her life. The cries of the panicked passengers rose to a hideous crescendo.

Do something!

Rebecca evoked the strongest magic she knew of. Something she'd never tried before. She let out all the cautionary stops and did her damndest to save herself and the rest of those onboard. To hell with her inadequacies, to hell with what she could or couldn't do. Her trembling fingers absentmindedly located the infamous book and an electric charge bolted through her. Another charge, like a snake of lightning, crackled from one end of the plane to the other. Magic was everywhere. Strong magic. And the sound of both engines were back again.

The plane righted itself again. The lights came back on. The pilot was crying over the intercom. *"Were all right,"* he kept repeating in an hysterical voice over and over. *"We're all right! It's a miracle."*

The plane wasn't going to crash. *Not bad, Rebecca, for a second-class witch,* she congratulated herself shakily, deflating back into her seat. It seemed impossible . . . but she'd done it. Her magic had worked somehow—or had it? Deep down inside somewhere she suspected a greater power had stepped in and saved her neck. Her call for assistance had been answered. Someone had helped her.

She could hardly believe it.

She searched outside with strained eyes. The wing was empty. The demons were all gone. Every one of them.

Rebecca took the small black book from her coat pocket and just looked at it. They'd wanted it bad. What was in it that was so important? But she didn't have much time to dwell on the mystery. The energy she'd expended performing the magic necessary to save them, with or without someone's aid, had sapped every bit of her strength. Even as a relieved and proud Tibby was babbling away at her from her shoulder, she was already sliding into an exhausted, unwakeable sleep.

Magic exacted a heavy price.

She didn't wake up until they landed seven hours later at Heathrow Airport. Even then someone had to help carry her off, she could hardly stand. They thought it was because of the trauma of the near crash and they wanted to send her to the hospital. She resisted them adamantly and had them call her a cab.

"Take me to 777 Cherry Lane in Richmond," she apprised the cab driver as she was escorted into the backseat of his cab by two airline attendants. As usual for England, it was drizzling a fine steady mist and the night was chilly. At least it wasn't snowing.

The driver, a burly guy with a cigar and a funny-looking cap, gave her an exasperated glance in the cab's rearview mirror. Probably thought she was sick or drunk, the way she was acting.

"Jet lag," she told him gruffly, and he seemed to accept that. He had to wake her up when they arrived at Winifred's; the rain tapping on the roof had lulled her back to dreamland.

As Rebecca was unloading herself and her bag out of the cab, the cottage door opened and a rotund figure bounced out.

Winifred was in a long pink flannel robe and fuzzy pink slippers, her snow-white hair tucked up and pinned in the back. She looked like a huge pink whale barreling down on Rebecca.

"About time you arrived, boss," Winifred greeted her affectionately, giving her a bear hug. "I was beginning to get worried about you." They were friends as well as associates.

"And judging by the way you look—awful—I guess I

had reason to." The Briton was studying her friend in the light reflected from the inside of the cab.

"Thanks. Let's get in out of this rain and I'll fill you in. On everything."

"Deal."

"Why does it always rain in this bloody country, Winifred?" Rebecca teased as the woman took her bag.

"Doesn't rain that much. You just catch us at the wrong times." Winifred watched as Rebecca paid the cab driver and then led her into the warm cottage. It was a small place with only three rooms, and the archaic way it looked, Rebecca always expected to see someone in seventeenth-century dress walk through it, not someone like Winifred in pink slippers.

Winifred tucked Rebecca's bag into a corner. There was a blazing fire going in the main room's stone fireplace. The table was set for visitors with Winifred's finest tea set and china, an overladen plate of tiny sandwiches and the ever-present scones Winifred was famous for.

"I mean," Rebecca said, "I've been here now at least twenty times and every time it's raining. Or foggy. Doesn't the sun ever shine?"

"Sure, every other month or so for a few hours, dear. But I love the rain, especially on my days off from the university. I can stay here shut up all cozy-like in my little cottage before the fire, with a good book before my old eyes. Listen to it rapping at my windows."

Winifred's shrewd eyes regarded Rebecca for a while, and then she said, "Had a bad trip, 'ey? You do look like death warmed over, child."

"I should." Rebecca slipped her hand into her pocket and brought Tituba out. He rubbed his eyes, awake, and she set him down on the table. Winifred, who knew Tibby well, and had a soft spot for him, broke off a piece of a scone and handed it to him.

The familiar flashed her a big grin and started nibbling. Then he scurried off the table and perched before the fire to warm himself.

"We had a rough flight over here." Rebecca met Winifred's curious eyes and held them. "Somebody didn't want us to make it. We almost didn't."

"This find of yours must be truly important."

Rebecca had settled down in one of the cushioned rocking chairs facing the bright fire, dropping her coat down on the hooked rug beside her. She exhaled a pleasurable sigh of relief as she stretched her short legs toward the flames to unfreeze her feet, which always seemed to be cold these days. Old age, probably. Not to mention that grueling hike yesterday in the woods and the banging around on the plane which had left her body feeling like it was a hundred instead of forty.

She glanced up at the old woman hovering above her and said, "After you give me some of those delicious-looking scones and a cup of hot tea, I'll tell you all about the book. The wild airplane ride. About the trouble my sister Amanda has gotten herself into, and my assessment of it."

Rebecca's usually stiff face had softened, highlighted by the flickering fire to a glowing pink. She was warm and dry and soon she'd be fed, and it felt good. "I need your advice. Any help you can give me."

Winifred's eyes beamed at her over her shoulder as she leaned over, rubbing her hands like an old witch before the fire. "Then I'd better get you some food and tea and let you begin your story. . . . You know me, my curiosity will kill me if I don't hear it all right away. I hate mysteries. Just waiting for you to arrive after that strange phone call of yours has been torture enough."

She moved quicker than a woman of her size with a gimpy leg would have been expected to, and hobbled over to fetch the tea and scones arranged prettily on a wobbly old television tray. After she had set it down between them, and Rebecca had bitten into a scone smeared with strawberry jam, Winifred, sipping a cup of tea, inquired, "Well, where's this book that had you hightailing it over here like a fox running from the hounds, dear?" The Englishwoman's accent was subtle, but very evident.

"Here." Rebecca picked up her coat and recovered the book from its pocket, handed it to Winifred, and went back to eating. She'd discovered she was very hungry.

"Delicious scones, Winnie," Rebecca said with a full mouth and grinned. Winifred made everything from scratch and was an excellent cook. "Delicious."

In the meantime Winifred had sat down in the other rocking chair and was examining the book. Leafing through the pages.

"It's got me stumped," Rebecca informed her. "Can't make head nor tails of the thing." Rebecca shook her head and tossed her frizzy hair back from her face. "And understanding it, I believe, could mean life or death for my missing sister," she said, her tone ominous.

"My, my," Winifred clucked. Leaning back in her rocker, she pulled out her glasses and kept studying the book in her hands.

Rebecca began her story from start to finish. The cult, Amanda's bizarre disappearance, Black Pond, Rachel, and everything that had happened since. What she thought it all meant.

"Well? What do you think?" Rebecca asked when she was done.

"I think you're right. One-hundred percent. And I think you're in extreme danger. You found this under the willow at Black Pond?" She was referring to the book she still held in her hands.

"Yes. Or Tibby did." The mouse was curled up, asleep, on the hooked rug before the fire.

"So you believe Amanda's back in the seventeenth century somewhere? But she could be anywhere, maybe even . . . dead."

Rebecca's face turned dark. "I'm not that good of a witch to be absolutely sure. I just have this feeling that Amanda isn't dead, that's all. I believe I'd know it if she were." Rebecca gazed into the flames, running her hands down the rocker's curved arms nervously, her thoughts far away. "I also believe that book there holds the key to saving her."

"Well, as you thought, this"—Winifred tapped her squat fingers on the book in her lap—"does seem to be a book of spells. Black magic. And, yes, it's in the Old Language of the witches. What was used centuries ago by all witches. I've rarely come across actual samples of it before, but I've studied it. Though, I, myself recognize what it is . . . I can only decode *some* of it on my own."

Her eyes gleamed in the dim room and her forehead puckered. "But I can tell you this: the witch who wrote this was very powerful. And the witch was Rachel, I'd bet a gold coin on it. Her name is mentioned in it." Winifred caressed the dusty old book.

"What doesn't make sense to me, Winifred, is why was the book buried there under that tree in the first place? Who put it there? Tibby told me that some *voice* ordered him to dig it up. Who . . . and why?"

"Maybe your sister discovered the book, couldn't read it, either, but suspected what it was, and hid it there for you to find. She might not have her powers, but she still has her wits. Or Rachel herself hid it so it wouldn't incriminate her. Who knows? The spells contained in this book are a death sentence. The American seventeenth-century, remember, especially in the New England states, was a deadly one for accused witches; they hanged and burnt them with much less incriminating evidence than this little goodie. I've never seen anything like this before in all my born days," she mumbled, shaking the book in her hand. "So much evil—from what I can decipher. The easier ones." She opened the book and turned to a certain page, showed it to Rebecca.

"I think this one spell is for maiming an enemy"— another page—"this one for murdering one, if I'm correct. No wonder she buried this thing. Whew. Talk about condemning evidence." Winifred shook her head and leaned back again in the rocker, humming to herself. It meant she was doing some deep thinking, that she was troubled about something.

It was distressing Rebecca. The way she was behaving. She'd never seen Winifred this disturbed over anything. Ever.

"What's the matter, Winifred?"

"Just speculating . . . After all you've told me, I believe, just as you suspected, that if we can get this book translated properly, we can find the solution to your sister's problem. There's most likely a spell in here we can use. Be a real joke on Rachel, wouldn't it?" A wide grin. "To use her own spell to defeat her and her Master?" A sarcastic chuckle.

"Wouldn't it?" Rebecca admitted, stifling a yawn. The tea, pastries, and warm fire nearly had her asleep again.

"You look ready to drop, dearie," Winifred said. "Why don't you just go back there into my bedroom and take a nice long nap, while I study this book a little more. Think on who I'm going to get to translate it."

How appealing the idea of a soft bed was, Rebecca thought. Her brain was fuzzy from her earlier adventures and the long flight and her body needed rest.

"I am weary. Every bone in my body aches. You're right, sleep is what I need."

Rebecca rose slowly from the comfortable rocking chair. At the door to the spare bedroom in the cottage, she looked back at Winifred in the rocking chair before the fire and smiled.

"If I haven't said so before, thanks for helping me with this, Winifred. Thanks . . . more than I can say."

The woman waved a hand nonchalantly at her guest, but her face was serious. "What are friends for?" she retorted and her eyes went back to the open book, her mouth moving. "Get some sleep. We'll talk more in the morning."

Rebecca retreated to the tiny cubbyhole where a narrow, but soft featherbed resided under a large window. She flopped down on the soft bed, still in her clothes, and burrowed under the warm comforter with a grateful groan. She lay there fighting sleep for a short while, listening to Winifred out in the other room, shuffling around. Before she knew it, she was asleep.

When she opened her eyes again, the birds were calling outside and the sun was shining through the window, brighter than she'd ever seen it. So England did have sunny days. She rubbed her eyes, yawned, stretched, and listened. No sounds from the other room. But something smelled heavenly. Eggs of some kind. Kippers. Winifred loved the smelly little things and sometimes had them for breakfast as well as lunch. Fresh sourdough bread. It reminded her how ravenous she was.

She rolled over and peeked at the clock on the night table beside the bed. Ten o'clock. She'd slept seven hours. Why had her hostess let her sleep so long?

Winifred was placing two breakfast plates on the small kitchen table as Rebecca strolled into the room toward the bathroom in her crumpled clothes.

"Don't talk to me yet," she begged Winifred on her way through as she grabbed up her traveling bag. "I need to do some quick repairs, change my filthy clothes. Be right out." She disappeared behind the bathroom door as the older woman chuckled and finished setting the table.

When Rebecca emerged a bit later, cleaned up and in fresh black clothes, she sat down at the round table.

The old woman lowered herself with a grunt into an adjacent chair.

"You didn't have to go to all this trouble for me, Winifred. A piece of stale toast or two would have been fine." But Rebecca was touched by her kindness. The English were a generous, good people, on the whole, she'd found.

"Not for me. I need a hearty breakfast," Winifred huffed and shoveled in another forkful of scrambled eggs. Gulped her steaming tea with a sigh of pleasure. "Looked like you did, too."

Rebecca took a good hard look at the Englishwoman.

"You been up all night, haven't you?"

Winifred leveled reddish eyes at her guest. She buttered a slab of bread and put it to her mouth. "Had a lot to do. Had some contacts to make. I got us a real expert on the Old Language and Black Magic . . . a real powerful warlock."

Rebecca's eyes lit up. "Yeah, who?" She knew quite a few warlocks.

"I'm not allowed to tell you his name. Yet," came out of Winifred's mouth. Her face was closed.

"You're not allowed to?" Rebecca repeated aghast.

"No . . . it's against the rules." Secretive.

"Winifred! What are you talking about?" When she

saw that the Briton still wasn't going to ease her curiosity, she reached over and touched her wrinkled hand. "If you don't tell me, then you're as good as saying that you don't trust me." There was hurt in Rebecca's startling blue eyes. Confusion. "After all, I trusted you enough to confide in you. Brought you the book."

Winifred stared at her friend piercingly. "All right. But what I'm about to tell you is in strictest confidence. You must not let on to anyone that you know. Have you ever heard of the secret organization called the Guardians?"

Rebecca was stunned. "Now wait a minute . . ." She almost stuttered. "Isn't that a myth? I mean, yes, I've heard of them. But I thought it was just a story. *Super witches* who watched over all of us and stepped in only when one of us had crossed the line, or when something catastrophic was about to happen to mankind? Everyone knows of the legend, but no one—none of the witches or warlocks I've known—has ever met one or even believed that they really existed."

"Well, dearie, believe me, they *do* exist. And they very, very rarely show themselves except when a white witch desperately needs their aid. Like when Satan is the enemy. Like now. They consider that cause enough to make contact."

Rebecca was flabbergasted. "You know them?"

"Yes. I'm one of their . . . scouts, which is the easiest way to put it. I was asked to keep an eye on you. I have. But I've also become your friend."

"Me?" Another shock. "Why?"

Winifred shook her head and gave Rebecca a soft smile. "I'm not at liberty to disclose that yet. Later. After Amanda is back, safe, I can explain everything. Not now. Now you have important work to do."

"And the Guardians are going to help me?" Rebecca's face was full of awe. She must be in a real load of shit.

"Here." Winifred handed Rebecca a piece of paper with an address on it. "This is where you have to go to meet with the warlock I told you about. It's a hole-in-the-wall rare bookstore on Charing Cross Road called Fletcher's. He's expecting you. But don't let on you know he's a Guardian. He'd have my hide for telling you. Take the book to him, let him look at it. Pretend he's just another warlock . . . one who has a knack for translating the ancient language. And listen to everything he says. Do what he says. That's all I'm going to tell you."

Rebecca eyed Winifred strangely, but her gaze was full of new respect. "I'll do exactly as you say, Winifred. I promise."

"Good," she replied, starting to clear off the table. She stopped a moment to look at the witch. "Trust me, Rebecca. Everything's going to be fine. Just fine."

Rebecca nodded, got up, and helped her friend clear the table.

"I can't thank you enough for your help," she told her.

Winifred patted Rebecca's hand. "Don't have to thank me. You know I'd do anything for you, Rebecca. Now, go see that warlock, then go and save that sister of yours. But be careful. I don't want to lose my best client."

Rebecca called a cab.

"Good-bye, Winifred," she said when the cab pulled up before the cottage and honked its horn. "After all this is over we're going to celebrate. I'll send you an airplane ticket and you'll come, won't you? To Canaan, or Boston, or wherever we are when Amanda comes home?" Rebecca asked.

"Wild pigs couldn't keep me away." Winifred

grinned. Then she waved in the doorway as the cab took Rebecca away into the day's sunshine.

Inside the cab, Rebecca leaned back, told the driver the address of the shop, and closed her eyes, letting the motion of the cab soothe her. Inside, her heart was beating wildly. She kept going over that last conversation with Winifred about the Guardians. The knowledge that they truly existed and were watching over her had taken a great weight off her shoulders. So much so that she almost felt like laughing out loud. She wasn't alone in this. Yet she was baffled at all the cloak and dagger mystery surrounding where she was going and who she was meeting. It was all so crazy. So clandestine. So . . . exciting. The game was afoot.

But then, she asked herself with a sly smirk, *you always did like excitement, Rebecca, didn't you?*

Maybe too much.

Tibby popped his head out of her coat pocket and scrambled up to stare out the window as the cab wound its way through the London streets. They were coming to a large intersection. The driver was obviously going to make a right.

Witch, tell him to go left. Now! Tibby squeaked, his tail whipping back and forth through the air violently. His face pressed to the glass. *There's danger!*

Rebecca knew better than to question her familiar. "Driver"—she rapped her fingers against the seat before her—"go left here. Not right."

"Ma'am, that's the wrong way to the address you gave me." The cab had stopped at the intersection, the man twisted in his seat to look back at her. His eyes did a double take when he spotted Tibby as he scampered back into Rebecca's pocket.

"Go left here . . . I'm sure there must be another way to where we have to go, isn't there?"

"Yes," he grumbled. "We'll have to go way out of our way, but I know another route."

"Then take it."

"As you say, ma'am. You're paying." But as he pulled the wheel to the left and the cab followed, he commented in his Cockney accent, "Ma'am, do you know you got a mouse in your pocket?"

"Yes. He's my pet. Goes everywhere with me."

"Oh." The man shut up.

What was that all about? Rebecca asked Tibby.

Demons again. Waiting for us that way. This way is safe. I think.

Thanks, Tibby, you're a lifesaver.

Tibby chuckled from her pocket. *Both our lives.*

Soon the cab braked in front of a tiny bookstore. The faded sign with the word *Fletcher's* on it in red flowing script swung in the breeze above the narrow wooden door.

Rebecca got out with her bag, paid the driver, and entered the bookstore.

It was dimly lit. So much so she didn't even see the proprietor until he stepped out behind her from a tall rack of dusty books.

"May I help you?" A soft rustling voice. British.

She turned to face the man. At first glance in the murkiness of the store, he seemed harmless enough. Not much taller than she, with silverish long wispy hair, going bald on top, a compact face with the brightest gray eyes she'd even seen. So bright, they seemed to send off sparks. A bulky deep-blue sweater topped a pair of dark slacks. An average-looking fellow. Until he smiled at her, and animated, he was transformed. Almost cute. Even though Rebecca recognized the depth of shrewdness and intelligence in his intent appraisal of her a moment later.

"You're Rebecca Givens, I bet," he stated without

preamble. And gently took her hand in his when she offered it.

Something like an electric jolt coursed from his fingers to hers.

Rebecca's face broke into a surprised smile. So this was the warlock—and if Winifred was to be believed, the Guardian—who was to help her. Not bad.

"How did you know?"

He let go of her hand. "Winifred described you to a T. Even down to the all-black clothes. Rather fetching on you. And . . . I saw a picture of you on the back of your latest book, *Of Witches and Warlocks*." The man crossed his arms and leaned against the book rack next to him in a casual pose. "Didn't care too much for the book. There's more to being a witch or a warlock these days than doing parlor tricks and divining the future."

That stung, but Rebecca hid it.

"But you're much better-looking in person, if I can be so bold as to say so, and I have a theory after Winifred updated me on your quest, that underneath it all there's a big heart." Charm just oozing out.

"Thanks for the compliments," Rebecca said mockingly. The way he was smiling at her softened the insult on her book. She also understood that Winifred had told him everything, that he knew all about her and Amanda's difficulties, Rachel, and the demons who were now chasing her.

Unexpectedly the warlock said in a low voice, "Don't worry, the demons can't touch you here." He spread his arms around the bookstore gracefully. "You're protected. I made sure of that." He offered the protection so easily, but Rebecca knew the strength of magic it must have taken to accomplish such a feat. The man had to be, without a doubt, a warlock of the highest magnitude. Level two, at least, or one. She'd never met one before, and she experienced a sense of humbleness before him.

As Rebecca and the man talked, someone else was observing them from a dark cubbyhole wedged between two tall books. A diminutive batlike creature with crimson eyes and tiny wings was behind her. It attended her closely and made little clicking noise with its claws. It grinned, and razor-sharp teeth gleamed like pearls. When Tibby waved at it from his mistress's pocket, it waved back. Old friends.

The warlock's name is Simon, Tibby secretly informed her. *Don't let on I told you, though. And yes, he's a level ONE. I'm impressed myself.*

Simon laughed aloud, and Rebecca realized that he could hear her familiar. He knew. She told Tibby to hush.

"Familiars can sometimes have minds of their own," the English sorcerer said to Rebecca, still amused. "I know, I have one just like him. Never know where he is half the time. Always getting into mischief somewhere. Sometimes I wonder who is the boss and who is the slave. You can call me Simon, Rebecca, I don't mind." His slender hand disturbed the air between them in a delicate gesture as his face grew serious. "I know you're one of us, a friend. Can I see the book?" his eyes suddenly mesmerizing as he waited with outstretched palm.

Rebecca took it from her bag, where she'd had it hidden and handed it to him. She trailed behind him as he took it to the back of the store, sat down on a battered old chair, and studied it under a strong lamp. His head bent, he started reading, and taking notes.

"Rebecca, behind you is a pot of tea. Cups. Help yourself. Then make yourself comfortable in that chair behind you. This could take a while."

Rebecca did as he advised her and waited. In her

usual way, when she found herself with time on her hands to kill, she yanked out a thick notebook and started jotting down ideas and notes for her next novel. The one she was working on now was going to be about werewolves, she thought. If she could find one to interview, that is.

After what seemed like hours, Simon closed the book, and looked up at her as if he were coming from the dark into the light. She was startled by the age reflected in his eyes, his countenance. And she had the strange idea that he was a lot older than even she would believe. As ancient as the book he held in his hands. She shivered. Silly notion.

"Rebecca, just listen to what I tell you. Write it down if you have to. But follow my instructions *exactly* . . . or your sister will never make it back alive—and Satan and his demons will have not only her, but you."

"I have a good memory. Tell me," she said gravely. Her jaw set. "I'll do whatever you want me to."

He spent a long time explaining what she had to do. And as Winifred had counseled, she listened well.

When he was finished, he murmured, "You're right. You don't have much time. Amanda will soon be facing death where she now is. That's why I'm going to do something I shouldn't do.

"You don't have to worry about the snowstorm that's raging in Canaan and the airline situation . . . or the demons harming you. You'll be protected, for a while—until you get to Witch's Pond and the book's been destroyed," he warned. "That's when you'll be most vulnerable. In the darkest danger. Remember."

The warlock handed her her traveling bag.

"Let me ask you something that's been bothering me?"

"Go ahead."

"When I first explained to Winifred on the phone

about finding this book at Black—Witch's—Pond, I had the premonition that she knew of the place."

He groaned. "Most of us do. There's an ancient legend about the place"—he stopped, his eyes narrowing as he seemed to decide something; he hesitated, then plunged on—"that concerns a promise once granted to a very evil witch by the Devil himself. She had disobeyed him and he reclaimed her powers as punishment. But she had been a favorite of His and on her brutal death he promised her she could live again . . . if she could find a pure good witch of the highest level to take her place. Then she'd be allowed to walk the earth once again in her new guise and have more black power than any witch in the history of the world." His voice had fallen to a whisper. "The possibility for destruction unleashed on our times would be almost unmeasurable."

"If that's true, why don't you stop her?" Rebecca was suddenly very afraid.

His eyes met and held hers firmly. "Because, there's the final part of the legend."

"Final part?"

"Yes." Softer. "Only another white witch bound to the lost one by deepest love will be able to save her. Only she, if she's true enough of heart. Maybe."

Oh, great, Rebecca thought cynically, *why did this have to happen to me? Of all witches. I'm nothing but a fake. A nobody.* Yet she couldn't say such a thing out loud. Too much was depending on her now, and she knew there was no way out but to take the path she had already begun. She had to try to save Amanda, her heart would accept nothing less.

Rebecca came out of her troubled reverie. She could feel the warmth of Simon's body, who'd moved closer, next to her and, for no reason, she had this unexplainable urge to put her arms around him. Wanted to have him wrap his arms about her. But she didn't. It was only her fear.

He smiled intimately at her as if he could read her mind. Then said, "It's time to go now, Rebecca. If you'll close your eyes for a minute, when you open them you'll be at Jane's door."

Rebecca asked no questions, showed no surprise, just obeyed and closed her eyes.

"You're a brave witch, Rebecca. Good luck. Remember what I've told you," was a haunting whisper in her ears as she felt the world spin around her. Dissolve away.

Suddenly she was freezing. A bitter wind tearing at her and her clothing. She opened her eyes. She was back in Canaan on Jane's very doorstep in the middle of a full-blown icestorm, bag in hand, and Tibby in her pocket, teeth chattering from the abrupt cold.

"Damn . . . it's cold," she breathed, and started pounding at the door. But there was a mysterious smile playing on her blue lips. That Simon was a heck of a sorcerer. A heck of a man.

She was elated when Ernie opened the door and let her in.

Chapter 14

Joshua had taken his tobacco harvest to Rivers Grove to sell at the market.

Be away at least three or four days, my love, he'd told her the night before under the moonlight after they'd made love. *I will not be any longer than I have to be.* For some reason he'd been apprehensive about the trip from the very beginning. Hadn't wanted to go. He'd been uneasy about Sebastien and the roundup of witches in the last weeks, the coming so-called trials which Joshua had learned would be no trials at all. He'd talked to his friend the chief magistrate about Rachel and he'd promised to try to help. To intervene for her with Sebastien, based on all the good things Joshua had recounted to him about her. Her healing. Her kindnesses to everyone. The way she cared so carefully for her own two children.

Yet Joshua had still been concerned; if the selling of his crops hadn't been so essential to the family's depleted coffers, he would have sent his overseer to sell the tobacco. But times were hard for all the farmers, competition stiff, and Joshua knew that he alone could hope to achieve a fair price in the marketplace. He had friends and connections whereas the overseer didn't.

So she'd seen him off the next morning and bid him

good luck. *Do not fret. I am sure I will be safe until thy
return.*

She couldn't have been more wrong.

That afternoon Sebastien's men pounded upon her
door and demanded she accompany them for questioning before Sebastien. She'd had no choice but to go
with them as she was, leaving the girls alone and terrified. She wasn't allowed to take anything, they were
so afraid of her magic. Her reputation.

She was taken to the town jail and herded into a
holding cell full of other people. All accused of witchcraft, apparently, or other crimes.

Some of them were peculiar old women whose only
sin was to be not fair of face or figure, not sound of
limb, or of possessing little wit or sense. In the twentieth century, Amanda thought, they would have been
simply labeled handicapped, mentally incompetent, or
simpleminded. A good deal of the prisoners were just
unfortunates who people had held grudges against, for
whatever reason, like herself, and had no true idea why
they'd been arrested. All of them had been taken from
their homes in the last week and incarcerated. All proclaimed themselves not to be witches. They were wretch-
edly frightened, hungry, and filthy.

The food and drink, when it came at all, were moldy
bread and dirty water. But then it would have been
hard to eat anything, with the foul stench of the place
and the dirt. Slop buckets weren't cleared out very
often, but left to stink, attract flies in the sweltering
cell, and breed germs.

It was so hot Amanda was soon drenched in sweat,
only adding to her misery. And she hadn't eaten since
an early breakfast, so soon enough the hunger pains
were gnawing at her like little beasts.

Most of the prisoners huddled in the straw-strewn corners in the dark and either stared into space or wept

as if they were lost souls. They all feared the questioning to come, for others had gone before them. "Most
never come back," an old woman with hair falling out
in patches revealed. "Tortured to death," she said, "in
another part of the prison. They die on the rack or
from worse persuasions. Thou canst hear them screaming and begging come sundown."

The name of their accuser, Sebastien, could not be
mentioned aloud without revulsion and fear.

"Aye, the guards come every evening and drag some
of us away. For interrogation, they calls it, but," an
empty-eyed girl of about eighteen, her voice filled with
horror, informed her, "if thee confesses thy guilt, I have
heard, the torture halts and thee are condemned to
die. All those be taken to another cell to wait . . . 'tis
rumored the hangings will begin in a few more days."

Amanda had been silenced and pushed into dismal
apathy by that news. For the first time as she'd listened
to what the other prisoners had had to say, she'd actually accepted the hopelessness of her position, the
irony of it. If she didn't confess to being a witch, they'd
torture her until she did; then, as a professed witch,
they'd hang her. That was justice in the seventeenth
century.

It seemed all of the prisoners were familiar with the
charges that were to be leveled against Rachel. She was
the scandal of the day.

The old woman who seemed to have taken her under
her wing from the first rambled them off for Amanda
in a hoarse whisper: "The worst be that thee be accused
of murdering thy married lover, Darcy. . . . He was
found dead this very morning in his barn. Sectioned
up like a hog sent to the butcher. They say Sebastien
wants you to hang for the crime. The lesser charges:
that thee have inflicted pestilence upon the crops of
the honorable farmer Block and withered them as they

stood in the ground, sent diseases to sicken his cattle, fever to the Watersons, and lastly, tainted the wells of certain of thy neighbors, Mistress Jacobs, and Mr. Ackerson."

"Those are lies," Amanda moaned, staring into the darkness about her at the shapes sleeping in the straw, yet also keenly aware that some of those things could have been done by Rachel before she'd come. But not Darcy's murder. Unless Rachel was still here somewhere, or she'd had someone else do it. Amanda could only guess.

"They say also," the wrinkled old woman in the tattered shawl and loose-fitting dress wound up with a cruel mocking in her tone, "that thee hast sold thy soul to thy master, Satan, as all of us have, in exchange for these powers . . . and that thee art, therefore, a witch."

Amanda cringed at the charges. Hopeless.

"I am innocent," Amanda cried softly.

The old woman laughed bitterly. "Are we not all? And are we not all fearful of Sebastien's branding irons, knives, and the rack?" the woman spat. "I had had hope, in truth, that thee were the powerful witch that they claimed thee to be . . . then thee might have freed all of us with one glorious spell." But again the woman's words were full of frantic sarcasm.

"I am sorry that I do not have that power for I would surely use it to save all of you," Amanda said.

The other woman chuckled sourly.

"Someone must stop this travesty," Amanda exclaimed angrily. *Oh, if only she still had her powers!* If only . . . cows could fly and the earth was flat.

Night had arrived and the cell had become an impenetrable blackness. The guards had come a while before and had taken four of the prisoners away, wailing and pleading for mercy, to face Sebastien. Amanda wondered when her turn would come, and a deadly chill crept over her, freezing her limbs as well as her mind so that her body began to shiver and wouldn't stop. She was sure that Sebastien had not forgotten her, not with murder as one of the charges. He'd just wanted her to have time to taste the fear.

Amanda felt her sanity slipping away for the first time in her life at the thought of what she would soon face. Making herself small in a corner of the cell, her ears tormentingly alert for the screams of the tortured, and her eyes wide open in the gloominess, she feverishly prayed that Joshua would return and save her.

But he was on his way to Rivers Grove and had not an inkling of her imprisonment. He wouldn't be back for days. Yet as the hours crawled by, she obsessed over that impossible rescue more and more until it clouded her mind, violently shoving everything else out. She thought of Maggie and Lizzy and Amadeus, and missed them all as tears trickled down her grimy face. She'd never felt so alone. Lost.

She missed her old safe life, too. Her sisters. Her friends.

Jake. She sobbed silently to the walls around her. *Oh, Jake, what I wouldn't do to be back in your arms in our little cabin in the woods.* But Jake was dead and that cabin was just smoking ashes, and she was centuries and worlds away from both of them.

She knew that no matter what she said or what she did when Sebastien questioned her . . . she was doomed. Better to admit what he wanted to hear right away and get it over with. The noose would be more merciful than the rack or the branding irons.

It was like being in a horror movie, except everyone else knew the script—their lines—but her. Torture To be hanged by the neck until she was dead. Her eyes froze in shock, and then glazed into a raging fury.

And then the hideous screams began somewhere else in the building. The nightly questioning. The other prisoners awoke; some wept at the agony of those undergoing the torment, a few prayed for them, some pounded against the walls in anger. Most were quiet, and like Amanda, covered their ears after awhile to shut out the bloodcurdling howling.

This couldn't be happening! Of all the times to be without her powers. All the years she simply took them for granted. She wanted more than anything she'd ever desired in her life to just be able to snap her fingers and have Sebastien and his friends all go to hell where they belonged. Release the ones being tortured. One woman screamed so hard her voice was nothing but guttural animal sounds.

Amanda thought, *I can't stand this. I can't!* The screams continued. On and on. She laughed insanely, scooting back like a terrified animal against the slimy wall. How truly alike Sebastien and his henchmen were to the demon high priest and his cult acolytes she'd torched in her own time. Except in the seventeenth century they were honored and given power over others' lives and deaths. The people couldn't see what they really were. Monsters.

Somehow they'd followed her here and soon would have their revenge for her destroying them then.

What had she ever done to deserve this end? *You took lives,* came back the guilty answer. *You crossed the line and broke the Law.*

Now you must pay in spades. With your life.

Joshua, she whimpered amidst the condemned suffering around her, *where are you?*

But what answered her, looming above her in its translucent cowled robe of black, was Sebastien. His appearance startled her. How had he gotten in? What was he doing here?

The cries stopped.

Joshua cannot help you, witch. No one can help you. You are mine. Finally. The face hidden under the cowl was pasty white and had the taint of the grave about it, but when the thing glared down at her, its eyes were incandescent holes. *And later, when we come for you . . . you shall suffer far longer and more exquisitely than any here will. I have a special treat in store just for you . . . Amanda.* The phantasmal figure pointed a bony hand at her, and then laughed evilly. *A torture that will disfigure you slowly but not kill. Though you will pray to die. Beg to die.*

Amanda cowered back against the wall from it in the dark, folding in on herself like a broken child. No one else could see the thing, she realized. Or hear it. Just her.

It was the same high priest demon she'd incinerated in the future. Or one like it. She wasn't sure it was really Sebastien or something that was appearing in his form to torment her further. Even *Satan.*

God, to have her magic again. For the first time in her life she was afraid. Unprotected.

In the name of Jesus Christ, Amanda hissed in a barely audible whisper and made the sign of the cross in the air before her, *go away. Go back to hell.*

It scowled at her and stepped back a little. *I will for now . . . but we'll be back for you, my sweet, later. And your cries of pain will give me and my Master joy, and serve another purpose, as well.*

Amanda blinked and the apparition was gone.

No one around her had paid any attention to her mutterings. The prison was a strange, fearful place and people lost their minds all the time, even before the torture.

She rested her head on her drawn-up knees and slammed her eyes shut. *I must hold onto my sanity . . . I must.*

And I must find a way to get out of here.

Then the brief silence ended and the tortured began to scream again.

Amanda laid her face in her trembling hands and wept like she hadn't wept since Jake's death.

Chapter 15

"This time I'm coming with you," Ernie insisted as he lifted up Rebecca's heavy pile of camping equipment. A large tent, cooking stove, and sleeping bag. Supplies of food. Lanterns. "If we need to we can just stay in the car if the storm gets too bad. Sleep in the back. I already have my camping gear in the station wagon."

"Ernie, I've told you it's too dangerous," Rebecca snapped for the tenth time as she preceded him through the old-fashioned country store toward Jane's station wagon parked outside. He didn't listen, like the other nine.

"And Rebecca, I've told you, I'm going. You'll never find Black Pond in this snowstorm. You'll need me to help set up the tent and build a fire—if this storm will let us. Keep you from ending up an icicle sitting next to the frozen pond."

"I can handle the weather and the tent. I'm a witch, remember?" But Ernie knew she wasn't the same caliber of witch as Amanda had been, so that boast fooled no one.

"And keep you company while you wait."

Rebecca halted at the door, shaking her head. She gave up. Ernie was dead determined to go out there with her, something to do with a promise to Jake to protect Amanda. It would be nice to have a friend

along, though, she admitted, especially since Tibby had
up and vanished on her again this morning. Didn't
know where he'd gone to or when he'd be back, as
usual. The English warlock had cautioned her that it
could take as long as three days, maybe more, before
the spell would do its work and bring Amanda home.

"I just hate to take you away from Jane that long."
Rebecca tried one last time to dissuade him.

"She'll be at her mother's with the two boys. Jonny's
still in the hospital, but doing fine. Jane won't even
miss me. She wants me with you."

As if he could protect her.

Outside the glass windows it was solid white. Everywhere. Ernie and Jane had both agreed it was the worse
snowstorm they'd had in years, and it was still coming
down and icing up the trees and roads. Just their luck.

"Driving in this is going to be a real picnic," the
mailman said flatly, looking out at the snow. He didn't
tell Rebecca that if it got much worse they'd never get
out there, much less raise a tent up in it. It would be
the station wagon or nothing. Thank goodness the station wagon had new snow tires and a heavy-duty battery.

They'd guard the exact spot where Rebecca now believed Amanda had disappeared; near the willow tree
where the book had been found. She had this special
spell to perform. The one Simon had given her. Then
she was to burn Rachel's book of black spells as a sacrifice, scatter its ashes across the water . . . and wait.
Wait for the door between the worlds to open. It would
only open all the way when Amanda approached, was
near, and would draw her in. It could take days. Rebecca refused to think of it taking longer. It'd be freezing out there at the pond in this storm. And she never
had been much of a nature girl, not like Amanda. Her
idea of happiness was a plush hotel with all-night room

service, cable on a big screen, an olympic-sized heated swimming pool, and a sauna.

Oh, she'd have a hard time burning the book, too. It was priceless, no doubt. Not just for its age and historical significance, but for the spells. Rebecca smiled. Simon had ordered her to burn it, but he hadn't said she couldn't have copies made of it first on the town library's copier. Ten cents a page. She'd done that an hour ago before Ernie had brought her here to the store. The writer in her, as well as the witch, wouldn't let her destroy the book entirely. Her rubber-banded roll of xeroxes was safe in her overnight bag for later perusal and study.

"Well, it's not going to get any better out there and you did say that we had to get out to Black Pond as soon as we could," Ernie remarked.

"I'm ready," she answered and swung open the door. Winter rushed in at them, and shivering, they carried their booty out to the back of the station wagon and loaded it in as quickly as they could move. The wind shoving them around like cloth puppets.

Inside the station wagon, as they crept down the snowy road toward their destination, Rebecca kept dwelling on Amanda and where she might be at that moment. If she was all right. If she was scared or in danger. When Rebecca listened to the crying of the wind outside the car, she could almost hear her sister weeping. No matter how she tried; Rebecca couldn't get Amanda's sobbing out of her mind. God, did it mean she was already too late? That Amanda was about to die?

She found herself reliving vignettes of the last few times she'd seen her sister.

That weekend early last summer . . . Amanda grinning over a spinning pot out in her workshop; the childish pride she'd always had over her pottery. She and Jake so happy together. That silly familiar of hers, playing with Amanda that morning as they'd sat alone companionably munching hot bread and drinking coffee in her sunny kitchen, talking about life in one of their rare sisterly moments, as Jake had slept in the back room of the cabin that was now gone.

Amanda's haunted eyes and puffy face at Jake's funeral. Her pain had been so palpable it had made Rebecca wince. For as much beauty, power, and goodness as Amanda had had, it hadn't been able to bring the thing she had loved the most back to her. Jake. Oh, how jealous Rebecca had been of her and Jake. In some ways, she and her sister had been a lot alike, but not in that. Rebecca had never known such love and could not imagine the pain of losing it. But seeing her sister's grief that day had made her feel guilty for ever having been so envious.

Memories of Amanda filled her thoughts. Rebecca had never realized until this how much Amanda had meant to her. As long as she was there, even if they had hardly seen each other in the last few years, what with Rebecca's book tours and traveling, just to know Amanda was in that cabin in the woods when she did need her, had made all the difference. She missed her not being there.

She missed her, period, because she loved her.

They drove through a churning sea of white, the car chugging valiantly mile after tedious mile along the almost invisible road. Rebecca couldn't see how Ernie was driving at all. It was the worst blizzard she'd even been in. A miracle they were going anywhere.

What seemed like an eternity later, Ernie spun off the road and started through a shimmering expanse of untracked snow. Through the woods. "Here's the tricky part," he said through clenched teeth. "Getting close to the pond without actually ending up in it." And they had to arrive there without getting lodged in a snow-drift or caught in a ravine. They now had to get the station wagon through the land Rebecca had had to slog through a couple of days before. Wasn't going to be easy.

Rebecca silently wove a minor spell, closed her eyes, and crossed her fingers. They made it.

Ernie released a great sigh, switched off the car. "We're here." He'd tucked the station wagon under the skeletal willow tree for some protection from the gusty wind. Yet it still shook like a shivering dog.

"About time." Rebecca stretched in the seat beside him and squinted out the window at the frozen pond. The place looked different than three days ago. The water slick, solid ice, and all the surroundings covered in a blanket of sparkling white. "Brrr . . . looks cold out there." She'd wrapped her arms around herself and shivered.

"And I'm afraid it's too bad out there to raise the tent, Rebecca. The wind would tear it right out of our hands and into New Jersey."

She nodded, concurring. "So we stay in here. For now. It was a silly idea to have brought a tent in the first place."

"Yep," Ernie answered, watching the willow sway above them wildly as he turned the car back on to circulate more heat. Might as well be comfortable. He took mental stock of their supplies. They had more than enough food and water to last them. Warm clothes and blankets. High boots. Snowshoes, even. He'd gone along with the tent she'd wanted, but now he was real glad that he also had brought along extra cans of gas. They could stay there for days, running the car for the warmth if he was just careful. If he cracked a window now and then to prevent a case of carbon monoxide poisoning, and made sure the tailpipe wasn't clogged completely with snow. In fact, he'd have to check on that pretty soon. The snow was now as high as the bottom of the door crack. They could easily become trapped here. Snowbound. But Jane knew where they were and if they didn't return in three days, the allotted time, she'd send out the mounties.

Upward through the falling snow there was just the tinge of a pinkish winter sky, and an eerie solitude to the woods and fields around them, with its dark wet branches of a thousand trees lined with ridges of white going up along the horizon. To Rebecca it seemed as if the world had turned monochromatic, accented in black. And the hush of the icy forest was unreal. It was like she was in another place, an alien place, and suspended in time.

"What does your watch say, Ernie?"

He lifted his wrist and peered at it in the twilight inside the car. "Four-twenty. It'll be dark soon."

"Thanks." She still had over seven hours until midnight, when she was supposed to evoke the warlock's spell, torch the book of spells, and sprinkle its remains across the pond. She shaded her eyes from the white glare and examined the area right before them on the shoreline near the willow tree. It would be slippery.

"Do you think the pond is truly frozen solid?"

"Yep, I imagine it is. The weather's been subzero long enough. But I wouldn't stake my life on it."

"I can perform the ritual right there," she went on softly, almost more to herself than Ernie, pointing. "Before the car . . . in the headlights."

They fell silent for a while as the night closed in around them. The snow was still whipping around, but it made things bright enough to see by.

Ernie finally asked, "I brought some cards along. Want to play something? It'll help pass the time."

Rebecca turned and smiled at him in the dark.

Though the car was running, they'd left the lights off. Not just to save the battery, but because Ernie was afraid someone would find them waiting there. He wasn't taking any chances.

"Sure. I know how to play poker, spades, and pinochle."

"Great. Poker." He reached back behind his seat and brought up one of the lanterns. He lit it and the front seat was flooded with soft light. "I'll deal first."

And so they passed the time until twelve, the witching hour, playing cards and talking about Amanda. Jake. The past. Their lives. Ernie loved talking about Jane and her kids. At one point Rebecca almost spilled the beans and mentioned Jane being pregnant with his son (it would be a son), but something stopped her at the last second. Maybe Jane wanted to tell him herself. Rebecca could tell already that he'd be so happy.

Rebecca tried not to let the growing evil of the place that she could sense hovering around them get its claws into her too deeply, or she knew she would be lost.

At ten minutes to twelve o'clock, cramped from sitting so long, Rebecca took the metal container that Simon had given her, the book of spells, and Ernie's lighter, and hobbled out toward the pond. Tibby would have been of real help to her now, but he hadn't reappeared. She'd have to do it alone. She remembered that Simon had said that she'd be in the direst danger after the book had been destroyed. Yet the atmosphere of the place had become more threatening every hour since they'd first arrived. She could feel it in her bones. In the air like heavy static. Evil was congregating, waking up and flexing its muscles all around her.

It was still snowing like crazy. The whole world was illuminated with it as if the snow produced its own light from underneath. She could see perfectly well but Ernie still snapped on the car's headlights for her.

In their harsh glare, Rebecca, bundled up like an Eskimo, waddled to the edge of the frozen pond and began weaving the intricate spell that she'd memorized in a low chanting whisper that carried over the air. Performed the ritual ceremony. The snow was deep, higher than her boots. The wind moaned around her, sharp and cutting.

It took a long time and when she was done, her gloved but frozen hands placed the ancient book in the container as her tired body shook with the numbing cold, laid the receptacle on the snow, and set fire to the book with the Bic lighter. It burned swiftly as she watched with bated breath. The flames arched up in exploding colors. Rebecca was sure the cries she heard were captured souls being released.

She had to fight for a moment to keep her balance in the blustery wind. A great tingling had coursed through her body like a small electrical current. What was that? she thought, bewildered, then forgot about it. Yet she felt somehow different. Less fatigued, more confident.

When the book was only ashes, she lifted the container and crunched as close to the pond as she could get. Tossed the ashes out into the whining wind and watched the soot swirl away over the ice.

Slowly, above the pond, close to the shore, a tiny flicker of light began to glow. A pinpoint like a distant star.

Rebecca's eyes fastened on it and after a few minutes she was sure. It was expanding. The doorway.

I did it! she cheered to herself. Her clenched fist swatching through the night air in a gesture of victory behind the car's headlights so Ernie could see. Jumped up and down excitedly.

She ran back to the waiting car, hopped in. Ernie turned the headlights off.

"I see it," was the first thing he uttered, his chin resting on the top of the steering wheel in the dark and his eyes riveted to the light pulsating above the water. It was the size of a baseball now. "You really did it." Astonishment.

"Did you doubt it for a second?" she said proudly as she shivered next to him. "I also feel like a Popsicle. Turn the heat up."

Ernie slid his eyes to her reddened face. "I already did. As high as it'll go."

"Thanks."

"Why don't we take turns watching it?" Ernie suggested. "We both need some sleep. You sleep first, though, in case something happens. You'll need all your strength."

"Good idea." Rebecca leaned her head back on the seat's headrest, her gaze still on the growing doorway. She didn't feel like climbing in the back and fighting with a sleeping bag. "But you'd better wake me the instant something changes. Something happens."

"I will. Promise."

Rebecca shut her eyes and attempted to sleep. She was amazed, as excited and nervous as she was, that she was able to.

But not for long.

"Rebecca?" a sibilant whisper in her ear. Louder, more urgent, "REBECCA!" And someone was shaking her violently awake. Ernie.

Gasping, she came to, unsure where she was. Then her eyes flew open in startled terror as she saw what was framed in the station wagon's headlights.

Demons.

"*Oh, God!*" Ernie, sitting next to her in the semidark with his eyes popping, gulped. "What the hell *are* they?"

Rebecca had the obscene urge to giggle. Fright. These were real, honest to goodness inhabitants of hell. Snarling. Viciously menacing. Massive. No, some were Brobdingnagian. Each encased in a glowing aura of unearthly luminescence so that when they moved it appeared as if they were coated in some living light shield.

They looked like escapees from some state of the art special effects monster movie. *Aliens,* maybe. Or a cross between *Aliens* and every *Howling* movie ever made. Hulking around the car like vultures circling their dying prey.

"They're demons," Rebecca murmured to her scared friend, "from hell, is what they are. Burning the book must have brought them. Like sounding a trumpet of black magic."

One of the creatures, a bearlike thing with the face of a deformed snake, was hammering on the hood, peering in at them like they were tonight's snack. But was too stupid to figure out how to get to them. He whammed the hood again and the car bucked like a wild horse on speed. Rebecca knew what a sardine in a tin must feel like. Except sardines were already dead and she wasn't.

"What does it *want*?" Ernie's voice quavered on the verge of hysterics. His face was whiter than the snow outside.

"Us," Rebecca quipped, humorlessly. "They love human flesh. Raw. I believe they've been sent to dispose of us before we can help Amanda."

"By whom?"

"The Devil, of course. They're His minions, after all. Like Rachel is His creature. I had suspected Satan was behind all this from the beginning. Then that English warlock confirmed it. He prepared me for something like this. Said it could happen." Her eyes were glued to the supernatural creatures. "But thinking it may happen and it actually happening is a hell of a difference."

She had to give the mailman credit, he had courage. He didn't whimper or pass out. Looked like he was going to, but he didn't.

Another of the fiends, one of the ones that could have been a twin to the monster in *Alien*, pranced around to Rebecca's window and hunkered down; a sinister eye gawked in at them, rows of jagged teeth as large as pointed boulders salivated, and then a mammoth spiked tail slammed against the side of the car door. The glass cracked and the door dented in.

Ernie yelped loud enough to wake the dead.

Two of the monsters were tugging at the door handles, gibbering like mad apes, drooling with unearthly hunger as they studied the two terrified humans cowering inside. Another one, a dog-faced thing that stood on three legs and had lots of arms, was carving up the fender like it was cold butter instead of painted steel.

"Do something, Rebecca!" Ernie wailed at her. He was plastered as far back against the seat as he could get.

Rebecca said a quick, fervent prayer for help, and invoked the strongest enchantment to rid oneself of spirits and demons she could call up. Knowing even as she did it, that it wouldn't work for her. Couldn't work. She wasn't a powerful enough witch to pull it off. Yet she refused to stop. Refused to give up. Amanda was depending on her, too.

Suddenly a swirling, towering tornado of icy howling wind swept in from the night and literally scooped up all the demons like a steam shovel. Ground them up like hamburger in a blender. The sounds they made were terrible. Like a million angry hornets. Then the cyclone carried the remnants away back into the night sky through the drifting snow.

"I'll be damned," Rebecca gasped out in genuine

shock. "It worked. My God, it really worked." She turned to a gaping Ernie and the biggest grin spread across her face. Then she began to laugh. "I *am* a true witch. I am."

Then Ernie began to laugh with relief, as well, pulling Rebecca into his arms. He hugged her thankfully.

"Did you ever doubt it?" he finally and simply asked when they stopped laughing. "I never did." The look of respect and awe on his kind face as he looked at her was worth more to her than any five-figure royalty check she'd ever gotten.

Rebecca gazed back out over the pond. The doorway was now a swirling vortex of brilliant light the size of a manhole cover. And growing.

"Whoa, look at that thing," Ernie exclaimed.

And she did.

Tibby appeared on the middle of the car dash. His tiny eyes shining in the dimness. Ernie jerked, until he saw who it was; then he smiled.

"You did pretty good, old witch," Tibby squeaked at her, as if he hadn't even been away in her hours of need.

"No thanks to you," she said sulkily.

"Oh, so that's what you think?" the mouse huffed. "Some gratitude. When I've been helping you all the time. Me and some . . . friends. Behind the scenes. You just didn't know it."

Rebecca glared at him for a second, but eventually sighing softly, she reached out her hand and he scrambled aboard. "Thanks. I really didn't believe you'd abandoned me. But you missed all the fun." She set him on her shoulder where he most liked to be so he could whisper in her ear.

He cocked his little black face at her, his whiskers feathering the air. "Na, I saw the ghoulies. They ain't gonna win no beauty contests, I can tell you that."

"I didn't know he could really *talk,*" Ernie burst out, staring at the grinning varmint.

"Only when he wants to," Rebecca replied smugly.

The familiar laughed, then.

Ernie thought it was the weirdest laugh he'd ever heard. A little like a teeny-weeny hyena.

Chapter 16

Amanda didn't sleep. The sounds of other people suffering wouldn't let her. Time stood still and all she was aware of was the darkness, the heat, the cesspool stench of her prison, and the fear overriding it all. She kept waiting for someone to come for her as they'd come for the others.

She prepared herself. She prayed, and as the night wore on, found herself dwelling in the past, her past, more and more. When she wasn't deep in her melancholy, she attempted to comfort some of the other prisoners. Many were dehydrated, weak from malnutrition, or sick with terror. Without her medicinal herbs, or food and water, there wasn't much she could do, and it broke her heart.

In her desperation, she remembered the mysterious Gibbiewackett and how he'd probably helped her once before with Jonny's life; and although she knew it was pointless (he was, after all, centuries away) she called to him. Not just for herself, but for all the others, the tortured as well as the imprisoned.

Help us, Gibbiewackett. Please help.

It did no good. She was still a prisoner among other prisoners in a filthy jail in a century that wasn't hers.

At times, behind the tortured cries, she thought she heard Amadeus meowing outside somewhere. Was he really out there, searching and pining for her, or was

it just her imagination? Her imagination. Because
Amadeus still had enough magic that if he was close
to her, he'd find a way to get in. To be with her. And
since he wasn't, it meant he hadn't found her.

Eventually the screams of the tormented ceased and
an ominous silence settled over those around her.

"Often they come and take more of us," a young
girlish voice stated darkly. "Some nights the questioning
goes on until dawn."

"Aye," another voice from the dark, "they need live
witches for their hangings next week, not dead corpses."

The key turning in the lock could be heard like the
sound of doom and the thick wooden cell door swung
open. The prisoners scurried away, fleeing to the murki-
est corners to hide. Even Amanda. What was pride now?
The promise of great pain could turn anyone into a
coward.

A tall guard paused in the doorway with a candle
lantern. His shadowed face was hard, cold under his
helmet. His narrowed eyes searched the room.

"I have come for Rachel Coxe," the deep voice
boomed out. The man had a neatly trimmed beard and
massive shoulders under his dirty uniform. A musket
held cocked and ready in his hands.

Amanda swallowed, a great lump lodging in her dry
throat, as she sidled back against the wall away from
the dreaded light. Her fingers skimmed the ragged
notches in the wall behind her arched back, shaking.

"Mistress Coxe!"

"Thee must go," one of the shadows next to her
whispered. "It does no good to hide. They find thee,
anyway, and then it will be worse. A beating before the
questioning even begins."

Amanda swiped the tears from her face with the back
of her sweaty hand and moved forward on unsteady
legs.

"Here I am," she said.

The guard captured her by the arm, roughly escorted her from the cell and down a narrow corridor. Amanda's heart was thudding in her chest like a monstrous gong. She couldn't think, it was so loud. Her jailer ended up half-dragging her because her legs trembled so much she could barely walk.

She'd never been so afraid. Her mouth so dry her tongue stuck to her teeth, her gaze blurred. She was helpless . . . she was going to die. She'd always believed she'd be brave in such a situation, but it was never the same when you were the one facing pain and death. You couldn't make your body and mind behave, that was the problem.

They were outside. Amanda felt the night breezes caressing her face. The smell of roses. Of sweet late-summer grass and shrubbery. She gulped the fresh air down like she'd been starving for it as the sweat evaporated off her hot skin. The velvet black sky above her twinkled full of stars. The moon full and radiantly white floated above her like a unique Christmas ornament.

How cruel, she thought numbly, *to give me this brief taste of freedom and beauty right before they start tearing my limbs apart.*

Then it came to her. What were they doing *outside* the jail? The torture chamber was inside.

A huge shadow rose before them. Pranced skittishly. A horse neighed. And then, astounded, Amanda heard Amadeus meowing happily. Coins clinked. Husky men's voices saying something . . .

Without warning, the guard who had her in his grip lifted her up off the ground and she found a saddle under her and strong arms about her. Unprepared and jolted, Amanda cried out in fear at first. A warm hand was placed over her mouth to quiet her, and the arms drew her lovingly backward. A familiar voice whispered in her ear, "Hush, Rachel, my love, be not frightened, 'tis me. I have come to save thee." And hot lips covered hers as the guard shuffled back into the night.

Joshua!

"You came for me! You really came for me, Joshua," she moaned, her whole body quivering with joy. Her tears were now tears of happiness and relief as she pressed his arms tighter around her.

He calmed Gabriel with a few gentle words, and then said to her, "We are not out of danger yet. Sebastien could at any second discover thee missing and alert the other guards. Come after us. I expect it. I bribed the fellow who brought thee out to me. He is my cousin and believed me when I told him thou were no witch, but falsely accused. That we were to be married."

It was almost all too much for Amanda to take in. "How did you know what had happened . . . where I was?" She was so ecstatic that he was there and she was free she forgot her *thees* and *thous*—and didn't care. Her lover didn't seem to notice.

Joshua had pressed his knees to his mount's side and they were heading into the woods at a brisk trot. The crickets and other chirping night creatures produced the loveliest noise Amanda had ever heard.

"This is going to sound . . . strange . . . but all the way toward Rivers Grove I had this overwhelming *urge* to return. A tiny voice deep in my mind kept telling me that thee were in urgent peril. It would not leave me be until I had heeded its advice and turned back."

Again Amanda had the premonition that there was someone watching over her. Protecting her in the best way it could. Gibbiewackett? Or his Master. Rebecca?

"So I sent two of my best men on to the marketplace with the crops, and my overseer Griffin and I rode with all haste back to thy cottage. The children explained that Sebastien's men had come for thee. I knew where they would be holding thee. The jail. And I came. I bribed the guard to bring thee to me."

Amanda's manner grave, she informed him, "Do you realize what you've done, Joshua? Sebastien will not let me go so easily. I'm accused of murder as well as practicing witchcraft."

"Aye, I have heard so. The guard told me. But I know that be not true, Rachel. Thou art no murderess, either. The charges be lies. As are all his accusations." Hatred underscored his next words. " 'Twas the questioning, the torture, I would not abide for thee. Sebastien will not do to thee what he did to my poor brother, Jacob. Once I heard thee were imprisoned, I swore that. The very fact that he sent for thee whilst I was gone, gave his foul game away. And Sebastien will not harm any more innocents, as well. I gave my cousin more than enough gold to set the others free once we were away. All of them. Even the ones undergoing torture . . . if he can do it."

"Joshua, you are so good," Amanda wept, reaching up with one hand and touching his face gently. The very thought of the other prisoners still being trapped in that wretched cell, while she was free, had haunted her. Knowing that they would be released took a heavy weight off her heart. But Joshua had taken such risks.

"Yet by saving me, my love, you have become what I am. A criminal."

He sighed understandingly as they moved, ducking in the saddle, under some low branches. "That be true, yet I do not care, Rachel. I love thee and soon I will make thee my wife. I will gladly give up everything I own for thee. When I heard thee were taken . . . I believed my soul would wither from the pain I felt. The loss. My heart cried. And I knew then that thee are my life. Nothing must happen to thee."

Amanda let the tears slide down her cheeks. To find

such a love once in a lifetime was rare; twice was a true miracle.

"Where are we going?" she asked, trying to hide the fact that she was crying, as she furtively wiped away the tears.

"We are on our way to my Uncle Kasper, my mother's brother, who resides in Providence. We will stay there with him and his family until we know we are safe, then we will send for the girls and go west. There be land and freedom, a new life, for all of us. Far distant from this place and Sebastien's abominable inquisition. I have also sent word to my mother through Griffin to continue to run the plantation until she can find a buyer for it, and then she is to follow us, in secret. We will begin anew, Rachel. For thee, I would do all this and more."

Amanda was humbled by the love in his voice and the great sacrifice he was making for her. To go on the run. To leave his home and start all over again in a foreign place.

Then an awful truth dawned on her. "Send for the girls?" Amanda repeated. The legend of Rachel had also proclaimed the children's bloody butchering. Had foretold their deaths. "Oh, God, no . . . Sebastien will have the girls killed when he finds I've escaped. I know he will!" Amanda grabbed Joshua's arm with tight fingers. "We must go back to the cottage and get them. Now!"

"Hush, sweet Rachel." He laughed kindly. "I thought of their well-being, also. I ordered my overseer to take them along safely with him to my mother before I ever set out to rescue thee. She will hide and care for them until they all come to us."

Her fear fell away like magic. Maggie and Lizzy were safe. It was unbelievable, but Rachel's children, like her, had escaped their predestined fate. Had escaped death. And soon they'd all be together, Joshua, the girls, and her; away from this cursed place—and Sebastien. Amanda felt like singing with joy.

Joshua had hesitated, but finished with, "That is why I am alone. Except for an unexpected passenger I discovered on the way. He must have jumped aboard."

Amanda heard the meow. Amadeus popped his head out of one of the saddlebags, and then he was scrambling into her lap, licking her hands and rubbing against her as if he were thrilled to see her.

"Oh, Amadeus. You weren't left behind after all. You're coming, too." She kissed his furry head, hugging him so hard he growled in protest.

"Thank you, Joshua, for bringing him," Amanda whispered. "I love you."

Joshua slowed his horse down just enough so he could turn her in the saddle and take her fully in his arms. He gave her a long and lingering kiss as he held her tightly. There were tears on his face, too. A moment later, he sent Gabriel into a gallop again. The shadowy woods went rushing by.

They had to get away from Canaan. They had to hurry. Even Amanda sensed that. Joshua slapped the edge of the reins against his horse's flanks and prodded him into a full gallop. They were far enough away from town now to do so. She held on firmly and they rode hard.

It was then the exhaustion drowned her, taking all the strength from her muscles. She could talk no more. Think no more. Her eyes closed. She was with the man she loved and he would take care of her now. Protect her. She trusted him. Safe, in her lover's arms, and Amadeus in hers, she could finally relax.

They'd been riding for hours, the descending moon shining down on the man with the sleeping woman cradled in his arms, when Joshua first heard the pounding of hooves coming up behind them quickly. Too quickly.

Then a shout rang out on the still night air. Another and another.

Amanda came to with a start, her mind clouded with a foreboding of impending disaster. She'd been dreaming. In the dream her sister, Rebecca, was looking for her. Calling her.

She'd been found. She was to come home. To Witch's Pond. Now.

"What's wrong, Joshua?" she cried out, as the horse leaned in low and fast against the wind. Its gallop now a dead-out run for their lives, as tired as the beast already was. Amadeus clung to his mistress with all four paws, claws out, like a burr. Amanda gripped on to the pommel to keep from falling off.

"Sebastien and his men were pursuing us," he said breathlessly. "I have known it for a long time. Now they have found us. Our only chance is to outrun them. Or hide from them and lose them."

Amanda said nothing further as they raced into the night. She'd believed she'd heard her sister calling only in the dream. But she was wrong. As they fled, she heard Rebecca's voice yet again.

Amanda, come to Black Pond. Come now. Come home.

Or you will die. And all those with you.

You must return.

Amanda made her decision. She believed the warning.

"Joshua," she yelled at him against the wind. "Go back. Back toward Canaan and my cottage. To Black Pond. We'll be safe there."

Joshua yanked the horse to a standstill, looked into her eyes in the moonlight.

"Are thee sure?" Doubt in what she was asking him, not in her.

"Yes, I'm sure. We must go back. We must get to Black Pond. It'll save us. *Trust me.*"

"I do," he swore. He seemed to think for a few precious moments, then nodded. "And we will go. It might throw them off our trail, doubling back like that. They will not be expecting it." He reined the lathered horse around and headed back, slanting their path so they wouldn't head directly into Sebastien's way, but circle around him if they could.

And Amanda prayed she'd made the right decision. She was going to take Joshua back with her. To her time. To hell with destiny, and what was right or wrong. To hell with not interfering with mankind or time. She loved him and he loved her, and she couldn't—wouldn't—live without him. She would do it, or die with him at Witch's Pond. She'd not lose the love of her life twice. She would not.

They evaded their pursuers in the thick trees when they passed them. They were lucky in that.

And that's all. A short time later arose the furious yells of discovery. Sebastien and his acoltyes were riding hard behind them again, closing in.

Joshua's horse was stumbling on his feet as they drew near Black Pond. Musket shots rang out through the night and then Gabriel was crashing, falling beneath them.

The horse sprawled on the ground, dying, as Joshua and Amanda rolled free and came to their feet in shock. They'd run him to death. Joshua crouched over his horse until its last breath, comforting the poor beast. Then grabbed his musket, her arm, and continued to propel her through the woods on foot, because their enemies were so near.

In the end, Amanda didn't know what had happened to Amadeus. He might have been caught under the horse. Crushed or pinned. She hadn't seen him after

Gabriel went down. Not anywhere, though she'd whispered out his name frantically as Gabriel had lay dying. Amanda had to leave, not knowing if her familiar was still alive or not.

Amanda and her lover picked their way through the brambles and thorns toward the pond. Amanda's eyes full of unshed tears over Amadeus. Her heart reeling because she feared what might be waiting before them as well as what was behind them.

There was magic in the air, she could feel it. Getting stronger. Beckoning her on. It hadn't been that long ago that she'd been a practicing witch. She remembered. And she suddenly felt as if she were in the end of a dream. Her thoughts were sluggish, feverish, her movements painstakingly slow. The world spun around her. Nothing seemed real.

What did it mean?

Chapter 17

The demons attacked a third time right before dawn. Rebecca was ready for them, but Ernie wasn't.

They were in snake form this time, bathed in that same eerie luminosity as the previous demons; they slithered over the snowy ground and tried to cover the car like a slimy blanket. Serpents of all sizes and varieties. All of them as mean and nasty as blazes. With teeth and fangs, and some with acidy venom they could spray out for yards.

Tibby clung to the ledge of Rebecca's window and made faces at the demons from inside, sure he was safe. He hadn't said another word all night, even though Ernie had kept an ear on him. Not another blasted syllable.

Rebecca thought Ernie was going to have a stroke.

"I hate reptiles," he snarled, shuddering. His face was wedged against the windshield as he surveyed the monstrosities gliding and crawling toward them. He'd turned the lantern's light up as bright as it would go and snapped on the headlights. A particularly persistent group of the vipers were throwing their slippery bodies against the car. Hissing and biting at the vehicle because they couldn't get to the occupants.

"I loathe snakes. They act as if they know it, too," Ernie remarked sharply.

"I'm sure that's why they're here," Rebecca said. A tingling had begun in her shoulders and was now traveling to her fingertips. Power build-up. She could feel the magic in the air around them. A stronger magic than she'd ever been aware of before. It'd been protecting them the whole night.

"God, I thought that last batch—the ones that looked like huge locusts but with the human faces—was bad," Ernie stated. "Ugh, but these are really ugly."

The snow had abated, but it was so deep now that Ernie couldn't open the door. Rebecca would have to use her powers to get them out the next time. To get them back to Canaan. Outside the horizon was tinted with just a tiny rosy glow. Ernie's eyes were locked on to it as if it were his salvation. Rebecca had mentioned that most demons disliked sunlight immensely. He hoped she was right. He was looking forward to at least eight straight hours of no lurching, stalking, or flying nightmares. His nerves were shot. He was a strong man but he'd never seen the likes of what he'd seen in the last night, and he prayed never to see their likes again. If he hadn't cared for Amanda as much as he did, he would have been long gone. And if it wouldn't have been for Rebecca's strong magic, all three of them would have been long dead.

"Can you get rid of them, too?" Ernie asked, now openly alarmed. He could hear Rebecca's strained breathing next to him and Tibby's scuttling about. But he was afraid to take his eyes off the things attacking the car. If one of them got in . . .

Rebecca had dealt with the last plague of demons with some kind of sooty gray fog that she'd conjured up with her newfound powers. The killing cloud had come out of the nebulous doorway like a freight train and had choked all the locust-critters into oblivion. They'd rolled over on their spiked backs and stuck their grisly little legs up into the air and had dematerialized as the smoke ate them. Gruesome.

"I can try."

The demons were converging around, on, and under the station wagon by that time and abruptly the two lone humans in the car were plunged into blackness as empty as a sealed tomb. Couldn't see a damn thing. The lantern had gone out and Ernie couldn't seem to relight it for anything.

Something was thumping under their feet.

"Then do it now," Ernie mumbled in the funniest voice she'd ever heard. Reminded her of Tibby when he was scared witless.

Rebecca reached out for the magic she'd need and as with the other times, it mysteriously came to her and did her bidding.

The magic. She didn't know exactly where it came from, or why it didn't weaken her like magic usually did. How she even knew what to say. It was just there for her. After the second time, she was smart enough to accept the truth: it wasn't coming from her. Or, at least, not all of it.

"Do you feel that?" Rebecca announced in the gloom, as Tibby directed something private into her ear. She nodded a reply.

Vibrations were rocking the car, harder and harder. Quake size. And again Rebecca sensed that Ernie and she were in a protective bubble. The world outside the car was raucously shaking itself into a great fury—but they were untouched.

Light began to seep in. Ernie gazed over at her in relief. The car was shedding off the snake-demons, and as they fell they were breaking into thousands of pieces as if they were fragile glass. The vibrations were shattering them.

The carnage scattered about them on the cold white

stuff began to smoke and dissolve. Soon there was nothing left of the last attack force but sullied snow.

"Rebecca, you amaze me," Ernie sputtered. His face was upturned to the rising sun as if he'd never thought to see it again. "How did you do that?"

"I'm pretty sure I had help," she said thoughtfully. "I'm not so naive to think I did that all myself."

Looking out at the pond in the faint sunlight, she was the first to observe the doorway. Now it was as large as a boxcar. And inside it was summer. The trees that rustled in the breezes were lush and green. Grass on the ground. Birds flying by in a summer evening sky. As she watched the light in that other world fade to twilight, she was fascinated. In her world dawn was coming, in that world it was almost night. Warm there, freezing and winter-bound here. It was the most remarkable thing she'd ever witnessed. Heaven knew how much time had gone by there for Amanda.

In Tibby's eyes Rebecca could see the lights from the doorway reflected like miniature fireworks. Magnificent.

The witch didn't say anything to Ernie, but struggled back into her coat, hat, and mittens, and pushed at the door until she somehow got it open. The overabundance of snow didn't stop her.

Tibby jumped into her pocket at the last possible second like a stunt daredevil as she plunged out into the winter morning. Eyes riveted to the staggering light show before her, Rebecca slogged her way to the edge of the pond. Drawn to the growing window of light like a person in a darkened house would be drawn to a lighted room.

Amanda was close. She *knew* it.

What would happen to her, the witch pondered, if she just walked into that other dimension and went searching for her sister? Physically brought her back?

Too dangerous yet, a voice hummed in her mind. *Wait.*

Rebecca, tears running down her cold cheeks, stood at the rim of the huge hole into another time and called out her sister's name over and over, *Amanda, come to me. Amanda! I'm here.*

For some reason, she also accepted there wasn't much time left. Something terrible was about to happen in that other world. Something that involved her lost sister.

The witch studied the strange phenomenon for a long time even though her face, hands, and feet were soon blocks of ice. When she swung around and tromped back to Ernie and the station wagon, the mailman was outside inspecting the damage. Shaking his head and rubbing his red eyes.

"Those demons were nothing, Rebecca," he muttered with a grunt, "compared to what Jane's gonna do to me when she sees her car." He kicked out at the snow with a large booted foot like a little kid. "She's gonna kill me. She just made the last payment on it."

"It is a mess, isn't it?"

"Yep," Ernie said, a frown settling on his face, his hands stuffed deep into his coat pockets. There was frost glistening on his salt-and-pepper beard. The usual sock cap was pulled low over his head, his long gray-streaked hair streaming out from under it. There was a hole in the elbow of his heavy blue jacket. He truly looked pitiful.

Rebecca laughed then, and raised her hand over the car. There was a swirling of snow, a screech of metal realigning and rearranging itself. Then sunny silence.

The car was whole again. Unmauled and unscratched. The same exact car they'd driven out there in.

"I appreciate that, Rebecca." Ernie grinned at her. "You're really getting good at all this."

"You're welcome," Rebecca replied cheerfully, but

her face was lined with fatigue in the rising sun's radiance.

"And thank you for appreciating it," she said humbly. *Even though it isn't me doing it. Thanks, anyway. It feels good to be a winner, if only for a short time. It really feels good.*

Ernie then trudged through the snow and to the bank of the pond. He looked out at the glimmering doorway and whistled.

"Never would have believed it. It's fantastic. To the day I die, Rebecca, I will never forget this. Any of it." He meant the night they'd just passed through, as well.

Rebecca came up behind him as new snow drifted down. "Neither will I," she said softly. "One way or another. Neither will I."

Chapter 18

They were panting and staggering among the towering trees, the pond visible through the next line of bushes, and their stalkers were behind them on snorting, pawing horses closing the distance. Sebastien's men had stopped shooting at them. Their horse was dead; Sebastien wanted them alive.

Amanda, sweaty and exhausted, not only from the running but from her earlier ordeal, was wheezing heavily as Joshua guided her. Her dress clung to her, a tangle of cloth that kept tripping her, while her hair had come undone from its neat braid long ago and was wild and flowing loose around her shoulders. Seeking Amadeus, her eyes kept searching around the silhouetted underbrush and past the hulking trees. She couldn't accept that he was dead. Wasn't following her. It was like a part of her had died.

At least Maggie and Lizzy were safe with Joshua's mother. No matter what happened to Joshua and her, they'd be protected. It was something.

Gradually filling the air around them there was this faint . . . glow. It lit up the woods like strong moonlight. But the moon was no longer in the sky.

What was it, then?

"Sweet Christ," Joshua breathed in disbelief as they broke through the brush onto the bank of Black Pond.

Before them was a hovering entity of shimmering light covering the whole pond like a dome. In the center a spinning miasma of scenery that shouldn't be there. Couldn't be there. A circle of winter complete with icy trees and swirling snow. Just poised on the bank, stooped in exhaustion, as they were, they could feel the freezing shaft of air piercing into the warmth around them. Touching them with icy fingers and sending goosebumps along their skin. Amanda shivered, crossing her arms across her breasts, even though the chill air cooled her hot flesh.

"What in heaven's name is it?" Joshua glared at the sphere of light as if it were the very mouth of hell, which to him it was.

Amanda's eyes wide and startled, she stared at the vortex, too. Except she thought she knew what it was. The doorway into another time. Her time. Something exploded in her chest. A great yearning, a bursting joy. *Home,* she thought in wonder. *I can go home. Finally. Home.*

It was winter there now, she'd forgotten.

She glanced across to Joshua's illuminated face. The utter terror in his eyes slammed the truth at her like a brick wall.

Her earlier plans of taking him with her back to her time was a pipe dream. Totally unacceptable. She'd never told him anything about her other self, Amanda, a witch from the twentieth century. A time where huge metal machines flew in the air, smaller metal beasts darted around on concrete highways and one could flick on light with one finger. A place where you could talk to someone clear around the world, and see strange faces talking strange tongues in a tiny wooden box. Joshua would never be able to accept all those things. Never told him that she'd only taken Rachel's place. Wasn't really Rachel at all. Never prepared him.

And now there wasn't time. How to explain everything—and the doorway—to Joshua? He was clearly
horrified by it. He'd believe her insane, at the least,
or worse. Possessed of the Devil.

"We have to get away from this—" He couldn't even
think of what to call it, much less understand it. He
had his arms around her shoulders, still watching the
light as if it could chase after them like some hungry
animal, as he pulled her away from the pond.

"No . . ." Amanda protested, tearing out of his grip,
and lurching toward the light like one entranced. "I
should go. I don't belong here."

Then the voice came again, summoning her. It was
Rebecca. She was sure of it. Somewhere through the
doorway in the snow her sister was searching for her.
Crying for her.

Amanda was torn. She felt as if she were lashed to
three angry horses and all three of them were galloping
in opposite directions. Joshua and love on one end.
The bloodthirsty witch-hunter, Sebastien, and his heinous followers on another. Torture. Death. Her time,
home, on the last.

Rebecca, Jessie, and her old life. Sanity. Electric
lights, television, and no dank prison cells.

She was so distracted she didn't hear or see the riders
charging down on them. But Joshua did.

He shoved her behind him, raised his musket, and
shot the first man on horseback that reached them. A
blur in the faint light.

Later Amanda could never recall what truthfully occurred after that first shot. It was like a nightmare. The
pack was upon them. Horses and men screaming,
thrashing about, and colliding into each other in savage
turmoil once they'd seen the doorway. It scared all of
them so badly they retreated like beaten dogs.

Amanda was knocked to the ground, almost falling into the water.

But Sebastien ignored his men's flight and bore down on her, anyway, even as the others fell back in panic.

"Thee shall not suffer a witch to live!" he shouted. His eyes gleamed diabolically as he aimed his gun and shot her point blank. Through the right shoulder.

Even through the blazing pain, Amanda was aware of the irony of the wound. Same place as last time. As if the two worlds, her two lives, were paralleling and now converging as the doorway loomed over her. She fought to stay conscious, rising to her knees. There was something she had to do.

Joshua had yanked Sebastien from his saddle and was pounding him mercilessly with the butt of his gun, enraged. "Thou shall never hurt anyone I love ever again!" he cried out as he battered him into a bloody pulp on the ground.

So, Amanda thought, *Sebastien wasn't a demon. Not yet.*

Joshua stood over the still form in the dark, shaking. "Thou shalt never accuse or imprison unjustly or torture another person, either. Never! Thou were the Devil's spawn, Sebastien, not those poor bastards thee put in chains. *Thou.* And thee deserved to die."

More shots and Joshua crumpled at her feet.

Amanda looked down at Joshua's body in the shadows and something went numb inside her. She crawled to him, hovered over him, took him into her arms as her shoulder bled, and rocked him like a baby. *I've been here before. I've lost you before, my love . . . not again . . .*

Amanda's scream echoed around the pond like a banshee's haunting wail. Or that of a dying animal.

"No, no, no . . ."

Blood trickled down her right arm and mingled with that of her dead lover.

Sebastien's followers were running away. Leaving her.

Something that had come out of the light had frightened them that much.

Someone was standing above her. A hand was placed gently on her trembling shoulder as she sobbed inconsolably.

Amanda gazed up with dead eyes.

Looked up with Rachel's eyes. Her face and hair Rachel's. It startled Rebecca at first until she recognized her sister behind the mask. But where was her familiar, that cat? Wherever Amanda was, he always was.

"Amanda . . . are you all right?" the woman was asking her. Love, compassion in large dark eyes.

The woman had called her Amanda.

Amanda's vision cleared and in the bright light from the doorway, she finally saw her sister, Rebecca. Really saw her. She was dressed, of all things, in a heavy winter coat, cap, gloves, and big boots. Silly woman. It was summer after all. Hot as blazes. Here, anyway.

"Rebecca!" she sobbed out in genuine happiness, throwing herself into her sister's waiting arms. "You're here. You came for me. Risked your own life and soul for me."

Rebecca, her eyes misty, too, nodded. She held her sister tighter. "Did you ever doubt that I would?"

Amanda didn't answer; instead, she pulled away weakly and asked, "Did Jonny make it? Is he still alive?"

"Yes," Rebecca hurriedly replied.

"Thank God!" Amanda gasped. "But how did you get here?"

"I'll tell you all about it later. Right now we have to get out of here. We have to go back." She looked over her shoulder at the constricting light. The doorway was smaller already.

"Right away. Or we could both be trapped here," she said in a lowered voice. "And if those rude friends of yours find their courage again, they'll be back. Looked like a lynching party to me."

"It was."

Rebecca's eyes fell on Joshua's body. She recognized the grief in her sister's bent form.

"Who is he?"

Amanda stared up at her sister with eyes shining full of tears. "It's Jake, you know. Reincarnated. In this time he was known as Joshua," a yearning sigh on the wind. Her shoulders shook and she swayed like she was ready to collapse. Blood was dripping onto the ground.

"I loved him . . . and that damn Sebastien—that demon—is responsible for his death."

Rebecca wondered if her sister was insane. Jake reincarnated? Ridiculous.

"I can't leave him like this, Rebecca."

"And we can't take the time to bury him, sister. I'm sorry. The doorway's closing. We have to go *now*." Rebecca tugged on her sister's arm.

Amanda muffled a cry of pain, clutching at her wounded shoulder.

"And you're hurt, too!" her sister exclaimed, realizing it for the first time. Even in the semidark she could see the black blood slick on her sister's dress when she looked for it.

"You need medical attention." Yet at the same time she was trying to recall a healing spell that would do the trick. But she didn't have time. The doorway was dissolving quickly now. Rebecca glanced back at it. As big as a car. Shrinking. In the distance the sound of horses' hooves returning. Their leader, their god, had been murdered and they wanted revenge.

"They shot me. They shot poor Joshua . . ." Amanda rambled on inanely as she huddled down next to the body and cried softly. "What else do they want of me?"

"Amanda!" Rebecca suspected she was going into shock.

Amanda seemed to recover herself a little and kissed her dead lover's cool lips one last time, then let her sister help her up from the ground. Let her half-carry her toward the ball of light with the snow scene dancing in the middle. Amanda's eyes never leaving Joshua's dead body lying in the grass.

They never made it. For manifesting itself between them and the doorway, was a blurry, shapeless form. For a moment, Rebecca was sure it was a huge man dressed in black with demonic gleaming eyes as crimson as fire, long dark hair, and a beard. A cloak blacker than night flowed around him like a living thing. His face, lit for only a heartbeat, full of sinister unearthly knowledge. Of sly avarice and cunning. Full of hell.

Satan.

Then his shape reworked itself, remolded and compacted into another form . . . a dark haired woman in a dress similar to the one Amanda had on. Grave-white oval of a face with black holes for eyes. Her arms groped out toward them. Her mouth opened into an iniquitous snarl, showing teeth like ragged needles.

"It's *Rachel,*" Amanda choked out, as Rebecca forcefully swung her wounded sister away from the ghostly grasping arms that tried to capture her.

"She wants you, Amanda . . . she wants your life, your soul," Rebecca hissed, feeling the apparition's black magic writhing around them like a yawning hungry maw. "Fight her."

But Amanda was too weak. Her body and her spirit. She had no powers of her own, she couldn't fight.

She yelled out as she was sucked from Rebecca's arms and missiled through the air toward the ghost. The greatest cold she'd ever experienced enveloped her, a darkness closed in around her. Rachel was gathering her in like a tiny helpless animal caught in the jaws of a trap.

Rebecca watched helplessly as her sister was encased in the dark caul of Rachel's embrace, frozen like a specimen. Only her eyes, terrified and huge, seemed alive. Begging for help as they touched her sister.

"No, you can't have her, Rachel. Give her back!" A vehement demand from Rebecca. Her hands pounded against her thick coat.

Tibby, hiding all the while in her pocket, yelped with pain. But never peeked out once. Let the witches handle this. He was out of it. He didn't do Devils.

The ghost laughed.

"I'll fight you for her!"

Satan's bride smiled jeeringly at her. Began to dematerialize, taking Amanda with her. Amanda had no magic with which to stop her.

The power came as before from nowhere—and everywhere. It rose up around Rebecca like a sentient being. A presence. It crackled like heat lightning through her body and haloed her hands and fingertips.

And Rebecca knew she could stop Rachel. Knew what to do.

The white magic jettisoned from her fingers in bolts of flashing lights and encircled the ghost, spinning around her like a horde of angry bees.

Instantly the ground beneath the spectre yawned open like a set of jaws and swallowed her; tearing Amanda from the black witch's arms, holding her safely aloft until the churning, grinding earth fissure below her resealed with an ear-shattering crack. Then it settled her down gently by the edge of the water on her back. She'd fainted.

"Way to go, Rebecca!" Tibby cheered from her pocket.

Rebecca ran to her sister, scooped her up as best she

could in her arms, and staggered toward the diminishing portal. Not only was the circle of radiance almost gone, but Amanda's rude friends had returned, as Rebecca had predicted they would. They were charging at her even now on their horses, shooting and hollering at her.

Time to go.

Rebecca had to wade into the water to catch the lip of the portal this time, to get into the light.

Then in what seemed like an instant later, wet from the waist down, and sputtering from the freezing cold that blasted her, she and Amanda were in Ernie's helping arms. And Amanda looked like Amanda again. Dressed like Amanda was the night she'd disappeared. Blue jeans and a sweater.

They'd made it!

"God, Rebecca, I thought you'd never get back. It's been a whole day! Was I worried. Then all that ungodly commotion. I heard gunshots—" Ernie went blubbering on about one thing after another. But Rebecca was so happy to be back, safe, with her sister Amanda, she didn't hear a word after he'd said *a whole day*. To her it'd only been a few moments.

"You waited for me all that time, huh, Ernie?" she marveled aloud, as Ernie took an unconscious Amanda into his arms and they made for the warm station wagon under the willow tree. The snow had stopped but it was over waist deep in some places. It was colder than before, if that was possible, and a sheet of ice glittered across everything. The sky a low-hanging gray ceiling.

"I wasn't going back to Jane without the two of you," he threw in. "She gonna be OK?" referring to Amanda with a bleak face.

"I pray she will . . . She's been shot."

Ernie had gotten to the car, opened the tailgate, and

had settled Amanda in the back of the station wagon on a pile of blankets. Rebecca was right behind him. Her lower body already feeling like an icicle. She was shivering so hard, she could hardly walk. She had to get out of the cold, out of her wet clothes. Saving Amanda had taken more out of her than she would admit.

"Where was she hit? I see the blood," Ernie declared. He had skillfully and quickly cut the material away from Amanda's shoulder where the red stain had been with a pocket knife he'd produced from one of his pockets. "But there's no wound."

Rebecca leaned around him and gawked down at her sister. He was right. There was no wound. Now. Just clear creamy skin. And Amanda was beginning to wake up.

"Well, I see she has her power back," Rebecca said with obvious relief. "She'll come around pretty soon now, I'd guess."

"Good," Ernie quipped. Shutting the tailgate. "That means we don't have to rush her to the hospital. We can all go back to Jane's and get some hot coffee and some supper. We can gloat over our success. Our survival. And on the way back you can tell me exactly what happened on the other side. What it was like and why it took so long. Then at Jane's we can embellish and retell the tale.

"Then I'm gonna sleep for a month." He yawned, resting red-rimmed weary eyes on his companion a second before he plodded through the deep snow, got back behind the wheel. He waited until Rebecca had slid in on the other side before he started the car.

Its wheels spun in the clinging snow for a few minutes and then Rebecca snapped her fingers. The car fairly leapt across the crusty snow, seeming to float above the crust until it got to the road, where Ernie and the car took over and drove them back to town.

Rebecca looked back at her sleeping sister, and smiled to herself. *Haven't lost my touch, either.*

Amanda was going to be all right. Everything was going to be all right. She'd done it. Truly done it, and made it out alive to tell the tale. Damn, what a book it would make.

She'd never felt so good.

Chapter 19

Epilogue . . . six months later

Amanda sat at the wheel, her hands molding the last pot she'd been consigned. Jane would be relieved to see that she'd finished all of them in time. Lately the supply never seemed to be able to live up to the demand; yet, she supposed, she should be glad that so many people loved her creations. That they sold so well.

Outside the open window the April breezes playfully teased the budding branches of the trees by the side of the road. She lived in town now. Three doors down from Jane's Gift Shop, which she was part owner of. And she spent a couple days a week working in the shop itself to ease Jane's burden, since Jane had had little Christopher, Ernie's son.

Amanda's hands stopped moving, her restless green eyes staring out the window at the town. So many things had changed. Jane and Ernie had gotten married right after she'd come back from Rachel's time. She was happy for them. They truly loved each other. Ernie was building an addition on the back of the shop to make room for everyone. Amanda could hear the hammering even now. Ernie's good-natured swearing when he missed a nail. She smiled wistfully. It was good to be in town, so close to all of them. Jane's boys were always underfoot and Amanda had decided she liked it.

When she'd first come back the town had wanted to make amends for what they'd done to her, for burning down her cabin. So they'd offered to build her a new one, or to give her a house in town.

Amanda had opted, after very little thought, to take the house in town, instead of the new cabin way out in the woods, alone. Something had happened to her those months she'd spent in Rachel's time. She'd been needed by someone other than herself. She'd been loved and had loved. It had felt so good. There was no going back now to what she once had been. A loner, a recluse.

She knew she didn't want to live that way anymore. She wanted to be accepted by the townspeople, wanted to be liked. Respected. And, besides, the town had made it quite clear that they'd wanted her, as well. She was a hero, saving Jonny and destroying the cult like she had, and everyone had wanted to be her friend. She'd decided she wouldn't mind that, either. To have more friends. A different kind of life.

A new life. So she'd moved into the one-story frame house down the street from Jane's, redecorated it so she'd have her own art studio in the back, and then had asked Mabel to move in with her. Telling her she needed her, which she would soon enough.

Rebecca was living with her English warlock in London and was as happy as she'd ever seen her. In love and content with herself for the first time in her life. She still wrote the books, but she'd stopped being a celebrity witch and had become a true one in every sense of the word. She still possessed the great powers that the Guardians had given her six months ago to help save Amanda.

The Guardians . . . now that was one of the strangest

developments of all. They really existed. Always had. And they were very powerful. Worldwide. They'd had their eye on Rebecca and her since their birth, if everything they'd told her could be believed. Rebecca was already one of them and active in their adventures. Using her magic to help other witches in trouble. To right wrongs or to prevent them, like Rachel trying to take Amanda's body and soul to wreak havoc on the modern world.

Amanda stood up then, arched her back, her hand braced in the small of it, and strolled toward the window. Her hugely rounded belly pushed at her long dress.

Amanda would be inducted into the Guardians herself in a few months' time. After her baby was born. They'd wanted her to get her head straight, too. She'd almost grieved herself into a grave when she'd first come back over Joshua's death and Amadeus's disappearance.

Joshua's dying . . . had been like Jake dying all over again. She'd stayed in her bed and refused to see anyone . . . at first. Then her other sister, Jessie, had arrived and between Rebecca and her, and the discovery that she was going to have a baby, Amanda had begun to heal. She still was. The Guardians wanted to be sure she was all right before she reported to work, so to speak.

Though her sisters had left a few weeks after she'd been settled in her new house, they both had promised to come for the birth. It'd be wonderful to see them.

Joshua's baby.

She smiled sadly at the thought of Joshua. He'd died trying to protect her, avenge his brother, but he would never be completely dead now. She would have his child. A girl. A girl she'd name Elizabeth Margaret. After Rachel's children. Lizzy for short.

Amanda had looked up Rachel Coxe in the library and had found nothing on the woman at all. Even Mabel and Ernie couldn't recall the legend of Rachel and Black Pond any longer. The memory, as the legend itself, had faded from their minds. Faded like the words Rebecca had had copied from Rachel's book of spells. They only knew of Rachel now as the witch that had kidnapped Amanda into the seventeenth century. That was all. And even that was beginning to melt away in Jane's, Ernie's, and Mabel's memories . . . along with what had actually happened at Black Pond. The demons. Rachel. Satan. Along with the knowledge that Amanda was a real witch and that the baby she was carrying belonged to a man who had lived almost three hundred years ago. Soon all of them, even the town, would forget what Amanda really was. What had occurred. She supposed it had something to do with the Guardians, or human nature. What people didn't understand, they chose to forget. Sometimes they succeeded.

Simon Fletcher, Guardian, friend, and lover to her sister, Rebecca, had sent her a strange dream message a few months ago. It seemed that in the history of white witches there had been a blind witch around seventeen hundred, named Elizabeth, who'd later married an Emil Givens. She'd had a sister named Margaret. No mention of their mother. But they were both famous as two of the most powerful white witches of their time. Each had been one of the first Guardians.

Both had been her ancestors.

Amanda had truly changed history by going back and doing what she'd done. In more than one way. She'd completed a circle that had had to be closed. By saving those two children, she'd indirectly saved many people's lives, including her and her sisters. Without Elizabeth Givens, there would have been no Amanda. And no child to come. Simon had explained that was one of the main reasons she'd been chosen to go back. Chosen. The Guardians had been behind all of it. The fact that Rachel's ghost had chosen her to take her place. Her attacking the cult and losing her powers. Going back and meeting Joshua so that he'd be the instrument to save her and the girls. All planned. Except this baby. An extra bonus. Amanda's face grinned again.

Simon and the Guardians knew of Joshua's baby, of course. Simon had told her in her dream that the baby would be special. Very special. A leader of witches. The most powerful witch in seven centuries. Amanda smiled again, a secret smile, as she rubbed her swollen belly gently. *A leader of witches.* Well, well.

The light was going with the day, so Amanda slowly ambled from her studio into the kitchen. Mabel was cooking them supper. It smelled like fried chicken.

The old woman turned and grinned at Amanda as she came in. Made her sit down and take it easy. Told her, as always, that she worked too hard. That she'd better rest before that baby came. She wasn't as young as most women having a first child. Like a mother hen.

It was chicken. Mashed potatoes, and corn on the cob.

Amadeus loved chicken.

"And don't worry," Mabel bantered in a lighthearted way. "There's more than enough chicken for that crazy cat of yours."

"Good. Because he just let me know how hungry he was."

Amadeus appeared out of nowhere in Amanda's lap. He tipped his one ear to the side and winked at his mistress. Amanda hugged him so tightly he squawked and jumped out of her arms, sashaying away like he was mad.

But Amanda didn't care. There were tears in her

eyes. He'd come home just last week. After being gone
all those months. No explanations. No fuss. He'd just
been there at her door one morning, wet, bedraggled,
and starving. She'd given him up for lost or dead a
long time ago, had mourned for him every day.

She was just thrilled to have him back. No matter
how eccentric he was. How smart-mouthed or pushy.

For a few seconds Amanda was back in the seventeenth century. Maggie and Lizzy. The Indians. Sebastien. She relived the horrible helplessness she'd felt
in that dark, filthy cell, the hideous screams of the tortured, that run for her and Joshua's life through the
night woods. She remembered Gabriel going down, the
pain of losing Amadeus. Joshua dying. The agony of
being shot, the disbelief and joy when Rebecca had
shown up. Jessie had been right all along. They had
underestimated Rebecca, all right.

Amanda laid a protective hand on the baby in her
stomach, her eyes far away.

She had loved Joshua so much. As much as Jake,
perhaps more, because she'd lost him once before. How
she missed Joshua even now. But after the worst of her
grief had subsided, she'd known the truth: she'd meet
Jake/Joshua again someday in another life. It was preordained. She'd never really lose him. She'd always have
his love. And how miraculous to be having his child—at
her age when she'd long given up all hope of having
children. The child she and Jake had never been able
to have. A gift from God. She was blessed, wasn't she?
Yes, the answer came from her heart. Blessed.

*You have loved and been loved, you have your family and
friends, and soon you'll have your beloved's child. You are so
lucky.*

"You ready for supper, Amanda?" Mabel asked, awakening her from her daydreaming.

Amanda blinked, and then met Mabel's soft eyes.

"Yes, I'm ready. More than ready."

And, together, the three of them sat down to supper. Amadeus, too.